VANQUISHED

VANQUISHED

Book 1 of the

End of Empire series

by

ALEX JANAWAY

First Published as 'End of Empire' in 2015 by Browncoat Books
and in 2016 by Fantastic Books Publishing

This Edition published as 'Vanquished' in 2017
by Fantastic Books Publishing

Cover adapted by Gabi from the original cover design by Kirsty O'Rourke

Map illustration by Fez Baker

ISBN (ebook): 9781-912053-64-3
ISBN (paperback): 9781-912053-65-0

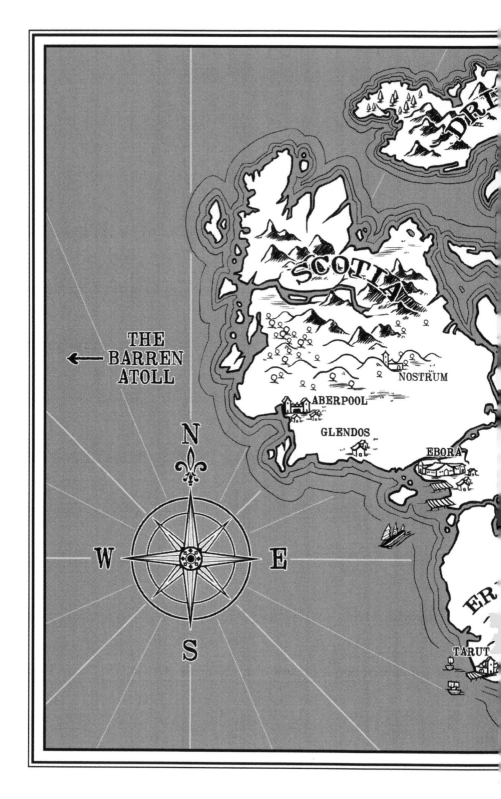

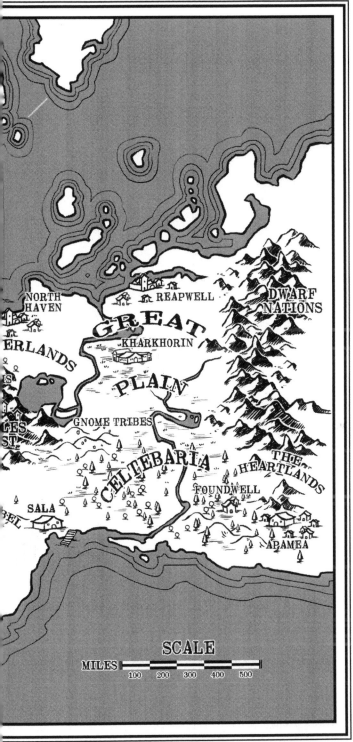

Part One

The Last Night

Owen Derle stepped on to the launching platform. Set on the highest level of the Roosting tower, it gave him a perfect view of the day turning to dusk. A few stars were already visible, bright white pinpricks that, on any other night, would have been a joy to look upon. The sky was covered with patches of oppressive, grey-black clouds threatening heavy showers. The breeze would keep those clouds away from the city; it was just a pity plenty more were coming in from the high country, and they looked nastier. It would be touch-and-go whether the battle would be over before they hit.

Owen turned his attention back to the matter at hand, and made his way across the platform.

'Arno,' he murmured. 'Are you ready?'

The young male eagle watched his approach and extended his wings, giving them a little stretch before settling down. Arno was still growing, big enough to take his weight but small enough to take only half the space of the platform, a rough semi-circle some fifteen feet at its widest point, and a similar depth. Owen put his foot into the stirrup and hauled himself into the saddle. Below him, Arno shifted restlessly. Owen knew the bird was eager to launch, to get into the air, where he would feel free. Owen was less eager. He knew what this night meant, this late autumn evening on the edge of the Empire. He was in no mood to rush what were likely to be his last hours in this world. He was as scared now as he had been on his first flight, as conscious of his own mortality as that day he'd first entrusted his life to Arno. Yet it just didn't seem real, not possible that he and everyone else would soon be dead.

Owen twisted his body and leaned forward, watching his fellow Eagle Riders busy themselves with their own mounts. He hoped they might look over; he wanted to wave at them, maybe hear them shout some words of encouragement. This might be the last chance to speak to someone human. He heard laughter in his head, a light, feminine sound. Someone was pulsing to him, sending a message straight from their mind to his.

'*Are they ignoring you, Owen? You are practically falling off your saddle to get their attention.*'

Owen recognised the voice and looked about, trying to spot the speaker. Maybe she was already airborne, watching him from the sky.

'*Down here.*'

Owen looked down into the gap between him and the adjoining platform. Below, Jenna was looking up at him, a broad smile on her face. He felt blood rush to his cheeks, his forehead grow uncomfortably warm. Even in the dark he couldn't hide the rush of embarrassment he always felt when someone called him out. And it had to be Jenna who did it. He often wondered what she saw when she looked at him. A lad barely grown into adulthood, a shock of red hair, green eyes, ruddy cheeks, and just the barest hint of stubble. Not exactly the image of a warrior born, or the finest example of an Eagle Rider from the Highlands of the Tissan Empire. Whatever she saw, it wasn't going to be anywhere near what he saw in her. A proud, confident woman with sparkling brown eyes and braided chestnut hair pooling down her lithe body.

'*Sorry. I just wanted to say good luck,*' he pulsed back to her.

'*I know, Owen,*' she responded, her bright smile fading, her lips pursing into a tight line. She raised her hand.

'Good luck. See you on the other side,' she shouted up at him.

Owen raised his hand in reply. 'You too!' He wished he had something else to say, but was grateful she'd given him that much.

She nodded and looked away. Her eagle stretched its wings, and in one powerful down stroke took to the air. Owen watched her head into the night and turn to her left, moving beneath his platform, out of his line of vision. There was no reason to stay any longer. Owen swallowed and blew out a breath of air, trying to settle the fluttering in his stomach.

'Time to get started,' he said quietly, trying to exude a calm he did not feel.

He settled himself into his saddle, and reached down to gather in the two ends of the thick restraining belt that emerged from either side. He buckled the belt across the tops of his legs, making sure it was tight, but not too tight. It was easy to cut off the blood. He'd done it enough times to know better. He adjusted his position, leaning forwards and slipping his hands through the leather hoop straps on the pommel. Happy that he was secure, he sent a pulse, ordering Arno to launch. The eagle approached the edge of the platform, its claws digging into the crude wooden decking. Repeating the manner of Jenna's launch, Arno down stroked his wings, then once, twice more, and lifted off and away from the tower. Their brief climb became a swift tipping motion as Arno angled down to gain airspeed. Owen felt the familiar lurch of his stomach, that rush of excitement as he and his mount swept towards the onrushing roofs and spires of the city below. The cityport of Aberpool. The last city of the Empire. Directly ahead, the paved square of the city council hall started to expand and fill his vision. He'd done this a thousand times, swooping over canyons, off mountainsides and treacherous cliffs, yet still he held tight to his pommel, hands crushing the reins within them.

The custom-made saddle forced him to lie almost horizontally, towards Arno's beak, quite unlike riding a horse. The lower profile gave the eagle more speed, reducing wind resistance, and he was glad of that. His legs tightened on either side of his thick cloth seat. He could feel powerful muscles move beneath him as the eagle angled its wings, caught the air currents, and flattened out into a glide. Not for the first time he felt the launch tower had not been built quite tall enough. Full-grown eagles had little difficulty gaining the air, whilst Arno had to work that much harder. Owen breathed deep as the eagle began to beat his wings evenly, getting into his stride, using his speed and the thermals to keep them level. Owen loved flying with Arno. He trusted his eagle more than most of the folk he knew. He reached out and patted Arno's neck, feeling the thick feathers slip under his leather glove, smooth as running water.

'Nice work, Arno. Nice work,' he said.

The eagle gave a long, slow screech in reply to his words. Owen often swore he sensed amusement when Arno responded like that. His fellow Riders would just scoff, reminding him that eagles were not known for their sense of humour.

He bid his eagle turn widely so they could circle the tower as the other birds in the six-strong squadron launched from the platforms that ringed the structure. Many of them had been hastily built to accommodate the other squadrons that had arrived in the city. The tower was only supposed to house one. It occurred to Owen that as one of the younger riders, he had been assigned one of the highest platforms.

He spotted his Leader, Cadarn, take flight, and quickly gain the updrafts. It was hardly a surprise, as his mount was so much bigger than Arno, with at least six feet extra wingspan. Owen had no doubt that Arno would grow larger, but for now, carrying a rider with growing of his own to do, the young predator was large enough.

Owen felt Cadarn enter his mind, after a gentle push. Where many others would force their way in with scant regard, he always knocked first. Their Leader was good like that; he led like he flew, calm and level.

'*Squadron, that's all of us away. Now get to your patrol sectors and keep a sharp eye. Remember, stay low, the light is good tonight. The other squadrons will stay higher and push out further. They'll keep the buzzers off our backs for as long as they can. If you spot the target, head for the tower and let them know. The rest of us will converge and try to give the target some top cover. Good luck.*'

Owen pictured his direction of travel and pulsed the image to Arno. The eagle dipped into a gentle turn, curving away to the north. He could have pulled on the reins but his father had counselled him against that. The gruff voice played in his mind: '*An eagle isn't a horse. Be gentle oft as you can be, else that beak of his will tear you open a little, just to remind you who's boss.*' Sound advice; his father had lost an eye to an irate eagle.

Now the excitement of taking flight had faded, the task at hand forced its way back into his mind. There was a fight coming and it was all he could do to keep himself from turning Arno and flying for cover. The trouble was, there was nowhere left to go to, nowhere left for anyone to run to. Owen felt another surge from the simmering pool of anger that lay beneath his immediate thoughts. It gave him energy and a desire to act, but there was nothing he could do except his duty. He had to keep a handle on it no matter how frustrated he felt, as it was liable to get him killed sooner than he expected. There were no choices left for him or any of his friends, or the others that were gathered around the city. The order to light the fire trench that circled the city waited upon the outcome of their mission. To those charged with its lighting, it mattered not whether they succeeded or failed. All that mattered to them was the timing.

Aberpool rushed past beneath him as he winged northwards. No one travelled through the city save for patrols coming to and from the walls and harbour, their torches often lost amidst the buildings. He had watched from the sky as the evacuation had been called two days earlier. Evacuation didn't feel like the right word, expulsion felt more fitting. Most of those who lived in Aberpool had been forced from their homes and out into the hinterland about the walls. Only a few had been allowed to stay, and those had been escorted to the docks and wharves to board waiting ships. What had shocked him was the lie that had been told; that the docks were too full, that people should move to the beaches to be collected. Thousands had left the city and joined the tens of thousands already encamped outside the walls. By the time they realised they were not going to be saved, it was too late. The gates were closed, the walls were manned with Tissan soldiers, and nobody would be gaining entry, no matter the pleas for mercy.

It didn't sit right with Owen but what could he do? He couldn't go against the decisions of his Church; they always knew best, they worked for the Blessed Emperor. At least, that is what they were all supposed to think but Highlanders had always had an independent streak, a distrust of anyone that tried to impose too much control. Years of Imperial rule had yet to breed that out of his people.

On his left was the sea, lights sparkled and shone upon the water, enough of them to rival the stars in the sky. He could not tell how many ships were out there, but it was a vast number. Everything still afloat within a hundred miles had been gathered in and around Aberpool, waiting to collect their precious cargo before heading west. Beyond the walls and completely surrounding them was another sea of lights. A refugee camp the size of which Owen could scarce comprehend. A desperate press of humanity huddled around large bonfires with nowhere left to go. Owen felt a cold knot form in his stomach that had nothing to do with flying or the fear he felt for his own life. There were people down there, terrified and frightened, who had done nothing wrong, unable to do anything but wait. They said it had been a nightmare back in the east, when the central cities of the Empire fell, hemmed in on all sides and their populations slaughtered. He'd tried to imagine what it must have been like to be penned in with no room to manoeuvre, but he had no point of reference. Eagle Riders lived their lives without boundaries or constraints.

As they crossed the city wall, Owen looked down upon the rows of soldiers, city guards and militia. Their faces were a blur, their arms and armour indistinct, the glow of hundreds of fires, braziers and torches stretching away in a semicircle, trailing off along the entire stretch of the parapet and the three gatehouses. Beneath the wall ran the trench, filled with the carcasses of the warehouses, slums and homes that were closest to the walls.

Beyond the city now, they passed over scrubland, bare rocks and the woodlands further inland. He had flown over this ground many times over the last ten days, flown for miles and none of the Eagle Riders had spotted their target. Their perimeter had shrunk further each day as the enemy drew near, content to command the skies and herd the Tissan stragglers towards Aberpool.

On the shoreline north of the city, a stretch of shingle and coarse sands, he could see groups waiting as rowing boats and skiffs shuttled to and from the shore to the larger ships anchored further out to sea. It was clear that not all the fleet had listened to the Church's orders to be selective of who they saved. The captains of those craft would know the enemy was almost upon them, even if those on the beach didn't. Good for them. At this stage, the most natural thing to do was to save as many as they could. It was the right thing to do, these folk weren't just Tissans, they were the last of humanity. He pulsed Arno lower so he could get a better view. There was a still a semblance of order. He saw women and children being sent forward, their menfolk sacrificing themselves. *How long before it fell apart?*

'Stop worrying about things beyond your control and look for those damned buzzers,' he chided himself.

At least you could hear them coming. The noise of a buzzer, a single giant bee, was hard to disguise, let alone a swarm of them, but if you didn't hear them, then your eagle could spot them more than a mile off. The birds' sharp eyes had given them the initiative in countless skirmishes. Unless the buzzer was ridden by a sorcerer. Those bastards could cast a spell to deaden the sound of the bees' wings, create illusions to hide their approach and blast you out of the sky before you got close.

Night was truly upon them now and that complicated things. Eagles did not have good night vision, they were day hunters. But at least the buzzers were no better and it would require their pilots to control them in any battle. In that respect the Eagle Riders had an edge, the eagle and rider had a closer form of contact. He looked about, concentrating on the dark horizon, yet he saw nothing, just the black silhouettes of his fellows. He had to rely on them to keep his back safe.

He switched to scanning the ground before him, as Arno winged over the wide, dark forests that ringed Aberpool. He had to focus and stay alert. The existence of the Empire depended on it.

General Cord wiped his hand across his mouth, passed the mug back to his aide and burped loudly.

'Another, Major Willets, if you please.'

The aide eyed his commander with concern and a measure of disbelief. 'Sir, is that wise?'

Cord laughed. He'd allowed himself to go to seed and his ample belly shook with mirth, but given the circumstances, it didn't matter much. Even standing upon the exposed battlements of the gatehouse, it was far too warm for comfort. He could feel the heat of the brazier against his mutton chop cheeks and a bead of sweat working its way down his back. He liked to think he was beyond fear, so it had to be the heat.

'It's the last night of my miserable life! Do you think a little indulgence is going to matter? Have a draught yourself. Might be the last chance you get.'

His aide tugged at his collar.

'Sir, we are forbidden …'

Cord waved his hand irritably. 'Forbidden, my arse. I retired five years ago. They only put me in charge here because there was no one else left to command this sorry rear guard. We lost all our generals when we lost the Emperor, and our colonels, and anyone else competent to command an army. All we have left is the Church and the Empress to give the orders and it was just my luck to decide to spend my last days living in Aberpool. So if the Empire wants me to save what's left of her, then that's what I'll do, and I'll gladly give my life to do it. But the least the Empress can do is bloody well stand me a drink.'

Cord squinted and studied Major Willets. Did they really make majors that young? His beard was full and tidily trimmed, but his eyes gave away his age. Too much innocence there, too much worry and doubt. This one was an Aberpool guard commander, he would never have left this city at the edge of the Empire and had likely spent his life catching thieves and locking up drunks. He wasn't a soldier and had probably never fought in a scrap before. Cord leaned forward, placed his hands on the battlements and frowned. He had two thousand men manning the walls, scores of artillery pieces, and none of it would do any good. This city was not built to withstand a determined assault, and the single curtain wall would be next to useless against what was coming. He may be old and well past his prime but he still knew his business and his duty. Their best defence was out there, in that seething mass of frightened souls, the remaining dregs of humanity left on this forsaken continent. Right now that mass was calm but that would change when they caught sight of the enemy forces. In the meanwhile, most folk were just staying put, waiting for a miracle, perhaps hoping that the Emperor would save them. Good luck with that. The Emperor was dead and his heir was out God-knows-where. His fellow Tissans didn't know that their last acts would be to slow down the advance, break its momentum, and buy time, time for the heir to get through to them. He knew, and his men knew. If he was younger he might have let it get to him, but now he just wanted it done. He wanted one chance to cause the enemy some pain, to bleed them a bit, before Tissan finally went under.

A bright beacon flared into life away to the north. This was it. They had arrived.

'Runners! Spread the word. All forces stand to and be ready to engage. They are upon us!' he bellowed.

Behind him orders were barked and men ran along the walls and down to the catapult crews below. He reached out and collected his battered helmet from its spot on the wall. The purple horsehair crest running from the front to the back still stood proudly, if a little more ragged than when first he wore it into battle a lifetime ago. There was a large tuft of it missing right at its peak where a Celtebarian spear had smashed into it and brained him senseless. He'd missed the rest of the battle but they had still won the war. He placed it on his head and fastened the strap. At least it still fitted him, unlike the rest of his armour. Instead of his old breastplate, all he could find was a mail shirt to cover his expanded waistline. Once the helm was snug, he sighed and stood to attention, his hands tucked into his sword belt.

Beyond the walls, the word was spreading among the refugees. At first it was like a low moan, faint, and carried on the wind, but as it travelled it grew, building in urgency. It minded him of the Erebeshi songs, a mad display of ululating cries, whirling and leaping. Those songs had all told a story, though he had never understood them, but this song he could understand. This shrieking and wailing, growing louder and louder, came like waves to drown out his very thoughts. It was a tale of man's ending and the sound of it chilled him to the bone. The many thousands of displaced citizens of the Empire stood and swayed, rippling to and fro, undecided which way to go. Soon they would surge for the walls. *Blessed Emperor, help them.* The tide quickly gained a sense of purpose and started to flow towards the sea and even into the trench. He had expected that and tried to ignore the screams of those falling on to the wood, desperate to get out.

'Well, Major, gather your strength. The Tissan Empire, bitch that she is, expects us to do our duty. We are going to witness something terrible tonight and you must not look away.'

'No, sir,' said the aide quietly.

Cord noticed movement to his right. He looked down and saw his mug, refilled and proffered by his companion. He grunted and smiled ruefully.

'Now you're getting the idea.'

'Raise the flags. It's time to make our run in,' ordered Captain Sabin Fillion of the Imperial Scouts.

Two riders hoisted up poles, little more than crudely cut branches. Large pieces of white cloth had been tied to them, their ends hanging limply. Captain Fillion turned his gaze upon the litter. They were still three miles out and to the north of the city walls. He could plainly see the lights of the refugees camped around Aberpool. The enemy was right behind them and their arrival would start a panic. As always time was against them, they had to move fast or the press of bodies would make it impossible to reach the wall. At least he had spied eagles in the dark sky, his excellent vision one of the few benefits of his maternal heritage.

It was his birthright and his curse, to possess the flawless skin, the pointed ears and the almond eyes of an elf. And as far as he knew he was the only half-elf fighting for the Empire; humans and elves seldom mixed so closely. Fillion nodded. The game wasn't done yet. If they still had air cover then they might spot the flags and the city would receive word they were on their way. Night was upon them and the lack of light would help as much as hinder, hiding them from both rescuers and hunters.

'Get those flags nice and high. I want the birds to see us as quickly as possible,' he said, though he didn't need to explain it. His men knew what had to happen.

Once more he looked towards their ward, the unconscious man was leaning forward like a drunkard, stretching the ropes that held him to the horse and saddle. It was going to be a rough ride and he did not trust those binds to keep him safe. Nor did he like the thought of the animal's reins breaking free from his man Cayden's grip.

'Right, get him off there. Cayden, he's riding with you. Albin, Kally, give Cayden a hand. Then you'll be riding close to each flank to make sure he doesn't slide off.' Not the most dignified arrival for the heir to the Empire. Just their luck the Prince had fallen from his mount, smacked his head and was now out cold. Fillion wondered whether the Prince's mind might be addled beyond repair; not a good sign for their new God. Three days and the Prince hadn't regained consciousness, but at least he was breathing.

The men dismounted and got to work as he turned in his saddle to address the rest of his troop. Including the three on the ground, his band numbered fifteen. For three days they had pushed through the forests that dominated western Scotia, using the cover to hide from the enemy above and behind, staying barely one step ahead with no time for rest. Now, finally, he could hear those hunters drawing closer. No more cover, it was open ground all the way to the city, apart from the mass of Tissans between them and their goal. He shook his head, trying to force down the frustration. It shouldn't have been like this, they should have had plenty of time, but the enemy moved too fast, could seek them out too easily.

'The rest of you, I want an arrow formation. Cayden and the others will be in the centre. If we are spotted quickly enough we'll make a circle and give the eagle enough space to land and pick our charge up. If we don't have time, or the opportunity, then we'll get him there ourselves. We do not stop until we hit the walls.'

'Captain? We can't just ride through, we'll be hitting our own people.'

Fillion turned and looked at the man asking the question. Donal. A young scout who lacked the harder edge of those around him.

'If they get in your way, then ride them down. If we start to slow then we'll never make it. Remember why we are doing this and what we have already sacrificed to see it done.'

A few stirred at that but none questioned him. Donal swallowed hard but nodded his assent. Fillion maintained eye contact for a moment and gave a curt nod in return. The lad had at least learned not to question him, though Fillion realised it was hard when Donal looked at his captain and saw the face of the enemy looking right back. This action would be difficult but there was no choice. There hadn't been any choices for a long time.

'He's ready,' said Cayden. The Prince sat in front of him, ropes binding his body tightly against the scout.

Fillion nodded and drew his blade. He could hear the enemy drawing closer. 'Ride hard, don't stop and I'll see you on the other side. For the Emperor!'

'For the Emperor!' cried his scouts.

He kicked the flanks of his dray and they emerged from the gloom of the forest into the evening light. The snorting of horses, the dull clumps of hooves upon the ground, and the urgent encouragement of their riders, masked the sounds of their pursuers. They had a clear run for a short distance and he allowed himself a moment to enjoy the acceleration, the power of the horse as it ate up the yards.

'Riders behind us!' came a shout.

Fillion jerked his head round and watched forms emerging from the forest. Even in the dark Fillion could see them clearly. The horses were all dark skinned, the riders clad in an array of differing outfits of cloth and leather. They were wood elves. Without the protection of the trees, his men were vulnerable. These bastards only needed to keep pace and they could pick them out of their saddles. Fillion looked ahead. They had another half mile to go at least. It was too far.

The wood elves had merged into a ragged line and began to notch and loose. They were experts with many human lifetimes of practice, which gave them almost flawless judgement, choosing the moment to release perfectly. A few of the first volley fell amongst them while many fell short. The scouts still had a slight advantage in distance and speed, but it wouldn't last. More arrows fell amongst his men, now a loosely spread pack. He used his knees to guide his mount, turning left for a few seconds, then right for a few more. Constant movement, that was the best defence, never let them predict his movement. He knew everyone, even Cayden and his flankers, would follow the same drill. He leaned forward, pressing down towards the horse's neck, lessening the target. His sword arm hung down, the weapon waving loosely. He wished he'd got the damn thing back in its scabbard but it was too late now.

He heard a scream. Looking back he saw a horse had been struck, flinging its rider into the air as it reared in panic. It was Donal, the poor sod. He wouldn't be the last; even with the lack of light the elves could still bring them all down. *Damn it!* They were so close, had almost made it.

'Come on!' he roared.

He felt a rush of air as a black shape passed over him, moving fast. He heard more cries and shouts from behind. This time he didn't look back. It must have been an eagle. They'd been spotted but it was too late. Ahead of him a bright light flared into life. It was high above the ground, sitting upon the dark shape of the city wall. He steered for it, knowing his men would follow suit. That light was their guide in, their marker, at least somebody was still thinking straight in there. He noted the arrows had stopped falling around them. As he hoped, the eagle was running interference, likely strafing the line of wood elves with its talons. More dark shapes were homing in on their position. They were free of their pursuit, but they were by no means clear. They couldn't rely on the eagles to stop the enemy for long or pick them up, and the skies would be full of buzzers.

They were seconds away from the refugees and many of them had seen the approaching riders. Others had spotted that beacon and were turning towards it. The crowd was still relatively light here, but he could see movement to the left. A surge of figures was coming their way and behind them the sky had started to glow with the power of sorcerous energies and a thousand flaming brands. The attack had begun.

'Tighten up!' he shouted. They had one chance to get through. The horses wouldn't charge a tightly packed mass of people; they weren't heavy cavalry, trained to smash into bodies of troops. He and his men had to rely on folks' natural fear and instincts, that they would sooner get out of the way of a charging animal. That only worked if there was space to do so.

He kicked his horse once more and aimed for a gap in the milling humanity. And then he was into them. People screamed, faces flew past and folk threw themselves from his path.

'Move! Get out of the way!' he shouted.

His momentum stalled, the refugees started to fill the small space he had created and they sensed an opportunity. Arms reached out to him, voices pleading, begging to be taken with them, to be saved. He felt a tug on his leg. A young child, a girl was reaching up to him. Then she was gone, her place taken by a thin-faced, ragged looking man. He looked back and his men were right behind him, urging their horses forward, cursing and threatening those on foot. Albin, Kally, and two of the others flanked Cayden. His charge was still attached to his back. *It won't last.* He saw a man get between Albin and Cayden, reaching up to pull Cayden off his horse. Albin punched him and he fell away. His group was splintering, being pulled apart by the desperate jostling crowd. As soon as they were separated, they were lost. He knew what he had to do. *Gods forgive me.* He raised his sword and held it high.

'Clear the path! Get out of the way!'

A few souls took note of his drawn blade and tried to step back, but those behind did not. Pleas for mercy were replaced with shouts of anger. On his left, a hand reached out, trying to clutch his reins. Fillion swept his blade down, biting deep into the wrist. He raised his arm and slashed the sword down his right flank. It struck a woman's face, her head whipping back in a spray of blood. More hands reached out for him and he responded fiercely, kicking his horse on and fixing his gaze on the beacon ahead. He cut, hacked and slashed, moving the sword left and right. He couldn't look, couldn't bear to witness the damage he wrought. He tried to block out the noise, the wailing, the terror of the moment, telling himself he had no choice.

Owen turned Arno and headed for the eastern ramparts, Cadarn's firm voice commanding his squadron to rally together. He had spotted the party as they had emerged from the woods to the north. As he started to pulse his sighting to Cadarn another voice entered his mind. *'I see them. I'm going in!'* It was Harwen, only a little older than Owen, yet still full of energy and optimism, where Owen only saw despair. The Eagle Rider had homed in on the line, strafing them with his eagle's talons extended. As they had pulled up, a few arrows had followed them, one even striking the side of Harwen's saddle. His sortie had given the riders the space they needed to escape but there was nothing more the squadron could do to help. A blazing signal beacon had been lit to guide the riders to the walls, and that would have to do.

The wood elves had regrouped and were cantering steadily towards the crowds. As he winged across the seething mass below, Owen drew next to Harwen who waved and grinned.

'Good spot', pulsed Owen taking station next to Harwen.

'*Bloody foolish, Harwen. Those wood elves will stick you with arrows,*' came Bryce's gruff tones. He was one of the older hands, a short, squat and powerfully shouldered Rider. The sour bugger liked to rip into the younger Riders, even when they had done the right thing. Owen couldn't see where he was. *Must be behind me,* he thought.

'*It was necessary, as much as it was foolhardy,*' responded Jenna, the squadron's best flier after Cadarn. She drew level with Owen on his left side, her eagle, Delwyn, screeching a greeting. Jenna nodded to Owen.

'*That's enough,*' pulsed Cadarn. '*All of you, join me above the eastern gate.*'

Owen and the others flew towards the gate, following the line of the wall. Owen watched soldiers scurrying to and fro. Ballistae crews were loading their missiles and archers were stringing their bows. Soldiers carrying shields and spears and torches gathered together around their lightly armoured fellows. They were preparing for an aerial assault. Owen spied dark shapes circling high above the gate. Other eagles were gathering. A number of large braziers burned upon its parapet, creating useful thermals. One by one, the squadron fell into a similar circling pattern, their eagles riding the rising heat to maintain height and conserve energy.

'*Buzzers have been spotted. Coming from the east and the south,*' pulsed Cadarn. '*The other squadrons are moving to engage. We are going to join them. We have to keep them busy for as long as we can. Keep them away from the city and the fleet.*'

Owen swallowed hard. This was it. Buzzers were just bees, but on a gargantuan scale that rendered them terrifying. They had the sorcery of the elves to thank for that.

'*Remember, work together, keep talking to each other, and stay above your target. Ready your weapons,*' ordered Cadarn.

Owen reached behind him and withdrew a small crossbow from a well-secured holster. Others would be doing the same, one or two would use bows. He wasn't yet good enough to fly and shoot a bow effectively, unlike their opponents. His crossbow, already cocked, held a bolt that was most effective at close quarters. Once the shot was expended he'd use his spear, he wouldn't get time to reload. With Arno's reins in his left hand and the crossbow in his right, he was as ready as he was ever going to be.

'*Everyone follow me. For Tissan and the Highlands,*' pulsed Cadarn.

One by one the squadron peeled off and headed east. Owen and Arno joined the others in a wide, flat line. Behind him in the far distance, the last dying rays of the sun created a warm glow, playing around the far horizontal edge of the sea. Ahead of him was the shadowed darkness of night. The clear sky and the many lights below gave them some light to work. They covered the ground quickly, passing over the picket lights marking the extent of the many refugee camps. The sound of humanity retreated to be replaced by another, more terrifying sound.

Buzzing.

It varied in pitch and tone but always constant and insistent. Ahead of him, dotted around the sky, shapes moved against the star-strewn backdrop. They advanced quickly, large and cylindrical, their rapidly moving wings invisible in the night.

As the squadron drew near, a bright lance of fire shot out across the night sky ahead of them engulfing an eagle in flame. Owen blinked, the sorcerous light blinding him. He heard the bird screech in agony as its feathers were consumed and its flesh cooked, and in his mind he listened to the long the cry of despair as the Rider pulsed unconsciously to those around him. There was a stab of pain deep in Owen's heart. The eagle, a blazing twisting ball of fire, fell to the earth, another eagle and Rider gone, another loss that could never be replaced.

As his sight returned, Owen caught a glimpse of a bee, black and yellow furred, body curled inwards, holding its position. An eagle shot down towards it, claws extended, ready to rake across the bee's body. The buzzers were only vulnerable to attack from above. It was the perfect strategy for eagles but it was hard for them to exploit it. What the buzzers lacked in manoeuvrability, they made up for in numbers, and the lethal elven marksmen that rode on their backs.

'*Get higher,*' ordered Cadarn.

Owen leaned forward in the saddle as Arno climbed. He lost sight of the battle beneath him as they gained altitude. He could feel the air getting colder through his fur-lined jacket. Ahead the leading eagles were levelling out.

He felt Cadarn once more. '*Pick your targets, take your run then get high again, don't give them time to shoot.*'

Owen struggled to contain his fear, his mind racing. He couldn't let his squadron down. He swallowed hard before pulsing to Arno. '*Hunt my friend, show them what you can do.*' The eagle began to search the conflict below. It spotted a buzzer and Owen felt Arno's excitement, the desire to attack, as he tried to hide his fear from his bird. Ahead of him he saw eagles peeling off, curving left and right. '*Go Arno. Now!*' The eagle responded, banking sharply, and as he completed the turn, Arno tucked his wings in close and dived.

Seeing through Arno's eyes he spotted the buzzer's pilot and an archer. They were both looking forward. Owen thanked the Emperor.

'*Come, on Arno. Pluck him from the skies.*' As they drew closer, Owen was aware of movement all around him, glimpsed images from the corner of his eyes, of eagles dodging and weaving. There was another explosion of fire, a body falling through the air. And always the buzzing.

Then they were upon the bee. As Arno opened his wings to adjust their speed and direction, the archer turned, saw them and loosed. *Too late.* The arrow sped past Owen's head and Arno struck. He knocked the archer aside, gripped the pilot in its claws and pulled the struggling elf free of his saddle restraints.

'*Release.*' Arno opened his claws and the rider was gone.

Owen whooped as the bee veered away. Free from its commanding influence it no longer had a sense of purpose. '*Quickly, Arno. Climb.*' This was the most dangerous moment. The bees were faster at gaining altitude and could easily chase a bird down. An archer could pick him out of his seat or worse the eagle could get caught, enfolded by the bee's many legs then stabbed by the stinger. Owen looked behind but there no one was following. '*First blood to us, Arno!*' But as they climbed, another eagle fell from the sky.

'What d'you think you're doing?' asked Squash-Nose.

Cade sighed but continued to work at the lock. She almost had it, just a few more tweaks.

'I'm getting out of here. What do you think I'm doing?' she replied.

Squash-Nose slammed his side of the bars that separated their cells.

'Careful, bitch. I've been nice to you so far. I might not be so nice when I break in and show you who's in charge now.'

Nice? If you called a constant stream of crude suggestions about the two of them having sex 'nice', then yes, he was the nicest man she'd ever met. Cade glanced over. Squash-Nose was well named. His hideous snout looked like it had been broken a dozen times. It was framed in a greasy, ragged-bearded face. His eyes were dark and blazed with an anger that would never be calmed. It was a face Cade had seen a hundred times on a hundred different men. It meant very little to her now. She focussed on the lock. It was a bit stiff which wasn't much of a surprise. Since the war began, the prisons had fallen into poor repair as many of the guards, and prisoners too, were hived off to fight in the front lines. Now there were no more guards, they'd just up and left earlier that day. Things must be bad. She'd waited a while just to make sure they weren't coming back. When they didn't, she'd teased the lock pick from the stitched lining of her smallclothes and got to work. Just her luck that the day she finally decided to make a break was the day the city was falling. It would make her escape a more interesting proposition.

The pick met resistance, Cade applied some gentle pressure, too much would snap it, and the resistance gave way. A loud click, and the door swung outwards. She turned and gave Squash-Nose a grin. He looked back open-mouthed.

They were the only two prisoners in this corridor, all the other cells were empty, and their doors open wide. She turned left heading towards the central guardroom.

'Hey! Hey! What about me?' called Squash-Nose.

She should have kept walking but something made Cade stop. She turned and looked at Squash-Nose. His arms were hanging out of the cell, his hands open, palms up. Pleading.

'What about you?' she asked.

Squash-Nose smiled, revealing a mouth half-empty of teeth. Those that remained were black-stained and rotten looking.

'Aren't you going to let me out?'

Cade shook her head.

'No.'

Squash-Nose slammed the bars with both hands. They shook slightly.

'What gives you the right?' he spat.

Cade cocked her head.

'The right?' She took a step forward. 'I earned the right. Every time I took a beating. Every time I had to fight to get away from the likes of you.'

Squash-Nose leapt towards the bars, his arms snaking through, attempting to grab her. She stepped back and spat at him.

'You're not worth saving.'

She turned and walked away.

'Damn you, bitch! I'll get out, and when I do I'll find you. Fucking bitch whore!' he shouted.

No, you won't.

Cade entered the guardroom. The place was deserted. There had been only a skeleton crew left and they had not hung around when the order had come to go. She'd heard the shout, then the whispered discussion, and the debate about what they should do with the prisoners. One had even talked about killing the pair of them. That would have been a very bad mistake for the guards, but it would have made her escape easier. The table where her jailers had sat and played dice was bare except for two empty plates and a tankard that had tipped on to its side. There were no weapons, no food or money, no clothes or shoes for her to steal. All she had was the plain grey prison tunic she was wearing. Cade cocked her head and listened. The place was quiet. Squash-Nose had thankfully shut up, yet she could hear a voice, muffled and distant, like someone shouting for help. It looked to her like the prison had truly been left to the prisoners. That meant then enemy must be at the gates and the war was almost over. *Ain't nothing left of the Empire west of Aberpool 'cept for sea. So, what to do?* Cade considered her options. Going out of the room, stairs led down and up. Above her were two more levels and two more below her, head down and she'd be at ground level. Then there were the underground cells for the serious criminals, the ones that made Squash-Nose look like a harmless rookery drunk. It was the kind of place they put you in and then threw away the key. Lucky she'd not ended up down there, no bars to reach out from, no lock she could have reached. But then she'd never killed anyone that important, or ever stolen enough money to warrant it. She took the stairs to the ground floor and stepped out into the night.

She stood in a nondescript street, Lord Achre's Row it was called. Considering the presence of the prison, it was not a poor neighbourhood, both sides of the street held a mixture of businesses and private residences. Where it met the prison, the street split and worked its way round either side of the building. There was a strange atmosphere to the place. She'd never seen it so empty of life, and it felt uncomfortable, almost oppressive. She could smell the sea, it was only a few minutes' walk to the docks, but there were no birds in the sky, none of the familiar calls of gulls. She'd seen the sun go down through her cell window, and in the early evening shadows, the houses loomed over her, like monsters ready to pounce, as if she was the last morsel to be cleaned up. She heard the creaking of wood behind her, but when she turned there was nothing there. It was too damned eerie. *This place is dead already.* Cade felt she'd escaped one prison only to emerge into a larger one. She barked a harsh, croaky laugh. *Get a grip, woman.* There was an inn not fifty yards from the prison entrance. It was not a bad place to start looking for something useful. She could hear something else now, a distant sound, low and deep, almost like a sigh. She'd picked up enough from the guards to know how bad things had become. Even before she was caught, there'd been a host of refugees camped outside the walls.

The inn door was locked. That was inconsiderate; did the owner seriously think they'd be coming back? Who was likely to break in? There was an alleyway to the side of the building, and at its end, on the right, a wooden fence, slightly over six foot, with a padlocked door. That was more promising. Her pick wouldn't work on such a small aperture, so instead she spat into her hands, rubbed them together and took a step back so that she was pressed against the opposite wall. She pushed off and launched into the air. Her hands grasped the top edge of the fence and the flat of her right foot struck the side of it. Using the purchase it gave her, she hauled up with her hands, shifting the direction of her momentum and swinging her legs up and over the top. She landed lightly on her feet upon bare earth. Another bit of luck, she could just as easily have landed on broken glass, but you didn't get anywhere by being timid. She stood in the back yard of the inn. There was a stable to her left, barely more than a lean-to. Ahead were a number of barrels and to her right another door. She tried it and this one was unlocked. She stepped through into kitchens and it struck her how hungry she was, but a thorough search yielded nothing more than a rotting onion, stuck behind an empty crate in the larder. *Oh well, could've been worse.* Munching the fresher looking part she continued into the inn to see what other treasures she could discover. Her earwigging of the guards' conversations back in the prison had told her that all the population of the town had either been sent to the docks or outside the walls. She wondered whether those who had dwelt here had made it to a ship. It seemed unlikely. It was obvious to her that they had decided to pick and choose who could escape rather than wait for a mad rush to the boats when the enemy arrived. She approved of that kind of careful planning and preparation.

Twenty minutes later she emerged from the alleyway with her riches. The owner and his family had left far more clothes than they had food. She now wore a pair of rough, dark brown, homespun britches, tied round her waist with rope. She'd found a pair of old scuffed boots that almost fit her, a son or stable-boy's perhaps. A dark green tunic replaced her prison garb, unwashed yet still smelling ten times sweeter than that grey rag. Her greatest find had been the store of wine in the cellar. She'd been tempted to stay amongst the bottles and ride out the storm above in a haze of grape-induced oblivion. Very tempted. Instead she'd downed half a bottle of red to celebrate her freedom then supped on the rest while dressing. Before leaving she'd looked at herself in a cracked mirror in the master bedroom. She'd lost some weight. Her raven-black hair was matted and hung lank and forlornly about her shoulders. Her high cheekbones made her gaunt and her thin, delicate nose had a little dirt on its bridge. But her eyes hadn't changed. They were hard eyes, a deep blue, flecked with green if anyone ever got close enough to notice. She couldn't remember a time when they reflected anything other than lies. With them she had hidden pain, pretended pleasure and falsified truth.

Back in the street, she thought about her next move. On her shoulder she carried a sack containing three bottles of red, and had one more in her hand. That should keep her going through the night. She doubted she would live to see another one, so would rather face her end drunk and insensible. The armies of the enemy no doubt ringed Aberpool. The final outpost of Tissan was set to fall. She had the run of the city and her options were north or south. She took a swig from the bottle, wiping her mouth with the back of her hand. South was the prison. *North it is then. Perfect.* She started walking, her pace slow, and her gait unsteady.

'Father Michael?'

He looked up. 'Yes, sergeant?'

'We have a signal from the wall. They are coming.'

Father Michael nodded. He pulled back the hood from his voluminous brown cloak, his wide sleeves falling down his arms, revealing well-muscled forearms bearing old scars. He looked up at the wall. Above him the signal beacon blazed away in the early evening sky. *Thank the Emperor, but they had left it tight*, he thought.

'Open the gate and get your crossbows out there. No one but the riders get through.' Reaching inside a pouch tied to his belt, he withdrew a large black iron key and handed it to the sergeant.

'Yes, Father.'

The sergeant gave orders to his men, a full platoon of thirty soldiers. Father Michael was in no doubt all of them would be needed. He stepped back to allow them room, it felt odd not to be the first out, but his role was not to charge into battle. He watched as the detachment moved to open the first of the sally port doors. The sergeant unlocked the door and pulled it outwards. He took a flaming brand and entered a short dark passageway, his men following. Two wooden planks, almost three times the length of a man, waited by the doorway. In the flickering light he saw the far door open outwards. A gust of wind blew the flame backwards for a moment. Beyond was the world outside the wall. The sergeant and his men stepped into the night; the soldiers carrying the planks followed on. Father Michael joined the rear of the party and emerged into a tumult. Gathered around him, on a small patch of ground, the soldiers looked out on a mass of refugees. Before them was the fire trench filled with oil-soaked wood. The trench continued around the walls, almost touching the stone foundations, the circuit leading nearly to the sea. For what they needed it to achieve, a moat would not have sufficed. Only here had the trench deviated from its proximity to the wall, deliberately forming an island. A second salient had been constructed on the southern side of the city in case those they waited for had come by a different route.

Ahead he could see a disturbance among the throng, horsemen forcing their way towards the island, swords flashing in the night fires.

'Quickly. Get those planks out!' the sergeant ordered.

The soldiers carrying the planks stepped up to the edge of the trench and started to push them out and over the span. They held on to the wood at waist height, feeding it through their hands, arms starting to strain as they fought to keep the wood level and steady. A number of nearby refugees were moving closer, begging to be let across.

'Bows, get yourselves a clear arc of fire,' said the sergeant.

A dozen men carrying crossbows stepped up to the edge of their island and aimed their weapons towards the crowd. The refugees took note, their desperate pleas turning to anger.

It is not for you we do this. There is no rescue, thought Father Michael. *There is nowhere left for you to run. Forgive us. Forgive me.*

The first plank touched the far side. It was joined moments later by the second, just a few inches away from it.

'Go, go!' shouted the sergeant, ushering men across. Another group of soldiers, armed with shields and short swords drawn, scurried across the planks, the wood vibrating to their footfalls. A man stepped on to the crossing, shouting at them and the lead soldier did not hesitate. He raised his shield and barged into the man, knocking him from his feet and back into the crowd. The soldiers gained the far side and spread out, making a small semi-circle around the planks, their shields locking together just in time. The refugees surged against them and the shield wall rippled, but did not break. The soldiers pushed back, using the flats of their swords to cudgel and cajole people away.

Father Michael watched the people, studying their reactions. They were backing off for now, but a determined surge could undo everything. Ahead, the first horseman was scant yards away from the soldiers.

'Open up, let them through,' called the sergeant, shouting at the men on the far side. The middle two soldiers forced their way forwards and outwards. Their neighbours moved accordingly and the semi-circle became a line, creating a corridor. The first horseman barged his way through the remaining crowd and charged down the line, dismounting by the planks. He sheathed his sword and looked to those following behind. Father Michael strained to see if they had their charge. *Yes! They had him. Emperor be praised.* The third horse to get through the press carried him in front of the rider and as it passed them, the sergeant ordered the protective lines of shields to close up. He watched as the remaining riders dismounted before the shield wall and forced their way into the circle. Not all of them made it. One was pulled away by the mob, wrestled to the ground and set upon, a focus for their anger and frustration. He did not rise again.

'Get him off the horse!' shouted the lead rider. Two men moved to help get their charge off his mount and he slipped off the saddle as they loosened the binds. Father Michael had not known what state their charge would be in and fear surged through his mind. Had they bought him a corpse? One man took the legs, the other the arms and between them they carried their charge across the planks. Father Michael stepped up, looking briefly at the face of the man they had all come to save. There was still some colour in him. He sighed. *Still alive.* A man joined him, the leader of the riders. Upon the left breast of his tunic he wore the fox sigil of the Imperial Scouts. The man looked odd, his face not quite right, his blond hair was tangled and hanging over his eyes. There was blood on his cheek.

'He took a fall and a blow to his head. Been unconscious for three days,' the scout said.

Father Michael nodded. The scout loitered, his face expectant. What did he want? *I am not your master.* He thought a moment. 'Take your men to the walls. They need support.' A look came over the man's face and his mouth opened to speak. Father Michael had no time for this. 'Quickly, go through, there's a cart waiting.'

The scout gathered himself, saluted and ushered his men into the tunnel. As they passed him by Father Michael called to the sergeant.

'It's time.'

The sergeant raised his torch high. Waving it left and right in wide sweeps, the light illuminated his visage one side then the other, trading with the shadows. It gave him a feverish, demonic expression. Father Michael watched the reply. All along the wall's length torches were thrown down into the trench. Moments later, barrels tumbled after them, smashing into the piled wood as they landed. The liquid inside exploded outward on impact, splashing the nearby material with yet more flammable oil. Where it touched naked flame it burst into life, spreading the fire, snaking along planks and branches like cracks in ice.

On the far side, those gathered let out another great cry of anguish. Father Michael had not thought it possible, yet there was more despair in this sound than in any he had heard before. He had dealt with death all his life and had despaired too, but he'd never been one of the baying crowd, one of the spectators watching the show. How could anyone take pleasure from this? From watching a fellow human die with no hope of rescue or reprieve? How many times had he been party to such acts of violence? Too many.

The remaining riders sprinted over the planks, past him and into the passage. The shield wall started to bend and contract as the soldiers struggled to withdraw in good order. The crowd had grown violent, desperate. There was nothing left for them to lose. The soldiers switched from bludgeoning to stabbing. It was a matter of survival. Yet even as the civilians fell, more took their place, scrambling over the dead and dying.

'Come on!' shouted the sergeant.

Three soldiers disengaged and started to cross the plank bridge. The shield wall buckled then broke, and the crowd engulfed the remaining men.

'Get those planks shifted, don't let them get across!' cried the sergeant, an edge of hysteria to his voice.

Soldiers stooped to pick up the planks. Even as they did so, the first refugees were already starting to cross, heedless of the flames starting to build beneath them. In their panic several of the crowd were pushed into the trench, their screams lost in the cacophony of panic.

'Crossbows, clear them off,' ordered the sergeant. There were not enough bowmen to stop the crowd, but they could hold a single crossing, if only for a moment.

A thrumming sound filled the air as a dozen bolts flew at those on the planks, most striking their targets. Three more bodies fell. It gave the soldiers enough time to lift and push the planks into the fire trench.

The soldiers stepped back. The crossbow men reloaded their weapons. The fires were starting to rage all along the trench and on the far side, their fellow citizens of the dying Tissan Empire stared at them. He could feel their hate, their anger and their fear as surely as he could feel the heat of the flames.

A few brave souls chose to jump into the trench and try to make their way across.

'Father?' asked the sergeant. 'Should we shoot?'

Father Michael shook his head. Those folk would die tonight without their help.

'Don't waste your bolts. Let's head in.'

He turned and strode back through the passageway. He knew they had done a dismal, despicable thing. Their own people, his own people, had been slaughtered to save one man. Yet you had to look at it with the right perspective. They'd acted in the name of a greater good. *A hundred, a thousand times I have done ill and will do it again. I was damned but the ills I commit this day and each day forward will save me.* Amidst the death he felt the stirrings of an emotion he had only recently become acquainted with. Hope.

'You've got one on your tail, Owen,' said Harwen.

'Where?'

'Break left!'

Owen pulsed the command to Arno and the bird executed a tight turn. He looked around and saw a buzzer coming right for them. Its pincer-like legs extended, the stinger a sharp shadow beneath its torso. There was a rider, but no archer and if that rider had been a sorcerer he'd already know about it. A small mercy, he was a sitting duck.

As the bee turned to follow him, a blur of a shape broadsided the creature. An eagle dug its claws into the bee's head and Harwen thrust his spear into one of the large black eyes. The bee reacted violently, bucking and twisting, while the eagle released and was away. The bee was already on the way to the ground, its buzzing high pitched and shrill. *Thanks for the assist,* he pulsed to Harwen but the other Rider didn't respond.

He ordered Arno to climb in a wide circle so he could try and make sense of the fight in the half-darkness. It was as confusing as it had been at the start, shapes still danced in the shadows and cries and screams rode the air. If he had to guess, he'd say the eagles had the upper hand. There was no more flame in the sky, so perhaps the sorcerer had been taken out? They always made a point of targeting the spell casters first. No one had noticed him so he reached behind and drew out the crossbow from its satchel. It was his only weapon, other than Arno, since he had lost his spear in a clumsy charge.

Owen looked towards the city. The fire trench was well aflame, the walls glowing with light. Before it the crowds continued to surge, but now they flowed around the walls, not towards them. They were heading for the beaches, driven on by the advancing enemy. This was the first time he'd had a chance to see that enemy, his attention had been focused on the sky. A sea of torches had appeared, not a quarter mile from the walls. Armour and weapons glittered in the light. Slightly behind the line huge black shapes were rolling forwards. They were siege machines: catapults and trebuchets. He spied a low rectangular shape but its roof was rounded, like a dome, and he could just make out a black protrusion sticking out at the front. It was a ram, a big one. The sea of lights went on forever, almost the entire length of the eastern wall. How many machines did they have?

The city's war machines suddenly opened up now that elves had come into range. Owen watched as some of his fellows dodged the projectiles and winged higher. *Nice of the bastards to tell us.* Trebuchets flung barrels of incendiary oil into the massed ranks, followed swiftly by archers releasing flame arrows, hoping to ignite the substance. Ballistae shot their large harpoons with powerful thumps. The damage must have been terrible. Here and there a shield flared, as sorcerers deflected a projectile, and protected their own siege weapons. *They must know the city is empty, surely. They could just starve the few defenders out.* But then that wasn't the purpose of their attack. The enemy wanted to end this tonight.

Owen jammed the front end of the crossbow against his pommel and leaned back in the saddle hauling on the string. The trigger caught and he fished in a saddlebag for another bolt. The elves were responding to the barrage, flinging missiles, rocks and boulders towards the city. He saw a chunk of parapet smashed into oblivion, large pieces of stonework tumbling into the fire trench. The front lines were parting as the siege towers and rams began their run towards the walls. The fire trench would stop them. It was too wide, too deep to cross.

He felt Cadarn reach out with his usual calmness. *'There is another wave of buzzers coming in. We have to keep them from the walls for as long as we can.'*

Owen fixed his gaze back on the aerial combat. He could just make out the buzzers ahead, a cloud of black forms covering the night sky. There were so many, they could not hold out for long. With that many bees in the air the eagles wouldn't get a chance to gain altitude between strafing runs.

Owen could feel Arno's concern too. It was strong and building. The eagle was fighting against his own primal instincts to flee and Owen didn't blame him. *'Climb higher, Arno. Higher!'* he pulsed, unable to hide his fear, and Arno screeched in response.

Cade leaned against the shadowed corner of the intersection and took another drink. She was feeling quite merry. She raised the bottle to her mouth once more. Nothing came out but a solitary drop. How many bottles was that? She watched with interest as a number of men emerged from the lane opposite her. A grim looking lot, some carrying torches, all of them armed. A wagon followed them on to the far broader street running west and east. The turn was sharp and the driver had difficulty manoeuvring the cart round it. The soldiers fanned out, weapons pointed in all directions. They looked antsy.

'Where you boys headed, then?' she asked.

The one nearest her stepped back in surprise. He raised his crossbow, ready to shoot her.

She raised her hands.

'Whoa there, just being friendly.'

'Lower your weapon!' barked another man, dressed similarly to the first, but with a purple feather sprouting from his helmet. The first did as he was told and stepped back, eyeing Cade warily.

Purple feather man stood before her, his hands resting in his sword belt. He gave her a once over and she smiled back sweetly.

'Problem, sergeant?' asked a third man, walking towards them. Cade cocked an eyebrow. This one was big, even in his heavy brown cloak.

'No, Father. Looks like someone got left behind. A drunkard. No doubt she's been comatose in a cellar the past week.'

'Oh, *Father*, is it?' said Cade. 'I suppose it's too late to ask the Emperor to absolve me of my sins?'

'Take a care, wench,' growled the sergeant.

The one called Father pulled his hood back and stared at her. *My, but this one is pretty.* If you liked your priests raised in one of the Emperor's arenas. The man was bald, his head shaven rather than through hair loss. The left side of his head was dented, as if it had been smashed in. In her book that should have been a killing blow but this fella didn't look like he let things like that slow him down. His jaw was big, solid-looking. He had a thick brown beard but no growth on his lip. A scar ran across his nose and the top of his right ear was missing. About his thick neck he wore the sun symbol of the clergy, a small brass disc with flames etched upon it. He looked more like a thug than a priest. Except for the eyes. In the dim light they looked dark, probably brown. They also looked … sad.

The priest remained quiet a moment longer, gazing into her eyes. It made her feel uncomfortable and she stood up straighter. He shook his head gently, pulled the hood back over his face and turned away.

'Leave her, sergeant.' His voice was deep, but not as gruff as she had expected.

The soldier gave her one more disdainful glance and followed on.

Cade spat on to the ground. *Damn priests, damn soldiers. It was their fault. They got us all into this mess in the first place.*

'Sergeant. Take half your men to the market square. No doubt they will need your assistance.' He spoke his words quite precisely, but it sounded like an effort.

'Father? Is that wise?' replied the sergeant, his voice pitching a little higher than before.

The priest stared at him, his eyes blank, betraying nothing. 'You know your duty.'

The sergeant paused a moment, then nodded. 'Yes, sir. First squad. East to the square.'

The soldiers hesitated and looked at each other.

The sergeant drew his sword.

'Now, dammit!' he shouted.

A number of soldiers formed up behind him and together they ran off down the street in a clatter of armour and the dull stomp of boots upon the cobbles.

The cart had finally turned. The priest gave her a look, like he was sizing her up. She straightened her shoulders and looked back. He blinked, turned away and gave the order to continue on. She watched them head west toward the docks.

Cade cocked her head. There was a definite sound of fighting coming from the east. She stepped out from the shadows and looked down the street. The horizon was glowing. A light arched high into the sky and fell into the city somewhere ahead of her. A great ball of flame expanded from the point of impact and a second later she heard the explosion and felt the concussion hit her body. Well, that wasn't a good way to go. West was where the soldiers were going and she had just come from the south. *Keep north, then.* She hefted her sack, hearing the clink of the bottles within. She threw the empty bottle over her shoulder and started walking. As it smashed, she began to whistle.

'Where's my aide?' shouted General Cord, as he kept low behind the battlements. 'Where's Major Willets?' Above his head a blazing ball of fire sailed past. The heat washed over his face and he could swear he could smell his eyebrows singeing. Beside him his men squatted behind the wreckage of the wall. Large chunks had already been eaten away by magical detonations or torn out by the massive artillery pieces that had all found their range.

A younger officer, face blackened, tunic torn, scrambled over.

'He's dead, General, got hit by one of them rocks. There's nothing left of him.'

'Really?'

'Yes, sir. He was standing right by you.'

To his left was a gaping hole. He could see open air and the red, glowing trench below. Cord scratched his chin.

'Congratulations then, son. You have just been promoted.'

The young officer stood a little straighter. 'Yes, General!'

The fire trench was starting to burn out, the fuel was still glowing red but the flames had died down. It wouldn't be stalling the advancing army for much longer. The gatehouses had been reduced to rubble, and it was only the Tissan refugees that had given the enemy any cause to slow down. He watched as all along the defences enemy fliers ranged above them, the bees hovering in place for the crews to shoot at will or choosing to fly low, using their legs and the threat of their deadly stingers to drive men from the heights. There were still eagles fighting up there, the Emperor alone knew how they were holding on. There was precious little counter-fire coming from his men now. Either the crews were dead or the men had run out of ammunition. It didn't matter much either way, the massed fire from the elven archers was heavy and relentless, most of his men couldn't move from the protection of the merlons for fear of becoming pin cushions.

In front of Cord, the city burned. There were enemy troops within the city now. He had seen a flight of buzzers drop them off a short time ago, not many but enough to start causing real harm. He didn't need to look to know that there were no more refugees out there beyond the trench. They were all dead. The walls could no longer be held, but they could still buy some time. The fight wasn't over yet.

'Pass the order. All troops are to pull back and gather at the market square. We'll make our last stand there.'

His new aide saluted and hurried away as fast as his bent-double form let him. Cord pushed himself up and moved from the protection of the wall. He pulled down his breastplate, cricked his neck and stepped slowly towards the ramp leading down into the city. It wouldn't be good for the men to see him scrambling away, there had to be some semblance of order. Behind him, as the word was given, his surviving soldiers ran along the walkway but once they gained the ramp, they slowed. No one attempted to run past him. He smiled to himself. *Good lads to die with,* he thought.

Captain Fillion shook his head, trying to blink the dust out of his eyes, and to stop the damned ringing in his ears. He wasn't sure where he was; he wasn't even sure who he was. Then it came flooding back to him. He and his men were running through the streets, heading for the east wall, and they'd run into a bunch of elves coming the other way. Weapons were drawn and blood was spilled. He'd gutted the lead elf personally. Then there had been a shouted warning to get down, take cover, followed by a great whooshing noise, a mighty cracking sound and then something hard had struck him. Whatever it had been, he now had one bastard of a headache. He coughed, hacking up a thick mix of dust and phlegm. He looked about, tried to get his bearings. He was on a street and it was still night. To his left a building had been utterly demolished. A sharp pain in the side of his head made him wince. He gingerly put a hand up to touch the source of the pain, his fingers probing through his hair. It was sticky, warm and wet. *Not good.*

'Ah. Ow.' He pressed. More pain, stinging this time but there was no obvious puncture wound, nothing hard sticking out. *Better.* A little down the street a fire was blazing and crackling away merrily. Above him, drifting trails of smoke obscured the sky. He stretched a little, realised his back was against a wall and his legs were stretched out in front of him. The street was empty of life, friendly or otherwise. Someone, probably one of his men, had pulled him out of the rubble and left him here. Was the battle over? He couldn't be sure. He heard a buzzing sound, and one of those damned bees flew over. If nothing else, it confirmed the enemy hadn't been beaten, as if that had ever been possible, but were the walls were lost yet?

That's it, then. What do I do now? I can't walk. I sure as hell can't fight worth a damn. Where is my sword anyway? His weapon was gone. So was his cloak. He looked about once more. His vision must be improving because he saw he wasn't entirely alone. There were others on the street, mostly elves, some of his men too. Nobody had thought to treat them so kindly as to prop them up against a wall, so he guessed they were all dead. He tried to stand but a wave of pain washed over him. His vision blurred and he had to fight against the overwhelming urge to throw up. At this point he reasoned that crawling might be a far better option. He relaxed his body, letting himself slide down the side of the wall until his shoulder was touching the street, then he rolled on to his front and slowly crawled across to an elf who looked up at him with sightless blue eyes. Lightly armoured, it wore an ornate, leather breastplate full of fluting scrollwork, greaves and vambraces. Clothed to move fast, he must have been dropped in by the buzzers.

Fillion thought for a moment, a germ of an idea forming. He got to work undoing the straps of the armour covering the elf's forearms and shins. Struggling against the pain and his aching body, it took a few minutes to get them secured on to his own limbs. Then he went for the breastplate. That was hard bloody work; he started with the buckles on the side nearest him, loosening the breastplate a little before he switched to the other side. He worked those buckles free then he flipped the front of the armour over the elf's head. The last bit was going to be the hardest and he took a few breaths, stealing himself for the pain. He sat up slowly, got his hands underneath the body and pushed. He rocked backwards and forwards a little to get some movement then with a heave he pushed the body over and away from the back half of the breastplate.

'Ahhh ...' Fillion sat back and threw up between his legs. 'Shit,' he whispered hoarsely, wiping his mouth. He reached over, pulled the breastplate over his head and did a strap up on either side. It the best he could do, he felt dizzy, his body going limp. *Quickly, before I bloody pass out.* He reached up and gathered his long blonde hair and pushed it back behind his ears, making sure their pointed ends were prominent. *No point dying just yet. I can still serve.* He lay back down with a sigh, tilted his head so his profile was obvious and closed his eyes.

'*We've lost the walls,*' pulsed Cadarn. '*Fall back, head for the fleet.*'

Owen didn't need to be told twice. The second wave of buzzers was larger than the first and it was all he could do to avoid the arrows, stingers and fire blasts of new sorcerers entering the fray. Each time he'd tried to make a run, another buzzer had sought to block his attack. It took every ounce of Owen's skill and Arno's instinct to keep from getting hit by arrows coming in from every direction at once. They banked, wheeled, dipped and climbed to the point where even Owen's stomach, inured as it was to flying, wanted to empty itself.

Arno tipped his wings taking a tight turn and Owen looked back. He couldn't see many eagles disengaging from the melee. The buzzers seemed in no hurry to chase them, however, thank the Emperor for that. Arno used the thermals to gain height as he passed over the battlements.

He flew directly west, towards the sea, his eyes trying to look everywhere at once. He scanned the sky for any friendly fliers and saw one low and to his right, a couple more far off to his left. There were a few shapes, winging their way ahead of him in the night sky. *Is this all that's left of us?*

Below in the city he saw the glow of lights, a lot of them. As he drew near, Owen discerned the wide, open space of the market square. Within it were gathered the remnants of the defenders, the last valiant soldiers of the Tissan Empire. He dropped Arno lower for a closer look. Men were scurrying about, manning crude barricades of overturned wagons that had been placed at all the entrances to the square. A few stragglers were making their way in from the north, scrambling over the obstacles and taking their places. In the centre another small knot of troops were gathered together. Owen ordered a low swoop and Arno screeched a greeting to the men, a figure in that group waving back as they passed over. And then he was beyond them, beyond the square and through the dark, empty and dying city. A short distance away, the docks appeared, a few lights bobbing on the calmer water within its protective barriers. There were virtually no lights further beyond that. The ships had been told to run without them, and most would be well underway by now. Part of Owen's orders had been to fight in the line then withdraw to provide air cover for the fleet. Not all the squadrons had had that order, some were told to stay about the walls and fight to the last. His squadron was one of the lucky ones. They still had a chance to live.

He did not spot the figure perched on a rooftop near the lower wharfs, but Arno did. Owen turned his head as he felt Arno's reaction and tried to focus. Whoever it was, they sat on the high-sloped roof of a grand looking building. Arno changed his course slightly to get a better look. The building was a church, the structure was four stories in height, with a wide frontage of steps leading up to a porch held up by a row of tall pillars supporting the red tiled roof. The figure, a man, sat on the apex of that roof. He must have been missed when everyone was made to leave, another soul left behind, another human who would die before the night was out. The man would have a good view of the Empire's final death throes, he'd give him that. Owen shot past, getting Arno back on track. He chewed his lip for a moment, looked out towards the sea, and then turned his head sharply. There were no buzzers behind him. *Damn it all.* He pulled hard on the reins, eliciting a wave of irritation from Arno.

'Sorry old friend,' he said aloud. '*Go back, land on the roof,*' he pulsed, picturing the building for Arno.

The eagle swung around, taking a few moments to reach the church. Arno flared his wings, extended his talons and gripped hold of the rounded capping tiles that ran along the top of the gently sloping roof. Arno took a second to steady himself, and then tucked his wings in.

'Hey!' said Owen.

The man looked over at him. His legs were dangling over the far slope of the roof, his hands clasped in his lap. He had black, closely cropped hair, a forked beard and a long, thin face. He wore the black robes of a novice.

'Want a lift?' asked Owen.

The man raised his hands.

'And go where?' he asked in a good-natured voice.

'Where do you bloody think?' asked Owen. He was already regretting his act of kindness.

'The world is ending, my friend. I was going to sit here and watch it,' said the man, smiling.

'It's not over yet. One time offer, get on board.'

The man tilted his head and looked at Owen.

'Very well.' He pulled up his legs, placed both hands on to the central line of capping tiles, got his feet between them and stood unsteadily. 'It appears I am granted a bird's eye view with which to witness our final hour.'

The black-robed man picked his way towards Owen, his arms held out to keep his balance.

Owen reached his hand out.

'Come on, almost there.'

Two feet away, the man thrust his right arm out and seized Owen's hand. *Strong grip*, thought Owen.

'See the stirrup here? Put your foot in that then step up. You can sit behind me.'

The man nodded. Owen withdrew his foot from the stirrup and watched the man place his left foot there.

'Alright, up you come.'

As the man lent forward and pushed off, Owen hauled him up. In one smooth action, the man stepped and swung his right leg behind Owen, his body coming to rest on the rear of the saddle.

'Nicely done. Now hold on tight. This will be tricky.'

He felt arms snake around his stomach.

'Arno. This is going to be hard. Away you go!'

The eagle unfolded his wings once more and took three powerful beats, trying to gain some lift.

Owen felt Arno's struggle. He was not used to this much weight.

The eagle left the roof, lurching down slightly as he switched his flying angle. Arno fought to stay level, his wings moving rapidly to counteract the downward force upon his back. He turned towards the west heading along one of the wider streets. Owen ground his teeth. They were moving, but they couldn't climb. He kept Arno following the course of the street. There was no way he was going to clear any of the tall tenement buildings on either side. At least they were only a few hundred metres from the wharf now.

'Come on, big lad. Keep going,' he muttered while pulsing thoughts of encouragement to Arno. They just had to reach one of the larger ships. They had special platforms for eagles to land on, and he could drop this one off then get back in the air.

Arno struggled on, slow, unsteady, straining with every motion. Owen watched the skies. The way ahead was still clear, but their progress was far too slow. There were no discernible sounds of buzzers, so they had a chance. He spotted a mass of shapes coming along the coast from the south moving at speed. They had wings. He felt a surge of relief. More eagles, and their paths would meet in the harbour.

'Looks like we have some friends, Arno. Almost safe.'

As they started to converge, he was able to see them clearly. Yes, they had wings, and four legs, and no riders. Just as quickly as it came, his relief was replaced by fear. They were gryphons, intelligent and vicious, with the head and wings of eagles and the body of lions. Gryphons hunted in packs working together to bring their prey down. They were the enemy. Smaller in size than an eagle, this had led him to believe they were further away than they truly were. He could hear them screeching to one another. They didn't need riders, they wouldn't have allowed it anyway, they were too proud.

'Shit.' Owen thought fast. They couldn't climb above them, couldn't fly around them. *If we didn't have this damned extra weight, Arno's speed would have carried us clear.* Once the gryphons spotted them, they'd be torn to pieces. But they hadn't yet. Arno was lower than them, the city buildings providing a screen. A hundred yards away the street ended, emptying on to the wharf.

'Arno, right!'

The eagle obeyed, seeing his rider's intention. Another street opened up, running north. Arno banked sharply, dropping even lower, barely a dozen feet above the ground. Owen looked behind him. No pursuit. They were hidden in shadow, far below the vision of the gryphons and moving away from their direction of travel. They'd be after the ships and he pitied the poor folk who were picked for the gryphons' attention.

'Change of plan!' he called back to his passenger who had been clinging on silently.

'I noticed,' came the cheerful reply. 'You can drop me anywhere if you'd like.'

Owen shook his head. This fellow was quite mad.

The street they flew along was mercifully straight, but also heading directly north, away from where he wanted to go. His mind raced as he tried to figure out a solution, painfully aware that Arno was growing more tired with every beat. Pretty soon they'd all be on the ground.

A large, tall building with lights blazing from a dozen points, hove into view. It was the Roosting tower, but it was likely to be empty, there'd be no help there.

His mind wandered back to earlier that night. *North. What was north?* Then he remembered their flight path.

'Hold on, we're taking you to the beaches,' he shouted.

He pulsed his directions to Arno. They just had to keep going this way and they'd be across the wall, out of the city and over where he'd seen the boats loading refugees, hoping there were still some left. As they struggled along the street Owen allowed himself a small measure of satisfaction. It was a good plan and it was working. Buildings shot by left and right of him. When lanes and streets met his route the night sky was revealed for the barest of moments. To the east, occasional flashes of light, and the brighter glow patches of countless fires. To the west, ships were heading further out to sea. And ahead, the street was coming to an end. In its place was a wall. It was too high.

'Arno, please,' Owen pulsed. '*One more effort, climb. Give it everything Arno. Climb!*'

Arno responded, his wings beating harder, the range deeper, biting down into the air. And they rose, slowly, barely. Owen felt the stress Arno was placing on himself, using his last reserves. 'Come on. Come on, come on …' said Owen, whispering his new prayer to any God who would listen. Ahead the wall rose to meet them, a grey, unyielding mass. The walkways were empty of anything except for few braziers glowing red, some scattered bodies and one or two wrecked artillery pieces. Owen reckoned the distance: thirty yards, twenty, ten. Too close.

Arno breasted the battlements, skimming along its lip, his talons scrapping the top of a merlon. Arno gained more height, a precious extra few feet, then trimmed his wings, started to glide. He had nothing left.

Owen whooped. He clapped Arno's neck and shouted, 'You beauty!'

They slid over the smouldering ditch and across the wreckage and detritus of abandoned campsites. There were no enemy troops crawling around yet, but that would change. He could see a mass of torches in the distance. *Oh.* He realised his mistake, they were already there.

The beach was a nightmare, crawling with a heaving mass of people sandwiched between the sea and a slow-moving line of enemy troops. No cavalry, no siege weapons, just a line of soldiers. They were hard to pick out at first, and as he drew closer he saw they were wearing blackened armour. They were totally covered from head to foot in the stuff, utterly enclosed. The dark armour meant that nothing shined, that nothing was able to reflect light. They were carrying axes, spears and war hammers, similarly blackened. Dwarves. That's how they chose to fight, in the dark, where their night vision could be used to best effect. As he winged over them it was like crossing a barrier of silence. They marched soundlessly; there were no shouts or battle cries, no barked orders. These dwarves were a stark contrast to the screaming mass of humanity, and they marched inexorably on, cutting down anyone too slow to stay ahead of them. It was clear to Owen they were driving those people right into the water, not caring whether the Tissans died by their blades or the cold, briny sea.

He watched the throng splinter and spread as many entered the water, swimming out beyond the thin, shallow sandbank to where the ground swiftly fell away into the murky depths. It reminded him of how a drop of blood dilutes in the water, losing form and colour, merging into the greater whole. There were still a few boats out there, but they were several hundred yards from the beach. Most of those people would never make it. He knew he couldn't have, he wasn't a strong enough swimmer. He'd drown before he got halfway.

He urged Arno to head out. They had made it just in time, those boats were pulling up sails, readying to leave. Most were little more than fishing skiffs, but a trading vessel, small of draft and beam, designed for river use, lay ahead of them. A small rowboat was heading towards it. That would have to do.

'Listen, we can't land. You are going to have to jump,' Owen shouted to his passenger.

'Alright.'

Owen marvelled at the calmness of the man.

Arno flew in between the ship and the rowboat, not twenty yards separating the two.

'Good luck. Now!' Owen barked.

He felt the man let go of his waist and push himself away. Arno helped by tilting his body to the right.

'Ow!' The man's foot clubbed Owen in the back of his head and then he was gone. Arno immediately responded to the lightened load. He flapped his wings, gaining some extra height. Owen looked back. He could see the man in the water, a hand raised. Someone was pointing at him from the rowboat and Owen thought he heard shouts. It would have to do.

Now what about us?

They were heading at an angle back towards the land. They'd reach the headland where the beach ended, behind the line of the dwarves. It was rocky and forested and beyond that was hill country, rugged and windswept. Arno had gained some relief but he was still dead tired, they both were, and his soul felt empty. Those damned gryphons were behind them, ranging around the fleet. It was going to be too dangerous to go that way. But what of his orders and his friends? He had to get back to them, didn't he? He was still an Eagle Rider and that meant something, didn't it? If the enemy were busy at the city, it stood to reason they wouldn't be wandering around elsewhere. Everyone would want to watch the end, so nobody should notice the pair of them coming in from the sea. *Am I really going to do this?*

He pulsed Arno with directions; they'd head north and east into the hills to lie low. Arno acknowledged with a twist of his neck. *As for tomorrow*, Owen thought, *we can figure that out later.*

The driver hauled on the reins, stopping the wagon. He reached down and pulled on the handbrake. Father Michael walked past him and along final few yards of the pier. Behind him tired soldiers, breathing heavily from the pace he had set, got to work gathering their cargo on to a stretcher. He looked back towards the city. It was surrounded by a low, orange and red penumbra. Bright flashes in the sky highlighted the aerial battles. But the battle was already over. The flashes were the death throes of the last defenders.

The pier reached out the furthest from the wharf. The harbour itself was empty. He had expected to find the Emperor's ship, *The Fist of Tissan*, waiting for them. Instead a cutter rocked against the side of the stone pier. It had a crew of twelve oarsmen and a man on the tiller. There was precious little space left for anyone else, certainly not all of his party.

'Where is the Emperor's ship?' he demanded.

'Out to sea,' the man on the tiller responded, pointing towards open water. 'The captain said it would take too long to put off from the harbour.'

Father Michael blinked and nodded.

'Very well.' He turned to the four soldiers carrying the stretcher. 'Take him down, put him in the boat.' He stepped back, turned around to look at the city and breathed deep. Ahead of him the remaining half dozen men of the platoon waited. They looked nervous.

He turned to watch their cargo; the stretcher had been handed across into the cutter and lay in the centre where the boat was slightly wider. The four soldiers had taken all the available space left. There was just enough room for someone to sit by the tiller. He looked at the steersman.

'Get ready to cast off,' he said.

He then turned to the men by the wagon. *I must try at least.*

'Men, return to the city, aid in its defence. You work is done and you have the Emperor's gratitude.'

The soldiers eyed each other.

One, the driver, placed a hand on his sword. 'Why should we? The city is lost and there is still space on that boat.'

'True, but not for all of you. It must leave, now.'

'Are you going?' asked another. This one had a crossbow. It was loaded.

Father Michael nodded.

'I am required to. I must see my charge delivered.'

'Looks to me like you done that, priest,' said the driver icily.

So be it. He looked at each man in turn. Assessing them. The driver's sword was still sheathed. Three men had crossbows, only one loaded, on his far right, and the last two carried spears. Who would attack first? He should force the issue, just to be sure. He took a step towards the nearest spearman on his far left and held his hands up. The soldier responded by raising his weapon, the point not a foot away from Father Michael's stomach.

'Your Emperor commands that you defend him unto death! Do you disavow him? Do you betray him?' Father Michael asked. He raised his voice, adding an edge of arrogance to it.

The driver took the bait.

'The Emperor won't know we betrayed him because you won't be there to tell him, priest. Take him!' he growled.

The spearman thrust his weapon towards Father Michael who stepped to one side, twisting his body. As the spear passed through empty space and the soldier overbalanced, Father Michael grabbed hold of the shaft, and with his left arm yanked the end of the spear up and into the soldier's jaw, his head snapping back with a grunt. Father Michael saw the crossbow rise. He heaved on the spear once more, yanking the man around in a circle. Another grunt and the soldier released the spear, a bolt buried in his back. Father Michael once more assessed the danger. The driver was drawing his sword and the other spearman was charging him. Of the three crossbowmen, two were frantically trying to load their weapons, and the third stood numbly by, still shocked by what he had just done. Father Michael stepped up to meet the charge; this spear was again levelled at his stomach, held tight to its wielder's side. He dropped to his knees, swayed his head out of the way of the approaching point and whipped his own weapon round in an arc, slamming it into the legs of the soldier. The wood snapped, as did at least one bone in the man's left leg. He fell screaming.

Father Michael stood and strode towards the driver, who had finally gotten his sword out. He was gripping it tightly in both hands, point levelled forward. Father Michael glanced at the bowmen and none were ready to fire yet. The driver raised his blade and shaped for a downward slash. *Sloppy.* He stepped inside the driver's reach and with his right hand jabbed his outstretched fingers into the throat, while using his left to check the descent of the blade by gripping the driver's wrist. The driver gagged, let go of the sword and clawed at his neck, his windpipe crushed. Father Michael took the blade and moved towards the bowmen. One of them gave up loading his weapon and swung it. Father Michael jumped back, letting it pass him by, then thrust his sword deep into the bowman's exposed belly. The second bowman had his weapon ready and was bringing it up to fire. Father Michael ran towards him then dropped to the ground and scissor kicked his legs away. The bowman was swept on to his back, his breath escaping loudly as he hit ground. Father Michael saw a dagger sheathed in the soldier's boot. He reached forward, pulled it out and stabbed it into the man's left eye. Then he looked up. The soldier who had shot first was just standing there, open-mouthed. They looked at each other for a moment. Then the soldier turned and ran. Father Michael collected the cocked crossbow, noticing that the bolt had fallen out. He picked it up and calmly placed it back into the weapon.

He raised it to his eyeline and took aim. The runner was almost fifty yards away.

'The Emperor bless you,' he said. He fired and the bolt hit the soldier's lower back. He stumbled on for a few more paces, a hand reaching behind him, feebly trying to pull out the bolt. He collapsed, falling on to his side. Father Michael could have given him a chance to live a little longer but more than twenty-five years of conditioning had left little room for pity or mercy.

Father Michael lay down the crossbow and walked towards the steps leading to the water. The wagon driver was still alive and making strained hissing noises. He ignored the dying soldier. He *could* have given him a merciful death, if the man had deserved mercy. That one had started the fight after all. He climbed down into the cutter.

The two ropes holding the boat were released and the oarsmen pushed them away from the pier.

'All together, haul away!' said the man on the tiller. The oars dipped into the water and the men pulled in unison, practised and efficient in their business. The boat gained speed quickly and the swishing of the oars in the water was strangely calming. The harbour was eerily quiet. Not at all like he had known it in earlier times, constantly busy, always alive with the comings and goings of fishermen, coastal traders and Imperial warships. He knew he was in an open space, knew that there were thousands of people, a hundred ships and a wide open ocean nearby. But right here, right now, it felt unreal, like they were alone in the water. He recalled a time when they'd cut a channel to the sea and flooded the arena, creating little islands and bridges for them to fight on. For added spice they'd thrown some sharks into the water. The first man to go in had thrashed around for a bit and climbed back out, the beasts hadn't been interested. But when the blood started flowing and poured into the water, that's when they got interested. He'd watched a man get his arm ripped clean off. Lucky for him he was already dead. The craft soon left the protective wings of the harbour moles and entered clear water. Ahead in the dark, Father Michael spied three grand-looking craft. These ran no lights, but he could easily identify them: two large war galleys flanked an even larger vessel, easily half again their size. That was their destination. He took one more glance behind him. *Is this the last time I will ever look upon the Empire? Or land for that matter?* He watched as a flock of winged creatures flew towards the harbour from the south, gryphons by the look of them. They curved westwards. For a moment he wondered if they had spied the ships. No, another one, a vessel a half-mile off to … port. That was the word. Bad luck for that ship, good luck for them. Whatever was attacking that one would be too busy to see them leave.

The cutter sliced through the water, waves lapping against its prow. A north-easterly wind blew against the side of the boat, scented with brine and the odour of fish.-

'A fair wind,' said the man next to him. 'It's needed.'

Father Michael didn't respond. To him, the fair wind smelled foul.

Part Two
WINTER

CHAPTER 1

Cade awoke to darkness and pain. She shut her eyes again. Her head was pounding, like her brain was going to burst through her skull. Her mouth was dry and her body ached. She felt around her, finding a hard, cold surface, stone that had been deliberately smoothed out. *Oh Gods Below, am I still in prison?* She groaned, and placed her hand on her forehead. It was hot. *Am I still locked away? Is this a fever? Was it all a dream?*

'Water, I need water,' she croaked. There was no answer.

Fine, you bastards. Let me die here then.

She rolled over on to her stomach. Her arm touched something hard; she pushed it away from her. She heard it roll across the floor and make a clinking noise as it struck another object.

'Huh?' She raised her head, opening her right eye just a little. It was gloomy but there was light, it was coming through the base of a door. That wasn't right. She opened the other eye, waiting for it to stop being blurry. Where was she? It was no cell. She pushed herself up and rolled on to her backside. A few yards away was another door, a thin sliver of light along its bottom edge. She was in a passageway of sorts, as wide as two men. She stood up and a wave of nausea swept over her.

'Oh Emperor …' she moaned. She placed one arm against the side of the passage and bent double. She started to cough, readying herself for the surge of vomit. After a few moments the sensation faded. Cade righted herself and walked to the far door. It had bracing and a lock. She wasn't getting out that way, so turning about, she went to try the other end.

'Ah, there you are.' Cade crouched down and picked up her sack. The bottle she had kicked against the passage wall was empty but the sack

53

still held one more, which was, thankfully, full. *It could be worse*, she thought. She tried the other door. It also had a lock but someone had neglected to secure it. She pushed it open. A flood of light dazzled her and she threw an arm across her face. Then, once the after-image on her retinas had faded, she took another peek. Ahead was a street. To either side other streets ran left and right. She turned and looked up at the top then back down at the passageway she had emerged from.

Some sense of where she was started to filter into the part of her mind that wasn't throbbing. Her new accommodation was a sally port. She was likely somewhere in the northern part of the city, if memory served correctly. Parts of the previous night were coming back to her. After that encounter with the soldiers she had continued on her way and had somehow made it to the walls. After all the wine she'd tamped down, an open door offering a safe place to hide was probably the last coherent thought she'd had. Though she did seem to remember a great deal of ruckus at some point during the night, lots of shouting and folk moving about. Not that it had bothered her. Whoever it was had carried on their merry way and hadn't stopped to pay her a visit.

Another spike of pain centred itself on her forehead. She had to do something about that, so she reached into the sack and withdrew the last wine bottle.

'Hair of the dog,' she announced. She bit into the cork, pulled it out and spat it to the ground. Then she tipped a generous helping of the red stuff into her mouth, a few drops sliding down her chin. She sighed. *There you are, feeling better already.*

She squinted into the sky. It was a clear day, and crisp. As good a day as one could hope for this time of year. A few clouds were lingering over to the west, well out to sea. The sun's position looked like it was beyond midday. The city was deathly quiet. No birds, no nothing.

'I must've missed all the fun,' she said. The eternal Empire of Tissan had run out of time, everybody was likely dead, and she was hungry. Cade was now the ruler of all she surveyed and somebody must have left some damned food somewhere in this open grave. She took the street ahead of her working out a plan of action. She'd head to the centre of the city; the market would be a good place to start. If there was no luck there, then she'd just have to work outwards and explore the rest. As she strolled along the street, she started to get her bearings. It was nice to be out and about, not that she'd been locked up for that long. Shame she got caught in the first place, but the city had been crawling with soldiery, so maybe she'd been too ambitious. Not that she regretted anything; it had been a damned fine job. Her best, if you forgot the bit about being arrested.

The merchant's property had been on her hit list for years. It had always been too well protected, too hard to get to. He'd had guards on the guards, traps, alarms and the only set of keys to half the rooms. She'd gleaned all that from two years of study, her pet project, the one big score that could set her up for life.

Then the war had started.

For all the Empire kept saying they were winning, Cade had known it would not end well. She'd never listened to the priests and Imperial lackeys, with their smiling words of victory and their tales of the Emperor's martial prowess. She knew what a lie sounded like. So she'd had to stop putting it off and get on with it. The plan was sound: go up through the sewers and into his gardens via a convenient hatchway. Cade had drugged his dogs, crept into the kitchens, swapped clothes with the serving wench she had already paid off, and taken the bugger his evening wine. He hadn't even noticed she wasn't one of his servants as she smacked him with her cudgel. After trussing him up it was away with his keys and after a half hour of searching, she found the mother lode. A private stash of gold and jewels was hidden under the floorboards of an unused bedroom. She'd been impressed by that, it wasn't where she'd expected. Either way she'd come away with the largest haul of her life. Money wasn't going to mean much soon, but she was going to have a party. How was she to know that the bastard had employed a Reader? They had sniffed her out only hours after completing the job. She'd barely finished her first flagon.

Oh.

Cade stopped.

The remains of a barricade of wagons and sundry large wooden objects lay smashed and largely dismantled across the middle of the street. Beyond that was the market square, it was the largest, widest open space in the city, where for most of her life she had spent her time browsing the stalls of a hundred traders, hawkers and grocers. Where she had tasted spices from far Erebesh, felt fur from the ogre lands to the north, and played with tribal trinkets from eastern plains. When she hadn't been doing that she'd been eyeing up her next mark, the next purse to be picked. She would have felt almost nostalgic if not for the sight before her.

At the entrance to the square, trails of smoke rose lazily from a dozen piles of smouldering wood. The place was littered with weapons, pieces of armour and scraps of clothing. Bodies lay spread amongst and across the wreckage, all of them human, all torn and bloody, all Imperial troops. Crows, big black ones, enjoyed the carrion. She stepped gingerly over a blackened timber and into the square. It smelt of burnt flesh, of boiled blood and soiled breeches. More bodies lay scattered on the paved slabs and cobbles. In the centre, fire-blackened and dirty, stood a large rectangular dais, the height of a man, built of large blocks of stone and faced with marble. Friezes decorated each side, displaying scenes of the lives of the Emperors, leading armies, hunting for stag, passing laws, and being generally godlike. Often lawyers and petitioners would stand upon it to seek judgement for petty crimes, while at other times executioners would use it to discharge the sentences handed down by those same judges. And in the same day, it would become a clown's stage, to entertain the people well into the night as the wine flowed. She walked towards it. There was a whole heap of the dead gathered on that stage. Cade had never been afraid of death, but nothing could have prepared her for the sheer scale of slaughter she saw before her. Hundreds must have died in this place, maybe a thousand. Upon the dais stood a banner, leaning almost horizontal, its pole half splintered. Hanging lifelessly off it was a scorched rag, barely a few tatters, yet she could see the faintest outline of a ray of light, a small fragment of colour amidst the black. The Sun Banner of the Tissan Empire.

This was the last stand, the place where the defenders of the Empire had gathered to die. Then it struck her.

'No others,' she whispered.

There were no dead elves, no dwarves, none of the enemy fallen. Did they attack at all? Or did they just use sorcery to pound this place and the Tissans' flesh to oblivion? Cade stopped at the nearest body, a young looking girl with a mop of roughly chopped auburn hair. She had a startled expression. There was a pool of red underneath her and a ragged looking wound in the stomach. Something had punched through her mail and left a nasty hole. It smelt awful; the weapon must have punctured her bowels. Another dead soldier, a few paces away, was missing an arm at the elbow. It didn't look like sorcery. This lot were dealt with up close and personal, which meant the enemy must have taken their dead with them. What had been left was a whole host of weapons, just human ones, but she wasn't being picky. She wandered through the slaughter, looking for the choicest items. A nice looking dagger perfect for tucking into her boot, a shortsword which she buckled round her waist, a crossbow that she slung over her back and a bag of bolts she tied to her belt.

Before she left, she noticed one more thing, a small, triangular blade, no more than four inches deep and three wide. Almost like an enlarged arrowhead. Its centre was open, not solid and the base of the triangle was shaped like a handgrip, the two sharp sides cutting back into it. It reminded her of the shape her fingers made when she touched her thumbs and forefingers together. It was a nasty looking thing, designed for thrusting, a close-quarters weapon. She liked it, this weapon was for keeping secret, so she found a piece of cloth, wrapped it around the blade and shoved it into the back of her britches, underneath her tunic.

Ready to move she stood for a moment before the dais, studying the carnage. A last stand. What brave idiots they all were. They sacrificed their lives so a few high and mighty fools could live a little longer. As she stood there, she remembered something very important. She was hungry. Cade turned and walked to the western side of the square, where there was no barricade. Perhaps they'd thought to leave an escape route, maybe they just hadn't had time. She moved on, enjoying the solitude. The city was undamaged and there were no more corpses to bother her. As she was ambling down Silver Street, halfway through her last bottle, she was pleased to find that the alcohol was finally starting to take the edge off her headache. It gave her a chance to think clearly. There was a problem with her plan for dealing with her hunger. She had got lucky with that onion the other night. Food had been scarce in the last few days anyway.

As the Empire had shrunk, so had the trade routes and caravans. Once those refugees had started showing up it had been impossible to get any food into the city from the outlying farmlands. Thank the Gods Below that they lived next to the sea. The fishing fleet had kept them all alive. Of course, the powers that be had been stockpiling for months. She'd also seen plenty of requisitioned ships out in the harbour; trading cogs from the north, whalers, merchantmen carracks from the far east of the Empire with no more spices to carry, anything with a hull and a barrel to put food or water into. An honest girl like her could never hope to get near that, not with the wharf swarming with guards. It hadn't been too bad to start with; she'd gotten sweet with a couple of them: a female corporal who was in charge of manifests and a young lad who was one of the warehouse sentries. Got herself a nice line in dried fruits and salted pork, right up to the point the corporal discovered her draped over the lad. She never would have thought the corporal would have come round for a *romantic* surprise. Good thing the bitch had been angrier with the lad than her. She snorted. *No more pork for me.*

'Where to go?' Cade asked aloud.

Twenty minutes later she stood outside the same mansion she'd raided not so long ago. In a flash of brilliance she remembered something from that night. When she'd been changing in the kitchens she'd taken a cursory glance in the larder. It had appeared well stocked. There was no way that merchant would have taken all of it, surely?

She folded her arms and inspected the frontage. A high wall ran to either side of a finely wrought double-doored gate. Lines of iron wove around each other, curving and looping, creating a scrollwork of metal branches and leaves that someone must have bust a gut to design, let alone make. Peering through the gaps, she could see the house set well back in the gardens. The place looked deserted. Obviously. She tried the gate, reaching out and grabbing hold of the iron and giving it a shake. Unsurprisingly, it was locked. *Right, needs must.* She spat into her hands, rubbed them together, placed her foot in a gap between two branches and climbed. All this lovely artistry meant plenty of handholds, and she was up and over in no time. She jumped lightly to the ground and set off along the wide driveway. Designed especially for his carriage, it was laid with thousands upon thousands of white pebbles. They crunched underfoot as she made her way along. The gardens still looked quite neat, and benefited greatly from a lack of canine presence. She doubted her drugs had killed the beasts, so they must've gone with their master. She hoped.

The house itself was all white marble. A temple-like facade was built around the entrance while the rest was a flat surface arrayed with several windows to either side. The windows were set high on the ground floor, only half the size of the ones on the floor above. Those ground windows were impossible to reach for most folk, designed with security in mind. A third floor was made up of balconies to the west and east, both with tall windows looking north and south. There was a plentiful supply of gargoyles and other creatures looming out from the corners and edges of that final level. She walked up three steps and passed between two pillars and a triangular lintel. The tall double doors were locked. She tapped the wood with her index finger, and then strode back down the stairs and around to the rear of the building.

Deep in the recesses of the garden was the sewer access. She looked into the trees and changed course, her professional curiosity piqued. There it was. The same iron plate. Now there was a brand new chain link and padlock attached to it. *It's a bit late for that.* Still, nice to know she'd left an impression.

Cade turned back and walked towards the rear entrance to the building. She passed by a stable block. The stalls were all empty and the carriage missing. She stopped, walked into the stable and found where all the livery was kept. She found a set of tools and selected a large square-headed hammer. That would do the trick perfectly. She walked out, swinging the hammer backwards and forwards and humming contently.

The rear door to the mansion was locked as well but that wasn't her way in. To the right, set into the ground, was an oversized wooden trap door. It was also padlocked. Cade squatted before it and raised her hammer. A few well-placed strikes and the lock fell apart. She grinned, pulled the handle and, using both hands on the iron ring, lifted the door. It thumped on to the pebbled pathway that ran around the outside of the house. The sound was louder than she had expected and startled her, as well as a few birds who took to the air with hard flaps and the creaking rustle of branches. She'd forgotten how quiet the city had become.

Wooden steps descended into a cellar. She walked down, whistling a tune. At the bottom she allowed her eyes to adjust to the gloom ahead. A little way on another set of steps, these ones stone, led up to the kitchens but she wanted to check something important first. She passed through an archway made of thin bricks into a room lined with plaster. Against each wall were wooden racks. *Ah, the most important room in the house.* The racks were set up row above row with shaped braces to hold wine bottles. They were all empty.

'Bastard,' Cade hissed. She looked around the rest of the cellar. There were three crates stacked in a corner. She stepped over, dropped the crossbow from her shoulder and used both hands, to lever the lid off the first. Inside she found straw. Pulling that aside ... *paydirt.*

There was a row of dark bottles, all sealed. She picked up the first and shook it. There was something in there that sounded good. She pulled the stopper and tipped the bottle to her mouth. It tasted good. *Hah!* She reached down, grabbed another bottle and headed towards the kitchens. That door was not locked, and neither was the larder.

Inside she found it a little bare compared to her last visit. At least there was some cheese and pickled herring, and some sort of cake. It was half eaten but looked in good condition, barely any mould. She wrapped it up and tossed it all into her sack and proceeded into the house. It was dark and cool; all the shutters had been closed but she had committed the layout to memory. There were audience chambers, offices and servants quarters on this floor. She passed along a corridor lined with plinths. All were covered in sheets, disguising the various busts and likenesses of family members, as well as rulers and other great men of the Empire. Wide curving stairs leading up from the entrance hall took her to a long corridor overlooking the hall. There were several doors along the wall, all of them guest bedrooms. She passed them all by.

A further staircase, this one curving more acutely, almost a spiral, was her destination. Cade climbed, she wanted the best, finest room for herself. The floor at the top was the merchant's own private quarters and she entered into his sanctum.

The large room had been furnished to look as cosy and welcoming as any she could have imagined. Drapes hung from the walls, carpets covered the floor, and two long sofas covered with sheets were positioned facing each other, tilted slightly towards the windows. Thick red curtains were pulled to, blocking most of the light. Two high-backed leather chairs sat before the fireplace built into the far wall opposite the windows. That was right where she had nobbled the old fool. She crossed to the bedroom door and entered. *Ah, but it is a fine room, this one. Too dark though.* She headed towards the windows to draw back the curtains.

A thought of caution slipped unbidden into her mind. *Best not to open the curtains. Anyone could be watching.*

She returned to the fireplace and located a number of candles made with whale oil. They were expensive, but they always burned bright and long. Cade found the phosphorous sticks nearby and struck one against the stone. As it flared she brought the candle to the flame. Once it was burning nicely, she thrust it into one of the three-pronged holders arrayed on the fireplace mantle. She repeated the operation twice more then took the holder and returned to the bedroom. The light chased away the gloom, revealing a huge bed, enshrined within four posters, sitting on a low plinth. There were no sheets, just a thickly stuffed mattress. She placed the holder on the floor next to the door, dropped her gear, undid the sword belt and threw herself, arms wide, on to the mattress, bouncing a little as she hit it. She wriggled about then turned over and looked up at the ceiling. Some kind of fresco had been drawn there, all clouds and blue sky and winged cherubs gazing into a sun. Lovely. Cade turned herself around, crawled to the end of the bed and reached for her bottle and her sack. She spread the food out on to the bed and reached for the bottle.

Cade saluted the sun above her. She was the richest woman in the entire city of Aberpool. *Nay, the Empire.* A few frantic minutes followed as she crammed in as much food as she could manage, almost choking in the process. Each mouthful was washed down with wine. She stopped only when her stomach started to protest. It hadn't needed to work this hard in a long time. She lay back and sighed, clutched her complaining belly and closed her eyes. Cade was content.

She opened her eyes.

Shadows played among the clouds above her head. How long had she been asleep? She sat up. The candles were still burning brightly, but they were almost out, no more than an inch remained.

She rolled off the bed and stretched. Her head wasn't aching and she felt quite rested. She wandered over to the curtains. Behind them were glass doors that led out to the balcony. She stepped between the heavy material, unlocked a door, and went out into the early evening dusk.

She breathed deeply, taking in the smell of the city, and found it unfamiliar; the horse dung, the stale beer, the sea, were all gone. Instead her nose was filled scents of pine, shrubs and soil. This was how the other half lived, in another world. She could appreciate the desire to get on in life, if just to get away from the shit most folk found themselves surrounded by. She looked to the west and saw the sun low on the horizon. She heard gulls calling though she couldn't see them. Walking across to the southern end of the balcony she looked down into the gardens. Some small creature was scurrying across the grass. She watched its passage as it ran towards some bushes growing up by the side of the wall. It disappeared within them, the branches swaying as it slipped through. She smiled briefly then lifted her gaze to look out over Aberpool. The city was dark. In the east she could barely make out the buildings. She rubbed the back of her neck at the prickling of an itch. Her skin had goosebumps. *Why do I feel like I'm being watched?*

She looked down at the gate. There was someone there. She stepped back from the edge. Another survivor? Had they seen her? She pressed herself against the bedroom window and eased her body forward. She peeped around the corner. They were still there, a dark figure, details too faint to make out. And she could also see down the line of the building and the dark recesses of the windows on each of the floors. Dark except for one, there was the faintest light showing from the windows in the solar. Those damned candles! They had given her away.

Cade withdrew into the bedroom, scooped up her sword belt and ran down the stairs, cursing herself for her error. Whoever it was must know she was there, so she couldn't take any chances. She'd be damned if she was going to share her find. *Where is my crossbow? Fuck. In the cellar.* If she had it, maybe she could take a shot before they thought about climbing the gate. As she reached the ground floor, she heard a sharp twanging sound followed by a thump, coming from somewhere ahead of her. But not the front of the mansion. Someone or something was in the back garden. At the kitchen she turned and made for the cellar steps, all hope of driving the watcher away forgotten. She jumped down into the gloom and ran to the crates. Cade snatched up the crossbow and started to pull the string back.

A loud crack came from the kitchen. Someone was battering at the door. She yanked hard, felt the string slip into the trigger and reached for a bolt from the bag. It slotted into place as the door above shattered. She scuttled back into the far corner of the cellar, resting on her haunches, leaning into the three wines crates. If she was quiet, whoever had just broken in might pass her by, then she'd make a run for it.

Clump, clump, clump. She listened to the heavy footsteps above, and then they stopped. She heard another set of feet walk across the floor. Words were exchanged but she couldn't make them out. They were deep, guttural sounds. There was a short bark of laughter. Then one set of footsteps retreated the way they had come seemingly all the way out of the door. There was still someone above her. She just needed one shot. If the bastard poked his head down, she could take him out, then finish the other with her sword. She heard the footsteps again, further away, slightly muffled, then clearer, crunching against stone. Oh. The damned trapdoor. She'd left it open. The gloomy light coming from the opening was blocked by a figure.

'You get one chance,' called a voice from the kitchen. 'Don't make me come down there. If I do, you die.'

Ah, shit. They knew. And she wasn't stupid. Where there were two, there was likely to be more.

'You promise?' she called back.

The voice grunted. 'I don't have to promise. Just make your bloody mind up.'

Cade thought about it, but only for an instant. She was trapped. At least they didn't want to kill her. Maybe.

'Alright, I'm coming up.'

Another grunt and the voice switched to that other tongue and spoke to the one outside. That one laughed, again. She recognised the language now and her heart sank. She'd heard it spoken many years ago, when she was just a girl, running wild down by the docks.

Cade lowered her crossbow and climbed the stairs up to the kitchen. As she stepped into the room, she glanced towards the back door. It had indeed been smashed open, broken almost in two and resting at a crooked angle against its hinges. A figure stepped in front of it to bar her way.

'Don't even think about it,' said the voice behind her.

Cade turned. A dwarf stepped from the shadows and stood in the hall doorway. He was six inches shorter than her, and she was no more than five foot. He was armoured lightly, no helm, no plate, just chain and leather. She couldn't see much of his features; his hair, possibly a dark red, was long and plaited, a sharp pointed beard ended just below his neck. Several earrings clinked together from both ears. One hand was tucked in his belt and the other carried a large hammer.

'Be glad I'm in a good mood,' the dwarf said. His voice was deep and growling. He could speak the Imperial tongue well, even if his accent chewed up the words. 'The war is over. But no-one said I couldn't make a profit.' His eyes gleamed in the dark. 'Now, drop that weapon or I'll drop you.'

Cade nodded and very carefully placed the crossbow on the floor.

'Turn around and step out that doorway.'

She did and walked slowly past the splintered door and over the threshold. She could see evidence of passage from the back of the garden. Flowers had been stepped on and crushed. They'd come through the bloody sewers. Bloody dirty, stinking cave dwellers.

'Hold your hands out.'

She did so and a second dwarf stepped forward from their place at the trapdoor. He held a set of manacles. He pressed her arms together and clicked one cuff, then the second into place.

Cade sighed. It could be worse. She was still alive.

CHAPTER 2

Father Michael placed his hands on the railing and looked out across the fleet. It was an impressive sight as white sails bloomed in the wind, carrying craft of all sizes, literally anything that could sail. They stretched out on all sides of the ship he stood on.

The Fist of Tissan, the newly dubbed Imperial flagship, dwarfed everything else upon the seas. Three-masted, and three decked, only the flanking men-o-war were of comparable size. The rear of *The Fist* held two more above-deck levels, the accommodations for the captain and passengers of note. The first lower deck held small ports for oars to be shipped out of if the craft was becalmed. The middle had slightly larger holes designed for ballistae crews. The crew numbered almost five hundred. Some of these were marines, manning the weapon mounts: a number of ballistae and small catapults ranged along the sides, front and rear of the ship. The rest were employed in tasks Father Michael had little understanding of, yet they scurried around the tops deck and swarmed over the rigging with purpose.

The *Fist* and her two sisters were the only fighting ships in the fleet and none of them had seen action, all of them freshly built and recently launched. He was aware that a squadron of frigates had set off a month earlier, but he knew not where they were now. All other Imperial ships had been refitted to take stores, supplies and people. There had been no point in trying to maintain any kind of navy. There was no fight left in anyone.

It had been two days since the flight from Aberpool, the land now long lost to their sight. That didn't stop a constant flow of Eagle Riders acting as a rear guard, flying to the edge of their range, watching for enemy pursuit.

And he had no doubt that they were out there. Those elven ships were sleeker and faster than the human ones. Though from what he had learned from his time with the Arch Cardinal, there weren't that many left, most having been lost in the one major defeat for the enemy in this long war. The shipwrights of the Empire were the best in the known world, the human craft the most advanced ever to sail the seas. Everyone knew of the industry of the Imperial shipyards, it was talked about with pride even in the arena pits.

Almost a year earlier the Imperial fleet had fought the enemy to a standstill at the Battle of the Sound. The enemy had sailed in two great fleets, moving along the northern and southern coasts, laying waste to all the fishing villages and towns in their path, destroying any craft they found on the sea. The Imperial Capital, Vyberg, was left untouched, no craft sailed upriver to invest it. That city was too strong a target, its walls too thick for any waterborne assault. But the great trading hubs of Erebesh had burned and their huge wharves and docks were smashed. A thousand years of shipbuilding was made ash. But the Empire had reacted swiftly to that move, and had already withdrawn their military ships to the coast not far from Aberpool. There, untold numbers of elven cutters, dwarf merchantmen and ogre longboats had merged to surround the Imperial fleet. But they had miscalculated. The Empire's newest ships, designed for deeper waters, struck them from the west. The wind was with them and the ambush was complete. It was heralded as a great victory though it wasn't public knowledge at the time that barely a handful of human craft had survived. This war was not to be won on the seas but it was hoped that there would be peace talks, a chance to stop the advance. Yet there was none, and four months later Vyberg fell. It was at that moment that the remaining lords of the Empire realised the truth. The enemy wasn't going to stop until every one of them was dead. All that victory had done was to give them a chance to evacuate.

Every hour counted, the further they could get into the open ocean, the wider the space to hide in. At least that was the view of the Council, such as it was: half a dozen old men, some clerics and the Empress.

Though it may be that title would no longer be appropriate. He left the aftcastle, walked down a flight of steps and entered the interior of the ship. At the end of the corridor were the chambers of Her Grace. Before attending her and yet another endless discussion, he stopped at the door to his right, knocked gently and entered. The room was bright, the window open wide to allow in the brisk, salty air. A thin bed was pushed up against the length of the bulkhead. A table with a washbowl filled one end of the room, a dressing cabinet to the right. Upon the bed lay the man he had played a part in rescuing. Prince Tigh, the third son of the Blessed Emperor and now the only living heir to the Tissan Empire.

A man sat hunched over him, his hands upon the Prince's brow. He sat back, placed his hands upon the lap of his brown robe and turned to look at Father Michael. The man was older, his hair was greying yet still thick, and swept back from his head. He bore the third eye tattoo upon his forehead, marking him as a Gifted from the School of Reading, one of the four schools that made up the order.

'There is no change since last you looked in, Father Michael.'

'Then I will keep checking until there is, Father Wild,' he replied.

Father Wild shrugged.

'I don't need to be a Reader to sense your thoughts, Michael.' He stood and placed his hands on Father Michael's shoulders. 'The Emperor saw fit to bless me with two skills. One tells me he will recover, the other that his mind is at rest.'

There was a knock on the door and a young lad walked in carrying a jug. He had shoulder length blond hair held back with a band of black cloth tied around his forehead. When he saw Father Michael, he took a step back, his eyebrows arching. Father Michael was used to that; his presence was known to intimidate people.

'Forgive me, I should have waited,' the lad said.

'Nonsense. Come along,' said Father Wild. 'This is Uther, the Prince's squire. Though they have yet to be introduced to each other. He is a nephew to Lord Aban, I believe.'

Uther smiled with genuine warmth. 'Hello, Father. It is good to meet you.'

Father Michael nodded. *What was it squires did? Polished armour? Dressed their lords?*

'How old are you?' he asked Uther.

'Thirteen.' He answered confidently. His voice was cultured. He had breeding.

'You know how to fight, lad?'

Uther shook his head, 'I know how to ride and I have trained with a sword, but I've never fought anyone, not for real.'

'Then train harder.'

Uther swallowed and nodded.

'Father, don't scare the lad,' said Father Wild. That was something else he had yet to get used to, having people chastise him.

Father Michael scowled. Father Wild smiled gently and patted him on the arm.

'Please go, Michael. Be at ease. Attend Her Grace.'

Father Michael nodded and withdrew. Father Wild shut the door behind him. Father Michael could not be at bloody ease, Emperor forgive his words. This was a desperate time. The Empire could not be allowed to fall. He turned and walked the few paces to the end door. An armed man barred his way. He wore a thick black leather breastplate with starkly defined musculature, blackened steel shoulder guards and leather trousers. On each hip was a sheathed shortsword. He wore a smooth black steel skullcap, the top half of his face obscured by a metal mask fixed to the headpiece. The mask was shaped with high, flaring ridges about the cheekbones and eyebrows, the decoration making the wearer look like some demonic creature. His mouth was uncovered, as were the lower parts of his cheeks and jaw. On the left cheek he bore the lightning tattoo of a Shaper, another of the four Schools of the Gifted. This one seemed young and watched his approach with arrogant eyes. Father Michael knew how to read eyes. When you face opponents sheathed in armour, the eyes were still exposed and they always told you what they were thinking. The Shaper had to be young otherwise he would have attended the Emperor during his last hours. It was likely he had not even finished his training when the Emperor ascended.

He nodded at the guard and the man stepped away from the door. Father Michael reached for the handle and let himself in. He remembered fighting a Shaper once, in the arena. His opponent had not been skilled in his arts and he'd never been inducted into the Schools. The Shaper had still given him quite a knock before Michael had skewered the man with his own trident.

Beyond the door the cabin spread out before him. It was a grand room befitting the ruler of the Empire. The beams were covered in gold leaf, the walls adorned with portraits and fine sculptures. The ceiling was covered in alabaster, a mural painted upon it, showing the first Emperor, Ivan, receiving submission and obeisance from the old Gods on his rise to immortality and the rule of the heavens. It stirred Michael whenever he looked at that picture, it was inspiring and the scene gave him strength and resolve. In the centre of the room was a large round table, a dozen chairs arranged around it. On the furthest side, overlooking the others was a golden throne studded with jewels. It was a bizarrely shaped creation, full of carvings of beasts and monsters. Dragons breathed fire, lions fought with bears and two hippogriffs were shaped into armrests. Two marble statues flanked the throne; one was of the Emperor Feodor, the other was of his son, Prince Slavis. Both were now dead and they had ascended to join their forebears.

All the seats were occupied and upon the throne was the Empress. She cut a dignified figure. Her strawberry blonde hair was gathered up in a pile above her head and held in place by a lattice of small pearls. She was in her early forties and had a regal face, although if truth be told, Father Michael always felt her light blue eyes betrayed the many doubts she always seemed plagued with. Father Michael did not expect her to lead. She was the mother of Emperors; that was her role. He would obey her but she would never be the Blessed one.

Around the table sat her advisors, the Council. Baron Ernst, a Scotian merchant, prince turned ruler of Aberpool, plump, red-cheeked and self-satisfied. He'd learned little humility from the events of the last year. His control of the longest surviving trading hub meant he had wielded undue influence and earned himself a place at the table. The other four lords, Crisp, Florence, Albine and Fisk were all from the central Riverlands. The ancient, grey-bearded Chamberlain, Aban, was from Erebesh. Father Michael had decided the man had a sensible head on those old shoulders. As he had come to expect, they all sat together, forming a block. Opposite them were the clergy. Arch Cardinal Vella, leader of the Imperial Church, sat with his arms on the table, his hands clutched together. His eyes were bright, his grey hair closely cropped where it still clung to his head. To his right was Cardinal Yarn. She was the only surviving head of the four Schools of the Gifted and so now represented all of her remaining brothers and sisters. Her chin bore the tattoo of the Speakers, a black half circle with the curve facing downwards. She was still young, only in her mid-thirties, her dark hair tonsured. She glanced at Father Michael, her skin dark, her eyes slanted downward like all her people, the Plainsfolk, from a vast land filled with horsemen and shifting tribes. He had seen no others of her nation since arriving at Aberpool. For all he knew she might be the only one of her race left.

Welcome to the beating heart of the Empire, Father, she pulsed to him, amusement in her tone. He nodded to her in return. In truth he did not like the whispered conversations the Speakers could have amongst themselves. Or the Readers prying into minds unbidden. These things should have no place in a room such as this.

There were two other Cardinals present, Lucian and Hammerdal. Lucian, black-haired with a forked goatee falling from his chin, had ministered to Aberpool, while Hammerdal was the personal religious advisor to the Empress, a man in his fifties so thin he might snap with the slightest touch. Admiral Lukas occupied the final seat at the table. His skin was dark and leathery and his close-cropped beard was bleached blonde, though his hair was a light brown and tied back into a ponytail. Father Michael had heard it said that the Admiral was only recently appointed, and looking at the man, he looked a little too rough and ready for this audience, a little like himself. The Admiral had stopped talking when Father Michael entered the room.

'Father Michael,' acknowledged the Empress. 'Please continue, Admiral.'

Father Michael took station to the side of the door, folded his arms within the wide sleeves of his robe and listened.

'As I was saying, Your Grace. Our eagles continue to give us eyes for many leagues in all directions. There is still no sign of any pursuit, nothing on any horizon.'

'And what of the second fleet?'

The Admiral shook his head.

'Still we have heard nothing from the frigates. Three weeks, now.'

'We had a Speaker on the flagship, our most powerful. There was a trading cog on station with an Eagle Rider. They pushed as far as they could go in an effort to keep contact with them. That ship returned to us two days ago,' added Cardinal Yarn.

'Are they lost, then?' asked the Empress.

'We can't assume anything by that. It would have taken them two weeks to go beyond any known waters,' said Admiral Lukas. 'Not to worry, Your Grace, those ships have never been as strongly built. They can weather the seas and storms better than any that have sailed before.'

The Empress looked doubtful, although the only expressions he'd ever seen her wear were doubt and fear. 'And what happens if we are found?' she asked.

'Nothing has changed, Your Grace,' said the Admiral. 'In the event a strong enemy force catches us, the fleet must scatter. Though there was no attempt to stop us, they know full well about our direction. If I were a gambling man, I'd say they haven't recovered sufficiently from the Battle of the Sound. It takes time to build a ship and they don't have the strength to stop us. That being so, we will reach the Barren Atoll in another week.'

'Can their flyers follow our eagles?' asked the Empress. *There's the doubt*, thought Father Michael. *This ground has been covered before.*

'Those buzzers of theirs don't like the water. We are too far out for them to reach us, and besides, winter is upon us, they can't fly in that weather,' said Baron Ernst, waving a hand dismissively.

'There is still sorcery,' replied Arch Cardinal Vella. 'They can use their powers to scry us out.'

'Nonsense,' said Baron Ernst. 'Even if they have powerful wizards on their ships, they are still looking blind. It is no different to the challenges faced by our Watchers. They need a fixed point to work with. We are a speck in the ocean for all our size.'

'Is not the Barren Atoll a fixed point? They have hunted us remorselessly, bringing us to the edge of extinction. Why would they wish to stop now?' asked the Chamberlain.

'Because they have everything they want!' replied Baron Ernst, his flabby face coloured red. The other lords nodded and murmured in agreement. 'We have been ejected from the Empire and they are masters of a land almost half the size of the known continent. They can sit back and enjoy the fruits of their labour.'

'Was it not our labour that brought us to this sorry state of affairs?' asked Cardinal Yarn. Father Michael closed his eyes. She was being deliberately argumentative. Why dredge up the past?

'The actions of a few greedy people are no longer our concern,' said the Lord Crisp, haughtily. A noble looking man, with fine cheekbones and piercing blue eyes, Father Michael thought him the very image of rank and breeding, in stark contrast to Ernst.

'Indeed not,' agreed Fisk, an odd sort with weeping eyes and crooked teeth. 'What we must look to now is the future.'

Father Michael watched as the Arch Cardinal moved his hand to gently touch the arm of Cardinal Yarn. The message was clear, her face unreadable, though at least she did remain silent.

'The future, yes.' The Empress stood. As the others moved to stand with her she shook her head. 'No, my lords. Please. The throne is just ... uncomfortable.' She stepped away from it, her hands clasped behind her back. She wore a red gown with gold filigree worked around the fringes of the hems. Over it was a cloak made from the skins of badgers, a soft black and white arrangement with a silver clasp around her neck.

'Father Michael?' she asked, looking towards him.

'Your Grace?' he replied.

'How is my son?'

'He is stable, Your Grace. His body is exhausted, it is repairing itself.'

She nodded.

'That is good. Very good.'

The Empress turned to her councillors.

'Thank you all, my friends. You may take your leave. We shall gather again tomorrow. Admiral, please inform me of any changes.'

'At once, Your Grace,' the Admiral replied.

She nodded again, turned her back on them all and walked towards the rear of the chamber. Broad windows framed the seas and the dozens of craft trailing in their wake. It was an impressive sight, something Father Michael had never dreamt he would see. A large merchantman kept station not thirty yards from their stern, upon its prow was a mermaid, wielding a trident in front of her, pointing the way. A sailor was crouched just behind it, trousers hanging around his ankles. It ruined the scene a little.

Taking their leave, the group stood and walked past Father Michael. He acknowledged each in turn saving his most respectful bows for the Cardinals. Once they were through the door, he followed them out. The clergy had rooms below these and the lords had similar accommodation either in the bowels of the ship or on their own craft.

At the end of the corridor stood the Arch Cardinal. He was waiting for him and smiled warmly as Father Michael approached and bowed.

'How can I serve you, Your Eminence?'

'You can walk with me, Michael.' He placed a hand on Michael's arm and guided him out on to the deck. They walked in silence to the centre of the ship. An area had been cleared to either side of the main mast and crude shelters erected. These provided a degree of protection for the four eagles that were stationed aboard *The Fist of Tissan*. All were abroad, amidst the skies. On either side of the deck a landing platform had been built, projecting out from the craft and shored up by a framework of sturdy timbers that ran diagonally and horizontally into the hull itself. The men-of-war had similar landing points for other eagles. Nine had made it back to the fleet. It wasn't many, but they were invaluable. He and the Arch Cardinal stood together on the starboard bow, watching as an eagle touched down on to the platform of *Pride of the Emperor*, one of the two warships.

'The Empress is worried,' Father Michael said to the Arch Cardinal.

'The Empress, Emperor bless her, is always worried,' the older man replied.

Father Michael studied his mentor. While the Cardinal wore the same simple brown robe as he, the heavy iron sun chain that hung low about his neck held a diamond at its centre, denoting his rank and position within the Imperial Church. From within his black hood, his brown eyes were kindly under grey eyebrows. Father Michael knew well enough they served to disguise his fierce intelligence.

He smiled at Father Michael. 'She thinks of the future, of what will happen to her son and to us. She is, at least, wise in that.' He leaned closer and spoke quietly.

'The future is clear to me. Those lords that still circle her, those that make loud noises and pointless protestations. Their time is over. They believe they are entitled, yet they have nothing to give. They own nothing except a few ships. They command nothing.' He reached out and put his hands on the bow railing. 'The Church is the future. The new Emperor will need us more than ever. He will need our guidance. He is our Living God and his will must be expressed through the teaching of the Church. The people will need their Church to be strong.'

'The Church has always been strong,' replied Father Michael.

'True. But politics has also played its part in our society and the greed and vanity of selfish men have wreaked havoc among the faithful of Tissan. It has corrupted the promise of a better, purer way of life. Think about when I found you. The baser passions of others had turned you into a monster. You knew of no other path than to destroy everything that got in your way. Their plans for endless expansion, their desire for profit and gain ended up destroying us all. That was not for the good of the Empire, it was for the good of themselves. We should have shared the message of the Emperor with the other races and helped them come to worship him as we do.'

Father Michael nodded. He remembered all too well the day that he had been reborn, almost two years ago. Taken as the Champion of the Arena to pay homage to the Emperor by men who had grown wealthy through his skill at arms. He had killed so many times for them he had lost count. He had been toasted then led away to a side room while his masters had feasted and drunk and congratulated themselves. He remembered the tears rolling down his face as he despaired of what he was and how worthless he felt. Then Cardinal Vella had found him, recognised his potential, and saved him. His old name was forgotten, his old life forgiven, he was Michael and he was the sword and shield of the Emperor.

'There will be testing times ahead, I've no doubt. The old guard will not go quietly. The Empress was wise to allow the Church to select only the most pious and faithful to accompany us on this journey. Good Tissans who understand that they must serve the Emperor more diligently than ever, that those we left behind had failed him as much as his councils and noblemen.' He reached out and placed his hand on Father Michael's shoulder. 'Those citizens of the Empire that we have saved are loyal to the Church, but that cannot be said of the remaining nobles and their men at arms. You must be prepared to do what is necessary,' said Arch Cardinal Vella.

'I will,' replied Father Michael.

'Of course you will. You were always meant to. Now, I must return to my chambers. There are many thousands who look to us for succour and I must communicate with our brother and sister clergy scattered amongst the fleet. The Emperor bless you, Michael.'

'And you,' said Father Michael, bowing low.

He watched the Arch Cardinal return to the stern of the ship, then glanced around him. No one was nearby, the crew were about their business and the stables were empty. The Schools might have a Reader close, but they were of no threat, the Church looked after its own, the Church *was* strong. He looked at his hands, big, covered in the criss-cross of scars caused by countless nicks, slices and cuts. His fingers were thick and unadorned, his palms calloused and rough. He touched his chain of office, the only jewellery or adornment he had ever worn. *No man, woman or creature will touch my Emperor, as long as I have breath.*

CHAPTER 3

Owen used a stick to prod at the small fire, trying to stir some life into it. It was a cold night, the sky was clear, the stars beautifully bright. After three weeks of roughing it with no warmth, he had finally relented and broken his own rule. They had needed to bed down properly and rest. The cave they were now settled within was the best they could find in the circumstances. He hadn't spotted anything in the air or on the ground since their arrival. It was too cold for the buzzers; there was no way they could survive in such low temperatures. But there were always the gryphons to worry about, and they liked a cave as much as the next flesh-eating monster.

He leaned forward and tore a strip off the rabbit that was suspended over the fire. He had created a crude cradle for the spit out of some pine branches and the whole frame wobbled a little. Juices from the meat fell into the flames, making them flare and the wood sizzle. It was one of the many benefits of having an eagle as a partner, hunting for game became easy. Owen was also grateful for Arno's feathers and size. Until this very night, he had slept snuggled up to his friend, with his saddle used as a bedroll. It was common practice for Eagle Riders when away from home. And he'd been away from home for a long time now.

Home. That was something he had been thinking about for a few days now. The first two weeks he had little else on his mind other than survival and guilt. They had gone deep into the foothills north of Aberpool. That first night, the two of them had gone only a few leagues before Arno had been forced to descend. The eagle had outdone himself, had flown longer and with more weight than had ever been asked of him before. Owen had taken them down into a shallow valley, settled Arno down and climbed up the slope to watch the events to the south. The city was lost, even from this distance he knew that. There was still a bright glow coming from the edges of it, where the enemy hosts were gathered. Of the fleet there had been no sign. There had been a few flashes near the coast, sorcery perhaps. He saw a plume of fire upon the water, a ship in flames. His place should have been out there with the rest of the squadron. Yet here he was, having left them to it.

He felt fear, knowing how isolated he was. He also felt shame, shame that he wasn't still in the fight and that he had somehow let everyone down. But he had done nothing cowardly, he *had* fought, in two battles, and he hadn't run away, he'd just made a choice to spend his last days free. He told himself that he had played his part, had even saved a life. *Then why do I not believe it?* It was a habit of his to brood, and there was nobody to talk to but Arno, and that one never gave any advice.

Owen was mightily glad they had found this cave, high up in between two steeply sloping peaks. It had a relatively small opening but was just wide enough to accommodate the eagle, and once inside it opened up with room for Arno to turn. Had they gone any further north they would have been in true mountain country. There'd be virtually no game and no shelter, just snow and ice. They had stayed in the cave for the last four days, leaving before dusk to collect food, water and wood for the evening's fire. They had seen campfires scattered amongst the lower slopes for the first couple of days but now they had disappeared. The enemy must have finally called off the hunt. Maybe.

This territory was perfect for ogres, yet he'd seen none abroad. The ogres were unpredictable at the best of times. Often as not they'd turn up when least expected, cause a ruckus and then they'd turn around and go home. They mostly kept themselves to themselves back on their island of Drifa. That place, from what he'd heard tell, was even colder and more inhospitable, yet they seemed to like it there. The Drifa coast was full of inlets, and each one held its own ogre family. The ogres of old tended not to be interested in expansion or conquest. They were perfectly happy to fight among themselves, they hadn't raided a town or village in his father's lifetime. The Empire had come to a truce based on mutual interest; the ogres liked the weapons the Empire sold them and the Empire liked the furs they traded back.

What was it the elves had said to the ogres to convince them to attack in such numbers? The port of New Haven had had it worst. Stripped of its defenders who had gone east to the front and with no ships left in its harbour, the night had been one of blood and terror. Even in the short time left to the Tissans, the stories of the carnage had become almost a legend. Could it truly have been worse then what he'd seen at Aberpool? Considering the ogres had no issues with eating human flesh, it must have been. Owen shuddered, and this time not from the cold. He just had to hope they had gone home.

Home. He'd like to go home now, he'd like to go and visit his father. No doubt it would be as cold there as it was here. At least he would be ready for it. The Highlands caught the chill early in the autumn, whereas those living in the lower, fertile lands surrounding them got to enjoy warmer days for longer. He reached forward again, sliced off another long sliver of rabbit, forced it all into his mouth and chewed. Once it was gone he looked towards Arno who sat on the far side of the fire, his wings folded tight into his body. The eagle made a useful shield against the fire's glow. Owen had made sure to check it couldn't be seen from the cave entrance.

'What do you think, Arno? Is it almost time to go home?' Owen asked while licking his fingers.

Arno cocked his head and blinked at him. Owen reached out and felt his friend's feelings. The eagle was at ease and well rested, but at the same time there was concern, a sense of the threat around them. Owen reached inside his jacket and retrieved a square of thin, folded leather. He opened it up, revealing a crude but clearly drawn map which displayed the Empire in all its vastness, if not entirely accurately. What it did show were the major roads, the Emperor's highways that linked all the larger cities together. They at least were easy to navigate by. He was in the top left corner of the map, an area bordered by peaks and ice marks. To the south was Scotia, a wild and rugged place at the best of times, a land of steep hills, deep valleys and grey mountains. The Highland air was cleaner, crisper, the land was more vivid. He recalled the times he would go flying, just him and Arno. He'd take them to the west, to the foothills right on the edge of their country. He'd sit there, on top of one of the bigger hills and watch the sun rise. He loved the solitude, the sense of space. He couldn't help but wonder at the beauty of a mist-covered landscape emerging into light, of glistening dew drops held in the strands of a spider's web.

If he returned to Scotia, he'd eventually hit the Aberpool highway. He placed his finger on the thick black line that indicated a road. He could strike east and pass right through into the Riverlands and its dozens of cities and ports. Beyond that was the Great Plains and there was nothing much for him there. He could go straight south, past Aberpool and beyond, meeting the southern coast and skirting round. That would take him towards the fringes of Erebesh. It was a safer route and he couldn't imagine anyone wanting to hang around there. It was empty of anything but scrub, dust and desert, though the gryphons seemed to like it. The problem was he had no experience of the territory and wasn't sure he could live off the land. In the end, the choice was simple. They would have to go east then take a sharp turn to the south when he hit the highway leading towards the Highlands. He'd been hiding out long enough that he was sure that the armies had a good head start on him. He folded the map and smiled at Arno.

'Yes, Arno, I know exactly what you are thinking. I'm getting quite miserable living in this damned cave as well, and I sure as hell don't want to die here. Let's give it another couple of days and we'll make a run for the Highlands.'

Two nights later Arno emerged from the cave mouth. It was a little after sundown and a cold wind was blowing in from the north, sweeping down from the heights above them. Owen did one final check of his saddle, making sure everything was stowed properly. His crossbow was loaded and ready to be drawn out if needed. His water bottle was full and he had a fair supply of meat wrapped up in cloth. They'd still need to stay away from any highways and settlements but that suited them both fine. The land would give them all they needed.

Arno stretched his wings and took off. They swept along the valley, gaining speed as the wind at their back pushed them forward. Arno angled his wings, flapped powerfully and turned to the east. Owen kept them on, straight and level and not too high. The air was too cold for comfort, even though they had both grown up flying through the frost and chill of the Highlands in the depths of winter. After an hour he pulsed Arno and nudged him south. They wouldn't go far tonight, just back into the foothills. It would give them some shelter from the wind, and he still wanted to be cautious. The country would open up soon enough.

As the skies started to lighten in the east, Owen looked for a place to land. Below them was a grey, colourless patchwork of hills, copses and frozen streams. He blew his cheeks out, giving an involuntary shudder as his body reacted to the cold. He was frozen rigid.

The land beneath was still but he spotted something, a small steading, nestled in between the shallow hills, a wood climbing up the slopes to either side. Arno flew lower, giving them both a better look. The place looked deserted. Just two buildings, a cottage, and a barn off to one side, twice the size of the cottage, near the western wood. Owen thought he could get Arno inside there at a push. They circled around for another look. He was sorely tempted to land though he was surprised the place was untouched which aroused suspicion; it was well within the rangings of any patrols coming from the south. The last thing he wanted to do was to be caught, after all they'd been through, just because he got lazy. They continued to circle. He could sense Arno's increasing irritation at Owen's indecision, and the bird let out a gentle shriek to prove the point.

'Alright, we'll go down.' Arno dipped a wing and took them into a slow, gliding descent from the north, heading directly towards the steading. He touched down not twenty yards from the cottage. Owen slid off the

saddle, carrying his crossbow, and walked towards the building. Behind him Arno shook himself with a rustle of feathers. Owen reached the porch and looked inside. The door was wide open, as were the shutters to the two windows on either side. There was mud on the floor, frozen hard, little icicles criss-crossing the mud's uneven surface. There were also boot marks, scuffs and gouges in the gathered dirt. Someone had been here recently.

Bow held up to his shoulder, he stepped inside and into a large room that was a mixture of timber and daubed walls. There was a hearth to his right, a table upended, a smashed chair. A large cooking pot lay on its side by the empty fireplace. To his left was a bedframe. A straw mattress had been pulled out and cut up, the dried stalks spilling out on to the floor. He took a closer look; there were dark stains on the mattress. Blood. There was blood too on the clay wall, a spray of it. Someone had died in here. Unusual, then, that the enemy patrol, if that was who it had been, hadn't bothered to burn the place. It would have made for a fine, warming fire. Either way, it was a boon to him.

He walked back outside and over to the barn. It was a solid looking construction, made of shaped logs, no doubt taken from the woods. He reached for the sliding bar to look inside and heard a *click*. It had come from within the barn itself. He stopped and lowered his crossbow to horizontal, pulled his hand back from the door and gripped the stock. He stepped away, his nerves on edge, his breath quickening, his body reacting to danger, steeling itself for action. *It might be nothing.* The barn was shut from the outside, yet his senses were screaming. He knew there was something in there. He breathed deep through his nose, the cold air stinging his nostrils, trying to steady himself. He couldn't let his fear to get the better of him. If the enemy were here, they would have already jumped him.

He let go of the bow with his left hand and reached out for the slider.

'I wouldn't do that, son,' said a voice.

Owen froze. A strange sense of calm descended, his breathing slowed. They had him and that was it.

He turned. Emerging from the woods behind him came four men. They were dressed in leathers and furs, which were both functional and well made, designed to keep them warm in the cold nights. The men were grubby and bearded, with the looks of those who had been living rough and were used to it. All of them were armed; two with bows, their arrows stretched taught, two with spears.

'You can lower that, too,' said the same voice. The man gestured with his bow.

Owen lowered his crossbow.

'Who are you?' he asked.

'I might ask the same of you,' replied the man. ''Cept your bird gives you away.'

His accent was strong, his words coming out slow, the last syllables drawing out in a long ending. A Scotian accent, it was thick, difficult to understand. Owen figured this man had little contact with those living in the cities, where they had softened their tone to accommodate the Imperial tongue.

'I guess it does,' said Owen.

The man smiled. He was big, broad shouldered, well into middle age, his nose pockmarked and shining.

'I'm Gerat. Welcome to our little home.'

'You live here?'

'For the time being. We've had some rich pickings.'

'Pickings?'

Gerat walked past and pulled back the bar, opening the door to the barn, and gestured to Owen to go inside.

He stepped through. Directly opposite him were several bales of hay stacked together to make a crude, chest high barricade. There were two crossbows pointed at him.

'It's all right. We've found a stray,' said Gerat, gruffly.

The crossbow disappeared from view and two females emerged from around the bales.

'He heard you,' said Gerat, reprovingly.

'Sorry, Gerat,' said one of the two women. She looked only a little older than Owen.

Gerat shook his head. 'No harm done, Myra.' He closed the door behind him. 'This is our merry band. The rest are just over there.' Two more women and three young children emerged from the shadows.

Owen nodded to them and looked at Gerat.

'I need a place to hole up for the day. Any chance I can get my eagle inside?'

One of the children clapped its hands, its face a picture.

Gerat looked at him, his weathered face scowling. 'Fine, if you want. But you can move those bloody bales yourself.'

An hour later, Arno was ensconced on one side of the barn. He looked asleep, his eyes tight shut. Owen knew he wasn't. His friend was very aware of the children who, against the wishes of their parents, were edging towards him to smooth his feathers. He called them away. Arno was not a pet, he was a hunter, and whilst he'd tolerate being amongst people, he wouldn't think twice about giving those young ones something to remember him by.

A small fire was crackling away in a pit dug into the floor of the barn. Above it was suspended an iron pot and within that pot porridge was bubbling. Owen could practically taste the oats.

'We tend to do most of our sleeping and eating in the daytime,' Gerat was saying. 'You can see them coming so we can afford to have only one of us on watch.'

Owen was only half listening. Myra, who had been introduced as Gerat's daughter, was ladling some of the porridge into a bowl.

'Careful, it's hot,' she warned, handing it to him. 'There's a little honey in it.'

He cupped his hands around it and smiled his thanks. The bowl was indeed hot and the sensation felt wonderful.

'Oh, here,' she then passed him a wooden spoon.

'Thank you,' he replied.

He scooped some of the porridge into the spoon, blew on it briefly and shovelled it into his mouth. Owen rolled his eyes. Then he repeated the action, this time not pausing to cool it. It was too damn good. He noticed that Gerat had stopped talking. He stopped eating, the spoon mid-shovel and Gerat started to laugh.

'Been a while, has it?' he asked.

Owen swallowed. 'Yes, this is the first sweet thing I've had in a while. The first properly cooked thing too.' He nodded towards the fire. 'You're not worried about smoke being seen?'

'Nah, the wood is dry, it's been stored in here for a while. Doesn't smoke much and we keep the fires low.'

Owen left it at that. Far be it from him to tell these people what to do. Earlier, as he was settling Arno down, Gerat had told him some of their story. His people were crofters, herdsmen and trappers. People who made their living on the fringes of the Empire. They'd gathered together when they realised the enemy was coming, and begun moving between safe places, never sitting still for too long. 'No one knows this land better than us. No one but us would want to live here. We can lead any damned elf, dwarf, gnome or ogre a dance,' Gerat had said. Owen believed him.

He lowered his porridge to get some breath back.

'How long have you been here?' he asked.

'A short while. When we got here, the folks who owned it were already dead. Damned bunch of those little critters, gnomes, were rooting through the place. There was a fair store of food and supplies. We did for the gnomes then took their bodies and buried them back in the woods.' Gerat spat into the fire.

Owen felt a small measure of alarm.

'Aren't you worried that more of them might come looking?' he asked.

'Maybe they will. We'll do the same to them.'

'The war's done. We lost,' said Owen. Now wasn't the time to start alerting the enemy to their presence.

'War's just starting,' replied Gerat with a gleam in his eyes. 'We'll let 'em get comfortable first. And maybe they'll forget about us. Then we start hitting back.'

Owen started to feel plain uneasy.

'You want to start raiding?'

'That we do.'

'But, up here you know how to survive. You could stay low. Rebuild. Start a new community,' said Owen.

'We could. Ain't no way to live, though, hiding in the shadows. We want to hurt them, don't we, love?' he looked at Myra.

She nodded enthusiastically.

Owen shook his head. He couldn't believe what he was hearing. *These people might be the only humans left alive in all the Empire. And they want to throw it away?* He had to make them see sense.

'Look, there has to be a better plan. I agree that I don't want to spend my days hiding in a cave. Surely, if we just let them pass by, it's a chance for life.'

Gerat laughed.

'Not much of a life, lad, living in the wild, sometimes cold, sometimes hungry. You do it because you have to. Least in the Empire I didn't have to worry about every damn species wanting me dead. I didn't live in fear for my life or for my family.'

Gerat spat into the fire, shared a look with Myra. She smiled and reached out a hand, placing it on her father's shoulder. He patted Myra's hand and pushed it away gently. 'What's your plan?'

Owen paused. Now he had to explain it, it didn't sound very clever.

'I'm going home.' He felt his face redden a little.

'Back to the Highlands?' Gerat shook his head in disbelief. 'You want to head back into the heart of the Empire, and what do you think you'll find? Same as here 'cept more of them.'

'Maybe, maybe not,' said Owen. 'There isn't much left to take, from what I've heard.' Even he knew how weak that sounded.

'Tell you what, young Owen. Stay here with us. That eagle of yours, we could do with its eyes. You could spot the enemy for us. Give us an edge.' There was a gleam in Gerat's eyes that was more than firelight.

Owen thought about it for a moment. He couldn't say he wasn't tempted. He looked up at Myra and she smiled shyly at him. *We could just stay here. Perhaps I could talk some sense into Gerat.* No, he was a Highlander. He wanted to see home even if it was a fool's errand.

'Thank you for the offer, and your kindness, but Arno and I have to decline,' he said.

Gerat's face clouded over for a moment, his eyes growing hard. He scratched his cheek and shrugged. The tension left his face.

'That's a shame. But I'm not going to force your hand about it. Seems to me every man has to make his own decision.'

Owen felt relieved. Gerat had the look of a man with some very deep-running passions.

'Thank you, again,' said Owen.

'Least we can do to help our fellow man in these trying times. Go get yourself some sleep. We'll wake you at dusk,' said Gerat. He stood and made his way to the barn entrance, disappearing outside.

Myra watched her father go and then glanced towards the eagle.

'That's its name? Arno?'

'Yes, in the the tongue of the Highlanders it means wolf.'

Myra warmed her hands by the fire and shivered.

'It's cold.'

Owen nodded.

'Yeah.' He'd been colder, not two nights earlier, but it wouldn't have helped relations to bring that up.

'Father says he can't remember a more bitter start to the season.'

'I believe that.'

She looked across at him, her face questioning and her eyes bright.

'You're a Gifted. I've never seen one before.'

Owen smiled and shook his head.

'I'm an Eagle Rider.'

'There's a difference?'

Owen opened his mouth to answer, to say that there was a world of difference, but, when he thought about it, there wasn't.

'I have a Gift. I'm a Speaker, of sorts. But I don't bear the mark. I don't belong to the Schools. I'm from the Highlands and I fly free.'

'But you still served the Emperor.'

'In my way, I did. There's no Emperor anymore.'

'What's it like?'

'What?'

'Your Gift.'

'Oh.' Owen rocked back and pulled at an earlobe. 'Well, how to explain it? It's just a part of who I am, like a limb. I can push my thoughts out to someone and they hear me. It doesn't have to be words. It might be an image, a set of pictures or even just an emotion, a feeling. We call it Speaking or pulsing.'

'Is that how you control your eagle, then?'

'Yes, although it's not just one-way. Don't ask me how but us Highlanders have an affinity with our birds, we can communicate with them, it's both ways. I can feel his thoughts too. Speakers from elsewhere don't have that ability.' Owen shrugged. 'That's the best I can describe it.'

'Can you do it to me?' she asked. Her face was a little fearful.

'You should get a blanket, if you're cold.'

Myra jumped.

Owen smiled. 'Sorry. But you did ask.'

Myra smiled back weakly. 'Can you do anything else?'

Owen shook his head. 'That's not enough?'

'There are other Gifts,' she prompted.

'Yes. Shapers can move objects, Watchers can see places, and Readers can get inside your mind. But I can't do any of that stuff and I'm glad of it too. They would have taken me away from my home and sent me to train at the Schools.'

'It must feel good to be so special.'

'Special?' Owen was a little nonplussed. When he was fighting for his life in a maelstrom of stingers, flashing blades and bursts of sorcery, he never felt that special. 'No, it's not special. It's a responsibility.'

Myra frowned. 'Why do they hate us?'

He'd heard that question before, spoken around the campfires of his comrades, asked by his kin in the safety of their homes. The question had outlasted most of those who had uttered it. 'I have no idea. One day we were at peace and the next we were at war. I don't know what changed. We did nothing to provoke them.'

'I've never even seen any of the other races. At least, not until we found those outside,' she said.

'The gnomes.'

'Yes. They look strange. Like little ugly children.'

'Don't make that mistake if you have to face one down,' Owen advised.

'I won't.'

Owen spooned in the last spoonful of his porridge and sighed. 'None of the questions really matter that much. They won.'

'I suppose.' Myra didn't look satisfied.

Owen ran his finger round the empty bowl and licked it.

'I'll take that,' said Myra, holding out her hand.

'You sure? I can go clean this up.'

'Uh huh.'

'Here. Thank you. It was good.'

'I'm going to go and wash up. You probably want to rest a bit.'

'That I do.'

Myra stood and left the barn.

Owen lay back, his belly felt full, even a little uncomfortable. He hadn't eaten that much but it was more than he'd had for a while. His stomach wasn't used to it.

It felt good to be amongst people again even if they were strangers. Arno was not one for conversation at the best of times. He knew he ought to be thinking about the next leg of his trip but he just didn't have the energy. He was tired, and for once there were others who could worry about their safety. It wouldn't hurt to stop playing the role of protector just this once. Protector? Who was he fooling? There wasn't a role for him anymore. That life was gone. There was no expectation, no requirement, and no duty. It was every man and bird for himself.

He walked over to Arno, picked up a blanket and rested his head on his saddle. It was warm in the barn. Warmer than he had felt for a long time.

CHAPTER 4

Fillion dreamt he was lying on a boat in the middle of a large, quiet lake. A lake he had spent years beside, growing up in Celtebaria. It was summer, the day warm, the skies clear and empty and the sun's heat was upon his face. His body rocked with the motion of the water, the boat bottom rolling to one side, then the other. It was calming, soothing, and he felt at peace, contented, surrounded by the familiar and the safe. Lying there, sounds gradually started to invade his serenity; a creaking noise, words softly spoken, and the snort of an animal. To begin with he was annoyed, then curious. He allowed himself the time to make sense of it all. There was no rush, no danger and after a while he realised he was not on a boat but a wagon that was moving. He could sense others on the wagon with him, and two people were discussing the state of those aboard it. He wasn't dead then, that was a good start. The warmth he felt was not from the sun, but the heavy pressure of blankets. They enshrouded him, his movement restricted, though it didn't feel uncomfortable, quite the opposite. He was still drowsy, in that state between sleep and wakefulness, when the body was still calm. He hadn't felt so relaxed in a long time.

He focussed on the conversation. They were speaking elvish, the words lilting and melodic. It took him a moment to get used to it. He always thought in the common tongue of the Empire. He seldom spoke his own native language, though his elvish came easily enough when he tried. His mother had insisted upon it and so he had spoken it every day for the first sixteen years of his life. But hearing it spoken now told him that his crazy plan had worked, that he had been found by the enemy and mistaken for one of their own, an elf from the Heartlands.

'I think Carla is foolish to expect us to ride all the way home in this,' said a feminine voice.

'Oh, and you want to argue with her?' replied a male one.

'No, I'm not that foolish,' replied the first voice.

'Exactly. Besides, we'll be stopping at the way station near Breda. We'll be offloading the seriously wounded there for treatment. We'll have more space then.'

'I suppose so.'

Fillion heard boots shifting. The light filtering through his closed lids darkened. A hand was placed upon his cheek, the pressure light, the skin warm. He couldn't remember when someone had last touched him like that, though it was likely to have been his mother.

'This one has some colour about him. His breathing is settled too.'

He tried to swallow. His throat was dry and hurt like a bastard.

'Water,' he croaked in elvish.

The hand withdrew.

'And he awakes,' announced the female voice.

There was a pause and some shuffling. Then the hand returned, sliding under his head and applying gentle pressure, lifting him up.

'Open up,' the male voice commanded.

He complied, parting his lips, feeling the tender skin stretch and sting a little. A stream of cool water entered his mouth. He swallowed, wincing at the pain, then forced himself to drink three more gulps.

'There, better?'

He grunted.

'My but you are a talkative one. Definitely a soldier.'

He was lowered back down. He felt some kind of furred hood covering his head and a cushion beneath that.

He opened his eyes. He just needed to check. He was looking up into dark, cloudy skies. The shadow moved into his vision.

'How are you?' it asked. It was the female.

'Alright, I think,' he responded.

'Good. Just rest now. You're not going anywhere. Not until that leg has healed.'

'Huh?'

The shadow laughed, the sound was soft and light.

'Your leg. The one with the splint on it.'

Fillion lifted his head. He was covered with several dark grey blankets. A wind played across his cheeks, cold and biting, a winter wind. He could see the outline of something long, tied to his left leg.

'You have a broken bone,' continued the female elf. 'It's reset. The surgeon says it should knit without any lasting problems, you just need some time. But if you want a healer to mage it better it might be a bit of a wait. We have far worse injuries.'

He looked back at his carer, his vision adjusted well enough to examine her. The elf's hair was chestnut and delicate, kept back with a leather headband. Her eyes were almond shaped, like a cat's. She looked young but it was always hard to tell with elves.

'Let him sleep, sister,' said the male voice.

She smiled.

'Good advice. Close your eyes. We'll reach the way station soon.'

He did as he was told.

Damn but how did he miss his broken leg? He must have been in shock when he had changed his clothes. He turned his head to get a better look at the wagon. There were some other injured elves either sitting or lying on the wagon bed. The good news was he saw no guards, and there were no chains around him so he wasn't a prisoner. His ruse had worked perfectly. The next step was figuring out what to do next.

Fillion sat on the tailgate of the wagon with his back propped up with blankets. He toyed with his broth and surveyed the way station. It was quiet; apart from his small group there was hardly a soul about. A little surprising considering how large it was and how many elves he knew were here, but snow would do that, muffling sound and life. Above him the sky was dark grey, constantly threatening to dump more snow on top of them as it had done for the last two days. On the ground and on the trees, everywhere he looked, it was white. The ice-covered tents and wagons scattered around did little to bring much colour to the scene. The snow was deep, and where it had been travelled over it had compacted, rather than turning to slush.

The encampment was set back in woods a short distance from the Emperor's Highway. If all else had fallen back into the earth, then he was confident the roads of the Empire would outlast even the near-immortal elves. They were, and had been, the arteries of Tissan. When the first Emperor of Tissan had set about conquering the Riverlands, he had proven himself as much a logistician as a warlord. He had realised that to govern you needed good lines of communication and a means to move armies around swiftly. The Empire had been forged by ingenuity as much as by blood. As far as he knew, the elves had never built such a wonder. A series of straight and level roadways, of soil packed and raised three feet above the land they crossed, paved with shaped stone brick, fired in countless forges. It was the endeavour of generations of Tissan workers and their legacy, at least, would last longer than the Empire they had dedicated themselves to.

The elves called this place a way station but he thought of it more as a staging post. The invading armies had marched all the way along this route, burning everything and killing everyone, and now they were heading back. He couldn't be sure just how far this place spread out, but he had seen hundreds of elves. Most of them were casualties, the walking wounded. Several pavilions further back was the field hospital and he had watched a number of stretchers being carried in. Occasionally one would come out again. The elves were very skilled in medicine, and they had their other sorcerous crafts, but even they couldn't cure all ills. Their culture took death very seriously, their lives so long that the passing of an elf was momentous. No doubt there was a pyre somewhere, piled with shrouded bodies, ready to be lit. Then the Death Priests would start their interminable chanting. If he was lucky, he would be too far away to have to listen to it. Being injured meant he wouldn't have to attend the ceremony.

Behind him, he heard the muffled drumming sound of hoof beats. Moments later a large number of cavalry rode past, heading east. He'd heard many units go by during the morning; at least three regiments worth. The elves truly had emptied all of the Heartlands to finish the job. Fortunately for him they hadn't quite succeeded.

He looked around at his fellow travelling companions. Two others were members of an archer battalion from the northern Heartlands, good hunting country from what they'd told him. A third of their number was in one of those pavilions with a gangrenous arm. He doubted the fool would ever shoot a bow again. It gave him grim solace. The female elf who had tended him was called Alica, the male was her brother, Hedra. They sat close together by a tree, talking quietly. He had been right in his assessment. They were both still children. No more than a hundred years old and considered too young to fight, they had volunteered to help the wounded with their older sister, Nadena. There she was now, emerging from behind the wagon, dressed in a simple blue cotton shift, and over that a leather apron. She wore stout walking boots and a broad leather belt around her waist. Her sleeves were rolled up and she carried a pail of water in each hand.

Her long auburn hair was plaited into one strand that fell over her left shoulder and threatened to enter the water at any moment. The way she dressed suggested someone from one of the border regions of the Heartlands. With what he knew of the elven people, the city folk would never condescend to wear such … practical clothing, yet her cultured and precise accent suggested that was exactly where she came from.

She brought the pail over and placed it by the wagon next to him. She stood up and flicked her hair back. She smiled at him, her cheeks dimpling with the spread of her wide mouth and lips.

'Sabin, are you well?' she asked.

Fillion nodded. He had used his first name, the elven birth name given to him by his mother. His surname was Celtebarian and they didn't need to know that.

'I am well,' he replied.

'Good to hear. Your hair is starting to grow out.'

Fillion ran a hand over his head. It was starting to get a bit shaggy. Normally he kept it cropped short; it was one of the obvious ways to look more like a human than an elf, at least at a distance. Too close and the ears gave it away. He had usually worn a bandana when amongst those who did not know him. It stopped his own side from shooting him by accident. Nadena's face took on a solemn cast and she called over to her kin. 'Hey, you two, the Death Dirge is about to begin. We should be heading over. Sabin, would you like to join us?' she asked while rolling her sleeves down.

Join you? I'd rather eat my own shit. Fillion smiled sadly. 'I cannot, the pain is still too much to bear. Please forgive me, I will grieve in silence.'

'I understand,' said Nadena with a concerned look. 'We shall see you on our return.'

She walked away and met the two younger elves. All around him, the fit and the injured walked or hobbled their way to some place behind the pavilions. At last he could have a bit of peace. The only elves left were either unconscious or too injured to move. He leaned his head back against the cushion and sighed heavily. All this damned courtesy got on his wick. When he and his men had been chased across the Empire they hadn't had time to sing Dirges or give burial rights. You were left where you fell.

Time to go scrounging. He pulled his good leg back and planted the foot firmly on the wagon bed, then did the same with both hands. Nicely braced, he pushed himself forward, the good leg protesting at the strain on its muscles as the one strapped to the splint sent sharp shooting pains right to his head. He shunted himself to the edge of the tailgate and allowed his legs to drop quickly. He had to work at getting his good foot on the ground first to get his balance and provide the push up. The broken leg touched down a moment after. It hurt like a bitch but would have been infinitely worse if he had taken his time about it. He clung on to the side of the wagon and took a breath as his vision blurred temporarily. There was sweat on his brow. He composed himself then twisted his neck around so he could look into the wagon bed. He could see nothing useful, just blankets and bandages. He'd have to look elsewhere. There were plenty of supplies piled up nearby so there ought to be something good.

A plaintive wailing had started drifting over the trees. The ritual had begun, and they'd be at it for hours. It was just as well, as he wasn't going anywhere fast. He reached for a crutch on the wagon, and got it tucked under his arm. He took small, shaky steps forward, half expecting to go flying at any moment. He forced the crutch into the snow, digging it down to give him a stable platform as he hobbled forward. Each movement was jarring, his passage less than smooth.

'Ah, fuck, shit. Shit.'

He made it to the first pavilion. He had to be careful now; some surgeons could still be in there and no doubt some attendants too. If they were in the process of saving a life, they had special dispensation not to attend the Dirges. He started to search the various crates, packages and piles stacked near the entrance. It was mostly useless junk, though in one set of boxes, packed with straw and linen, was a selection of glass vials and jars. Ointments and potions; he'd like to have some of that stuff, but he had nowhere to put it, save the pockets in his torn trousers. He did find a sewing kit: strong silken thread, needles and a tiny wooden pot of some kind of poultice. He stuffed it into a pocket. On the far side of the supplies he found what he had been looking for; a small pile of weapons, no doubt stripped from the dead. They were all daggers and knives, a few arrowheads here and there, none of the bigger stuff. He rummaged around and found two promising items. The first was a fine steel dagger still in its scabbard of black lacquered wood. He tucked that into his boot. The second was a real find. It was a short, wide, stubby blade, with a grip like a knuckle-duster. It was meant for bloody, direct work. This was no infantry weapon. Perhaps one of the assassins or infiltrators had been using it. He wasn't even sure it was elven; the design seemed too simple, too straightforward, it lacked any of their usual flourishes. He liked it immediately, wrapped it in a strip of bandage, and tucked it into the side of his trousers, trapped snugly against his hip.

Satisfied with his requisitions, he made his way back to his place by the wagon, sweating and swearing. Looking back, the route looked like some wading bird had come to visit, leaving a set of deep, uneven holes marking its passage. Hopefully no one would notice, otherwise he'd have to come up with some excuse. It was worth it. Now that he had the means to defend himself he didn't feel so naked. *Speaking of which, I'll need to ask for some new clothes. I can't keep walking around like this in the Homelands.* Paupers didn't exist there, and he needed something better to hide his knives in.

'Your accent is very strange, you know,' said Alica, as she dangled her legs over the back of the wagon.

Fillion raised an eyebrow and smiled.

'So is yours.'

Alica laughed. 'I guess it's because you live on the borders?'

'That is correct, right on the western fringes.'

'Did you meet many humans?' Alica asked, her face serious, a little fearful.

'A few, quite a few, I suppose. In the early years,' he replied.

'Can you speak their language?'

'A little. I expect that is why my accent has become so odd. I let them taint me.'

She reached out and touched his arm. He stopped himself from flinching.

'They are gone now,' she said softly.

'Yes, yes they are,' he replied.

He had never considered himself particularly duplicitous but there'd been occasions that demanded it. The conflict had found many uses for his unique physical traits. He had infiltrated enemy encampments, stolen information, assassinated leaders and none had ever thought that one of their own might be responsible. The guards had never once questioned him or his provenance. This act of intimacy, touching his arm, had shocked him a little. It was something he would have to get used to. The elves had always been a tactile race and his mother had been a fine example of that.

'Thank you for letting me stay on with you,' he said. It had been a week since they had left the way station. In that time he had slowly insinuated himself into their affections. He kept himself quiet and courteous, an agreeable travelling companion. It had already yielded some good results.

Alica smiled and inclined her head.

'It is a pleasure,' said Hedra, turning to look back at them from his place on the driver's bench.

'Though you'll need to start walking alongside us if you want to get your strength back,' said Nadena sternly. She sat next to her younger brother and had the reins.

'I will.'

They were passing the white-covered, burnt-out remains of a small village, one of a hundred just like it upon the Emperor's Highway. He judged they were well into the Riverlands, where the Empire had first come into being. He studied the buildings. Though he had no idea what the village was called or how many had lived there, he knew it anyway. There were so many just like it. It would have had a coaching inn, a blacksmith, and a victualler; all the usual industries concerned with servicing travellers. Farmers would have come in from outlying properties to sell their produce to the larger merchant businesses. That produce would have flowed along the Imperial arteries.

The enemy had been remorseless. They had not sought to salvage anything or reuse the buildings, let alone attempt to colonise. They had tried to wipe the place clean. Easy enough to do when you were dealing with wooden buildings, harder when you were facing bricks and mortar, stone and marble. He did wonder at that; he hadn't stayed near one of the Imperial cities long enough to see what had happened to them. Word had it that the dwarves and gnomes were going in and dismantling them one piece at a time.

'Are we going to go around their capital?' he asked.

'No,' said Nadena. 'It is not a place any of us wants to visit.'

'I heard tell it was a horrible battle. So many died there,' said Alica. 'Were you there?'

Fillion shook his head. 'I was not part of the army that attacked it. I was to the north.' He was in fact very aware of what Vyberg was like. At least what it used to be like. It was Vyberg that he had first travelled to when he had buried his father and left Celtebaria. It had taken him weeks but once there he had marvelled at the sight. A city unlike any he could have dreamed of. Walls taller than two oak trees end on end, running for leagues to either side of him, their tops crowned with battlements and dotted with soaring towers, their pennants snapping in the wind. Vyberg had been home to hundreds of thousands of people from across the Empire, all of them crammed into these circling arms of stone. He had thought it would be chaos, and it was. Yet it was beautiful too. He had come from a place where each man could find a space amongst the woodlands and carve out a living. In Vyberg everything and everyone was on top of each other, houses built in different ages leaned against each other for support and folk jostled for space, shouting to be heard. He had lost himself for a time, wandering down shadowed lanes, crowded streets and then broad avenues along the Way to the Imperial City, a city within a city, that was lined with imposing statues of great emperors, princes and generals. Soaring pinnacles of man-carved stone thrust into the sky and a great tower, home to eagles and their riders, stood taller than any other. He watched as those eagles took to the air and sped hither and yon, whilst others seemed to hang, suspended on the currents, silent watchers observing the masses below. As he passed through another great wall, he saw on either side massive marble and stone structures built to accommodate the servants of the Empire. Each one was a work of great craftsmanship, covered with friezes and paintings of great men and women. One of them he had entered; the Headquarters of His Imperial Majesty's Army. And his life had finally begun.

'We were there,' said Hedra, breaking into Fillion's private reverie. 'I never knew just how evil the humans could be. They gave weapons to everyone, even the children. Then made them all charge.'

Like we had any choice? He knew about that battle, where every citizen stood and fought. The Tissans of Vyberg had always been particularly pious and loyal to the Blessed Emperor. They had streamed out of the gates before the enemy had had a chance to encircle the city. Even so, they were cut down in their thousands by bow fire and the massed ranks of elven spear. That host of humanity had quickly broken and been run down by chariots and cavalry. It was said two hundred thousand souls had perished that day.

'Do you remember the human fire-bombs they made, sister?' asked Hedra. 'They strapped some kind of explosives to themselves then set them off as they hit our lines.'

'Enough, Hedra,' snapped Nadena. 'We do not need to talk of this.'

'Sorry,' mumbled Hedra.

Nadena continued. 'The road leads us to the city but we are going to turn south and cut cross-country. The whole army is going that way. It's the shortest route home.'

Everyone was quiet for a time.

'Are you sure you want to ride with us all the way to Apamea, Sabin?' Alica finally asked. 'It's a long way into the Heartlands. Wouldn't you want to see your home on the borders first?'

Fillion shrugged. 'I have lived all my life on the borders, they aren't going anywhere. Now we have peace, I thought it would be good to travel a little. I'd like to see the cities.' And the capital of the elven kingdom seemed like the perfect place to start for his purposes.

'They are a little different from what you are used to,' said Nadena. 'Buildings, temples, people. More than you have ever seen packed into the same space.'

'You mean tighter then standing in a spearline, or having to share a sleeping space with nine others? I'm used to crowds, my lady,' responded Fillion.

Hedra laughed easily. 'He has you there, sister. He's marched across the whole continent with a hundred thousand others!'

Nadena did not rise to that.

'Just make sure you walk that leg, Sabin. We have another two weeks of travelling before we reach the plains. Then I want you running.'

Alica grinned at him. 'She's a taskmaster. Don't think she won't hold you to that.'

'I am glad she will. I need to get my muscles working again.'

He would need them soon enough, he had to get every part of him strong. He had found the perfect opportunity in this family. They lived in the capital of the Heartlands and now they were going to carry him all the way there. It was a good start though it was also the easiest point of the journey, if you could call what he'd pulled off so far easy. He had a mountain to climb and he was barely into the foothills. Life was going to get very hard for him but what did he expect? He wanted to kill a king.

CHAPTER 5

Owen was lying flat on the slope, the snow making a gentle crunching sound beneath him, his feet sliding and slipping as he struggled to gain purchase. The slope was quite steep and he wasn't sure if he'd ever get to the top of the hill. After some energetic and alarming scrambling, he finally reached the crest and looked across at Gerat. The man hadn't noticed his difficulty or had chosen not to mention it.

'Can you see that small copse?' he said.

Owen took a moment.

'Just to the left?'

'That's it. Now, track along it a little further left. See the fold in the ground?'

Owen couldn't, it was all white and hard to spot anything that wasn't the size of a tree or a small hill.

'Yes,' he lied. He didn't want to come across as anything other than a competent soldier, he had a feeling respect was easily lost with Gerat.

'They're behind it.'

'How can you tell?'

'Smoke.'

'Oh.' *Damn.* He could see it now, the whitest wisp of cloud drifting lazily into the sky. *Easy enough to miss in this landscape.* That's what he told himself anyway.

'Why are they in the open and not in the wood?' he asked.

'Maybe they are. That fold might give them better shelter from the wind. Doesn't matter, these wood elves are strange at the best of times. I hear that even their city cousins don't like 'em much.'

Gerat pushed himself away from the slope, sliding back down below the crest. Owen followed.

'Do you think they'll come close?' he asked as he lowered himself down gently, digging his hands deep into the snow, using them as an anchor.

'Does it matter?' asked the Scotian. His face was obscured by the thickly furred hood of his jacket, his body angled away from Owen's

Owen looked hard at Gerat. What was he talking about?

'I thought we were just coming to look?'

'You got that wrong, then, didn't you?'

Owen felt his face flush, the warmth making his cheeks sting in the bitter cold.

'You want to go after them?' he asked, already knowing the answer.

'Yes.'

'Right.'

He hadn't expected this. When one of Gerat's lads had come in from a hunt and told them he'd seen a party of wood elves in the distance, Owen had thought they'd hunker down. Maybe they'd set a trap just in case, then lie low and wait for them to pass by. Instead, they'd walked for thirty hard minutes through the snow and now Gerat was shaping for a fight.

'We need to know how many there are,' he said, though in truth he had no desire to find out. Maybe there was a way he could talk Gerat out of this. The Emperor knew the man was too stubborn to make it a simple task.

'We'll know that soon enough,' replied Gerat. He motioned with his head. 'Here come the others.'

Oh. There were three more figures at the bottom of the slope. Gerat slithered down towards them. Owen bit his lip. What were these folks about? He followed, taking the hand proffered to him by Bedwyr, a stocky man, only a few years older than Owen. The other two were Dill, a man in his fifties with terrible teeth, and a woman called Renna, his wife, as leathery and wild looking as he was.

'There's a bunch of the crafty bastards just over yonder,' said Gerat. 'We'll wait and see what Howell has to say.' The others, their faces covered, nodded. He could only see their eyes, but they all looked determined. With their mouths and noses obscured, their breath wasn't misting in the air as much. He had left his own scarf back with Arno. For some crazy reason, he hadn't thought he'd need it.

They waited, Owen uncomfortable in the silence. He wasn't afraid, he didn't think. Yet there was that familiar cold sensation playing about his gums. Gerat was an intimidating man and it would be hard to refuse to be a part of what was coming. He'd never fought anyone hand to hand before. He felt the eyes of the others on him. Were they judging him? It was a stupid thought. They had no knowledge of him, only that he was an Eagle Rider. That made him a soldier in their view even if he didn't think of himself as one.

'Here he comes,' said Dill.

Howell jogged into view, his body moving up and down in an exaggerated fashion as the snow pulled against his steps.

'What did you see?' asked Gerat.

Howell pulled his hood back and yanked the scarf down from his face. His high cheekbones and long thin nose gave him a hawkish aspect. He was breathing hard.

'I got into the woods, didn't see anyone. Then I pushed on through, almost right to the edge and got myself a good look at them.'

'Need to be careful, they can smell you out,' said Dill.

Howell shook his head. 'I stayed downwind, they didn't know I was there.' He coughed and spat out a big gob of phlegm. 'There's five of 'em, and a few spare mounts. They're tucked away in a draw, out of the weather.'

'Any look-outs?' asked Gerat.

'None I could see.'

'You sure there's none in the woods?' asked Owen, repeating his question from earlier. Gerat gave him a look and he felt foolish for asking it, but he wanted to be sure.

'It's pretty thick in there. You couldn't get a horse inside, so I reckon it's just a source of fuel.'

'They ain't expecting trouble, so let's give 'em some,' said Gerat. 'Five of them, six of us. We'll take 'em in a crossfire. Owen, you and Bedwyr go straight for 'em over this hill and work your way to the top of that slope. Stay just below the lip, keep quiet and keep low. We'll go through the woods and use our bows. Chances are we won't have to get into a scrap. When you hear the shouting, that's your time to join in.'

He made it sound easy.

'Right. Let's get to it.' Gerat took his bow and pulled out a string from a small pouch on his belt. The others followed his lead apart from Renna who humped a crossbow, a little larger than his own. The men carried staves as tall as a man. Owen could never hope to get any kind of pull on those great beasts. You needed a lifetime of practice and arms like tree trunks. His skill was in flying and his bird was nowhere near. He put his crossbow on the ground, placed his foot through the small stirrup and hauled back on the string. As it caught in the trigger, he placed a bolt in the groove.

'All ready?' asked Gerat. The group nodded and muttered their agreement. 'Good. Let's be off. Bedwyr, Owen, give us a few minutes before you move. It'll take us some time to get through that wood.'

'Right y'are,' said Bedwyr, his voice muffled by the thick woollen scarf wrapped around his head.

Owen watched them head away, trudging slowly through the snow.

'You any good with that?' asked Bedwyr.

'What?' asked Owen.

'That flatbow.'

'Oh.' Owen shrugged. 'Not bad. I'm used to shooting at targets that are larger, but they tend to be moving faster as well.'

'Long as you can shoot.'

They stood together in silence for a couple of minutes. Owen cradled his bow, rocking back and forth on his heels.

'Let's start. I'm going to have to climb that one-handed,' he said.

Bedwyr grunted his assent.

Owen led the way back up the slope, stepping into virgin snow, using his free hand to keep his balance. Once at the top, they started down the shallower slope, heading towards the pillar of smoke. Owen had to be honest, he might have been nervous before, but now he felt downright unhappy. They might be hidden from the sight of the elves right now but Gods of Old, they were exposed; two men walking across an empty, open space with nowhere to hide. He felt his breath quicken, his body tense. It wouldn't matter how quickly he ran, even a drunken wood elf was liable to drop him without too much effort.

After a tense few minutes, they made it to the bottom of the far slope and Owen breathed a sigh of relief. They stopped for a moment and listened. Voices drifted down to them, vague and indistinct.

Owen looked at his companion and placed a finger to his lips, not that Bedwyr likely needed it, but at least he had the good grace to nod, his eyes determined.

The climb up this incline was a lot easier, the footing surer. Owen settled down and crouched low. Bedwyr got into position next to him, his back against the slope, his bow resting across his legs, an arrow nocked against the taught string. Owen kept his crossbow and head pointed forward. Then they waited. The voices were a little clearer up here but he couldn't understand any of it; he'd never had much skill for languages. The conversation seemed easy, casual. There were pauses, another comment then a laugh. Everything was as it should be.

Owen started to feel calmer. There were no surprises and they had the easy job. All the attention would be on Gerat and his fellows. *It'll go well. It'll go well.* Owen felt a little breeze on his skin, the muscles in his side starting to complain at the angle he was keeping them in. He shifted a little so he could lie on his side. It wouldn't be long now. He could afford to let the cold seep through a little. Bedwyr raised a hand. Kinked his head. Owen froze. A voice, loud and clear, spoke up. A figure appeared at the top of the slope. It was a wood elf. He was wearing a long cloak of stitched leather patches, the fur on the inside. It was unlaced, revealing a black leather jerkin and bright green woollen britches. His hands were working at the belt, loosening it and starting to undo the small leather ties around his groin. His head was turned, looking back the way he had come, speaking to someone on the far side. Owen stared, his mouth open. He was at a loss. The elf turned, black eyes taking a moment to focus on what was ahead of him. His mouth fell open.

'Shit!' said Bedwyr as he struggled to stand.

The elf shouted, started to back up. Owen raised his bow and pulled the trigger, it was instinctive, and he wasn't even aiming. He didn't have to, as the elf was no more than a yard away and the bolt hit him in the top of his thigh. He fell backwards with a strangled yelp and disappeared from view.

There were more shouts. A horse started to whinny.

Bedwyr was scrambling up the slope. 'Come on!' he shouted. His steps were exaggerated as he climbed, his bow waving wildly.

Owen shut his mouth and scrambled after him. He wasn't thinking, just reacting, but he felt a rush of excitement and satisfaction. He had scored a hit! He reached the top and looked down into the draw. To his left a number of horses were panicking, rearing high and twisting around each other in the tight space. The campsite was small, a fire in the centre with bedrolls and blankets clustered round it. Two elves were already down. One was running towards the wood and another knelt by the fire reloading his bow. An arrow just missed him and was lost amidst the horses. The elf Owen had hit rolled down the hill and was crawling towards a grounded saddle, blood staining the snow behind him.

Bedwyr stood and loosed just as the horses crashed through the camp. Spooked and wild, they were away and running. The elf that'd been shooting was thrown to the ground. The fire was trampled to smouldering pieces. Owen's wounded elf was dead, Bedwyr's arrow through his back. The horses were clear and off, scattering away from the mouth of the draw.

'Look out!' someone shouted and Owen ducked as an arrow flew over his head. He heard the whirr of the shaft as it passed him by. Bedwyr already had another arrow notched and flying. Owen scrambled back and started to reload his bow.

'Hang on,' said Bedwyr. He had another arrow ready but it hung loose. He dropped to one knee and leaned forward. He stood. 'It's done. Shit, that last arrow was one of ours.' Owen released the tension on the string. That would have been a great way to go, shot by his side. He pushed himself up, and pulled out his knife, just in case. Joining Bedwyr, he looked down. There was no movement in the camp. All the elves were down, all of them had a shaft stuck in them somewhere, apart from the one run down by the horses. He might be unconscious, or just feigning it.

'Here they come,' said Bedwyr.

The others emerged from the trees and stalked their way across the short distance to the campsite. All had their bows out except Howell. He walked behind the others, a hand clamped to his arm.

Bedwyr climbed down the slope and Owen followed.

'Got 'em all?' asked Gerat.

'Looks like it,' replied Bedwyr. 'What happened to Howell?'

'Got sliced by a shaft,' replied Howell. 'Hurts like bloody hell.'

'They only got one shot off. Almost made it count,' said Gerat. He stopped in front of Owen and smiled. 'When I saw that elf take your bolt in the leg, we took them as they all looked the other way. Not quite how I expected it to go, but it worked out fine.'

Yeah. I almost got pissed on.

'Right lads. Better check 'em.'

The group split and went to the bodies. The campsite was a wreck, kit and equipment strewn amidst churned up, bloodstained snow.

'This one's still alive,' said Dill. He stood over the trampled elf.

'Finish him off, then,' said Gerat with a wave of his knife.

Dill pulled his knife out of his belt, lifted the elf's head and drew it across the throat.

'Ah!' Dill stood up and shook his hand, red drops flying in an arc. 'Got some of his dirty blood on my hands.'

'Least he's dead now,' said Renna. She held her own knife, large-handled with a wide, serrated blade. She stuck it into the elf sprawled out in front of her. She caught Owen's eye. 'What? Just makin' sure.'

'Start stripping,' ordered Gerat. He looked at Owen. 'A good haul this. If we can catch some of those horses, we can get all their stuff back to the barn. You any good with horses?'

Owen was tempted to say no, but then he looked at the others as they started to loot the camp.

'Yeah, I might be able to talk 'em round.'

'Good. Get to it, we'll finish up here.'

Owen walked away. He spotted a horse loitering not far from the wood and started to tramp through the snow. He hadn't tried to speak to an animal other than Arno for some time, but at least horses were smart. More importantly it gave him time to think. They'd been lucky and he'd been lucky and only Howell had taken a wound. It could have easily been worse. Gerat was set on fighting back but Owen wasn't and he didn't like the way they did business. There was a brutality to what they did. It made him feel uneasy. You could say one thing for flying into battle; you never had to see death up close.

Owen tightened the straps and gave his saddle one final check over. He looked up at the night sky. It had clouded over, which would be useful. He rubbed his hand through Arno's feathers.

Heading off again, Arno. He smiled as Arno pulsed back feelings of excitement. His bird wanted to get up there and do what he was born to do. Owen placed a foot into a stirrup and hauled himself on to Arno's back.

'Here.' Gerat handed him a cloth wrapped package. 'Some meat and dried fruits.'

'Thank you` Gerat. I don't mean to be stealing your food.'

Great waved a hand. 'Bah, we can look after ourselves.'

'I guess you can.' Owen pursed his lips. 'Gerat, don't do anything brave. There are only a dozen of you.'

Gerat folded his arms.

'I know that. Thought we might look for others. Now we got ourselves a supply of weapons folk can use, we can get stronger. I know there are more like us out there, smart enough to hide out where the bastards won't follow.'

Owen wasn't pleased to hear that. Looking for others was a good plan; leading them to war wasn't.

Gerat reached out and slapped his leg. 'You sure I can't convince you to stay? You can fight.'

'No, I need to go. But who knows? I might come back, once I've done what I need to do. Keep a fire burning for me, would you?' said Owen.

Gerat raised a hand. Owen raised one back.

'*Come on then, Arno. Fly.*'

Arno stood up, stretched his wings wide and with a powerful down stroke, he took to the air. Arno followed the path of the small valley north of the hills, then turned and flew directly south, back over the steading. Owen looked down; he could make out a number of figures, gathered in the dark. He waved and Arno screeched, then they were gone. He angled Arno south and east.

'Have I done the right thing, Arno?' he spoke quietly. He was turning his back on the first set of people he had come across. *Running again.* He had a nasty feeling they might be the last people he'd see. A short time later, he left the hill country and passed over the King's highway. It was empty. Far away to the right was Aberpool. He fancied he saw a glow on the horizon. If there was anyone there he doubted they'd be friendly. Arno turned due east, aided by a following breeze, his keen eyes scanning the ground for movement. Owen watched the skies.

CHAPTER 6

Cade was sweating hard. The tunic was stuck against her back and her crotch was sticky and chaffing. The westerly breeze felt cold as it blew against the wet fabric. She was also thirsty, her head ached and she felt weak. She humped another marble bust into the waiting cart, dropping it loudly on to the back tailgate.

'Careful,' hissed Evan.

Cade looked up at the boy. He looked terrified, afraid that he might be spotted at any moment.

'Or what? You going to call over the dwarf, get him to whip me?' she asked. 'You want to be the good toady?'

Evan shook his head quickly.

'No, no. They'll hear you that's all. Then they'll check. If there's a scratch they'll hurt us.'

His voice was whiney. She wasn't in the mood for it.

'If you squeak another word, *I'll* hurt you,' Cade whispered.

Evan swallowed. His adam's apple bobbed in his scrawny neck. His face turned red and he leant over, lifting the bust up by its head and dragging it to the back of the cart with the others.

'And don't scratch it,' she hissed.

Cade spun on her heel and headed across the dusk-shadowed road towards the large building previously owned by the Guild of Navigators. She took care not to slide on the icy cobbles while she studied the guild house. It had four bloody floors and long, wide corridors. And each of them had a parade of these bloody busts. Vain fools, the lot of them.

Looking left and right along the road, she watched several other work parties emptying similar buildings of their riches.

'Eyes down,' growled a dwarf guard as she passed through into the entrance.

She tipped her head, gaze fixed on the ground. She'd already learned not to antagonise her captors. A smack to the back of her head with a cudgel had made her see stars. Another captive had given them a sideways look and had been knocked to the ground. He never got up again.

Once past the dwarf she looked up, her eyes gazing around the interior. The first three floors had already been emptied of anything of value. Not for the first time she debated taking off when nobody was looking. She could just hide somewhere inside and wait for the greedy bastards to clear out. Surely they wouldn't notice if one of their captives was missing; they sure as hell didn't give a damn about their lives. There was nothing wrong with her plan, except for that dwarf standing high above her, leaning on the balcony. He was watching her every move. Dwarfs had excellent night vision, that's what came with spending almost all your time underground.

'Fuck it,' she muttered, and wiped her forehead. She climbed wearily up the wide, sweeping steps to the top floor landing. The dwarf had turned to follow her passage, his back now against the banister, his arms folded. She risked a quick glance his way. He looked bemused.

'You do that every time you walk into this place,' he said.

Cade didn't look at him, and didn't respond.

'I don't know where you think you will get to,' he shook his head and pointed. 'I reckon there's one more down that way. Give your friend a hand.'

Cade walked past him and down the corridor. She didn't understand why that one was so damned talkative. After he had found her in the mansion, he always had a word or two for her. The rest of his kind couldn't give a toss and stuck to their growling language, switching to the common tongue when they wanted something done.

At the end of the corridor she saw a figure, a young woman, wrestling with an object.

'This one is heavy,' she said. She looked a little older than Cade, maybe mid-twenties, slim with long, mousey hair and light brown eyes, probably from a small town in the hills of eastern Scotia. She had her hands around a short, flat-topped marble pillar.

'They are all heavy,' replied Cade.

'You going to help?' she said.

'Like I have a choice,' Cade muttered.

'Thanks all the same. Name's Meghan.'

Meghan took the top end and tilted it towards her waist. Cade got on to her haunches and got her arms around the base, taking the weight and lifting up. She felt her legs creak.

Together they shuffled back towards the stairs, Cade having to turn her head to watch where she was putting her feet. They took the stairs even slower, Cade feeling the weight in her arms, her biceps complaining. At the first landing she had to stop for a breather.

'Come along, women. This is the last one. Time to go,' urged the dwarf.

Cade screwed up her face.

'You can help if you want.' She regretted it instantly. She was going to get battered for that.

'Just pick it up,' replied the dwarf, his voice dropping. 'Or I will leave you here.'

And I won't be breathing when you do, thought Cade.

'I'll take that end,' offered Meghan.

'No,' snapped Cade.

She leant down and collected the pillar once more. The pain returned and by the time they got to the cart, her arms were shaking and sweat was pouring freely from her brow. If nothing else, she wasn't feeling the cold anymore. Evan hurried forward and guided her end on to the cart. She let go and watch her two companions shunt the pillar further forward.

The dwarf walked past her, shouting commands. Along the street the other groups were gathering, falling into line behind the carts. Cade hadn't noticed it before, but the dusky, darkening sky was glowing. She looked closer. It was not just in the west where the sun should be setting, this was all around them; a shifting red and orange hue gilded the roofs of the city.

She stood straighter and was joined by Meghan, Evan and a few others. This was a drill they were well used to now. For the last three weeks they had moved systematically through the city, divesting each street of anything of value. Sleeping in the nearest available building each day, then venturing out at dawn to start the pillaging once more.

A dwarf further down the line shouted something she couldn't understand and they moved off in convoy. The small carts laden with treasures were pulled by stout looking mules and driven by dwarves, and made a steady clip through the streets of Aberpool. They were almost at the harbour so there was nowhere to go but east, and as they walked towards the centre of the city, Cade spied activity. Dwarves were moving into buildings, carrying torches and barrels. On their return they were empty handed. She watched a house ahead of them, with a bright flickering light coming from the windows. As she passed, one of those windows exploded outwards, showering the group with glass fragments. She sneered as some of her companions gasped and shrieked in response. Tongues of flame licked out around the edges of the empty frame and inside the fire raged. Cade looked behind and watched the whole damned street being put to the torch.

The procession continued to wend its way through Aberpool, other columns joining them as they crossed the central square, then onwards along the Emperor's parade and past the rubble of the east gate. The heat was building around them now. She could feel it on the wind behind her. She could smell burning wood too, acrid and earthy. She could even hear a gentle roar in the night air. Cade worried her bottom lip. This was her last chance to get away, to try and fight through the flames that were surrounding them and put a barrier between her and her captors. But there were dozens of dwarves flanking the column on either side now. It would be next to impossible. More dwarves waited as they emerged from the city and her chances reduced even further.

Beyond the city walls, they moved along the road, an empty plain to either side of them. Any features had been trampled away by the feet of thousands, any buildings torn down for fuel. Ahead Cade saw a strange mound to one side of the road. She looked closer as they drew level with it. It was a large pile of freshly dug earth. A number of dwarves were gathered around an opening, a sloped hole leading into the ground. They were passing barrels down the slope, quickly disappearing into the darkness. A little distance away was another one of these mounds, and perhaps she could make out another one further on to the south, near the curve of the wall.

'They are sapping,' muttered someone behind her. 'Dug under the walls. Going to bring them down.'

Cade understood. The dwarves were finishing what they had started, making sure the city was left uninhabitable, a ruin, left to fade away for nature to reclaim. What she still didn't understand was why they were still alive. In fact, where were the rest of the bodies?

She got her answer soon enough. Coming from the head of the column she heard muted voices, a cry of horror. Then a dwarf shouted something, quieting the crowd. A great mound, nothing like the sapping piles, rose up to meet them, towering over the convoy. How did she miss this? But the answer was obvious. It was so big and the night so dark, it had just blended into the background, disguising the horizon behind it. It was smouldering in many places, but the burning couldn't hide what it was. It was a pyre. The heat had cleared the snow back by almost twenty yards. Bodies were stacked upon bodies. *Gods Below! How many thousands?* Arms, legs, and torsos emerged from that mound of flesh. Bones jutted out at strange angles. Skin was burnt and blackened. In other places the fire had not caught hold, and the bodies were rotting. The smell was intense, putrid, and terrible.

It awoke memories of burnt meat and Cade felt her mouth salivating against her will, and she felt ashamed. The emotion was not something she was used to but this was beyond anything she had seen before. There were faces within the chaos, sightless, mouths open, screaming in silent agony. She wanted to look away, but Cade forced herself to pay witness as they passed by the dead. *By all the Gods of Old. They have done it. They have ended us.* Sounds reached her, the plodding of the mules, the crunching steps of hundreds in the snow, the creaking of wheels. Over all of it she could hear the sound of weeping. The dwarves did not try to quiet it. Perhaps they were as awed as the rest of them or perhaps they wanted the lesson to sink home. The convoy passed beyond the mound and they continued on to only the Emperor knew where. *And I'm still alive.* She kept hold of that small crumb of comfort. After all, it could be worse.

Cade hunkered down next to the fire and drew her blanket close around her shoulders. She looked up at the overcast sky, the moon just a dim white disc behind the grey veil. They were well into winter, and she'd never known it to be so bad. Each day they awoke at dawn, blankets snapping and crackling with the ice that had formed over them. Then they marched through the day, stopping as the sun had cleared the horizon and only the faintest glow was left.

The humans were corralled into groups, fed, and then guarded until dawn. They had been on the road for a week now, and while her feet were sore, the going hadn't been that bad. They travelled at the speed of the carts and their dwarf captors, who weren't known for their fleetness of foot. What they *were* was relentless. They stopped for five minutes every hour with no longer breaks for food or rest. Just five minutes every hour. It could've been worse; at least the days were short. If they'd come during the summer, she would have had less sleep.

She held her battered pewter mug close and dunked a chunk of bread into the thin, watery gruel that slopped about within it. She could see something floating around in there. It might be carrot. Could be a cockroach. Either way, she'd eat it.

'Hey, how'd you get that?' asked Issar, a thin, swarthy man from far Erebesh.

'What?' she replied, just before she stuffed the bread into her mouth.

'That bread you just didn't share,' he said angrily.

'Was she supposed to?' asked Devlin, a lean-muscled, middle-aged thatcher from the Riverlands. A straight talker, Cade liked that quality.

'She should share,' Issar said, petulantly.

Cade swallowed the bread in one gulp. 'When you get good enough to steal food from under their noses, then I might think about dealing with you.'

'Some of us aren't as gifted as you,' muttered Issar. Cade knew his type, the Erebeshi was all piss and vinegar, happy to make noises but never to act.

'How do you do it?' asked Meghan, from across the fire.

Cade shrugged.

'A misspent youth.'

'Not so misspent now,' said Devlin.

'Speaking of youth, I had a look round the camp,' said Cade. 'There ain't no-one here over the age of forty, I'd say.'

Devlin gave a short, bitter laugh. 'That's me buggered then.'

Cade had been slowly sneaking her way around their part of the convoy during the night. Moving between fires, listening to conversations, studying faces. The guards were attentive but their minds wandered just like anyone's would.

'How many of us do you think there are, Cade?' Meghan asked. The woman had taken to treating her like she was the smart one. Cade couldn't argue with that.

'It's a long column. I'd say a mile or so,' said Cade.

Issar whistled. 'I reckon there may be a thousand of us.'

'More 'n that,' Cade added.

'Just fit ones and young ones, though?' said Devlin.

'Which sort are you?' asked Cade.

Devlin grunted.

'I ain't young, so I guess I fooled 'em into thinking I was still fit.'

'How many dwarves?' asked Meghan, throwing another small branch on to the fire.

'A lot,' said Cade, simply.

'They are pulling back, taking everything with them as they go,' said Devlin. 'You see how every night we get fed and watered, how they let us have fires. It doesn't matter to them. Each morning we reach a supply point. Then after we leave, they collect what's worth salvaging and pull down the rest. We are as much a prize to them as all the shit they made us gather. Gold, silver, jewels, marble and people.'

'Why do they keep letting us die, then?' asked Meghan.

'Weeding out the weak and unruly. Keeps the rest of us in line,' said Cade. Each morning they found another body. Frozen over, claimed by the cold. She'd thought it had been bad in the rookery. The homeless and desperate always suffered during the winter. If you were smart, however, there was always a way to keep warm. Warm enough at any rate.

'I thought they wanted us all dead,' said Issar. 'That was the point of all this, wasn't it?'

'Maybe it was. You see any elves, any of the other races stick around in Aberpool?' asked Devlin. 'I didn't.'

'Clearing out before it got too cold,' said Meghan.

'Hey, Devlin, you seem pretty clever. Like you've been taking notice,' said Cade.

'Did some time in the army. Long while ago now. I guess it never leaves you,' he replied, a rueful look on his face.

'Why weren't you called up?' asked Meghan. 'I thought they called up all reservists.'

'I'm no reservist, I did my time. That was enough.' Devlin's tone said that was an end to the conversation. It didn't bother Cade, what he said was right. They were on the last convoy out of the Empire. There was nothing left for them here. She lay down, turned her back to the fire and tried to block out the conversations around her. She reached down into the deep pocket of her britches, felt the reassuring presence of her 'assassin's blade', as she had dubbed it. The dwarves had rid her of all her weapons bar this. They had never thought to check. She was just a woman after all. The first chance she'd got, she had transferred it to her pocket. Having the blade gave her a sense of confidence. It made her feel she still had some kind of control over her life. She chewed at a fingernail. If they were all prizes to the dwarves, that did not bode well. Something else was going on as well, though she hadn't shared that with rest of her travelling companions. The four of them had been thrown together by ill luck and she was yet to get anywhere near trusting them, but there was a difference to the way they and the rest of their group were treated, compared to others. Some of the other groups were in a worse way than them, being beaten for no reason, being fed less and given even worse shit to eat than they were. She knew different standards were being applied and she had an idea why that was, but she was biding her time to check if she was right.

Her chance came four days later. A heavy snowfall had blanketed the land, rivers had frozen over and a cold wind swept down from the north. They were trudging through a white, empty landscape much changed from what they had travelled through before. Gone were the steep valleys and vales of Scotia. They had been replaced by gentler, rolling country, with plenty of grazing and the ground good for cultivation. There were numerous copses and small woods to either side, with large square areas marked out by hedgerows. This country looked managed in a way Scotia never had been. They were entering the heart of the Empire, she was sure of it but she had seen nothing resembling a house or barn anywhere near the road all day.

Everyone was swaddled in their blankets, staying on the right side of the carts, trying to gain some shelter from the wind. Cade had her arms wrapped tight about her body, clutching the folds of cloth to her. The edge of the blanket was pulled over her head to make a crude hood. At least in their place, midway down the column, much of the snow had been compacted by the vanguard, making the going easier.

A cart was by the side of the road, one of its wheels cracked and splintered under the weight of its load. A group of dwarves stood by it, watching a number of humans unload the cargo. A young man slipped and fell on to the vase he was carrying and it shattered. A dwarf, uttering a single, angry sounding word, stepped up behind him, drew a dagger and slid it across his throat. The blood rushing out of his severed neck turned the snow a stark, bright red, its heat melting the top layer to mush. She felt her temper rise and saw a familiar face stride past. She pulled back her hood so that she would be easier to recognise.

'Hey, is this stuff really worth it?' she asked.

The dwarf stopped. He wore a thick brown cloak over his broad-shoulders but his head was bare. She could see flakes of snow caught within his thick hair and his beard was frosted white. His earrings tinkled gently as he turned his head towards her. He looked at her a moment then fell into step with the group, though he kept his distance.

'You have some mouth on you, girl,' he replied looking back towards the broken cart. 'You think you are worth it?'

'Depends on what you expect me to do for you,' she replied.

'You'll do whatever I ask of you.'

'I don't doubt it. I'm a fine strong woman. But what do you want with all that crap?'

The dwarf grunted and shook his head.

'This "crap" is what is going to make me rich. A hundred years from now, folk will want to have a memento, a relic of your kind. It's shoddy workmanship but it'll sell. As for the gold and precious metals, they can be melted down, remade.'

She'd been right. This dwarf was a merchant not a warrior. *And I'm a commodity. No wonder he's holding back on the ill treatment. There is an opportunity here, if I can work it out.*

'You going to sell us, too?' she asked.

The dwarf shook his head, spat into the snow and picked up his pace, moving further along the line, Cade forgotten.

'That was a ballsy move,' said Devlin, behind her. 'You got a death wish or something?'

'Didn't you see what they did to that man? They just slaughtered him!' whispered Meghan heatedly, walking up to her shoulder. 'You shouldn't talk to them.'

'I'm not, least not to the others. They don't want to talk to us. That one,' she said watching the dwarf head up the line of carts, 'he's different. He spoke to me.'

'Don't get sociability mixed up with something else, Cade,' warned Devlin. 'Dwarves are unfriendly bastards at the best of times. Remember, from what I heard, they were the ones who started this.'

'I heard that we had upset them, moved into their territory or something,' said Meghan.

'I heard the Crown Prince had raped an elven princess,' piped up Issar.

'Bullshit,' replied Devlin.

'No, honest as the Emperor, I heard it from a man who worked on the Duke of Aberpool's staff,' said Issar.

'Oh him. I heard stories about that man. Heard he liked lying with young male prostitutes. Didn't have you down as one of those,' said Devlin.

'Piss off,' grumbled Issar.

Meghan laughed quietly. Cade liked that sound, it was genuine. She hadn't heard one like it for a long time. Her life had been spent amongst scoundrels, thieves, killers and bastards. The only genuine laughter she was used to hearing was the amusement shown as one sod kicked another when they were down.

'Hush,' warned Devlin.

A dwarf walked up to them, he face unreadable, his hand on his cudgel. Everyone looked away and put their heads down. After a few seconds he moved off.

Cade could feel the tension ease. She smiled to herself. That dwarf had been hanging around with the chatty one since the start. He likely worked for him and been told not to damage the goods. It proved what she had been thinking.

'Where are we now?' she asked quietly.

'Not sure but I'd say we are in the Riverlands. This is the true Empire,' replied Devlin. Cade had expected he'd be the one to reply first.

'Your old stomping ground,' she replied.

Devlin grunted.

It was obvious to her that they were heading to the dwarf lands in the mountains far to the east, beyond the plains. By the Gods of Old, this was going to be some trek. She wondered how many of them would be left by the time they got there.

The weather finally changed. The temperature rose, the wind lessened, but Cade was as miserable as ever. They were passing a burnt-out town buried under drifts of snow. The line of captives trudged their way along a road made into slush by thousands of feet, hundreds of hooves and dozens of wagon wheels. Cade's feet were soaking wet through, the leather of her boots blackened by the meltwater. It wasn't as cold today but the clouds were still thick and grey, there was no sun to warm the snow and ice. She passed a building that was nothing more than bare bones, a blackened framework of timbers, with no roof or walls. A pile of snow almost concealed the rubble beneath it. Long icicles hung off the front lintel, clear and smooth. They'd make a nice weapon if she could reach up, break one off and drive it into the neck of the nearest dwarf. Or she could thrust it into her own bare flesh and end this march, the constant cold and misery, with no hope of escape, rescue or freedom. She could do, if she was that way inclined. Things could be worse.

She entered a wide square. In the centre of it was a well, its roof and low stone wall clear of ice, melted away by the heat coming from the four braziers stationed around it. They were large, glowing red and pumping out warmth. Beside each one stood a dwarf, dressed like blacksmiths in their dark leather aprons, waiting for who knew what. Perhaps they were planning to re-shoe the animals, or put manacles on them all. Not that there was much point to that, they were too tired and cold to run anywhere. Up ahead folk were being separated. She saw large groups split off and placed on the far side of the square. Those nearest her were pushed into a spot on the north side. Dwarves patrolled the perimeter as the different groups in the column were separated out.

'What's going on?' whispered Meghan, sidling up beside her.

'Don't know.'

'They don't normally do this. Let us stay in a town, I mean.'

'They don't. Stop talking.'

Meghan pulled away.

Cade tucked her hands under her armpits and stamped her feet. More people were entering the square, the line still a long way from finishing. Something was up. A few of the other groups were being brought forward into the centre of the square towards the braziers.

'Oh,' said Meghan.

Yeah, she'd worked it out.

'What are they doing?' asked a ruddy-cheeked woman just in front of Cade.

This one wasn't so smart.

'Jessene, they are going to brand us,' said Meghan quietly.

The woman called Jessene turned and looked at Cade with wide, innocent eyes. She was probably of an age with Cade. Her long straw-coloured hair was piled up high on her head, except for a long lock that had fallen down and now dangled on the bridge of her nose. She was still carrying what could best be described as puppy fat and in normal times she'd likely be adding to it as she got older. Cade wasn't sure how she hadn't lost it in the march.

'That true?' Jessene asked Cade.

'Looks like it.'

'Gwillem. I'm frightened,' said Jessene reaching out and clutching the arm of the man standing next to her. Gwillem, her husband, reached up, took her hand in his and smiled weakly. His face, as youthful and innocent as hers, carried a light smattering of growth barely noticeable over his freckles. He was a lanky streak of piss and likely wouldn't last two seconds in a fight, but from what Cade had seen of him, he doted on Jessene. Very sweet. How the hell they had survived the war was beyond her.

'It's all right, love. This is a good thing. If they want to brand us, then they don't want to kill us,' he said, gathering Jessene to him.

'He's right,' said Cade. Gwillem was clearly the brains of the partnership. 'We've been upgraded from the walking dead to cattle.'

Jessene's ruddy cheeks finally lost their colour.

'Cattle? They want to eat us?'

Cade snorted. Now that tickled.

'Cade,' whispered Meghan. 'Stop it.'

'No love,' said Gwillem. 'They aren't going to eat us.'

'Thank goodness.'

'They'll be working us,' said Cade. 'That's what I'd do. Look, it's starting.'

Jessene and Gwillem continued to hold each other as they watched the activity before them.

Cade continued to wiggle her feet as she prepared herself for what was coming. A dwarf led a woman towards the nearest brazier and once they stopped, took station next to her, an axe at the ready. A second dwarf came up and took hold of her right arm. The dwarf by the brazier reached towards it and withdrew a long, thin bar. It was a brand. The woman ripped her arm away, screaming something incoherent. As she backed up the dwarf with the axe followed her and swept it round, hitting her in the waist. She slid sideways, falling on to her ass. The dwarf moved in close, and the woman threw her arms up as the axe chopped down into her neck. Those arms fell away as the dwarf worked his axe free, a fountain of blood following in its wake.

Cade felt a gentle sigh run through the crowd around her. It was the best they could do, everyone was far too used to this by now. Another woman was brought up and was made to stand next to the body of the first. The dwarf with the brand came toward her, spoke something that Cade couldn't make out. The woman responded by shrugging off the blanket she was wearing, removing the woollen tunic and the undershirt beneath. The woman stood with her bare breasts exposed, trembling with cold, or fear, but holding her ground. She took the brand on the inside of her arm, near the wrist, with little more than a whimper and a tightening of her shoulders. Cade saw a little steam rising from where the flesh met iron. The brand was removed and the dwarf stepped away with a nod. The woman gathered her clothes and was sent back. The next one in line, a man, had already removed his garments. He wasn't the only one, now all four lines were in motion. The branding took up speed as everyone realised what was expected. Cade watched with interest as the lines were managed. A number of dwarves were walking around the groups, speaking to the guards, directing them to the correct brazier. Each brazier held a number of brands, no doubt representing the mark of their various dwarf masters.

By the time Cade's group were brought forward, roughly half of those in the square had been branded. It was well into the day, the temperature dropping again. Amongst those already marked there were tears, groans and moans, a few folk crouched low with pain. One or two had fainted when the metal kissed their skin. They remained where they had fallen, their throats slashed wide open. No room for weakness, they should have known that by now. Cade stepped around a pool of blood that was already starting to freeze, and offered her arm up. She had taken off her cloak and tunic, and had rolled the sleeves up. No reason to take everything off, not like some of these idiots. Meghan walked by, clutching her clothes tight to her chest, her cheeks moist. She didn't look at Cade.

A dwarf took hold of Cade's arm, his grip tight, his arms slightly bent to react to any flinching movement. The branding dwarf came forward and placed the red hot metal on to the skin of her inner arm. He pressed it tight to her flesh. The other dwarf pushed as Cade's body reacted without thought, trying to pull away. The pain was sharp, searing, intense. She met the dwarf's eyes. *Come on you bastard. That the best you got?* She grinned. He stared back, eyes cold, uncaring, unimpressed.

She could smell her flesh and it was familiar, almost seductive. It reminded her that she hadn't eaten properly in days. It was strange, that thought coming to her in the midst of all that pain. It also reminded her of the bonfire. That dark memory was not enough to stop her feeling hungry. The dwarf removed the brand and turned his back on her, returning it to the fire and withdrawing an identical one for the next in line. Her arm was released and, without pause, she spun about and made her way back along the line. She tasted blood in her mouth and she spat out a large gobbet of saliva, tinged with red. She must have bit her tongue whilst she was smiling. She hadn't noticed. She spat again, more blood came out. A line of drool fell down her chin and she wiped her hand across it.

'You okay?' asked Meghan quietly, as Cade took station next to her.

That was just like Meghan. She'd just had a red hot poker thrust on her and she still had time to worry about others.

'Yeah. No problem.'

Cade looked at the brand on her arm. The flesh was a raw mess of cooked skin and meat, yet the mark was clear; a set of three columns with a horizontal stroke above them that curled upwards on either end, like some fancy temple you used to see in the better-off districts of the city. It was going to throb like a bastard. She looked at her feet, reached down and retrieved a handful of the more solid looking slush and held it tight to the skin. After a few moments, she felt the cold, mostly around the brand's edges, where the skin was not so deeply burned. The branding was still hot and the slush melted quickly, the water running through her fingers. It wasn't much but it took the edge off for a few moments. Could've been worse, she figured. The mark was clean and the burn deep. There was a good chance the wound wouldn't get infected. She knelt down again, scooped up some more slush. She noticed Meghan doing the same, gathering up a generous helping and pressing it against her arm.

'It hurts,' she said, with a weak smile.

'Keep it cool and keep it clean,' Cade advised. 'If you get some proper snow, use that, compact it up, like a ball, and press it down hard. It'll last a little longer. Ice is better.'

'There's some on that building behind us,' said Meghan.

'Great. Get me some.'

Cade looked up as another scream rent the air. She expected to see another corpse produced, but the screamer was still up and already moving back down the line. She shivered a little. They'd be at this for a while yet and she was tempted to hunker down. It was likely they'd be expected to stay here tonight. The temperature would continue to drop and the slush would freeze. She thought better of trying to sleep. The screams would probably keep her awake anyway.

CHAPTER 7

Father Michael stepped off the cutter and placed his feet on dry land. He took a moment to appreciate the feeling, but it still felt like the bare rock beneath him was swaying. As dry land went, it wasn't much to look at. The Barren Atoll was well named, a series of small, stony islands in the middle of a deserted sea. *There is no life here, no trees, no animals, just ... rock.* He wasn't completely correct, there was life here. First there were the birds. Gulls and auks and other species were clustered among the boulders and blue-grey shingle beaches. Their droppings covered much of the rock, giving it a dirty, off-white sheen. These birds reacted little if at all to his presence. He suspected half of them were from the fleet anyway, trailing along in its wake, stealing what scraps they could.

The second form of life was human. The Empress had decided that Prince Tigh might recover better if given some fresh air rather than being cooped up in his cabin. So the Court, such as it was, had decamped to this dismal place. Up ahead he saw the grand pavilion, the large structure that served as home to travelling royalty. It took up half the damned island. Flags and streamers were flapping vigorously in a strong wind. The pavilion was taking a beating on all sides from the both the weather and the sea and the salt water would rot it quickly. Several servants were moving around the structure, their constant duty to manage the pegs and securing poles, keep the pavilion clean of droppings, and the fabric taut. It was a losing battle.

No one else was allowed to come to the island or set up encampments, but some of the other lords had claimed the smaller islands as their new fiefdoms. It was a crazy notion as most were barely wider than a house. It was yet another example of their arrogance and stupidity. Father

Michael walked the short distance, no more than fifty yards, to the pavilion entrance. He passed soldiers, sailors and functionaries all purposefully going about their business, doing the Emperor knew what.

At the entrance to the pavilion he passed two Gifted, both Shapers, and entered into a reception area. Heavy dividing curtains separated off other sections of the pavilion. The curtain ahead had another guard before it. That one led to the Empress's rooms. The floor of the pavilion was carpeted with a fine Erebeshi weave, and to one side a small desk had been set up. Behind it stood a thin and officious-looking man wearing spectacles, doubtless a clerk. He bowed, but not too low, to Father Michael.

'I am here to visit the Prince,' he said.

The man deigned to offer him a thin-lipped smile.

'I shall inform His Grace and will return to you with his answer presently.' The man disappeared through a curtain to his right. Father Michael placed his hands within his sleeves and waited. Two chairs were placed further along the carpet, on the left side of the reception. On one of them sat Cardinal Yarn and he bowed in recognition, far lower than the official had done to him.

'Please, Father Michael, don't stand on ceremony. Join me,' said Cardinal Yarn, a broad smile on her face.

'Thank you.' He took the second seat, lowering himself gently on to a thick cushion. It yielded to his weight, sucking him into its embrace. He wriggled into it, adjusting his robes.

'Are you not used to sitting down?' she asked, amiably.

Father Michael looked over at the Cardinal, her eyes had the usual amused sparkle, and he felt his face redden a little.

'I'm not used to comfort.'

'No bad thing. I grew up knowing the harshness of the steppes and the joy of fur-lined sleeping mats.'

Father Michael could respect that. The Plains people had always been hardy and tough. He had always enjoyed fighting them.

'So Father, what brings you ashore?' she asked.

'I heard the Prince has recovered and is back on his feet. My place is at his side.'

Cardinal Yarn inclined her head.

'We are truly blessed by his recovery and he will be fortunate to have you. Although, it does strike me as a little odd that the Arch Cardinal felt the need to appoint you to the position.' She let the comment hang. Father Michael was not going to rise to that. He had heard it spoken enough times already to know better.

She smiled anew when he didn't respond. Father Michael saw plainly the knowing gleam in her eye. She continued 'It's just that the Empress and the Prince are already protected by my brothers and sisters from the Schools. They are more than able to detect and deal with any harm. You are a man of skills, I do not deny it. But surely the Prince needs guidance of earthly and spiritual matters, not martial ones.'

'I am happy to serve the future Emperor and the Church as the Arch Cardinal sees fit,' he replied. Was she playing a game with him?

Cardinal Yarn's smile was now tight-lipped. 'Of course.' She sighed loudly and sat back in her chair. 'Speaking of the Schools, I am here to report to the Empress on my assessment of our Gifted. It is a sad state of affairs. Of the four Schools, we have precious few brethren left. The war took so many. Did you know I was at the Monastery at Nostrum, our home and place of study, where all the Schools trained? When the war began to the east, we were aware but unafraid. We thought ourselves safe, that the enemy would never, ever reach us. Then the ogres came. They must have been marching for days to get to us. It was a terrible night. Our Watchers were looking to the east, not the north. They fell upon us, put the Monastery to the torch and slaughtered any that stood before them. We killed many of them, of that you can be sure, but we lacked coordination. I took charge of the younger ones and got them out, whilst the elders, the best of us, held off the brutes and the flames that surrounded us. They gave their lives willingly and gladly, but at such a great cost.'

Father Michael sat and listened, his face a mask of calm. There had been many who had sought him out, eager to share their tale of horror.

He had little and less to offer them, no words of comfort; he wasn't that type of priest. But he found that they didn't need to have him speak, they just needed him to listen. That was fine, they could unburden themselves if they wished, shed the guilt and their grief, he didn't care, it meant nothing to him.

'There are no more than a hundred Shapers, Speakers, Readers and Watchers remaining. Many of those are still young, still growing and learning the extent of their powers. You cannot truly call us four Schools now.' She sighed again. 'Not even a year ago one School alone could call upon hundreds of members.' Unexpectedly, she leaned towards him, placed a hand on his arm and squeezed. He shifted uncomfortably. 'I will be blunt. A man like you will appreciate that. When we realised the war was lost we should have marshalled the Schools and saved as many as we could. Their loss was nearly as great as the demise of our Emperor.'

Father Michael had been wondering what would happen with the Gifted. Those blessed with the Emperor's grace still had a role to fulfil, a duty to perform.

'What do you recommend for the future of the Schools, Your Eminence?' he asked.

'There are but a few senior clerics – those with greater Gifts – left. We must gather their knowledge and wisdom and ensure it is passed to the younger generation. We must ensure the remaining Gifted are given every opportunity to grow to their full potential. That is no easy task, I can assure you. The Schools are bereft of leadership and experience and no School can function on its own now. I am proposing that we merge them, return to a single School, like it was years ago, at the first founding.'

'And who will lead this new School?'

Another clerk emerged from the central curtain and bowed.

'Cardinal, the Empress is ready to receive you.'

Cardinal Yarn stood but continued to regard Father Michael.

'It is not my place to decide that. It is for the Empress and the Arch Cardinal to apportion that honour.' She adjusted her robe, nodded at Father Michael and followed the clerk into the rear chamber. Father

Michael had never been a shrewd man. His intelligence was based more on cunning, on understanding the calculation of behaviour and action. Yet he sensed that the Blessed Emperor had a plan in mind for Cardinal Yarn. She was strong-minded and sharp. Sometimes he had trouble understanding all the words she used, even though he had studied hard in the last two years to improve his own vocabulary.

'Father?' said the man with spectacles, emerging from behind another curtain.

'Yes?'

'The Prince will see you now. He is within.'

'Thank you.'

Father Michael stood and walked past the man, who held the curtain open for him. Inside he found another area, of similar size to the first. There was a desk, two chairs and a human shaped bust that carried a set of ornate, ceremonial armour. Another rug was laid upon the ground, this one circular, a bright orange sun, with sharp rays of light emerging like spikes from every angle. A second curtain opposite him was guarded by a Gifted. This one wasn't a Shaper, she was a Reader, and her left cheek was adorned with a flowering tree. That was, on the face of it, a strange thing. Readers were forbidden to use their power in the presence of the Emperor or his family. They could all read emotions but only the most blessed of Readers were able to sense thoughts. It would not do for anyone to pry into the private thoughts of the Living God.

'The Prince?' he asked.

'Through here, Father. His bedchamber.' The Gifted stepped back and pulled the curtain open. Father Michael felt a breeze on his face and saw daylight filtering through into the study. He walked through and heard the swish of the curtain closing behind him. This new chamber was bright and well aired. No wonder as one of the main pavilion panels had been undone and pulled back, opening a view to the world outside. A large bed was to his left, the covers thrown back. Standing just outside the pavilion, looking out upon the sea, was Prince Tigh. He was wrapped in a thickly furred robe, a bearskin by the looks of it.

Young Uther appeared, carrying an empty tray. He nodded at Father Michael and hurried out.

'Your Grace,' said Father Michael.

The Prince turned his head slightly, but did not look in.

'Come and join me, Father,' he commanded. His tone was friendly.

Father Michael approached the Prince and drew level with him. They stood upon bare rock, the sea only yards away. He looked at the Prince, a young man barely out of his childhood years. His face was pale, his hair a light auburn colour, gently curling to his shoulders. His beard was thin and straggly, not particularly full or noble-looking. He had yet to fill out properly, his frame still thinly muscled and wasted from his injuries. He would need time to recover and grow but Father Michael knew the Prince did not lack for courage. He had heard how the Prince had ridden into battle and slain an ogre before he had been thrown from his horse and wounded by a magical detonation.

'I can't remember the last time I saw the sea,' said the Prince. 'I like the smell of it. All I can remember of my last days at home is the smell of dirt and sweat and metal.' He spoke as an adult yet his tone was still high and youthful.

'I know those scents well, Your Grace. And all the smells of death that go with them.'

Prince Tigh grimaced. 'I remember those as well.' He looked over at Father Michael who saw his eyes were the same colour as his hair, though perhaps a little darker. 'Perhaps I am fortunate to have missed Aberpool's final hours. I understand it was a terrible sight.'

'You have been told?' asked Father Michael.

The Prince nodded. 'Yes, I have been told. I don't have much luck with staying conscious through engagements do I?' The Prince smiled ruefully.

'It took many days but they were able to get you to Aberpool just in time.'

The Prince had ridden with his father in the last great battle of the war, where the Blessed Emperor had fallen and the best part of his remaining armies with him. After that, there was no more hope of victory, just a desperate rear guard and a final sacrifice for a chance to save the Prince.

'What happened to those scouts?' Prince Tigh asked.

'I sent them to help defend the city. They died in your service.'

'That is perhaps not the best reward for their part in saving my life.'

Father Michael shook his head. 'They did nothing more than was expected of them, Your Grace. As do we all. You are the heir to the Empire, it is an honour and a privilege to serve you and give our lives if necessary.'

The Prince was quiet a moment then gave Father Michael a wry smile. 'And you, Father, are my new counsellor?'

Father Michael thought about that. The Arch Cardinal had described his role as such, but he had little counsel to give the future Blessed Emperor.

'I am to look after you, to ensure your person is protected and your needs catered for.'

The Prince laughed.

'I have many people who claim to do that for me already. I have Gifted standing outside my door night and day, servants, counsellors and a mother who has become even more protective of me.'

'You will also be our Living God, Your Grace. It is right and proper that the Church is at hand to assist you in governing your people, so that they may do your will better.'

The Prince shivered a little.

'Do I need spiritual guidance then? Will you give that to me?'

'I will give you everything I can,' replied Father Michael. It was the truth. He would give his life for the Emperor, because that was all he had to give.

Prince Tigh made a face. He did not appear satisfied with that answer.

'My mother has said that I must have a coronation as soon as possible.'

'The line of Tissan Emperors has been unbroken since the founding of the Empire two hundred years ago. Your people need you.'

'I understand what I must do, Father,' replied the Prince, harshly. 'Yet it would seem that I have precious few people left.'

'There has been a census undertaken, you have almost twenty thousand loyal citizens of the Empire left. That is more than enough.'

'Enough for what?' replied the Prince, his face hard, his jaws clenching. 'Where will I take my people? There is naught else here but this damned rock.'

'The Admiral says we sail west. There will be salvation, Your Grace. You will see to that.'

'I will,' said the Prince quietly. His eyes grew distant, his body still. Father Michael shifted, feeling a little self-conscious. The Prince shook his head. 'Thank you, Father. I am feeling tired, now, I wish to sleep.'

Father Michael bowed and withdrew. He retraced his steps through the pavilion. It worried him a little that he could not offer more guidance to Prince Tigh. *I must do more, damn it, I must think how I can serve him.* He passed through the reception area. The bespectacled man was back at his post once more, but there was no sign of Cardinal Yarn.

As he left, the man called after him.

'Father, I have heard the coronation is to be tomorrow. Emperor be praised.'

That was welcome news. He stopped and nodded his head.

'Then I must go and pray to the Blessed Emperor. Our salvation is truly at hand.' As he returned to the boat, Father Michael felt like a great weight had been lifted. With the coronation they would have a new ruler, and his value and contribution was clear to him. He had truly served the Empire and had played a part in saving the Prince, and now that young man would become Emperor. Their Living God.

The coronation took place at midday. The skies were grey and a wet wind blew in from the east. The throne from *The Fist of Tissan* had been transported across the water, and now sat in front of the pavilion upon a raised wooden platform that had been covered with a rich red carpet. Upon the throne sat Prince Tigh, his bearskin replaced by shining armour. He stared out to sea, his eyes fixed upon an unknown horizon. Father Michael was moved by the dignity that the Prince was displaying.

To the throne's left were gathered the surviving Church clergy, the Cardinals, Fathers and Novices. Together they sang a hymn praising the new Emperor. Father Michael had never been one for singing so instead he mumbled along whilst observing proceedings. He felt a little embarrassed that he could not so loudly proclaim his faith but it was in his heart, where it mattered.

To the throne's right were gathered the lords of the Council, other men of wealth and standing, commanders and captains. Seated in their centre and slightly forward of them all was the Empress herself. She would retain that title until the new Emperor found a wife. She looked resplendent in a shimmering silver gown, a white fox fur cloak around her shoulders. Behind the throne, Arch Cardinal Vella conducted proceedings. He held before him a simple golden crown, a circlet with a large ruby at its centre. And behind the Arch Cardinal were all the remaining Gifted, dressed for war. They all wore half helms, their eyes hidden behind their masks, in an impressive and intimidating martial display. Emperor forbid anyone tried to come close to the throne unbidden. Standing a little ahead of them was Cardinal Yarn, wearing their armour, but her head was bare. As he'd suspected she had indeed been given control of all the Schools and her first action was to unify them. She was smiling, enjoying the moment.

Arrayed before the throne were three lines of soldiers, almost a hundred per line, all that was left of the Imperial armies. Most were household guards, carrying halberds, wearing chain and leather over blue cloaks bearing a blazing sun. In the rear rank were different uniforms, the black cloth of a crossbow battalion, the fluted helm of a cavalryman, the kilt of an axeman from a Scotia regiment. Behind them were gathered servants, functionaries, and many of the professional classes. They took up every inch of available space. Most of the fleet would not get to see this spectacle. They would have to wait for their priest or captain to return and tell them what they had witnessed.

Father Michael returned his attention to the ceremony where the Arch Cardinal was making his final pronouncements.

'You are our Emperor. Our Living God. Lead us to glory, Your Imperial Grace. Emperor Tigh, ruler and master of the Tissan Empire!' he shouted, with gusto.

The Arch Cardinal placed the crown upon his head. The gathering erupted with shouts of joy and cries of elation. Many of his brethren openly wept. Father Michael could feel his own tears welling up. A part of his soul had been lost and now it was restored, and his faith was renewed.

The Emperor stood and the crowd hushed. He looked upon them, his face stern.

'My people, we have suffered so much. We have faced a terrible trial. Yet here we stand. The enemy meant to wipe us clean from the face of the world. They failed. We must look to our future, we must look to endure and rebuild. We will find a new home in the west. And in time, we will return and reclaim our Empire!'

The gathered hundreds erupted in cheering once more. The Empress smiled, the Clergy raised their hands to the heavens, the Gifted stood silent and the lords cheered the most enthusiastically of all. Father Michael guessed it was for the Emperor's final words, that the old Empire would be reclaimed. They no doubt thought it meant their places and privileges were assured. They would be wrong. Overhead an honour flight of eagles sped past, diving low and screeching loudly. They continued past the island and out amongst the fleet. The Blessed Emperor said they were heading west. No man had ever ventured further than the Barren Atoll, at least none had returned to speak of it. It was said that there was no land and that the seas continued on to infinity. If that were so then they were doomed to sail forever and the Emperor was wrong. And that is why Father Michael knew they would be saved. The Emperor was never wrong and they would find land. Those who were worthy and loyal and believed in the Empire would have a new life. He looked toward the Arch Cardinal and found him looking right back, a smile playing on his lips. *Yes, the worthy would live and prosper in this new land, but the unworthy would never be allowed to.* Father Michael turned his gaze back to the lords. It felt good to be worthy.

CHAPTER 8

In the grey covered skies of the Highlands, Arno circled above the old fort as the winter winds buffeted the eagle and his rider. Even from Owen's vantage, it was easy to mistake what he was seeing for a jumble of old stones and boulders. The snow added to the illusion as large drifts piled up against what were once walls and buildings. To either side, steep rocky slopes fell away leaving the fort virtually isolated, except for a thin trail leading up from a series of lower hills to the south and following a narrow, treacherous ridgeline. The fort had a further spur, running a hundred yards to the north that ended in sheer cliffs crowned by a circle of flat ground. They were flying in daylight; it was a risk, but Owen did not want to return like some thief in the night. It should be safe as they were almost in the middle of the Highlands and there would be no one watching the skies, not in this weather. He pulsed to Arno and the bird dropped down, heading towards a patch of white in the centre of the fort. Owen expected, hoped, it would be clear. Arno settled on to the ground with ease.

He leaned forward and clapped Arno's neck. 'Nicely done, Arno. We're home.' He sat back and gazed around. By the Gods of Old but the place had taken a beating. The dwarves had been through here and wiped it clean. He might not recognise it now but his memories of what used to stand here were still sound. Off to the left was the pump house, next to it the long, high-roofed roosting barn. Ahead was the great hall, where everyone would gather on winter days such as this to eat, laugh and live. He sighed and pulled down the flying scarf that covered the lower part of his face. His breath misted in front of him. Nigh on a hundred and fifty people had lived in this fort known as Eagle's Rest. They were folk he had known all his life, friends and family, and this was his home.

He pulled his feet away from the stirrups and slid off the saddle, his boots making a soft crunching sound as he sank into several inches of snow. He reached back and clumsily withdrew his crossbow from its pouch. He wore his supple leather flying gloves with extra cloth wrapped around the fingers. It was a good thing there was no trigger guard on the weapon as there was no way he could have put a finger through it. Cradling it in his arms, he crunched his way through the fort. He located a gap in the drifts where a small doorway had once stood. He passed through it to the northern spur. The wind was stronger here, and the going slow. Snow flurries went by left to right, and he kept his free hand to his face, trying to keep his vision clear. One false step and the snow would fall away and the last week would have been for nothing. It was fortunate that he knew the path so well, that he remembered where it kinked slightly to the right.

After five minutes of careful negotiation, the spur opened up on to a small plateau. It stood slightly lower than the fort and looked out upon the valleys on either side while taller and wilder mountains surrounded and towered over it. A cairn made of small, rough-edged stones stood in the centre of the plateau. It had been built by the people of the Eagle's Rest many, many years ago and had been added to ever since. Each stone represented a life lost, every man woman and child who had ever lived on this peak and within it. The riders had taken to leaving stones for their birds as well. It felt right; the eagles were as much family as any human was. He gently placed the crossbow on to the snow and fished around in his jacket pocket, withdrawing the small stone he had collected. He hunkered down and cleared snow from a section of the cairn, revealing the interlocking stones beneath. He placed his into the cairn, wedging it tightly into a gap.

He gazed at the stone for a while. He could feel the cold seeping into his body, the warmth generated by his struggle along the ridgeline starting to fade.

'There you go, Father. You can rest easy. You are with your family now.'

Owen had not been at the fort when the enemy had struck. He had already been away to the north, summoned to serve with the Emperor's armies even though he was barely old enough. His father had assured him that there was no way the Highlands would fall. The mountains were too inhospitable, impossible to navigate in force. They knew the ground and were too well dug in. It had taken years before the clans had agreed to join the Empire. They could wait out this new threat and the enemy would lose patience eventually.

His father had been wrong. The enemy wasn't prepared to wait. They had come down from the skies and they had burrowed up through the earth. The elves used their sorcery and the dwarves their mountaincraft to systematically reduce each fastness to nothing. No one had survived, only those few Eagle Riders who were able to escape and bring the news back to the squadrons fighting in the front lines.

Owen felt a degree of peace. He had achieved what he'd set out to do. After the weeks of cold and hunger, of hiding and flight, he had come home to say goodbye, to properly bury his father. He reached out and placed a hand on the stone. Emotion welled up inside him, his vision blurred as tears ran down his face, cooling fast in the frigid air.

'I'm sorry. I should have been here. I shouldn't have left.'

Even as he said it, he could hear his father's voice, telling him to 'show those wet, northern wastrels how true men fight, how Highlanders fight!' Owen smiled. They'd fought all right, and Owen hoped that somewhere his father had been watching him and had not been too disappointed with his efforts. Owen shivered as a blast of wind hit his face. Damn but he'd forgotten how grim it could be up here. He wondered whether the dwarves had destroyed the caverns below the Rest. It was where most of the families lived and there was always plenty of food and drink laid up down there. It was warmer too and out of this Emperor-forsaken wind.

He felt a jolt in his mind, a burst of emotion from Arno. It was a mixture of surprise and alarm.

Shit. What now?

Owen pushed himself up, gathered the crossbow and at a pace barely faster than walking, he returned to the fort proper. He used his footprints as markers, backtracking along the spur and through the slight opening in the wall. He was breathing heavily and he felt sweat forming on his brow. Why hadn't Arno taken off? If the eagle had been attacked, he knew better than to stay defenceless on the ground. Owen ran along the side of the great hall, the square coming into view. He saw Arno, standing up, facing away from him, but still on the ground.

Owen jogged over to Arno, gripping his crossbow tightly and raising it to his chest, ready to sight and shoot. He looked around but there was nobody there.

'Arno, what are you playing at?' he said quietly.

The eagle was facing the roost, his head thrusting forward, twitching side to side.

Owen squinted at the structure. It was barely standing, half the roof was gone and most of the walls on the left side of the building had collapsed in on themselves. Arno must've just caught wind of a familiar smell, a faint remembrance of his time there amongst others of his kind. Eagles had a good memory for the places they had nested.

Owen saw movement. He was sure of it. Where the wall of the roost still stood, there were many holes and gaps where stones and mortar had fallen away. He could swear that one of them had turned from dark to light, that something had been blocking it on the far side. Owen wasn't going to be caught out twice. He'd rather be a fool with nobody but Arno to see than have someone blindside him like Gerat had. He raised his crossbow to his eyeline.

'Come out. I won't tell you twice,' he shouted. Beside him Arno ruffled his tail feathers and scratched the ground.

Nothing responded.

'If you can understand me then I'll make it clear for you. Arno here is none too pleased about being startled. He's liable to come over there, pick you up in those mighty sharp talons of his and drop you down the side of the cliff,' he said.

No sound but the wind. Owen shook his head and lowered his bow. He'd been alone too long.

'He wouldn't do that, you know,' replied a voice.

Owen raised his bow, it sounded like it came from the roost, but it was hard to tell in all the wind. He turned and did a quick scan amongst the other wrecked buildings and piles of rubble.

'You had it right first time. I'm here.'

He swung back to the barn. A figure emerged.

'Hands up!' he shouted.

The figure complied. It was short, swathed in a dark hooded cloak. The gloved hands that emerged from the sleeves were small.

'You going to shoot me or let the bird eat me?' asked the figure.

'I haven't decided yet,' Owen replied. The voice was a young girl's. Her timbre was that of the Highlands.

'Could you make your mind up? I'm getting cold out here,' said the girl.

'You and me both.' Owen put up his crossbow and relaxed, a little. 'What are you doing here?'

'I live here,' she replied.

'What? Here?' Owen said.

'Yes, here. Can I put my hands down?' she asked.

Owen looked at Arno then back at her.

'Go on. Just be mindful. My eagle is very protective.'

The girl lowered her hands and pulled her hood back. She had light skin, which was smudged with dirt in places. Her raven-black hair was ragged, falling about her shoulders. 'I don't live *here*,' she said. 'We live down below.'

Owen was right about the caverns then. Perhaps some of his folk had survived, though he didn't remember this girl.

'You going to show me?' he asked, knowing full well where the entrances were.

'Yes. As long as you aren't going to shoot me.'

Owen shook his head. 'I can't promise that.'

She squished up her face in thought then she shrugged.

'OK. Over here.' She beckoned him forward.

Owen stepped up to Arno, placed a hand on his beak and looked him in the eye, pulsing calm thoughts.

Go hunt, Arno, return later. Arno tilted his head, opened his wings and took off.

Owen watched him go with fondness and concern. *Arno will be fine. This is his home, his territory as much as mine.*

He entered the roosting barn and found the girl was waiting for him.

'Nice eagle,' she said.

'The best,' agreed Owen.

The girl stood by a pile of shaped stones in the far corner. The walls there were still reasonably intact and the roof gave them some cover from the snow. She reached down and started to clear away some of the smaller stones and rubble. The outline of a sturdy wooden hatch emerged, as he knew it would. She reached down and pulled a round iron handle. With a grunt she hauled up the hatch to reveal a flight of stones steps.

At her signal he went forward and climbed down into what was the roost's storeroom. He waited for his eyes to adjust to the gloom. The chamber was much as he remembered it, except before the shelves had held saddle mounts, blankets, stirrups and satchels, and now they lay bare.

The girl followed him down and closed the hatch after her. The chamber went dark, only the slightest hint of light coming through the edges of the hatch. He heard a scratching sound. Sparks appeared and a small light blazed into life. The girl's face emerged in flickering, shadowed patches as she moved behind him, a candle in her hand, the light playing off the walls as she passed. Owen noticed how the candlelight bent away from the girl, as if caught in a slight breeze. *Impossible.* At the far end of the chamber she pulled a broken saddle mount away from the wall and then knocked. The sound was wooden, hollow.

'Wait a minute, that's not rock,' he said.

'Of course not,' said the girl.

He heard a noise, something scraping. Then the wall in front of the girl opened backwards and light streamed in. Owen blinked. The light was blocked briefly as she stepped through into whatever was beyond.

'Come on, you're letting all the heat out,' said another, male voice.

Owen hurried through into another chamber. This one was much larger, square shaped, its walls smooth, except for where alcoves had been chiselled out to hold lanterns and candles. In the centre of the chamber was a long table with several stools and chairs arranged around it. He knew this chamber very well. It was directly under the great hall and served as the hub for all the families who dwelt within the rock. The stair leading up to the hall was no more, in its place was a great pile of rocks and fallen timbers. The girl walked over and found a place at the table, joining three others, two men and a woman. The wooden door shut behind him and Owen turned to watch a thickset man lower a wooden brace into two crudely wrought brackets. The man wore furs over shoulders but his well-muscled arms were bare apart from iron and leather vambraces and copper bands on his wrists. He squinted at Owen with dark brown, almost black eyes. His closely cropped hair was black as well, and his black beard was long and braided.

'You sitting?' he asked, as he walked past Owen.

Owen followed the man to the table and took a seat next to the girl, facing the man who had spoken to him. Owen nodded to the others. The two men looked like twins, young but still older than Owen, they shared the same copper coloured hair, sharp looking noses and high foreheads. The only difference was that one was clean-shaven and the other sported a full beard. They didn't get many redheads in the central Highlands, could be these folk were from the south. The woman was older, perhaps into her fifth decade, but it was hard to tell, as her face was lined and careworn. She smiled at Owen. The others just scowled at him.

The black-haired man pulled across a jug and two mugs from their place in the centre of the table. He poured something into both mugs, liquid slopping over the side. He looked up at Owen but spoke to the girl. 'What have you found, Em?'

147

'He was riding an eagle, uncle. I was keeping a watch like you said. He acted like he knew the place.'

Owen raised his eyebrows. *And there was me thinking no one would be watching us in the daylight.*

'I know it,' Owen responded. 'This is my home. Eagle's Rest this place is called,' he said, leaning forward, 'but I don't recall you ever living here.'

The man leaned back and grunted, a wry expression on his face. He turned to the others.

'Think he'll like what we've done to the place?'

The clean-shaven twin spat.

'Do we care?' He spoke in the old tongue. That confirmed it.

'You are southerners, aren't you? You still keep to the old ways.' Like speaking in the Highland tongue when no Imperial is around to hear you, he added to himself, switching to that same language. He hadn't spoken it for more than a year but it came easily.

The twin continued to scowl, although the bearded one was grinning broadly, and the woman too. The older man looked ready to pounce on him and Owen squared his shoulders.

'Enough, Murtagh, show some manners,' said the older lady, gently but firmly, placing a hand on his arm.

Murtagh huffed, but after a moment slid one of the mugs across to Owen, picked up one of her own, and gestured towards the others.

'My name, you got. That's my sister, Naimh. The girl is Em, her mother is dead, but she's got us. The two lads are Erskine and Ernan. The hairy one is Ernan. You might've guessed already but they are twins.'

'My name is Owen. My father was the head man of this place,' Owen said simply.

'Really? Well, welcome home, Owen. Just don't be thinking you can charge us tithes,' replied Murtagh, drinking deeply from his mug.

Owen did the same. The smell had already told him what it was, ale, malty and rich. It tasted good. He drained his mug and slammed it down on the table at the same time as Murtagh, the bang echoed around the room. Perhaps it was because this was his place, and he felt more secure and he had nothing left to prove, but Owen knew what he had to do. He couldn't let this man ride over him.

'Tell you what,' said Owen, 'you give me your story and how you came to be here and I won't even make you pay for the ale.'

'Hah,' said Murtagh. He leaned forward and refilled Owen's mug, for the first time a friendly smile was playing on his lips. Murtagh sat back and poured himself another drink.

'Don't be shy,' said Ernan. Murtagh pushed the jug his way, then looked hard at Owen.

'You got the right of it when you said we were from the south. A town called Mallaig, but I doubt you've heard of it. It's in a valley, good pasture, and good streams to drink from. '

'I know Mallaig,' said Owen. 'I stopped by there once. Seemed like a fine place to live. Defensible as well.'

'We thought that too,' said Murtagh. 'Then we saw the size of army coming towards us. There was no way we could hold them back for long. So we used a different strategy instead.' Murtagh took a long drink then continued. 'We burnt Mallaig. Burnt it to the ground. Then we went deeper into the Highlands, used the country and stayed hidden.'

'Why didn't you try and get to one of the hill forts? It would have been safer there,' asked Owen.

Erskine grunted. It was a bitter, angry sound.

'There was nowhere safe. It was summer, with warm skies. They sent their flying beasties and spied out every village, town and fort,' said Naimh.

'And tore them down, one at a time,' continued Murtagh. 'We couldn't get near one if we wanted to. We were lucky. Most of us survived although some of us got caught. Our head man sacrificed himself, him and a few other brave souls, drawing the enemy away from us as we fled. We pushed on and found this place. By then it was empty. The enemy had already passed through.'

'Did they leave anyone alive?' asked Owen. He knew it was a foolish question but he had to ask it anyway.

'You know better than that. We found their bodies. They'd been thrown over the side.' Murtagh paused. 'I'm sorry.'

Owen nodded. There was a hollow feeling inside his stomach. He'd seen for himself the damage, had known the enemy would have shown no mercy. Yet there was always a hope that maybe somebody had survived. Now he knew for certain. He was probably the last of his community left alive.

'When we got here there was no point in trying to rebuild the place,' Murtagh continued. 'We found the entrance to the caves. We also found that they hadn't taken all the stores, so we decided to hunker down. First thing we did was work out where the dividing wall was between that storeroom and this room here and knocked through. Then we blocked the stairs leading down.'

'Nice job,' acknowledged Owen. 'And that wooden door to the storeroom is well hidden, I know this place and even I didn't notice it in the dark.'

'We didn't want to leave any sign of us. When they came back they found it exactly as it was left,' said Murtagh.

'They came back?' asked Owen.

Murtagh nodded.

'We saw them coming. A bunch of dwarves, must have been at least fifty of them. There were too many for us to fight so we locked ourselves in. They camped above us overnight, never got a sniff.' Murtagh and the others were smiling.

Owen shook his head. 'And you *thought* about fighting them? Sounds to me you had the right idea to stay low.'

Murtagh gave him a look.

'What do you expect? Those bastards have it coming.'

Owen let it lie. He saw the looks on all their faces.

'How many are you?' asked Owen.

'There are forty of us, most are down below. There's plenty of space,' said Naimh.

'Not many men, just us and four others. They're out hunting,' added Murtagh, 'and looking out for trouble.'

'I flew in from the northwest. I didn't see any troops ranging beyond the King's Highway. It looks like they have been pulling back,' said Owen.

Murtagh took another drink and scratched his chin through his beard. 'For now.'

Owen felt it was time to change the subject.

'Have you seen any eagles?' he asked. Eagle's Rest had sent all of its riders to join the war; only a few young eagles, less than a year old, had remained. There were plenty of eyries about, and the wild eagles had never been too precious about sharing the skies with their human-reared cousins. It was possible the younger ones had been set free.

There were shakes of heads around the table.

'I saw some,' said Em.

Everyone looked at her. She shrugged. 'In the distance. Around the higher peaks.'

'You are supposed to tell us when you see anything,' said Erskine, his tone was harsh.

Murtagh raised a calming hand.

'Easy now. Em, you know the rules.'

'I know, but they were eagles. Not buzzers or gryphons. I can tell the difference.'

Owen leaned towards her.

'Em, can you feel them?' he asked.

She shook her head. 'No, I haven't got it. I'm not a Speaker. I just like eagles.'

'We only ever had a few riders. They all went north,' said Naimh.

Owen nodded. He was a little disappointed.

The Highlanders had always produced large numbers of Speakers but almost none of the other types of Gifted. Virtually all the Speakers amongst them became Eagle Riders. When the Highlands had made peace with the Empire, their Gifted had been allowed to keep their faces unmarked in return for military service. It was important to the Riders, it meant they retained their freedom. It also meant they were not inducted and indoctrinated into the Church.

'I'll take a look when Arno comes back. They might even follow him, though it's unlikely, they would have learned there is no food for them here.'

Murtagh tapped his mug with his forefinger.

'That mean you're staying, then?'

Owen nodded.

'Why wouldn't I? This is where I belong.'

'We'd be glad to have you and that eagle of yours,' said Murtagh. 'It'll be good to have some eyes in the sky, and it'll help with hunting too. Question is, where we going to put him?'

Owen had already decided that one.

'We are right in the middle of the Highlands. It's winter. I'm willing to bet we won't be getting any visitors. I'm going to rebuild the roost, part of it at least. Enough to give Arno shelter from the wind.'

Murtagh shared a look with the others.

'I'll help,' said Em. 'It's better than having to stand there freezing to death.'

'I don't know …' said Murtagh.

'Arno will give you far better warning if anything is coming near,' said Owen. It annoyed him having to justify his decisions, when by rights it was his fort.

'He's right, Murtagh. We are well placed here, it's time we made things more comfortable if we want to stay,' said Naimh.

'I'll help you too,' said Ernan, standing up. 'I don't like living in the dark. Besides, it's your bloody fort.'

That was better.

Murtagh stood as well and proffered his hand. Owen pushed himself up and took it in his own. The grip was firm and Murtagh ended the shake with a sharp squeeze. He wanted Owen to know who was still in charge. That was fine by Owen. He had no intention of leading anyone but he wanted his say on the future if they planned on staying at Eagle's Rest. He also had no intention of starting another war. Why was it that everyone wanted to fight back? It was as if they had gotten a death wish when they had a chance to make a new life.

'We'll be eating soon,' said Murtagh. 'We'll call you down. Em, you are going back up, but I want you doing what you are supposed to be doing. Keeping watch.'

Em looked downhearted.

'Come on, Em,' said Owen, 'you can keep a lookout for Arno.'

The girl smiled and headed over to the door, Ernan following her. Owen nodded at the others. He felt their eyes on his back as he left the chamber.

The next day Owen got up early and set to work, though the day was as grim and cold as the one before. He wanted to get the roost as habitable as possible as quickly as he could. Arno was tough but he'd already been through enough.

He had spent much of the previous day working on the section of the roost near the trap door. It hadn't taken too much effort, especially with Ernan helping. They had been able to clear away the rubble, shore up the roof with a discarded beam and replace some of the fallen stones from the wall. Before it had been wrecked, the roost had been divided up into twelve separate stalls, each able to accommodate a fully grown eagle. In fact the barn was even bigger than the great hall thanks to the tall roof and wide exits that the birds needed to get in and out. Each stall had a set of barn doors, so that when the eagle was inside it could be protected from the harsh weather. It was a shame that the doors at that end had been ripped from their hinges.

Arno had returned a short while later and after Owen had him settled inside his stall, they had brought up some leather sheets and strung them up to block out the worst of the wind. Em had spent the time stroking Arno and speaking to him, after Owen had pulsed Arno to keep him calm. As he and Ernan tightened the sheets against the remaining beams, he'd smiled at the girl. She had no fear at all, which Arno picked up on, taking a mild interest in her fussing. Owen thought he was actually enjoying the attention. Her face was a picture of awe and happiness.

Owen and Ernan had spent the best part of the second morning moving two serviceable doors down from the wrecked end of the barn and putting them in place. The man proved strong and amiable. He'd even apologised to Owen about his brother. 'Don't worry about Erskine. He is a moody bugger but he means nothing by it. He's just frustrated. People like you got to go away and fight. He thinks we should have done the same.'

'Didn't do us much good in the end,' Owen had replied. 'They were all over us.'

'We must have hurt them, though, eh?' said Ernan, grunting with the effort to hold a door steady as Owen knocked a metal pin into the hinge.

'You can let go.' He'd stepped back and thought about the question whilst Ernan released his hold and blew into his hands

'Yeah, we hurt them some. They die just like the rest of us. The problem was there were so many. I only got involved towards the end but by the time the Empire realised what was happening, we'd already lost half of our armies. No one had ever thought we'd have to fight everyone at once.'

'Murtagh thinks we can still fight,' Ernan had said.

'I'd like to know what with. Look, I'm not saying you didn't have it bad but I was there at the end. They wiped everyone else out. We are all that's left.' It had been a white lie, but close enough to the truth that Owen didn't feel too bad about saying it.

'More reason to do something about it now, then,' Ernan had said simply.

'Then we just give them a reason to come back and finish the job properly.'.

Ernan had nodded but didn't reply.

Just after midday, Owen was satisfied that Arno now had a far cosier home, his stall enclosed on all sides and almost windproof. It was high time they got up and flying. He wanted to see if Em had been right, that she'd spotted eagles. She brought a lunch of ale and oatcakes and he quizzed her as to where she'd seen them. Armed with that information he took Arno north, towards another snow-covered peak. The day had brightened measurably, with glimpses of blue sky. It was wonderful to see, he'd grown so used to the dismal grey cloud cover. That had suited the situation and his mood but now he was home he felt more optimistic.

As they drew near the peak, he saw black spots moving against the sheer white mountainside. Those spots resolved into wings, gliding gracefully through the frigid, biting air. Eagles. He estimated their wingspans and of the three eagles he could see, none were larger than twelve feet. They were still young and it was possible they were wild but having three so close together was unusual. Wild eagles tended to be solitary for the most part, although not entirely unsociable. He let Arno get closer. He wanted to see their reaction to having a larger bird nearby. Arno drew level, keeping a respectful distance between him and the younger birds.

They watched warily but did not draw off. *That's a good start. Let's see if they understand me.* Owen reached out with his mind and pulsed images to the eagles. He pictured Eagle's Rest and the rookery barn before they were destroyed, trying to give them a sense of something familiar, a recollection of their time when they were hatched and reared by their surrogate human parents. As he pulsed, he watched their reaction. One of them screeched, and wheeling, it turned towards him. He smiled and continued with the images, creating a sense of warmth, of food and family. The eagle drew level with Arno, a little way off to the right. Arno turned his head and looked at the youngster. It was keeping station and looked comfortable. A minute later and the other two fell in behind; not too close, but they were following. He had a closer look at the one nearest them, clearly the bravest. It was hard to tell the sex of an eagle from a distance, but judging by the size of the beak, he'd say this one was a girl. The beak was larger in comparison than the rest of her body, always a giveaway.

Owen pulsed thoughts of joy to Arno. These birds were from Eagle's Rest, he was in no doubt. He felt elated, it was like finding family, and now Arno and he weren't the only survivors. He let Arno fly slowly, no need to rush this. He lay forward, trying to reduce his profile against the wind, enjoying the ride despite the freezing temperatures. He wanted the other eagles to feel comfortable in their presence even if it was too much to hope they would follow him home today.

After twenty minutes Owen felt it was time to go, besides which he was getting far too bloody cold. He set Arno on a course back to Eagle's Rest. The eagles followed them for a while before peeling off, heading back to whichever home they had made for themselves. Arno continued on, heading for the western side of the fort, turning wide and getting them on to a straight glide path, heading towards the barn.

As they drew near, Em waved at them from further down the barn. An icy wave of fear washed over him – were they under attack? No, he spied Ernan and his brother working on the building, lifting another door into place. He shook his head, his natural instincts were to fear the worst; it was their way of life now. He waved back as Arno landed easily on the ledge of rock before the open stalls. Owen slipped from the saddle, led Arno inside and then turned him around. Em stepped forward with a bucket.

'We got some spare meat, just the leftovers. Thought Arno might like it.'

Owen grinned. 'That he might. Here, you can leave it for him.'

Em stepped in front of Arno, a little gingerly for all her confidence of yesterday, and placed the bucket in front of him. Arno eyed her, then the bucket and dipped his beak inside, pulling out a hunk of flesh that he tilted back into his mouth. Em looked at Owen and grinned.

'Did you find them?' she asked.

'Yes. They're ours.'

Em's grin got broader.

'Where are they?' she asked, looking out at the sky.

'They won't come back straight away. It'll take a bit of time for them to get confident. They were forced away from their home. It would have been a terrible shock for them.'

'You think they would have fought back?' she asked.

Owen shook his head. 'No, my father wouldn't have let that happen.

If there were buzzers, or worse, gryphons, they wouldn't have lasted two minutes. My guess is they were forced out as soon as the enemy was sighted. It would have been the only way to save them.'

Em nodded solemnly. 'I hope they come home,' she said quietly.

Owen ran his hand through Arno's feathers.

'Me too ... wait.' He could've sworn he just saw a shadow in the sky. *What now?* He leaned forward his eyes squinting. Then he smiled. 'Hey, Ernan, you got those extra stalls ready?' he shouted.

Ernan looked over. Beside him Erskine wiped his brow and looked quizzical and slightly annoyed.

'Almost. Should be done by nightfall,' Ernan replied. 'Why?'

Owen pointed.

'Think we might be having guests sooner than we planned.'

Swooping low overhead an eagle passed them by. It was the female.

Em clapped her hands and made a delighted squeal.

Owen laughed. It looked like the family was getting bigger already.

Part Three

SPRING

CHAPTER 9

'Sabin, wake up, you're missing it!'

'Huh?' Fillion replied groggily.

'Wake up, sleepyhead, we're home,' said Alica, excitement in her voice.

He rubbed his eyes and his cheeks, then forced himself up off the wagon floor and turned his head to look around. He blinked a few times trying to focus. The spring sun was bright today and he had to squint. He turned himself about and crawled over to the side and looked out. They were on a road made up of marble slabs. No slab was the same size or shape, but they fitted against each other with the smallest of gaps between them. The going was smooth, the wagon barely shifted as it travelled along at a fair clip, the horses making a rhythmic clapping sound as their hooves struck the marble. They were passing through a wood or a forest, full of oak and beech. Sunlight speared through gaps in the canopy, playing upon fresh-grown leaves and fern bushes.

'Can't see anything,' he muttered.

'Look ahead,' said Hedra.

He leaned his head out further and tilted it to the side. *Oh. The Emperor be damned.* They emerged from the wood and into a wide area of green grass, grazing horses, cattle and sheep. No more than a few hundred yards ahead rose the city of Apamea. The capital of the Heartlands, a sea of dwellings sprawling across a range of hills. Sprawling was perhaps the wrong word; elves never built anything so vulgar as to sprawl. The structures were aligned in rows, following straight lines, flowing up the slopes. Set on the highest point he could see the roofs of very grand looking buildings, their size obvious even at this distance, likely palaces or temples. What struck him more than anything was the lack of walls. There were no defences of any kind, no towers, no emplacements, no ditches or moats. *The arrogance of them.* Granted the city was in the centre of their nation but still. *If I was in charge of defending this place I would have been hung drawn and quartered for leaving it like this. And I would have deserved it.* The road they travelled on was wide and busy with carts and wagons full of produce ahead and behind them. Coming the other way were official-looking riders carrying pennants on long shafts, small groups of cavalry, an occasional chariot, and plenty more carts and wagons carrying bolts of cloth or amphorae stacked perilously high. It had all the hallmarks of a busy, bustling, prosperous metropolis.

'What do you think?' asked Hedra. 'It's impressive, is it not?'

'Yes,' said Fillion, 'I have truly never seen the like.'

He pointed up the hill.

'What are they? Palaces?'

'Yes,' replied Alica. 'The one on the right, with the curved roof, that's the Parliament building, and on the left is the Temple.'

'To which God?'

Alica looked at him askance. 'All of them. It's a big temple.'

Fillion knew that the elves had a pantheon of Gods, worshipped as they saw fit depending on the requirement. It was little different to his Celtebarian upbringing, where his culture also had a number of deities that ruled the woods, the animals, the streams and rivers. His father had never given up on them and his mother had never given up on hers. The two respected each other's beliefs and found enough in common for it not to be an issue. For his part, he had never truly found solace in either, nor had he ever committed himself wholeheartedly to the Imperial Religion. It was enough to know which side he was on and why he fought for it.

Alica was still wittering.

'And you can't see it but there is a broad avenue between the two. It leads to the King's Palace. It's actually a long plateau up there, on top of the largest hill, so it's set right at the far end. Apparently it wasn't flat at first but a king from long ago ordered the slope removed. They say it's a legend. And if it's a legend for us, it must mean it happened ages ago.'

He nodded absently. His grip on the side of the wagon tightened, they had drawn nearer to the entrance to the city and finally he saw some guards. There were just two of them, both carrying spear and shield. *They weren't even armoured!* Long hair spilled over their shoulders on to white tunics and britches. They wore cloaks of light green, fastened with silver clasps. With each wagon that went past they exchanged pleasantries and just waved them through. Pitiful.

After leaving the last way station and finally entering the Heartlands proper, the column of elves had started to splinter. Groups peeled off to travel to other settlements and regions. Theirs was the only wagon to head on to Apamea. You'd never know they'd been in a war.

Then it was their turn.

'Where have you two come from?' asked one of the guards, a friendly look on his smooth-featured face. Had this one ever been in a fight? Probably not.

'Just got back from the war,' said Hedra proudly.

'Then welcome back. It's good to have you home,' replied the guard, waving them on.

They rolled past into the city. It took Fillion a few moments to take it in and to make sense of it all. After so long on the road he had forgotten what civilisation looked like. Apamea was a place of wide boulevards, leafy public spaces, clean streets and statues, and everyone he saw was moving with purpose. The buildings were well maintained, none more than three storeys in height. Built from wood, brick and glass, the workmanship was excellent, though it pained him to admit it. Each structure was a sequence of angular windows, curved walls and fluting roofs. It didn't change as they travelled deeper into Apamea. The buildings might have looked older, slightly weathered, but no different for all that. There was something disturbing about it that played on the edges of his mind. As the young elves sat in front of the wagon talking excitedly and pointing to familiar landmarks, it came to him. *The entire place is too damned … ordered.*

The elves claimed they lived in harmony with nature, but all he saw was a way of life that demanded conformity. Nothing was out of place. Nothing was allowed to be. Everyone looked happy and contented, to the point of inanity. Where was the shouting, the markets, the arguments and negotiation? It wasn't like this back in the Empire where the cities had grown naturally, with no plan or control. He'd loved how the streets were so haphazard, each house different, every one telling a story about those who built it and those who lived therein. Even the dwarves had a better sense of the value of individuality. The only elves with individuality were the wood elves. They were the opposite of their cousins, wild and passionate, little more than savages by comparison. He often wondered how the common elves suffered them; they cared nothing for the order the elves of the Heartlands craved.

They were climbing now, up the first of the procession of hills. The buildings to either side were kept level, shored up by a lower base of bricks. A group of children ran by, their faces smiling. He watched them charge off back down the hill. He had never seen a young one before, had never even seen a pregnant elf.

'Nadena!' cried Alica.

Walking down the hill was their sister smiling broadly.

'I thought I'd wander down and find you,' she called.

'We do know the way home, you know,' said Hedra.

'Of course you do, but I did promise father that I would look after you and see you home safe,' she replied. She smiled at Fillion as she continued past him to the rear of the wagon and leapt up. She sat opposite and rested her arms along the railing.

'What do you think, Sabin?' she asked. 'Apamea is something special, isn't it?'

He nodded, *oh yes, it's special*. 'I have never seen the like,' he repeated.

'The border towns are a little less developed,' she said, by way of an unnecessary explanation. 'The other cities are just as beautiful, in their way.'

'I can't wait to see them.'

'Well, there is no need to hurry,' she said, with a mock stern tone.

'How many live here?' he asked.

'There are over seventy thousand elves at the last count. That makes this the largest city by far,' she replied. 'Most other cities have no more than ten or twenty.'

He knew that. The elves liked to spread themselves out into smaller communities. Yet when they were called together, their host had proved to be significant.

'Is father at home?' asked Hedra.

'I sent word, he'll be back if he can,' said Nadena.

They levelled out as the wagon topped the first hill and drove through the middle of a large green square. A small group of elves was seated on the grass, arranged around another who stood with his eyes closed and his arms held wide. That elf wore robes a deep red in colour, signifying him a sorcerer. Those sitting around him were younger and were attired in sky blue, his apprentices. Fillion would have sorely liked to wade into them. The damage the sorcerers had wrought during the war had been horrendous.

Where the elves had sorcery, so the Empire had had magic of its own, in the Schools of the Gifted. Their intelligence gathering, communications and protection, had helped build and sustain the Empire, giving the Tissans a crucial tactical advantage. As the Empire spread outwards from the Riverlands, the Gifted had helped to defeat each of the human nations they faced. None of them, Celtebarian, Erebeshi, or Scotian, could counter the organisation and speed at which the Imperial armies could react. When the enemy had risen up against the Empire, these damned sorcerers with their elemental magic had changed all that. They could block Gifts as if it was the easiest thing in the world. They erected shields to blur the sight of Watchers, mute Speakers, and stymie Readers. Shapers fared no better, nothing they threw at the enemy could break through. Then the sorcerers unleashed devastating elemental forces; earth tremors, ice storms and fireballs. A sorcerer at the height of their powers was a truly terrifying thing to behold. No human had ever learned how to wield sorcery; the elves had always jealously guarded the skills of their craft.

They passed the group and the green and started to climb again, the buildings finally starting to differ. They were larger, grander, displaying more artifice in their design. The wagon turned left on to a slightly narrower lane and moved alongside a building of two levels, its shadow looming over them. The wagon turned again at a tall archway and they drove through the building into a sunlit courtyard. The ground was packed earth with trees dotted around the edges. Two wings flanked them, running from the front-facing portion of the building to the larger-looking rear structure. Each wing had a covered walkway, with another level above them.

Hedra pulled on the reins, halting the wagon. An elderly male elf emerged from an open doorway behind them, walking towards the front of the wagon and taking hold of the horse's bridle.

'Welcome home, youngsters,' the elf said.

'Thank you, Rabi, it's good to be back,' said Hedra.

Nadena stood and tapped Fillion on the knee.

'Come along, let's get some refreshment.'

He stood, jumped down and stretched. His leg complained a little but it had healed well and his muscles were starting to get their strength back. The rest of his companions were heading towards another lower archway with two open doors. He walked after them and entered a brightly lit interior. Another male elf, almost as old as the first, was waiting for the small party in a short hallway, wearing a light green robe with a purple sash around his waist. He stood with his hands behind his back, smiling at the arrivals. The two younger elves squealed with delight and ran towards him. He opened his arms wide, pulling them into an embrace.

'My children,' he said warmly.

Fillion stole a glance at Nadena, who wore a happy, indulgent look.

The older elf pushed Alica and Hedra away so he could inspect them.

'No, you don't look any different,' he said, shaking his head.

'We were away for less than a year, father,' laughed Hedra.

His father ruffled his hair then looked up at Fillion, his eyes narrowing slightly. He turned his attention to Nadena.

'And who is this fellow?' the elf asked.

'This is Sabin. He was wounded in the last battle. He asked if he could ride with us so he could visit the central Heartlands,' replied Nadena.

The elf stepped forward and offered his hand. Fillion took a closer look. This elf was even older than he had first thought. His hands had liver spots and there were flecks of grey in his long brown hair. His eyes were still bright and sharp however and he appraised Fillion, even as he welcomed him with genuine warmth. There might be nothing wrong with his mind but this elf was *very* old, and that was saying something.

'If you have never been to the city, I assume you must be from the borders.'

Fillion took the hand and lowered his head respectfully.

'That is true, Sir.'

'I'm Patiir, the father to this little brood.'

'Sabin, Sir. I understand you are a Representative as well?' said Fillion.

Patiir nodded.

'Yes, indeed. I hurried back from the Parliament as soon as I heard my family had returned.'

'I am honoured and fortunate to have had your children to tend my injuries.'

Patiir smiled. 'I am lucky to have them, even luckier that they have returned to me. We lost so many,' he said sadly.

'We have. I cannot count those who I have lost, but I remember them,' Fillion said.

'We remember them all,' said Patiir solemnly. 'Now, what are your plans?'

'I thought I might spend some time travelling. I am in no hurry to return home.'

'Then you must stay with us,' said Patiir.

Fillion feigned surprise and reluctance, even as inside he was smiling.

'Sir, I could not impose.'

Patiir reached out and clapped him on the shoulder.

'Of course you can. It is the least we can do. You fought for us all.

Nadena? You and your brother and sister don't mind if we have a house guest for a while?'

Alica smiled and Hedra laughed.

'Does that mean our sister will stop watching our every move?'

'No, it doesn't,' Nadena replied.

'Children, I am sorry but I must return to the Parliament. We are in session, and it was lucky that the King was not in attendance, otherwise I might not have been able to get away, even for a brief moment.'

'Father, since when has the King ever declined you anything? You are his oldest advisor,' said Nadena.

Patiir chuckled. 'In one sense you are right, my dear. Please do forgive me. Rest up, get clean. I will see you all tonight. You too, Sabin, our home is yours for as long as you wish it.'

Patiir strode out into the courtyard and through the archway. His children gathered to watch him leave.

'Father hasn't changed. He does too much,' said Alica.

'He does what he has to do,' said Nadena, firmly. She turned and looked back at Fillion. 'You seem to have charmed my father. It looks like you are staying with us.'

'And you had nothing to do with it?' he replied.

She flushed a little. *That is interesting.*

'I might have mentioned you had nowhere to stay,' she replied nonchalantly.

Fillion smiled and bowed once more.

'Then I owe you another debt. I am starting to lose count.'

She waved her hands in the air dismissively. 'You owe us nothing. Come along, I'll show you to your room.'

He followed her up a flight of stairs to the second level and along a passageway. The walls were bright white, clean and unmarked, except for a continuous line of twisting vines painted along the top and bottom edges, hues of green blended together. The artistry was very fine, the detail incredible, the shading subtle yet effective. She stopped at a door to her left and opened it.

'Your room.'

He stopped before the door.

'I cannot thank you enough for this,' he said, looking her in the eye.

'Well you can do me the favour of getting out of those clothes and into a hot bath. My father was too polite to say it, but I can only imagine how badly we smell after months on the road.' She pointed back down the corridor. 'Our bath house is on the other side, in the east wing. We'll no doubt see you there shortly.' She smiled once more and turned away, heading further along the corridor.

Fillion watched her disappear and entered his room. It was a good size. The walls were the same white plaster, with wooden beams painted gold and silver. In front of him was a wardrobe made of ash. To the right was a bed, big enough for two, with four posters and a white sheet suspended above it. He shook his head. What were they, nobility? It was certainly grander than anywhere he had ever laid his head before. Directly ahead was a window. The frame was horizontal at the bottom and straight on the sides, though at the top the frame had a high curve, the glass shaped to match it. He saw hinges and a handle and he moved to open it. The window opened outwards and he leaned out to get his bearings.

He looked down into the courtyard. The elf servant, Rabi, was busy unhitching the horse and leading it into a stable at the front of the house. Fillion's room was right in the corner of the yard, the western wing stretching out and away, just a little to his right. He stepped back, pulled off his shirt, and sat on the bed, the mattress nicely firm. He honestly couldn't remember the last time he had slept on a real bed. It must have been before the war.

Things had gone very well today. When Nadena had told him that her father was a Member of the Parliament and her family had a place near the centre of power, he knew this was a sign and that his cause was just. He could never have dreamed of such an opportunity. Here was a chance to get close. This Patiir was an advisor, was he? And what this aging elf needed was a helping hand. Someone he could trust and lean on. Fillion's mission was becoming clearer by the moment.

First things first. He lifted his arm and had a sniff under the pit. His nose wrinkled. It was time to get clean. He quickly undressed, leaving his clothes and boots in a pile at the end of the bed. He opened the wardrobe and found a white linen robe. He put it on, wrapped it around his body and tied it in place. Elves were scrupulous about cleanliness. They had a bathing ritual that bordered on obsessive. They also didn't discriminate between sexes and there was no understanding of modesty. It was going to be another ordeal for him. He would have to undress and slide naked into a bath with them, sharing their water, letting their foul stench cover him. Just thinking about it made him feel sick. *I've done worse, lived in worse. I can do this. I am far too close to my goal.* He stood and left the room.

He walked barefoot down the corridor. At the stairs he had to think. Which level would the bathroom be on?

'Hey, Sabin.'

He looked down at Hedra who stood in the corridor by the stairs.

'What are you doing up there? Come on, the baths are down here.'

He smiled. Of course.

He took the stairs quickly and followed Hedra to the east wing into a large marbled chamber. It was gloomy and warm. There was steam in the air and it smelt of some kind of herb with mint; it stung his nostrils.

Hedra removed his robe and hung it on a peg, then stepped down into a pool of water, sinking into it with a sigh. Fillion followed suit. The water was hot, almost scalding. He closed his eyes and let the heat wash over him. He felt cleaner already, and then he remembered who he was sharing a bath with.

'It really is good to be home. I have been dreaming about this for months, almost as long as we were away from it,' said Hedra.

'I can see why,' replied Fillion.

'We are lucky to have this. Most folk use the municipal baths. They are very good,' added Hedra quickly, 'but it is nice to have our own.'

The two of them floated in the water in companionable silence for a minute or two, then Fillion decided to broach a subject.

'Hedra, your mother. You never mentioned her on the trip home and your father was alone when he met us. Can I ask, has she passed on?'

Hedra was silent, his face obscured in the steam.

'Yes,' he said, finally. 'She died in childbirth. She died giving birth to me.'

'I am sorry, Hedra. I shouldn't have asked,' said Fillion. 'Forgive me.'

'No, it's all right. My mother was too old. She and Father had children late in their lives. He'd always been so busy with politics but mother insisted. And then she wanted a sibling for Nadena and Alica.'

'And your father raised you by himself,' stated Fillion.

'Yes. And Nadena of course. We can't go anywhere without her watching.'

'I am surprised he let you all go. To the wars, I mean.'

'We all had to do our part, and father couldn't very well not do what the Parliament was asking everyone else to do. Alica and I were too young to fight so we volunteered to do the next best thing. I think Father was, is, very proud of us. We helped save the Elven nation. And so did you, Sabin.'

Save it? Young idiot. I will yet see it torn to the ground and erased from existence. If we had done it sooner, perhaps the Empire would still be standing.

'I just played my part too, Hedra. And I'm sure your mother would be proud of you.'

He saw Hedra nod. The boy grew silent again.

The door opened behind them and he heard female voices, Alica and Nadena. The pair of them stepped into the room. They were chattering some nonsense as they disrobed and entered the pool. He caught a glimpse of Nadena. Her body was lithe and smooth, her breasts small, a little out of proportion with the rest of her delicate frame. He turned away. He didn't need to see that.

'Ah, that's good,' said Nadena. 'You found it then?'

'What, oh yes,' replied Fillion. 'Hedra showed me the way.'

'We'll be eating soon and after that, I think, bed. I could sleep for a week.' She sighed, splashing water into her hair and smoothing it flat against her head.

'I prayed to all the Gods for that,' laughed Alica.

'Would you like me to show you around tomorrow?' asked Nadena.

'I would like that but could you do it next week? I'll be sleeping,' Fillion said.

Alica snorted.

'Whenever you wish, Sabin. I'll be here,' said Nadena.

'Come on Sabin, let's wash this off.' Hedra stood and exited the pool. 'If the cold water doesn't wake you up, nothing will.'

'Right behind you,' said Fillion.

Now the game begins.

CHAPTER 10

Cade rubbed her earlobe and shifted her position as she sat with her back to the cavern wall. She glanced around at their new home, buried in the depths of a nameless mountain, in a range she had never heard of or imagined she'd ever see. The cavern was immense, like some vast, underground arena. Surrounding it was a series of tiers, working their way around and up to the ceiling. That ceiling looked solid enough, with a few small stalactites growing down. Water dripped from those fangs and fell the hundred yards to the cavern floor. On that floor was a jumble of crudely built dwellings, ramshackle huts and lean-tos fashioned from mismatching pieces of timber, sheets and blankets, all salvaged from an abandoned mining settlement. Along the tiers there were plenty of cave mouths, tunnel openings and wider areas where the rock had been excavated back. Every one of these had been claimed as accommodation.

The settlement extended to fill every available space except for two areas. The first was a large rectangular shape, cleared of rocks and detritus, set out before an iron gate, beyond which a tunnel led down and deeper into the mountain. The second was on the opposite side of the cavern, smaller, as was the gate that blocked the path leading upwards and outwards towards the daylight.

Cade sat just a short distance from the larger open rectangle. In front of her was a crumbling shack, and she could hear a whispered conversation coming from within. The building gave her little cover from view, if any of the dwarves were interested in her business, but she could make out the gate easily enough. She counted four guards, all armed with crossbows, arrayed behind the iron bars. Light blazed in semi-circular bowls set atop stanchions to either side of the gate, illuminating the open area. Behind them darkness crowded around the circle of light.

The Downside Gate (as it had been named) would open twice daily: once to admit workers into the mines, and then again to allow them back to their beds. Those guards seldom opened the Topside Gate (as it had been named) except to allow the daily food deliveries or the occasional contraband sweep. What they expected to find was beyond Cade. She suspected it was just to keep the inmates in line and in fear. Every morning and every evening, everyone would be called to the Accounting. Every single man and woman, there were no children, had to gather within the Downside Gate rectangle and take their allotted place in the line. Anyone missing would be checked against the previous day's roster, usually to confirm that they had died in the mines the previous day, as frequently from punishment as from accidents. Once done, they were marched down into the depths to work. Cade had made it her business to study the daily routine. The dwarves left them to get on with things during the off shifts but a lot of folk were just listless, sitting around waiting for the next shift. Some others were more active in their surroundings, trying to make the conditions more comfortable and liveable. And some, like Cade, were looking for an opportunity.

A kind of order had descended on what had been at first a chaotic, desperate fight to survive. As soon as everyone had realised they weren't going to be slaughtered out of hand and they finally had a place to settle, the old habits of humanity started to come back. People were inevitably falling into their natural places in the pecking order. The shock of capture and the casual brutality of the dwarves that had made people come together for a while, to help each other make it through the bitter march across Tissan, that had passed. She ran a hand through her hair and gazed up at the tiers. That was where it had started first. Why live in the filth and shit when you can live above it? The smarter ones had staked claims to the higher levels, the Heights they'd taken to calling them. Then the devious ones, the strong ones and the cunning ones, they worked it out as well and started to move in. There had been a few fights, some scuffles and then those ejected had returned to the floor, miserable, bleeding and just that bit more defeated.

The day before they'd had their first unexplained death. It wasn't hard to work out the why of it. Someone had decided they wanted something. Someone else had been in the way and had paid for it. Cade had been interested to see what the dwarves doing the Accounting would make of that and had been disappointed when they had done nothing, putting it down as *natural wastage*. She truly did admire their cold and unfeeling approach to business.

Cade rubbed with her fingertips just below her right wrist. Her brand was itching again. She looked at the blocky, angular symbol emblazoned on it. The burn was red and angry-looking around the edges, the raised, marked skin still felt tender. After the branding, they'd only lost a few to infection and they went fast, within a few days. The dwarfs had ended anyone who'd started to show the signs. Those of her branding group that had made it through the journey now numbered one hundred and forty-eight. A middling number, some brands had three hundred members. She and Devlin had estimated there must be almost four thousand humans living within the cavern and for all its size it was still a tight fit.

It had been obvious to all that they were entering a mine when they had come in sight of the great mountain ranges, stretching north and south beyond their vision. Devlin had said these ranges marked the eastern edge of the Empire, territory that neither they nor the dwarves had owned. Humans called them the Barrier Mountains, a name first given to them in the language of the Plains people, which had carried over to the common tongue of the Riverlands. Devlin had no idea what their captors called it.

The mountain they were taken to was only a little way into the first range, along a path that was accessed from the foothills climbing up from the Plains. The dwarves were supposed to live further eastwards in the heart of the range and only travel westwards into human territory to trade. Devlin – always thinking, that one – had also reasoned that this mine was owned not by one, but by many different concerns, and the brandings represented each of those who had their own workings within the mountain. He also suggested that there was at least one more entrance to the mountain, the route where the produce was taken out and the dwarves could enter. Issar had offered that maybe the dwarves just went deeper into the rock. He'd heard it said the dwarves had a massive network of roads that connected their cities and mines. Cade had heard that too and knew it was only partially true. Dwarves lived above ground just as much as they did below.

She pushed up off the floor, wiped her hands and headed back. She picked her way through tiny encampments, crude shelters populated by dirty, stinking men and women. Little light reached within the cavern but her vision had grown used to the gloom. A few fires scattered light here and there. The dwarves gave them a little wood each day, just enough to take the edge off the cold, although the cavern was a lot warmer than the winter they'd struggled through to get here.

She got the familiar stench of someone's slops bucket and darted around it as it hove into view. It was a relief that they'd found a small underground stream a couple of days after their arrival. It had started smelling like a gaol in here, people had taken a shit wherever they could find a free space, inevitably up against the cavern wall. The buckets had arrived a day or two later. The stream was in the lowest tier, a fair way back down one of the tunnels. By common consent no one had claimed that spot.

Taking a professional interest, she'd spent time studying the stream. It came through a hole in the wall a couple of feet off the ground and continued along a channel and down into another rocky tube heading to the Gods Below knew where. The hole was just wide enough for someone small to squeeze into and she almost pitied the first stupid bastard to try. She had no doubt they would end up stuck further along the passage and drown, panicking, cold and alone.

She soon located her patch, the territory her branded group had claimed, and negotiated her way past exhausted and sleeping bodies. Their group had all stayed together, having worked, marched and suffered together, and seeing their companions die together as well. It was quite the bonding experience and many of the other branded groups had followed suit. Cade stepped around the crude V-shaped barrier she and the others had constructed out of a collapsed ceiling and some spare pieces of planking. It faced the cavern wall and gave them a little privacy from the press of humanity behind them. Issar and Devlin were awake and sat before a miserable looking fire. Meghan lay curled up, in the crook of the V, her mouth open wide.

Devlin nodded to her. 'What did you see, Cade?'

'Nuthin' much.' She took a spot opposite.

'Here, saved you some food,' said Devlin, handing over a piece of cheese.

She took it, gave it a quick sniff, and jammed it into her mouth.

She nodded her head. 'Thanks.'

She would be the first to admit, she was surprised her three companions had stayed so close. She knew it wasn't friendship; she didn't want that, she didn't need that. But as events went on, she knew it was going to be useful to have someone watching her back. She studied her companions: Devlin, stolid, smart and far more capable than he let on; Meghan, quiet, caring and brave in her own way; Issar, a frightened mouse but with a knack for finding things out and getting where he shouldn't.

'I heard there's someone called Anzo, he's been making some noises. Big fella, mean-looking. Got a few folk gathered around him, mostly men, a couple of women, different brands,' said Issar.

So it begins. Cade chewed thoughtfully on the cheese. It was off, but only by a week or two. Her tongue tasted something sour but she ignored it. 'Don't know him. He sounds like muscle. Probably from some gang running in a rookery from one of the other cities.'

'Must have some brains,' said Devlin.

Cade shook her head.

'Not really. His sort are cunning, like animals. He keeps control with his fists.'

'The others, they look like rough types,' said Issar.

'Sure. There's bound to be a few criminals and low-lifes amongst us,' said Devlin, giving Cade the eye. She stared right back.

'I'll tell you what happens now,' said Cade. 'There will be some power plays. Anzo, maybe one or two others like him will try and create their own little fiefdoms. There will be deaths.'

'That's already started,' interjected Issar.

Cade ignored him. 'The weaker ones amongst us will pick a side, look for someone to be their patron. My guess ...' She paused and looked around the cavern. '... is you'll get two gangs. We already got one in the Heights, you heard about that branding group that's been turfing everyone else out? Somebody worked it out fast, got his whole branded bunch together and forced out any folk that weren't them. They might be just one group but they can hold the territory easy enough and then they'll take control of the water.'

'They wouldn't!' said Issar.

'You know they would. The other gang, maybe Anzo's, will take the floor. They will have the numbers because he's recruiting from all the brands. Food is the one thing we all want, so that'll be the currency, Anything else of value, clothes, tools, sex, will go to the bosses and they'll dole it out to their favourites.'

'You make it sound so final. How can you be sure? Haven't we all been through enough?' asked Meghan, her voice sleepy and quiet. She lay where she was, a hand tucked under her head between her cheek and the ground.

Cade shrugged. 'I've seen it before, plenty of times. It's what desperate people do. I grew up in a rookery. That's how people survived.'

'Did you join a gang?' asked Meghan.

'No. Never had time for 'em. And I wouldn't give my soul to some greedy, selfish, stinking son-of-a-bitch. No one controls me but me,' Cade said, with a determined edge. She meant it too. It was a matter of pride for her. A few had tried to bring her into a gang when she was just a kid. They'd threaten, cajole, promise and in the end just beat her, or worse. She'd just move on, slip away, and keep running 'til they got tired. After a while they all stopped bothering, there were plenty more kids they could use.

'If that is the way it's going to go down, what side do we pick?' asked Devlin.

'I'm not picking a side,' she replied. Devlin had used 'we,' like they were their own little gang. That tickled her a little; perhaps they were. 'Let's just hang back, watch what happens. Get some names, learn who the players are. Look after our own. I reckon they'll come to us.'

'We negotiate for the best price?' asked Issar.

'Something like that. We all keep our heads down. Start learning more about what we have here, skills, trades and so on. Then we start earning favours.'

'Favours?' asked Meghan

'Yeah. We start making friends, getting people to owe us. Trust me, I know that currency.'

'And what if they don't pay when we call the markers in?' asked Devlin picking the play up quickly.

'Then we make a few examples. Get folk to realise we won't be messed with.'

'Beat them?' asked Meghan.

'Kill them if we have to, whatever works.' Cade saw the look of horror on Meghan's face. This girl needed to grow up fast. She was kind, and strong in her way, but that wasn't going to keep her alive. 'I'll do it, if I have to. When it comes down to it either we hit first or we get hit.'

'I don't like it,' said Devlin, his face grim in the firelight, 'but I've got your back.'

Cade nodded. This partnership might work out.

'What do you think we'll be doing tomorrow?' asked Issar with a wry but weak smile.

'I'd guess smacking our pickaxes into rock and seeing if we can't find some silver,' replied Devlin. They had been at it since they'd started, working on a seam that ran deep into the mountain. They'd knock the stuff out as best they could, piling the ore into carts and pushing them up to a central gallery. From there they were taken away, but never under the eyes of the humans, along that route Devlin had talked about. Cade was already bored to tears. She'd never liked to do the same job more than two days in a row. Predictability was for losers and those who deserved to be robbed. And usually it was her doing the robbing.

Cade stepped into line and tried to work the kinks out of her neck. The crude cushion she'd made out of a scrunched up woollen blanket wasn't exactly the best way to sleep. Still, it could be worse. Beside Cade, the rest of her branded group took their places and around them the other brands formed up, gathering in front of the Downside Gate. Their brave army formed up on blocks for the inspection and parade. Just another day (or night), working for the Dwarf. Speaking of which, she hadn't seen their particular dwarf since they'd marched along the road into the range and had entered the cavern. Cade chewed her lip and thought about that road they'd followed into the mountains, beyond the Great Plains and past the borders of the old Empire. It hadn't escaped her notice that the road, whilst crudely finished, had all the hallmarks of Imperial design. There were mile markers written in the common tongue and occasionally she'd seen the ruin of an Imperial way station, which was odd, because Devlin had said the mountains were considered neutral territory. Yet clearly the Empire's reach had extended further than they had thought.

The Accounting started. Three dwarves were marching down the line, two of them armed with long-handled axes, armoured in chain, their faces hidden behind faceplates attached to their helmets. The third was an older dwarf, grey-bearded, carrying a ledger. He stopped by each human, made a stroke in the book and moved on. Where someone had died, his or her position in the line was kept clear. It made for an interesting if grim diversion, seeing what new gaps had opened each day, and it meant everyone was kept aware of their own mortality and how easy it was to lose it.

The three dwarves stopped at Meghan, the grey-bearded one looked up at her with a stern expression, marked his book and moved on to Cade. She smiled winningly and he scowled back. One of the armoured dwarves stepped up to deliver a blow but stayed his hand at a barked command by the ledger-bearer. The older dwarf glared at her, shook his head, marked the book and carried on. Her owner still wanted them all in good condition, then. It was one less avenue of potential violence for Cade to worry about.

The branded group standing just ahead weren't so lucky. A man who had been coughing bad was pulled from the line, pushed on to his knees and his head struck from his shoulders. A woman screamed, tried to intervene and was similarly dealt with for her efforts. Fool, she ought to have learned by now. Besides, the dwarves' pragmatism was doing them all a favour – any sickness that developed in here was likely to ravage the population. It was better for everyone to weed it out at the root.

After a few minutes, the various accounters finished their run down the lines. The old dwarf shouted a command and Cade's group turned and followed him through the Downside Gate, losing their carefully spaced formation and becoming a desultory pack of shambling souls. Before and behind them other branding groups were led under the gate. They marched in silence for five minutes, along the familiar downward sloping tunnel until it opened out into a larger, torch lit chamber. A series of entrances led deeper into the mines, and above each one, scratched into the rock, was the symbol of the owner. Before each tunnel was a cage containing their tools and a few small, wheeled carts for pushing their findings back to the chamber. Cade and her group started towards their usual tunnel but were surprised when the dwarf held them back, the guards herding them off to one side, as the other brands were issued their equipment and marched down into the depths. Cade shared a look with Meghan, her eyebrows raised. This was new. New could be good. New meant opportunity. The old dwarf spoke to his comrades and pointed at another tunnel opening, larger than the rest with no symbol etched above it. That was where the mined rock was taken.

'Today you work in the light,' the old dwarf shouted, in the common tongue for a change. 'You carry and you load. You try to run, you die.'

Sounded reasonable so far.

One of the armoured dwarves grabbed one of the others and pointed to the passage. He took a position in front, indicating for the humans to follow. The older dwarf joined him and together they marched off. One by one they all stepped into line and entered the passage, the last dwarf bringing up the rear. The passage continued along a flat path for a few hundred paces before Cade felt a definite change. A breeze was blowing down the tunnel, fresh smelling, and they started heading up. A few minutes more passed and she registered that it was becoming lighter, barely noticeable at first, but she could make out more of those walking ahead of her, grey shapes, like ghosts. They rounded a bend and she saw a circle of brightness, an exit growing in size as they drew near. There was a ripple of excitement amongst the line, whispers and gasps, as the circle grew brighter. She could see black shapes moving around, highlighted in the shining backdrop. Then she was through this circle and out into bright, dazzling daylight. Cade put a hand to shield her eyes and squeezed them tight, then she opened them again, blinking rapidly, slowly adjusting to the light.

As her vision sorted itself out, Cade took in the scene. They were at the end of a steep-sided valley, little more than a gap between two mountain slopes. They stood in a small cleared bowl, no more than fifty yards wide. She looked behind her. The tunnel mouth was cut into a third towering peak, running high above them and disappearing beyond a false horizon. The sky was blue, the sun was bright, but there was a chill crispness to the air.

Everyone huddled together, all hundred and fifty humans. Directly opposite were at least a dozen dwarves armed with crossbows pointed right at them. The thought occurred to Cade that they could rush the guards and make a break for it. Sure, a bunch of them wouldn't make it, but she might, and she knew she wasn't the only one having the same idea. But there were too many in the group that were already beaten and she couldn't rely on them to show some guts. *Another time, there'll be other chances.* Behind the guards was a great pile of ore. It was likely everything they'd been digging up for the last month or so, not nearly enough for the entire population but definitely their group's contribution.

The old dwarf stood in front of them, his ledger tucked under one arm.

'You will make the ore smaller, cut away the excess and place what remains into the baskets.' He indicated the baskets that were stacked next to the pile.

With that inspiring speech to motivate them, the group was separated into smaller parties of ten, and given hammers, chisels and smaller picks. Cade took a pick and got to it, sifting through the rocks, selecting those that sat in the palm of her hand and chipping away at the rocks, leaving as much of the silver as possible. Each time she had done the best she could, or could get away with at least, she took the ore and placed it into a sturdy-looking shallow-based reed basket. Cade took her time with that, using the chance to survey her surroundings. The guards were placed in a semi-circle overlooking the work. Some stood by the trail leading out, which was well used with ruts that had been worn into the ground edges that were churned up from a heavy bout of spring rain. She assumed it was spring as it didn't feel like they had been underground *that* long. A couple more guards were stationed by the entrance to the mines, though why they would feel the need to stop them going back in was beyond her. Occasionally dwarves would arrive, driving wagons or on foot, coming from wherever that valley started, before proceeding into the mines. A little later those wagons would return, laden with rock, and then disappear off down the valley. During a rest break Meghan joined her and pointed at another wagon emerging from the darkness.

'I think I see why we are doing this. Everyone else is taking the mined rocks somewhere else. Likely once they are there, somebody has to shape it down to something more manageable.'

'Yep. Our boss has figured he can get it done cheaper by us,' replied Cade.

Meghan was silent for a moment.

'You think there is a way out, through there?' She nodded towards the trail. 'Devlin said we aren't even in the dwarf territories.'

'Don't even think about it,' said Cade. For all they knew it led directly into some dwarf encampment.

'Just a thought,' said Meghan quietly, moving away when one of the guards noticed their conversation.

Later that day, a small convoy of five wagons arrived in the bowl. In the first wagon sat their master and when they halted, he dismounted to speak with the old dwarf. Cade watched them and decided it was time for another chat. They were almost finished with the ore anyway, so she manoeuvred herself to a place near where the full baskets had been piled up. Sure enough a few minutes later, the old dwarf barked a command and a score of workers were drafted in to start loading the baskets on to the back of the wagons. She shouldered her way through and picked up the first basket alongside a man called Anyon, a Scotian like her. Together they humped the basket to the rear of the first wagon.

'Hold on,' she said. She lowered her end and hauled herself up on to the tailgate.

'Lift it up,' she commanded.

Anyon nodded, went down on his haunches and lifted the basket up to Cade. Once it was resting on the edge she reached a hand down. 'Come on, we're needed here.' Anyon, red-faced from the lifting, took her hand and pulled himself up. Together they moved the basket to the back of the wagon and started to receive the others as they came forward. The going was difficult as they manhandled the ore and Cade lost her footing. She let go of the basket and dropped down to a crouch as the rocks spilled around her. She put her arms out to halt her fall and her right hand slipped between the two baskets at the front of the wagon. It made contact with something hard and sharp and Cade closed her hand round the object.

'Damn it,' she muttered.

Anyon reached over to help her up.

'Careful with that,' said the familiar voice of her owner. 'Those baskets cost money.'

'So do I,' retorted Cade, her back to him as she struggled up.

'Not as much as you might think,' he replied, a hard tone to his voice.

She turned and grinned broadly at the dwarf. He stood by the wagon, his arms folded.

'Oh, it's you. Might've known,' he said.

'Afternoon, boss. Clever idea this,' she said brightly, whilst mopping her brow with the front of her shirt.

He scowled.

'Clever?'

'You know, getting us to prep the ore for you here. Saves time and money, I reckon.'

A bushy eyebrow was raised. 'Aren't you the smart one?'

He gestured towards the trail leading out. 'Let the others employ someone to reduce the ore. I like to use all my assets.'

'You might as well get us to smelt it for you too. Then you don't need to employ anyone,' she said with a grunt, as she and Anyon lifted another basket on to the wagon.

'Now I'm getting business advice from a human. We live in an age of wonders,' he said with a shake of his head. 'Just get this wagon loaded and I might forget your insolence.'

'Yes, boss,' she replied.

The wagons were loaded and turned around within thirty minutes. As they disappeared round the bend further down the trail, the humans were rounded up and marched back into the mountain.

Once they were inside the cavern, Cade and the others gathered.

'That was a different day,' remarked Devlin.

'It was nice to see the sun,' said Issar. 'I'd forgotten what it looked like. Almost.'

'Cade, you are crazy, do you know that? Talking to the dwarf that way,' chided Meghan.

Cade pinched her lips together. Should she tell them? It wouldn't hurt.

'That dwarf and I go way back,' she said, waving a dismissive hand. She reached under her shirt and pulled out a dark, metal object.

Issar leaned forward. 'What's that?'

'It's a knife,' Devlin answered for Cade.

'Where did you get it,' whispered Meghan, her face fearful.

'Up above,' said Cade 'I …'

'They'll know. They keep track of everything they issue out,' Issar hissed.

She reached over and cuffed him. He squeaked and held his hands over his head.

'I didn't take it from our tools. Some idiot dwarf left it lying in the back of the wagon. By the time they realise they lost the thing the chances are they won't stop to think it's been nabbed. Besides …' She held it up higher so they could get a better look at it. 'I doubt they'll be upset. It ain't up to much.'

The knife had a short wooden handle. The blade was wide but barely four inches long, the end curving round to form a gutting hook. The knife was designed for hunting and skinning prey, not for fighting.

'That changes things,' said Devlin, with an air of approval.

'Why?' asked Meghan.

Cade snorted. Sometimes the woman was just plain stupid.

'No one else has one of those,' said Issar. He understood.

'Issar is right. It's a weapon. It gives us an edge,' explained Devlin. 'When the gangs start to form, they might want to get physical with us. They'll have rocks.'

'We'll have this,' finished Cade.

'Best you keep it out of sight for now. Save it for when we need it,' suggested Devlin.

'I know what to damn well do with it,' growled Cade.

'Okay, just saying,' said Devlin.

'Just don't say anything. To anyone. Right?' she said looking at each of them in turn, her gaze resting on Issar. They all nodded.

She smiled. Devlin was right. What she hadn't told them, what she wouldn't tell them, was that she had a second weapon, her wicked blade from Aberpool. That was just for her, for when things truly went to shit. It was her lifeline. With that dwarf knife, they had some leverage, amongst the humans at least. She still had to work on their dwarf master, but that was coming along.

'Any of you ever worked in a smithy before?' she asked.

CHAPTER 11

Land. Somehow Father Michael had expected it to take longer to find. He had imagined a voyage of great hardship, fortitude and waiting, a voyage that would have lasted at least a year. But he had never been a nautical man and had no idea how sailing worked, how fast ships could move over water and what it meant to travel so far from a port of safe harbour. He'd never had any doubt they'd find land, after all the Blessed Emperor was at hand to guide them. He'd just thought there would be more … suffering? Perhaps some kind of ritual atonement for their sins? Yet there it was, on the horizon, directly ahead of his position on the forecastle.

'Admiral, how long has it been since we took to the sea? Forgive me, I have lost track,' he asked.

Admiral Lukas did not turn to look at him, his eyes fixed ahead.

'Ninety-three days. If you don't include the time we spent hanging around at the atoll.'

'That does not seem like a great deal of time. It would take longer to walk the breadth of the Empire.'

The Admiral smiled at that, his grizzled face forming folds of skin as his mouth pulled back. His neatly trimmed beard had pearls of seawater caught on the tips of the hairs.

'I'm sure it would. Sea travel is different. No one has ever gone this far before. Leastways no human has come back to tell us. Until now our ships were never built to withstand a journey such as this. Our skills were just starting to solve this problem when the war started. We've always plied our trade close to the shore and even our whalers never strayed too far from the unfriendly northern coasts. When you go out to sea, you take your life in your hands. The food and water you carry is all you've got and when it runs out, there isn't any more to replace it. And if the weather turns against you … well. We have been very, very lucky.'

Father Michael understood. Perhaps they had already endured the test he had been expecting, including a week of hell, when the waves had risen high, the wind had howled, and the rain had lashed the deck. He had thought he might die (something he had considered but seldom cared about before) and for the first time he had felt his faith truly tested. He did not know what had been worse. The leaden-grey skies of the daylight, where you could see the waves towering before you, or the pitch dark of night, where monsters loomed just beyond the flimsy wooden walls of the hull and you never knew when they might strike. After that terrible ordeal, when the storms had abated and the clouds had lightened, a new census had been taken. They had lost almost half the fleet, most of them shattered and sent to the depths. Many of the others were damaged beyond repair. It had taken the best part of three days to reunite the scattered craft. The Eagle Riders, yet again their saviours, were flying from morning to well into night to guide solitary ships and tiny flotillas home. There was one final piece of good news. The small fleet of frigates they had sent ahead had returned, had found them in this vast ocean, and they had brought word of salvation.

'The Emperor provides,' said Father Michael dutifully.

The Admiral nodded curtly. 'As I said. We have been lucky. Not so the six thousand lost to that storm.'

Father Michael looked hard at the Admiral. The man was too unguarded with his thoughts and they often strayed close to disrespect. He probably thought his position gave him the privilege, which was not the case, not in this new world, but Arch Cardinal Vella had told Father Michael to not worry about the Admiral; he was blunt but loyal.

Father Michael watched from the corner of his eye as the Admiral reached into his jacket and pulled out a plug of foul-smelling chewing tobacco. He offered some of it to Father Michael who shook his head. Admiral Lukas shrugged and took a bite. Soon his teeth would be stained and he'd be hawking black spit over the side.

Together they watched as three eagles came closer, returning from their exploration of the land ahead. One peeled off towards the starboard man-o-war, the other two split and landed on either side of *The Fist*.

'Come along, Father, you might as well hear the news first before the Council starts hooting,' said the Admiral.

Together they descended the steps and made their way to the eagle shelters. They stopped at the port platform and watched the squadron commander, Cadarn, dismount. He saw them both and nodded but he didn't join them. Instead, he saw to his bird first, taking off the saddle and carrying it past them to an empty shelter.

'How did it go?' asked the Admiral, as Cadarn returned to the platform.

'Well,' replied Cadarn, continuing his work. Father Michael had noted the squadron commander was a man of few words, only saying what was necessary. He liked that in a man. Cadarn took the reins of his eagle, gently coaxing it off the platform and into the shelter. Only then did he stop, wipe his hands and look at them.

'The brief version is I don't think it's an island. Least, not a small one. I flew in for half an hour or so. The land is wooded with rolling hills. It reminds me of southern Scotia a little. And I saw a mountain range further west.'

'What about anchorage?' asked the Admiral.

'I sent my people north and south. Jenna says south is just cliffs and beaches, no protection. Bryce says there might be something further north. An estuary or something. Bryce?' He called across the deck to the far platform. Bryce looked up and walked across.

'Anchorage?' asked Cadarn.

Bryce nodded.

'You got a number of tributaries feeding into a basin with a lot of smaller islands. The main river is coming in from somewhere north west. Plenty of wildlife down there too. Birds and the like.'

'That might do it,' said the Admiral. 'Pity we lost all the river craft in that storm.'

Father Michael saw a commotion further down the ship and he turned to see the Emperor striding towards them.

'Gentlemen! We have news?' he called briskly. He was wearing a fine forest green cloak stitched with gold thread along its edges, underneath a red tunic and dark leather britches. His sword was at his waist, his hand resting on the pommel as he walked, looking quite the adventurer. Behind him followed two Gifted, keeping a respectful distance.

'Your Grace,' said the Admiral, inclining his head. Father Michael and Cadarn followed suit.

The Emperor waved his hand, dismissing their greeting.

'Leader Cadarn. What did you find?'

'Land, Your Grace,' he replied.

The Emperor looked at him askance for the briefest moment, then laughed. 'I know that much! But what sort of land? Is it an island, a peninsula? A volcano?'

'Your Grace,' interjected Father Michael. 'Perhaps we should continue this discussion out of the wind and back in your chambers?'

The Emperor gave him an irritated look and shook his head, sighing theatrically.

'Very well. It seems that even as the Emperor I have to consider my poor Council. They would get upset if they weren't there to hear the news and they have been gathering to await your arrival. Come along all of you. Leader Cadarn, with me.'

'Bryce, take care of Hilja for me,' ordered Cadarn before joining the Emperor. Father Michael and the Admiral fell into line behind the Gifted.

Admiral Lukas raised an eyebrow at Father Michael. He couldn't quite read what the sailor was trying to suggest, but he knew the man well enough now to know he probably wouldn't like it.

Ten minutes later the Council were gathered and Cadarn stood before them, delivering his report. Father Michael listened dutifully, his place now tucked in a corner, just behind the throne. He had the gist of what the man was saying so he allowed his gaze to wonder around the room.

The lords occupied one side of the table, the clergy the other, just as they always did. There were two notable absences: Lord Crisp's ship had been lost to the storm and poor Cardinal Hammerdal's heart had not been able to take the battering the elements had inflicted upon it. His seat, however, was not unoccupied. Another man, wearing a novitiate's robe, looked upwards from Hammerdal's seat, staring into nothing, a strange smile on his face. His lank, greasy hair was down past his ears, a ragged beard trailed below his neckline and a thick moustache obscured his top lip. Father Michael did not recognise this priest, but he had no doubt the man would have been carefully chosen by the Arch Cardinal, so he returned his attention to the discussion.

Leader Cadarn had finished his report. Father Michael had thought it quite thorough, but the Council kept asking for more details of him and his two fellow riders, who had joined him shortly after his report had begun.

'Perhaps we should sail further south if there is no suitable anchorage?' asked Baron Ernst.

'We'll need fresh water soon. If there is a river near, we should head there first,' argued Lord Fisk, the chamberlain.

'It's a consideration. Better to resupply, then we can think of striking south and north if need be,' said the Admiral.

'Is there wood to build within the estuary?' asked Lord Aban.

Cadarn looked at Bryce. 'A little. There is plenty of forest inland.' Bryce replied. 'I would like to go back and take a closer look.'

'Then you must head back immediately,' said Baron Ernst.

'Tomorrow we can, not now. The birds are tired,' said Cadarn.

'Or is it just you?' said the Baron icily.

Father Michael watched Cadarn for a reaction. The man was inscrutable.

'My lords, I think our Eagle Riders have done enough for one day,' said the Emperor. 'I believe we can all agree, getting off these damned ships on to dry land is the first priority. No offence, Admiral.'

'None taken, Your Grace. Even an old sea dog like me could do with looking at something other than these noble faces every day.'

Some round the table smiled or laughed gently, though Father Michael thought it a poorly disguised barb. Most importantly, the Emperor smiled.

'Quite so, Admiral. I believe Lord Fisk is right. Let us find a safe port of harbour, gather our strength and then strike out.'

'And Your Grace, I believe we should hold a public ceremony to celebrate your consecration and recognise your leadership in bringing us to salvation,' added Arch Cardinal Vella.

'Yes, of course,' said the Emperor. 'Admiral Lukas, How long do you think it will be before we reach the coast?'

'In this wind? Likely a day. If we tack slightly north, we should reach this estuary. Captain Cadarn can quickly locate it for us, I'm sure,' replied the Admiral.

'Then we shall proceed. Thank you all. I would like some peace to think on this news.'

As the Council withdrew, Father Michael watched Arch Cardinal Vella converse with the Empress and this new priest. He followed them out on to the deck and hovered nearby. After a minute, the Arch Cardinal bowed and withdrew, turning towards Father Michael. The Empress and the priest went below deck to her new quarters.

'Father Michael,' said the Arch Cardinal, 'I saw you loitering. You have a question?'

'Forgive me, but who is that?' he asked.

'Ah, no doubt you mean Llews? He is the new advisor to the Empress.'

'Is he not just a novice?'

The Arch Cardinal looked at him sternly. 'Does it matter the providence? He is a man of the cloth, as you are.' She relented slightly. 'That said, I can understand your confusion. Why go from a Cardinal to a novice? We are a little thin on the ground now, Father. The storm robbed us of many fine brothers and sisters. Llews wears a novice's robes, yet he is a fine preacher. I have been to hear his sermons to the people aboard his ship. He has fire, passion, belief. The people love him and he loves our Emperor. He shares my view, that it is time for a new way. A way of peace and progress. I felt that at this time of joy and renewal, it would be of great comfort to have a man like him giving faith and hope to the Empress. Do you not agree?'

How could I not? Father Michael bowed his head. 'Of course.'

Arch Cardinal Vella placed an arm on his shoulder. 'Our time is at hand. We will make our move soon, before those who would presume to power grow strong again. Go now, attend your Emperor.'

Father Michael returned to the Emperor's chambers and found his lord pacing back and forth behind his throne, his hands clasped behind his back.

'Your Grace,' he said.

The Emperor looked up. He appeared confused for a moment then his lips parted into a wide smile. 'Father. It is wonderful news, is it not? We have reached land sooner than any of us could have hoped.'

'We had faith in your guidance,' replied Father Michael.

The Emperor stopped, turned to face him and folded his arms. His face assumed a solemn cast. 'What do you think? Was my decision to head north the correct one?'

'Your decisions are not questioned, Your Grace.'

'Which means?'

Father Michael struggled to choose the right words to something that, in his mind, appeared as obvious as the day was long. 'You are the Emperor. If you say it is so, it is so.'

'Let me put it another way. If I was not here and you were required to make that decision, what would you have done?'

'I don't think anyone would have asked me for my decision. There are a long line of worthies far better placed to lead than I.'

The Emperor laughed. 'Honestly, Father, you are a terrible advisor. What use are you to me if I can't get a straight answer from you?'

Father Michael thought again. *What do I think? How can I say it?* 'I'm not a sailor. I can barely swim. The sooner I get myself off of this leaking, miserable barrel of a boat, the better I will feel, Your Grace.'

The Emperor slapped the top of the throne. 'That's more like it. I quite agree. The sooner we get to land the better. I have been cooped up in here far too long.' He paused for a moment. 'Did you see that fellow sitting by the Cardinals? He has a queer look about him. Yet I am told he is one of my Church.'

'Yes. Llews. I spoke briefly to the Arch Cardinal about him. He is your mother's new advisor,' replied Father Michael.

'Really? Then I pity my poor mother. Cardinal Hammerdal was little better for her, obsequious and straight-laced in equal measures. She needs someone to raise her spirits now that we are free and clear.'

'I understand Novice Llews is a most pious and passionate man, Your Grace.'

'Let's hope so. We could do with a little more passion around here. I can't remember when I had a decent drink.'

'We have a supply of wine in the hold, Your Grace.'

The Emperor eyed him. 'You know what I mean, Father Michael. I may be the Emperor now, but I wasn't raised to be one. I wasn't raised to lead armies and dictate the affairs of an empire. Being the third son meant I had time for other distractions. Most of them enjoyable.'

'You are the Emperor now. If Your Grace wants to get drunk, then you can do so.'

'And you won't stop me?'

'Only if it looks like you are going to drown in it, Your Grace.'

The Emperor laughed once more. Father Michael was pleased, he had allowed a little of his old self to come through and surprisingly, his lord seemed to approve.

'My priestly bodyguard. If only you could find me some worthy company to get drunk with. I fear my council are too old, too pious or too damned unsavoury to keep as drinking companions.'

'I dare say that Admiral Lukas could down a brandy or two. If you could stomach the swearing and insolence,' said Father Michael bluntly.

The Emperor pursed his lips. 'You might have a point there.'

The estuary landing took longer than the expected day. The Admiral insisted on conducting a proper exploration before the fleet entered. The eagles were sent up and undertook aerial surveys of the river mouth, looking for the best approaches and learning the tidal flows.

As he had pointed out, their larger sea-going vessels had to be certain of penetrating upriver to ensure they had adequate harbour from the weather. They had lost most of the shallower-drafted ships in the storm so the survey was painstaking and slow. Father Michael decided to stay close and listen in on the Admiral's business, it would be useful if the Emperor needed detailed information. He stood near the table in the Admiral's quarters as they prepared a map. The Admiral drew it himself, with a surprisingly steady hand, as the Eagle Riders clustered round, describing the terrain, the water and everything in between. A picture of their new home took shape. To the north a large, flat island sat close to the mainland, separated by creaks and marshes that grew and shrank with the tide. Surrounding it were scores of smaller islands, several displaying evidence of recent flooding. In the southern part of the estuary, there were many long and narrow shoals. The Admiral decided that their best bet was a passage running along a northeast to southwest route, not far off from the larger island. One of the smaller caravels went first, using its banks of oars to propel the craft forward at a walking pace, taking readings with weight and anchor. An eagle circled above ready to spot any lurking dangers just below the surface. After two hours the all clear was given and the fleet entered the channel. It was almost dark by the time the Admiral announced that everyone was through.

Once beyond the estuary, the river that formed it was wide and calm. Vessels weighed anchor, *The Fist of Tissan* and the men-o-war staying to the centre of the channel.

Even though it was almost dark, the landings commenced immediately. The Emperor's pavilion was erected a little way back on the southern shore, upon a patch of grassy and solid-looking higher ground. Lights blazed upon the water as boats and skiffs shuttled back and forth carrying people and supplies. Father Michael didn't like it. There was too much chaos, too much uncertainty about the way they were approaching this. They ought to wait and see what the new day brought. Let others go ahead and secure the land.

He voiced his opinion to the Emperor and was gently rebuked. 'We are perfectly safe. Our Riders have spotted nothing resembling a settlement and no sign of anything intelligent spying upon us.'

Father Michael left it at that. Despite his misgivings, you did not doubt the word of the Living God. He trailed through the haphazard camp towards the circle of lights that surrounded the pavilion. About him folk bustled, most of them with purpose, others in a daze, unsure what to do with themselves.

As he reached the perimeter, he saw at least a score of soldiers, facing outwards, their backs to the light. That was better, someone was clearly thinking straight. He was permitted entry by a grim-faced sergeant-at-arms and within the circle he spotted Cardinal Yarn in conversation with another Gifted. She turned at his approach, her face grave.

'Father, you look troubled,' she said.

'We should have waited. We don't know what is out there.'

'I agree. It is a risk but it was the Emperor's wish that we land. I have taken precautions, my Gifted are on hand,' she said, turning to the pavilion. 'I have doubled the guard and have people both at the rear and at the sides.'

Father Michael appraised the structure where four Gifted stood, two to each side of the entrance.

'I have also sent patrols of Watchers and Speakers to the south, east and west. The Watchers will return soon, having committed the place to memory. They will remain close by to warn us. The Speakers will remain out there and will call if they spot anything,' Cardinal Yarn said and smiled, not unkindly. *'Don't fret too much, Father. This is our business and we do it well,'* she pulsed to him.

Father Michael frowned.

'The Emperor is within. He is already drawing up plans for the conquest of this new land,' she continued.

'All I ask is the Blessed Emperor grant us at least a night's sleep on something which isn't rocking,' said Father Michael.

Cardinal Yarn laughed lightly.

'As do I.'

He bowed to her then continued on his way.

Within the tent he chanced upon the Empress and her new advisor. He bowed once more, this time a little lower, as they passed by. As he raised his head, he found Llews had stopped and was looking at him even though the Empress was still moving away. His eyes were dark black pools. A smile, the same one he had worn at the council meeting, was on his lips.

'You are Father Michael,' he said, his voice deep, his tone friendly.

'I am, Novitiate Llews,' he replied.

'Oh, I am no novice. I never undertook vows or study, this robe symbolises my faith.'

Father Michael was confused. 'Then you are not a member of the Church?' he asked.

'I am now. I chose to devote myself to preaching the Emperor's blessings amongst the smaller communities in Scotia.'

'How did you escape?' Father Michael asked.

'I was chosen. I had already made peace with my fate when instead I was plucked away and delivered to serve my Emperor and his blessed mother.'

'A strange and fortunate thing.'

'Yes, a miracle. The Emperor chooses his servants as he will. You would, I am led to understand, know something of this?'

Father Michael found himself bristling.

'I was lost and the Emperor's grace granted me a new beginning,' he replied.

'Yes,' said Llews, his head nodding eagerly. 'A new beginning. And we are on the verge of another one. A chance to truly make the world as it should be.'

Ah, now I understand. I hear the Arch Cardinal's words in his voice.
'Then we share a common view,' Father Michael said.

'Indeed we do. Together we can help to forge a world where humanity need not fear. Where we can achieve true greatness and bask in the Emperor's holy light,' said Llews with alarming intensity. His face changed, the shine in his eyes faded, his face went blank.

'Now please, you must excuse me, Father.' Llews bowed to him with a theatrical sweep of his arm. It looked comical and almost mocking, yet Father Michael felt it suited the manner of the man.

A new land. A new beginning. It was good to be reminded of that and Father Michael felt hopeful and optimistic. The feelings were as powerful as when he had first embraced the Imperial Church and its teachings. A better time is at hand, for those strong and worthy enough to earn it.

CHAPTER 12

'Good morning, Master Sabin,' said Rabi. The old elf servant was emerging from the stables leading a fine-looking grey stallion. 'I hear you are heading up to the Parliament today.'

Fillion placed a hand on the horse, running it along the sleek flank. One thing about elves, they did know how to breed fine horses. Not as powerful or useful in a fight as an Imperial courser but stallions often had a temper that could be shaped into a useful asset. It might serve him to get friendly with one.

'I am indeed, Rabi,' he said, smiling. 'Nadena is going to show me where her father works. Though putting it like that doesn't do justice to what he really does, I'm sure.'

Rabi laughed, 'I know what you mean. It is difficult to imagine just how important the master is.'

Fillion scratched the grey's ear, earning a snicker in response. 'Whose horse is this? I haven't seen him before.'

'Ah, no. That's because he's yours.'

Fillion stared at him in surprise.

Rabi grinned. 'Master Patiir thought it would prove useful in your travels.'

Fillion shook his head. 'Yes, yes it would.' *Am I really as good as all that? I'm no spy, I've had no training, and things are just falling into my lap. Nothing in all my days has ever gone this well. Elves are many things but they aren't stupid.*

'I don't know what to say. This gift is too much,' he continued humbly.

'Hardly. I think you have earned it,' said Nadena's voice behind him. Rabi bowed low in greeting.

Fillion turned to watch her walk across the courtyard. She was wearing a gown of purple and yellow silk, the colours swirling together, creating a mix of vibrant bright tones. It was, to a human eye, extreme. He was getting used to the elves' chaotic idea of fashion. The gown was worn off the right shoulder, revealing her bare pale flesh to the warm late spring sun. Nadena had a sly smile, her eyes sparking as she drew near.

'You have made quite an impression on my father. I can't imagine why that would be.'

Fillion copied Rabi's bow. 'I think he likes the company of another grown male in the house, no offence to Hedra.'

Nadena laughed. 'I'm sure there would be none taken.'

'You are looking lovely this morning,' he added.

She tilted her head coyly. 'You think? I just wanted to put something on which matched my mood.' She pursed her lips and looked him up and down, inspecting him like he was on parade.

'Sabin, you are odd sometimes. You are still wearing trail clothes. You are not at war anymore.'

Fillion looked down at himself. He wore brown trousers, a green tunic and sturdy black boots, pretty much what he wore every day. He had relented to earlier pressure and left his full length leather duster in his room. That had been easy compared with having to wander the streets without a sword for company.

'I'm sorry, I just feel more comfortable this way,' *and more human.* 'It must be my border blood. I'm just used to a life outdoors.'

Nadena sighed dramatically and slipped an arm through his.

'We'll make a city elf of you yet. What do you think of the horse?'

'He is truly magnificent,' said Fillion honestly.

'He comes from father's holdings to the north. Some good pasture country up there.'

'Does he have a name?' asked Fillion.

'He's called Amice, a little ironic considering his temperament. He is three years old and feisty.'

'That's the best way,' said Fillion. Amice. The old elvish word for friend. *He'd better be.*

ALEX JANAWAY

Nadena pulled on his arm. 'Come, you can ride him later. We have business elsewhere.'

Fillion nodded to Rabi and allowed himself to be drawn through the gate and on to the street. Nadena set a gentle pace, content to enjoy the weather.

'I'm glad you are getting a chance to see the Parliament. It is a rare honour,' she said.

'I am truly humbled to have received the invitation. I know that very few are allowed into the chamber.'

'Fewer than you know, and very few of those are not either related to a Member or a wealthy petitioner.'

'I would have thought the King was above all that?' said Fillion.

'The King is but his councillors are not. It is the nature of politics. The King rules the nation, he is our heart. But the blood of the realm is still money and favours and influence.'

'You sound like your father.'

'I suppose I do. I think he has a mind to put me forward for selection as a Member.'

'Can that happen?'

'Yes. It's not very democratic but my father has …' she shrugged, 'influence.'

Fillion chuckled. 'I'm not sure if politics is really what you want.'

She looked at him, her eyes holding his. 'Maybe not.'

They turned a corner and started up the slope towards the highest point of the city. The route was busy and Fillion had to keep making way for passers-by, each time done with a smile. Only the Blessed Emperor knew how damned hard it was to stop from screaming when all around you were the faces of the enemy. A thousand elves who would cut you down rather than look at you, if you happened to be a human.

After ten minutes they arrived at the plateau that served as the administrative and spiritual centre of the Heartlands. A broad tree-lined avenue separated the two halves. On the right side stood the imposing, steeply sided dome of the Parliament, the seat of elven government. The wooden building was painted bright white, and it gleamed in the sun. Opposite stood the huge Temple of the Gods, made of smooth marble and shaped stone blocks. So large that within its walls it held separate chapels to all the Gods of the elves, or so he had been told. He had not yet been inside, it hadn't felt right. Behind the temple, bordered by a low wall, was another small city of homes, offices and further worshipping places, all designed to support the priests and faiths of the elven pantheon. The Imperial religion had but one God, one Church, one faith. It demanded much less resource.

'Shall we have a closer look at the King's Palace?' Nadena asked. There was something like amusement in her voice as she mistook his disquiet for awe.

Fillion forced a smile. 'Yes, I'd like that.'

They strolled down the avenue, covering the almost quarter mile to stand before the Palace. He had never seen anything so ugly. It reminded Fillion of a bug or some kind of spider. Six towers, three to a side, flanked a central hub. Each tower, or leg, was attached to the hub by means of a thin bridge, itself supported by a deeply curving wooden arch. The hub was a smaller version of the Parliament but ringed with ornate curved walkways and large balconies that looked like eyes. It was also suspended off the ground, supported by the six towers. All of it was made in wood. He didn't understand how the thing could stay up, yet he was no carpenter or engineer, so perhaps it was something simple, angles, weight bearing and so on. He liked that it was all wood; he had visions of burning the damned thing to the ground. Each leg had an ornate doorway, all were open, with two royal guards stationed to either side. None of the casual, easy manner of the city guard about these ones. They hid behind bright steel armour with shining breastplates, greaves and gauntlets over clean, bright chainmail, looking like it had been freshly forged. They carried halberds that were pointed and well honed. These ones were looking for trouble. Those doors might be open but you weren't getting in there without a good reason or a fight.

'Incredible, isn't it?' Nadena asked.

'It is that.' *Incredibly ugly.* 'What's it like inside?'

'Grand. Magnificent. Beautiful. The palace has existed for centuries. It lives and breathes.'

Fillion stopped short. 'It's alive?'

'Don't look so surprised, Sabin.' She laughed lightly. 'There is no one alive who has not heard that said. It is a legend as much as the tree that grows within Parliament.'

Shit.

'I know, forgive me. But is it really alive? Truly?'

'Yes. Truly. The walls are alive. Living wood. Dormant in winter, vibrant and leafy in the summer.'

'But it looks like the wood has been shaped, cut. It isn't natural.'

'No, but is magic not natural? Sorcerers used their power and imbued the palace with life energy.'

'That *is* incredible.'

'Oh, Sabin. Your face is a picture. You can see it with your own eyes, yet the set of your mouth says you still have doubts.'

Fillion shook his head and forced a smile.

'I'm sorry, Nadena. I look and I see a grand, magnificent and beautiful palace. I don't see the hand of sorcery. It is not something I have much experience of save for the battlemagics used against the humans. That was vast and terrible. Sorcery and life do not go hand in hand in my eyes. Faith and life, the gifts and blessings of the Gods. That is something I hold dear.'

Nadena pulled her arm and drew him closer. She pressed a hand to his cheek, letting a finger brush across his skin.

'You are such an enigma, Sabin. At once you are both a simple, spiritual soul and yet you have such a presence, a confidence and an understanding of things.'

He reached up and took her hand in his, squeezing it gently. 'Should I be insulted or complimented by that?'

'Complimented, on both counts.' Her hand lingered a moment longer before she withdrew it. 'I like your innocence. It is refreshing. A person can become jaded, living here in the capital.'

'I don't believe that.' *Jaded? How? These people have such a perfect, ordered life. If you were happy being brutal murdering bastards.*

'Believe it, Sabin. Politics can drain the energy of even the strongest if you let it.'

'Your father might disagree.'

'My father is special. And he has us! Come on. We'll be late.'

If the palace was well guarded and closed to visitors, it was certainly not true of the Parliament building. A broad length of stone steps climbed almost ten yards to the entrances, a series of separate portals, high-framed and curving. Elves were bustling around, coming and going. Many more were sitting on the steps deep in discussion.

'It's busy here,' Fillion remarked.

'Any citizen is allowed access, whether to petition, bring information, provide a service or just to stand and look. Only the central debating chamber is off limits.'

'Isn't that dangerous?'

'What do you mean?'

'Anyone could come in and get hold of secrets. Where's the protection?'

Nadena shook her head.

'Honestly, Sabin, I must add to your list of qualities. Sometimes you can be infuriating. Why would anyone want to come in and steal something? There is nothing to hide. This place is for the people.'

'Politics, Nadena. The people and politics don't mix well.'

Nadena laughed and gave him a short bow. 'I acknowledge the riposte. Now you are just showing off how clever you are, Sabin.'

As they climbed it wasn't just elves he saw. Not far from Fillion were two dwarves, talking quietly in their own tongue in a deep bass rumble. They wore long leather coats fastened with wide belts, underneath were dark coloured tunics with golden filigree blocks on the edges of the shortened sleeves. Their arms were bare but for long leather bracers with black iron studs running their length. Their sombre attire marked them out more than their stature amongst the riot of colours the elves wore.

He wondered whether the dwarves had any hidden weapons. He wouldn't put it past them. They likely felt naked without something sharp close to hand, as he did.

In his previous explorations he had seen some of the other races, including a few gnomes and an ogre. That was unusual, those buggers hated coming down from the mountains. After some questioning, he'd found the dwarven embassy, set further back behind the Parliament. An Imperial building had once been sited nearby, or so he had heard many years ago. That had been harder to find, most didn't want to mention it. He'd finally gained directions after telling a palace guard he was a soldier who wanted to see what they had been fighting against. 'Don't expect to see much,' the guard had warned. When he had located it, along a quiet side street, he realised how right the guard had been. There was nothing there, just a patch of green, bordered by flowers and shrubs. They'd erased it, just like they had erased its occupants.

Fillion and Nadena entered the dome and found themselves on a curving, busy concourse. The bold white of the outside continued within, the concourse lit naturally through windows arranged in the outer wall at regular intervals, the white walls glowing. It was stark and spartan. Elves swept by, engaged in their own private affairs of state. Fillion and Nadena pushed through the flow, heading for another corridor leading into the interior of the building. As they drew away from the concourse windows set into the ceiling provided the light. From what he could tell, light was reflected down these vertical tubes by means of highly polished, reflective glass. He had seen similar devices used before as a signalling mechanism for their armies. It had worked well, as long as the sun wasn't obscured. He'd used it against them once, early on in the war, when they discovered a few elven scouts ranging far ahead of the main host. He'd flashed back a message that there was a huge Imperial ambush waiting for them. There wasn't of course, but it was good to watch an army stop in its tracks for a couple of hours.

At the far end of the corridor was a small wooden door. Before it stood a guard clad in a brown leather breastplate and chain hauberk. He wore a metal helm with high cheek guards, held in place by flaps laced under the chin. He carried a sword, sheathed at his belt and his arms were held behind his back.

Nadena and Fillion stopped before him. The guard nodded in recognition.

'You are welcome, my lady. The Parliament is in session so please be quiet as you enter.'

'Thank you, we shall,' responded Nadena.

The guard turned and pulled open the door. Nadena went first.

'It's like you own the place,' whispered Fillion in her ear, ignoring the look the guard gave him.

'Hush,' replied Nadena, obviously pleased with his comment.

They emerged on to a small balcony, overlooking a semi-circular bowl. The balcony had two banks of six seats, four of which were taken. Nadena took him to the front row and they settled on two seats furthest on the left. The balustrade running around the edge of the balcony was not high and by leaning forward he could get a good look at the floor below. Beneath him and fanning out to either side were banks of benches following the curve of the circle. Climbing up nine levels, they were bisected by two flights of steps running down from high double doors so that the banks were divided into equal thirds. More steps ran along the edges. At least two thirds of these benches were full of elves, male and female. They wore clothes of all colours and styles but each had the purple sash of rank around their waists. Patiir had told him there were six hundred Members of Parliament. Some represented regions, others headed up business and mercantile concerns. Then there were government officials, military and civil leaders, even sorcerers. Anyone with power and influence could be invited to join. Membership was, in a number of cases, hereditary. Patiir, as a major landholder, was one of them. It made sense that Nadena would take up the mantle when her father finally decided to retire.

The steps led to a floor, which was empty apart from a raised dais set nearest the centre block of seats. A wooden railing at waist height ran around its front half and two steps led to it from the rear. It reminded Fillion of a priest's pulpit back in one of the larger Imperial chapels, where the clergy would preach to the faithful, extolling the virtues of having a Living God to guide them. This platform faced towards the far wall upon which another larger construction sat. There were three levels of wooden platforms that overlooked the seated Members. The highest and central level was only wide enough to accommodate a single wooden seat. What was remarkable was that the seat was carved from within the trunk of a massive, living tree. That tree, old and weathered, rose up to the top of the roof of the dome. It was branchless along its length of travel. Only at the apex did limbs emerge and extend, a green leafing canopy spreading outwards. At first Fillion thought the roof was open to the elements, but this was dispelled when his sharp, elven vision spotted a bird alighting, almost by magic on thin air. It was glass, yet no less impressive for that.

To either side of the tree, on the next level down, were two chairs, this time just freestanding, with backs as high as a man. The chair on the left held an elf wearing bright red robes. The chair on the right was empty. On the final, largest and lowest level, a long table held several elves, quills poised over documents. No doubt they were officials recording the proceedings. The pulpit on the floor, as Nadena had explained, was where whoever was speaking would stand to address Parliament. The seat within the tree was reserved for the King, when he attended. Whoever was speaking, whether the King was there or not, must always face that tree-throne as a mark of respect, the relative heights of the platforms ensuring the speaker always had to look upwards. Currently that speaking platform was occupied by someone droning on, their voice echoing around the chamber

As Fillion got comfortable, he spied two more balconies left and right of theirs, spaced further along the walls. Both were empty.

'It's a quiet day, then,' he said softly taking advantage of the noise below.

Nadena shook her head. 'The session is only just starting.'

'Ah.' Fillion sat back and placed his hands on his thighs. 'What about those fellows in the red sashes?' He pointed at the scribes and at the elf in the cloak.

'They are Servants. They act as aides to the Members and also as staff to the Parliament itself. It's a great honour to serve. Many see it as a pathway to becoming a Member.'

'I understand. So who is that speaking?'

'I don't know, it sounds like a representative from one of the outlying regions,' she replied, her voice even lower. 'They are talking about crop forecasts and the like. Now, Sabin, please, I told you that we can't talk in here, only listen.' Her eyes flicked to someone behind them and she smiled apologetically. Fillion turned around and looked at a middle-aged she-elf, a look of irritation on her face. He smiled, with no hint of apology.

Fillion settled back on his chair and allowed the proceedings to wash over him. He noticed Nadena took a polite interest in what was being said. Hells Below, for all he knew she might be enjoying this crap. It was a bloody boring and mind-numbing affair. He had always wondered why politicians in the Empire had a reputation for skulduggery and intrigue. Now he felt he understood a little better. They needed something to make their lives interesting. Who in their right mind would want to do this? It was all tedious and mundane. The Parliament sat and listened to each speaker in turn, no one interrupted, no one looked outraged. Occasionally the elf in red would say something, the speaker would reply and then they'd carry on as before. The scribes scribed and no doubt the tree grew a little larger. At one point he was going to ask who the elf in red was, but then realized he really didn't care.

Finally, something vaguely interesting happened: Patiir arose and spoke. Fillion hadn't spotted him so he must have been sitting directly beneath them. He looked at Nadena, her face radiating pride. Patiir's subject was the repopulation of their western borders. Those lands had taken the highest toll in terms of casualties from the war, and the argument was that trade and produce would likely be affected for some time. Fillion took his own small measure of satisfaction from that.

During the war it was easy to forget that the enemy was losing troops as well. All he had had time to think of was the men they had lost, the next city to fall, the citizens slaughtered and the next place to fall back to. They never once pushed the enemy back, never got behind them, never retook land. Only a few units like his scouts and the Eagle Riders were able to get close and interdict supply lines, for all the good that had done.

'I would humbly beg the Parliament to approve subsidies for the encouragement of certain tradesmen and their families to move to our western regions. We have need of the wood that is harvested and the grain that is grown there,' said Patiir, his back straight, holding on to the railing, head raised high towards the platform. Fillion watched many of the Members nod their heads in agreement. 'And of course, our cousins in the west would like nothing more than to take what we do not want!' he said lightly. Gentle laughter rippled through the assembled Members.

Fillion figured Patiir was referring to the Wood elves, vicious bastards.

'Good thing Kanyay isn't here,' murmured Nadena.

Who was Kanyay?

'Thank you Member Patiir, your words are, I think, well received. I shall pass this to the King for consideration. You will hear in two weeks,' replied the elf in red.

Patiir withdrew from the dais and was replaced by a female who spent some time agreeing with Patiir before moving on to new matters as mundane as before. It took at least another hour before the Parliament was adjourned, the red-clothed elf calling the assembly to order. They all stood and waited in respectful silence as the elf retired through a doorway behind his seat. As the Members filed out, a low hum of conversation filled the air. The clerks on the lowest level busied themselves with collecting the piles of paper they had amassed during the session. Fillion stretched and looked at Nadena.

'I assume that means we can talk now?'

Nadena's thin eyebrows arched. 'You really are an impatient individual. Yes, let's go and meet father.'

They retraced their steps along the corridor and back on to the main concourse, following it around about a quarter of a turn until reaching a set of steps leading down, on to a second identical broad passage. Fillion guessed they were at ground level now, the same windows spaced high along the walls.

Members conducted their private business on this level. The curving route was populated on either side by a series of offices. Some doors were shut but others were wide open, with elves gathered around the doors. As they walked, Members passed by, flanked by aides. Functionaries hurried on carrying everything from single pieces of paper to large, leather-bound ledgers. Every now and then an elf would greet Nadena, who would respond with a smile or a nod but never stopped to talk.

On arrival and a quick inspection, Patiir's office was no different from all the others. They proceeded through the door into a small reception room. A young elf stood up at his desk, smiling as he recognised Nadena. He wore a red sash, wrapped round a purple robe made of silk.

'Simeon, how are you?' she greeted him warmly.

'I am well. Your father is indisposed at the moment, but I am sure he will be out soon.'

'Sabin, it is good to see you,' said Simeon.

Fillion nodded. He had met this elf a few times in the last couple of months. Patiir's assistant, he was from the family estates, sent to gain experience in administration. He was also frustratingly keen, constantly good-humoured and generally annoying.

A red, square-panelled door opened behind him and Patiir appeared, ushering out another Member, a female elf wearing a green and blue smock-coat over light blue leggings.

'Nadena, Sabin. May I introduce Tekla, Member for the Treasury.'

'Nadena, that is a lovely dress,' said Tekla. 'I feel quite provincial.'

She turned to Sabin and held out a hand. Sabin took it and bowed. As he looked up she was smiling indulgently. Her chestnut hair was done up in a mess behind her head and held in place with small pearl-handled combs. Her eyes shined with intelligence, yet she looked only slightly older than Nadena. It meant very little to Fillion unless they had lines or grey hair, their age could be anything between two hundred and six hundred years.

'Where are you from, Sabin? You have quite a colouring about you,' she said, looking at his hands and studying his face. Her hands held in contrast to his were painfully white.

'The western borders, a little place you will never have heard of,' he said. Fillion was getting used to these questions.

'He was with the army,' added Nadena.

'Ah, that would explain it. Then you would be interested to know we were talking about both subjects,' Tekla said looking at Patiir. 'He raised an interesting issue regarding our future recovery from the war.'

'Yes, we were in the chamber,' said Fillion. 'I must approve of Patiir's proposal. We have suffered so much.'

'And how much should we incentivise our people?' she said, a slight tone of amusement in her voice.

Fillion shook his head. 'Enough to get them started. It does not need to be money, what they need is tools, horses, cattle. Why would they not wish to come? The western borderlands are wild but beautiful.'

Tekla laughed lightly. 'The optimism of youth! But you have the truth of it. Patiir and I share the view that the King would baulk at spending any more money. Our revenues are stretched as it is. Yes, I believe we could couch it in different terms.'

'We have spare material, especially after the war. All we need do is redirect it,' said Patiir.

'That is all we need. We could use the carts that carried supplies, the horses that pulled them and the tents that housed the drivers,' said Fillion.

'Hmm …' Tekla placed a finely manicured finger upon her chin and studied Fillion. 'You should look to keep this one close to hand, Patiir, he has your insight.' She removed her hand and tapped it twice on Patiir's shoulder. 'Now, you must excuse me.'

She swept from the room like she was the queen of all the Heartlands.

Patiir smiled wryly at Fillion and Nadena. 'Come along inside. Simeon, I am indisposed for a short time.'

'Of course, Sir,' replied Simeon.

Patiir closed the door behind them. 'Welcome to my humble quarters, Sabin.'

Fillion took just a moment to survey the room. It was, unsurprisingly, minimally furnished. A solidly built table, taking up most of the available space, held a few unopened scrolls. Patiir's chair was made of oak and covered in a rich red felt padding. Two chairs were opposite, not so well upholstered, covered in green velvet. Fillion took one and Nadena the other.

Patiir took his chair and sighed.

'Tired, Father?' asked Nadena with concern.

'A little, but it was a productive morning. What did you think, Sabin?'

'It was ... instructive,' he said fighting against all his instincts to say something rather less diplomatic. 'I must admit, much of what was said was beyond me.'

Patiir smiled. 'Nicely put.' He leaned back and steepled his fingers under his chin. 'Although, I must say, you were quite eloquent with your comments to the Member for the Treasury.'

Fillion shrugged. 'I just said what seemed to make the most sense.' It was also the only thing that came to mind. 'I was just thinking about the war and the impact it has had.'

Patiir nodded, though his face frowned.

'These are the last dying days for us to explore the conflict with the humans. In most people's minds the war is done. The Empire of Tissan is, for the most part, dead and gone. It's time to move forward. In a hundred years it will be forgotten.'

In a hundred years, you'll still remember it and what you reaped. Trust me. 'Then it is doubly important that we do all we can to provide assistance to my folk.'

Patiir leaned forward. 'I admire your passion for this and I will do all I can. We are fighting against time. I fear that without a swift resolution it will all be too late. The Heartlands will not suffer overmuch but it will be harder for the communities that have lost their men folk. It will take them time to recover and I would spare them as much pain as possible.'

'Tekla seemed supportive of your position, Father,' said Nadena.

'And you know better than to trust anything that the Member may "seem" to be. She has managed the finances of the war and maintained the trade agreements with our allies for the last two years. Our common cause has avoided major damage to the coffers, but she is in no mood to spend more on the peace.'

'Surely, there was plenty of wealth to be taken from the humans?' asked Fillion.

Patiir raised his eyebrows. 'Sabin, you know better than that, we took none of it,' he said sternly.

Damn, careful now. The ignorant country lad routine would only get him so far, and this elf was far too shrewd to risk it.

'I know,' he said slowly, 'but I was thinking about other things: jewels, lumber, base metals. Raw materials the humans may not have worked on.'

'I understand, but we will not make exceptions. We will not touch anything they have wrought or owned. We leave that to the dwarves, and all the rest. They have no qualms about profiting from the war.'

'They do feel that they are owed it, in reparation for what was done to them,' said Nadena.

Done? Fillion wanted to ask more about that but it was a question too far. Besides, the dwarves were always ones to remember a financial slight. They were likely extracting a price for those of their kind they had lost. It damaged their workforce. They were a lot like humans in that respect.

'So, to finish your enquiry, Sabin, there is no extra money. Tekla was here to say as much. Therefore we must present her with another option. When Chancellor Nazar, you saw him today, speaks to the King, he may well be moved to support the motion. But he can be just as easily moved by any argument that Tekla will put to him about it.'

'If I can help in any way?' Fillion asked.

'Thank you, I will think about that offer.' Patiir placed his hands back on the table. 'Enough of the politics. How do you like your new horse?'

'Patiir, I cannot thank you enough for all your kindness. The horse is too much,' said Fillion, concentrating on his sincerity.

'Not at all. Nadena needs a companion to ride with, and if you can master that horse then he's yours. He has a … fiery temperament.'

'I will see what I can do about managing that,' said Fillion.

'Speaking of which, it is time we should be going,' said Nadena.

'Indeed. I have another meeting, more opinions to shape,' said Patiir, standing. 'Go and enjoy yourselves, the first summer of our new peace is almost here. Let it warm your hearts and hasten the passing of bitter memories.'

CHAPTER 13

'Steady, now. You don't have to worry. She won't bite you.' Owen had a hand on the female eagle's flank, pulsing calming thoughts. In response he picked up positive emotions, suggesting she felt safe, amongst family.

'I know that. She just doesn't seem to want to eat much,' said Em, her hands holding a plate with scraps of meat. The eagle's head darted forward, shifting through it.

'Oh, she just wants to get a smell of it first,' he said, with a smile.

Em looked thoughtful. 'She is getting bigger, isn't she?'

'That she is. She is not far from Arno's size. And she'll get even bigger than him, the females always do.'

The eagle took a chunk of meat and threw it back into her throat. The eagle had grown quickly, and would soon be able to carry weight on her back. Arno had grown too, he'd added another foot to his wingspan. Their eating, in both quality and quantity since returning to Eagle's Rest, had improved dramatically.

Em put the plate down and looked at Owen, her face set.

'I want to be a rider,' she stated.

Owen nodded. He had been expecting this.

'Then you have to name her.'

Em's mouth fell open. Owen laughed.

'You weren't expecting me to roll over so easily, were you?'

Em shook her head. 'No, I … I didn't think you'd let me. I thought only Gifted could ride them.'

'It's been that way for years. But only because we make the best pilots. We can forge a bond with our birds and communicate with other Gifted, both within the squadron and on the ground. It means we can fight and fly better. But the fact is, I don't know of any other Gifted around here, so we'll just have to make do. We all learned to fly our eagles using our voices and the reins. Our Gifted abilities just made that process easier. You'll have to do it the hard way.'

Em beamed at him. 'And I get to name her?'

Owen removed his hand, bent down and picked up some rope, starting to coil it in his hands. 'That's how it starts. You pick her name and every day from then on, you use it whenever you can. She already likes you, you bring her dinner.' Owen was enjoying himself. Of late he'd only been happy when he was in the air with Arno. It was good to spend time with someone else who wasn't always thinking about where their next meal was coming from. Em was watching the eagle closely, her face frowning in concentration. If there was anyone who was meant to be a Rider, it was her. He had already spoken to Naimh to get her consent. She was at once both proud to think her adoptive daughter may be a Rider and extremely worried for her safety. He had assured her that in all his eighteen years, he had not seen a single life lost in training. He didn't mention the screaming terror you felt on your first take off from height.

'I've got a name,' she said brightly.

'That was fast.'

'I'd been thinking about it. I'd like to call her Taru.'

Owen thought for a moment. '*Little Wind*,' he said. 'She won't stay little forever.'

'I know, but when she's grown, they'll never hear her coming. I'll train her to be silent and swift.'

Owen grinned. 'Then Taru it is.'

Em stepped up to the she-eagle and put her hand out. 'Taru … 'she whispered.

Owen laid the rope back on to the floor and returned his hand to the eagle's flank. He pulsed images of the roost and its warmth and then the eagle in flight, '*Taru*,' he pulsed, '*Taru*.'

A short while later Owen left the roost by the newly installed door. A notion came to him and he halted.

'Hey, Erskine?' he shouted back inside.

Erskine looked around from the last stall on the left. 'Yeah?'

'I think Em might forget to feed the other eagles. She's rather taken with her new bird.'

Erskine grinned. 'You told her then?'

'Yep. Go and meet Taru when you have a minute.'

Erskine waved in acknowledgement.

Owen waved back and made his way towards the great hall. The new roof was just about finished. Two men balanced upon it wielding hammers, nailing slate tiles back into place on the apex.

'Murtagh, you are a man with hidden talents!' he shouted up.

A figure at the top made a dismissive gesture, brandishing his hammer. 'Piss off!' he shouted back.

'Owen, Owen,' a voice cried his name.

He turned and Anneli, a girl of sixteen, her red hair flying behind her, ran across the open square. She carried her spear, waving it in the air like a mad thing.

'Anneli, calm down, what's the matter?'

She stopped in front of him, red-faced and wide-eyed.

'Just take a breath,' he said.

'Not under attack, are we?' called down Murtagh.

'I don't think so,' replied Owen.

'Good, I'm too bloody tired. And we just finished this roof. There'd be no justice.'

Owen placed a hand on Anneli's shoulder. 'I am right, no attack?'

She nodded. 'The hunting party are back. And they brought a friend.'

Owen raised an eyebrow.

'Hey, Murtagh. You might want to come down for this,' he shouted, and motioned for Anneli to lead the way.

The entrance to Eagle's Rest had been rebuilt. A high stone wall framed a new wooden gateway, put together from a mixture of old and new timber. The gate was a single door, wide enough to accommodate one horse and rider at a time. Behind it stood a crude watchtower, giving a view of the approach from the slopes below. It gave them ample warning if anyone was coming but, Owen reflected, they still needed to create a fighting platform for the walls. It had been quite a debate as to whether they should even go above the surface but having the eagles meant the point was moot. It was never a question of not having them, the eagles were family. Murtagh had pointed out that if they were going to rebuild the roost, then they might as well build everything and die in comfort.

He pulled up the crosspiece bar, placed it vertically against the wall and opened the gate, stepping out into a freshening crossways breeze. Spring wildflowers grew by the side of the path, bending gently, their blooming unaffected. Coming over the last hilltop before the gently rising path to the peak was the hunting party. He saw a deer strung up on a pole, carried on the shoulders of two men. Naimh walked next to them carrying her longbow. The woman had quite an arm on her and Murtagh swore blind she had once laid him out cold. He was drunk at the time but still, Murtagh wasn't the sort to give up on a fight.

Two men walked in front. The first he recognised, Larson, the best tracker and hunter they had. Well into his fifties yet fit as a fiddle, he was hardened by his years in the wild. The other was well wrapped up in furs and Owen couldn't see who it was. There were three more following a little behind. That added to the mystery. The hunting party had left with four men, not five.

As they drew near he walked out to meet them, Murtagh jogging up to join him.

'Looks like we have a visitor,' he remarked, tucking his thumbs into his belt.

The group stopped in front of them. Larsen, lean and leathery, got straight to business.

'This here is Saul. Came across him a little way's to the west.'

Owen extended his hand and the man reached out and took it. His grip was strong, his eyes a dark green.

'Not much out west these days. You been all by yourself?' asked Murtagh.

Saul pulled back his hood, revealing a brown beard turning grey about the chin, and an angry white scar running down the length of his right cheek.

'Sometimes I wish I was,' said Saul with a rueful smile.

'He's been doing what we have, hunting for food down in the valleys,' said Larsen.

'There's more of you?' asked Owen.

Saul nodded. 'A fair few. Me and my two comrades almost got into a shootin' match with your bunch, we didn't expect to see anyone else around.'

'Where are your friends, then?' said Murtagh, his face stern, his tone openly suspicious. Owen wasn't worried that Murtagh wasn't welcoming; he had learned well enough it was his way of meeting new people. Ever the cautious one was Murtagh.

'The other two went back to the others, to tell them what was going on. I'm here to make sure this is all what Larsen said it was.'

Owen nodded.

'Hey, can we get inside? This bloody thing ain't light, you know,' said Ernan, the back end of the pole on his shoulders.

'Go on in. There's some stew in the pot,' said Murtagh. 'Naimh, that your doing?' he asked, gesturing with his thumb at the carcass.

Naimh smiled as she walked past. 'What do you think?'

Murtagh grunted. 'I think we'll be eating well tonight.'

Owen waited for everyone to pass and fell in behind them.

'My brother still stuck in eagle shit?' asked Ernan over his shoulder.

'Yes,' replied Owen.

'He might want to get his hands dirty with something else for a change,' said Ernan bitterly.

Owen didn't rise. Ernan was a naturally aggressive and sour man. The fact he spoke to Owen at all was an achievement of sorts.

The news of the hunting party's return had already spread and the small community were gathered around the entrance to the Great Hall. Murtagh's wife, Jenni, was standing at the steps.

'We've got ale on the table and food on its way,' she said.

'Where d'you want this?' asked Larsen, pointing at the carcass.

'Straight to the cold store. We can butcher it later,' Jenni replied.

'We'll be back out day after tomorrow,' said Larsen to Owen. 'Weather's letting up. I want to see what the herds are like. We might need to go further out.'

'Fair enough. Let's talk about it later.'

As the day ended and the air grew cold once more, everyone gathered in the great hall. A fire blazed in the central pit as the younger children ran around the edges, playing games, laughing and joking, bringing life to a once-dead place. Meanwhile the adults listened to Saul's story.

'How many of you are there?' asked Murtagh, arms resting on his legs, hands clasped together, his body leaning forward facing Saul.

Saul took a long drink of ale and sighed as he breathed out, wiping his lips with the back of his scarred and dirty hand. 'Gods of Old, that's good. Twenty. Not all from the same village. Kind of found each other after the bastards swept through.'

Murtagh exchanged looks with Jenni.

'Twenty. We can manage that.'

Saul raised a questioning eyebrow.

'You'll be wanting to stay, no?' asked Murtagh.

Saul stretched, pulled his face into a frown. 'I can't say, not without speaking to my party. You have to understand, we've been on the move for a long time. We've … *I've* become used to staying low. I know some will be afraid to come here. It's so open.'

'It's hard, I know,' said Jenni. She reached out a hand and touched his shoulder. 'But how long do we wait before we can stop living like savages?'

Saul shrugged. 'The thought of putting down roots again. After all that has happened. It's fear. We've lost almost everything.'

'Not here, though,' said Owen. 'This was my home before the war. They destroyed it, and look at it now. Almost back to the way it was. We have survived and we can start again.' He pointed to the door. 'And we have the eagles.'

Saul scratched his head. 'Never thought I'd see those birds again. Not the tame ones. You know, we've got a lad, he was just starting his training when the war reached us but he was still too green and his eagle wasn't big enough.'

Another Rider?

'He has the Gift?' Owen asked excitedly.

Saul nodded. 'I imagine that's one vote for coming here,' he said smiling.

Owen's mind raced. Another Eagle Rider! That would be a boon. Arno was getting stronger all the time, but he could do with help, having another Speaker would take the pressure off. They could share the load in scouting the surrounding area and helping hunt for game.

'What happened to his eagle?' he asked.

'Oh, it's about.'

'It's still alive?' asked Em, from her seat behind Owen, ever his shadow these days.

'Yes, when the lad escaped, he released his bird. They still communicate but he doesn't fly him.'

'We can change that,' said Owen.

'How far away are you?' asked Murtagh.

'I'd say about a day from here, found ourselves a cosy cave system down near a valley, well hidden, got running water too.' Saul looked quite pleased with himself.

'Are you heading back tomorrow?' asked Naimh from a little further down the table.

Saul nodded. 'That's the plan. My people will want to hear all about this place.'

'Fancy some company?' asked Owen. Arno would like a decent stretch.

Saul picked at his tooth with a grubby nail. 'Company with a different face, sure. You bringing your eagle with you?'

'I plan to,' said Owen. 'You can ride on his back. He can take the weight for a little while now.'

'Then call it half a day's travel.'

Later that night, after most had retired to the caves below, Owen stood with Murtagh just outside the closed doors of the hall, looking out over the square towards the gate. A dark figure was moving in the watchtower.

'I was thinking,' said Owen.

'I could see the steam rising from your brain,' said Murtagh drily.

Owen flushed a little. 'I found you, and then we found Saul. I know it's taken a while but do you think … '

'That there may be more Highlanders out there?' Murtagh interrupted. 'Yes, I do as a matter of fact. Stands to reason. This country is a treacherous bitch but our folk know how to survive in it. With summer on its way, I reckon more will be popping their heads out from whatever hidey hole they've been sheltering in.'

'And the enemy. Do you think they'll come back? Now that the trails are open again.'

Murtagh pulled an earlobe. 'The weather never stopped them before but I can't see why they would.'

'Then this is our chance. I can start ranging further out and start looking for other survivors. I can train up the young ones, get a squadron flying.'

'Heh. Ready to go to war finally, Owen?'

'Not on your life, Murtagh. We leave well alone and we don't provoke anyone.'

'Well, that's where you and I differ, Owen. I won't forgive or forget. The first damned dwarf, gnome, elf or ogre I see, I'll kill the bastard.'

They stood in silence for a moment. Owen realised that he had to broach a subject, something they'd been skirting around, avoiding it by making compromises and gaining agreements, but never actually talking about it.

'Murtagh, if these people do join us, that's going to be another twenty opinions to consider.'

Murtagh turned to Owen. His face looked hard yet his mouth was set at a strange angle, a cold smile. 'And you're thinking, who is going to be in charge of this rabble?' he said.

Owen swallowed and nodded, keeping his eyes locked with Murtagh. Whatever happened he had to look strong, even if inside he was shaking like a mouse.

'We don't agree on everything, do we?' asked Murtagh.

'No, especially when it comes to our future. You want war, I want peace,' responded Owen.

Murtagh folded his arms and leaned back against the doorframe, his eyes closed.

'If it hadn't been for you, we'd likely still be skulking around down below. I like it up here. Do you want to be Head Man?' he asked.

Owen didn't know what to say. A part of him didn't want to go anywhere near it, but his father led the people of this fort. He had a legacy to live up to.

'I can't do it alone,' he said.

'No, you probably can't. Tell you what. I'll watch your back, give you a steer when you ask for it or even when you don't. Fact is, I don't want to have to be in charge if I can help it. I took over because there was no one else left to do it.'

Owen nodded, still not sure what he had let himself in for.

'I'll speak to Naimh,' said Murtagh. 'She suggested you should take over. In fact, she damned well browbeat me into agreeing to it. She thinks highly of you and I trust her opinion, more than anyone's. We'll spread the word then get everyone together. Then you can talk to them. Trust me, there won't be anyone here naysaying you. That way if we start getting more folk arriving, they'll know straight out how things run.'

Naimh. Trust her to smooth the path. That she had spoken to Murtagh already made a lot of sense. She was smart and he'd seen how she could influence her brother. Owen felt relieved; things could have gone another way. 'Thank you. I appreciate it.'

'Just keep your head,' warned Murtagh.

'We need to start thinking more about our supplies. We got through winter and the hunting hasn't been bad, but if we have more mouths to feed ...'

'We'll sort it. Naimh and Jenni, they'll work something out. And this place had a lot more people living here before.'

'True enough,' agreed Owen. 'And that wall. It'll take just one ogre with a headache to knock it over. We need to make this place more defensible.'

Murtagh snorted. 'True enough.'

'I want to take Arno out and lead the search for survivors. I know most of the nearby forts and settlements. If someone survived, there is a good chance they'll have stuck close to them after the storm passed.'

'And between our people and Saul's we should be able to remember where most of the main towns and villages are in the Highlands,' stated Murtagh.

Owen took a deep breath and expelled it loudly through his nose. He looked out across Eagle's Rest. Things were starting to move quickly, but he was excited, hopeful even. They had a real chance here now. If they kept their heads down, the Highlands could survive, it would take years and generations, but they could do it. *What would those future folk know of now? Only what we tell them. And elves and dwarves have long lives and long memories. We cannot provoke them. But perhaps, one day, we can ask for peace.*

Part Four

SUMMER

CHAPTER 14

Amice pulled on his reins, his head swishing left and right. He snorted and stamped a hoof on the ground, pawing the earth and digging grooves in the sun-dried soil.

'Come on, Amice, play nice,' muttered Fillion. At least the bloody beast hadn't bolted when he had first climbed on. He felt beads of sweat forming on his brow as the sun bore down on him from a clear blue sky.

Nadena drew up beside him. Her chestnut mare was a far more pliant and steady animal.

'It's a good thing we walked them out of the city before you climbed on,' she said with a smile.

'Can you imagine what he would have done? He would have been off and into the Temple of the Gods before you could blink. And I would have been left on my bruised behind.' Amice reared up again. 'It still might happen!' he shouted, making a show of struggling to stay in the saddle.

Nadena laughed. 'You are quite a rider. I expected you to have fallen off already.'

Fillion smiled. 'I might have been a simple soldier, but this isn't a first time I've handled a horse. How about we just go for a nice walk, Amice.' He'd had plenty of time to get used to managing unsettled mounts over the last twenty years. This one would have to try a lot harder if he wanted to unseat Fillion. However it was important that he look unsettled in front of Nadena; Sabin wasn't so experienced with horses. The stallion grudgingly set off at a gentle pace.

'Where are we going anyway?' he called back.

Nadena made a clicking noise and her mare drew closer.

'Let's head into the woods. You horse won't be able to get much speed up amidst the trees.'

'You hope,' he muttered.

She laughed and kicked on, guiding her horse in a wide arc to get ahead of the stallion. They were to the west of the city, not far from the main road to Apamea that he had first travelled in on. There was a fair amount of traffic and plenty of folk out amongst the pastures, taking advantage of the sun. It was already a hot day and the sun had still not reached its zenith. They headed towards the woods that flanked the road. As they entered the shade the temperature dropped to a much more comfortable level. The horses made their way through low-lying fern and bracken, whilst a mix of oak and birch trees soaked up the sunlight with thick branches covered in green leaves. Small rays of light dappled the forest floor, the beams moving over the stallion and then playing across Fillion's bare arms and face, warm on his skin. It was very peaceful; even Amice appeared settled. He remembered a time from his childhood, just like this, when his family used to go for picnics. The three of them would sit on the bench of his father's wagon, enjoying the swaying motion as they trundled sedately along a worn, rutted path that the foresters used to travel into the deeper parts of the wood. Times had been good; he even remembered his mother being happy then.

He and Nadena let the horses guide themselves around the trees and bushes, content to meander without purpose. A prickle on the back of his neck made him glance over at Nadena. She was watching him.

'Yes?' he asked

'You looked a little distant,' she replied.

'Just thinking about home,' he said.

'Are you missing it?'

'It feels like I haven't seen it in an eternity.' *And I'll never see it again. Your kind made sure of that.*

'It's the war. I think it has affected all of us.' She paused for a moment. 'You could always go back.'

'No. I don't want to. I have enjoyed my time here, I am still enjoying it.' He looked at her, concentrating on her eyes. He smiled, and then looked away. 'Your family have been so good to me. I have grown to respect your father and his ideals. I would like to stay and be a part of that.'

'Really? You wish to get involved in government? That's is a change. What about your plan to see the rest of the Heartlands?' she asked.

'I still want to see them, but there is no rush. I have plenty of time. Besides, I suspect I have already seen the best, and the most beautiful places and people of the Heartlands.'

Nadena laughed. He stole another quick glance as he guided his horse around a shallow depression in the ground. She had two small spots of colour on her cheekbones.

'I'm not sure about that, Sabin, there are many wonderful things to see further east.'

'And I'll see them. Just not yet. Besides, I don't know if I'd want to go see them alone. Maybe you'd like to come?'

There was not an immediate reply. He imagined she was smiling.

'Perhaps. If you keep in my father's good graces, he might condescend to see us go together. He is quite traditional, you know. It's one thing to allow his family to head off west to the war. That was obligation. It would be quite another to see his eldest daughter go travelling with a man who is not her husband.'

'Well, that is something I'll have to work on,' he said.

That was the hook baited. It was the best he could do and he felt clumsy and awkward in the doing of it.

'I could speak to my father. You may have forgotten that Simeon is due to return home shortly. His time of service is coming to an end.' She didn't rise to feed on the hook so easily.

'I remember,' said Fillion. He hadn't forgotten at all.

'He'll need someone to help in his office. Scheduling meetings, making sure he is where he needs to be and when, that sort of thing. It's a little different to what you are used to,' she warned.

'I am a quick learner.'

'Oh, I don't doubt that. I've seen how you've been going out and inspecting the city. You know it as well as any who live here, I'd warrant.'

'I like to know my bearings,' Fillion said. He was surprised at that observation. He didn't know she had been keeping such a close eye on him over the last weeks. There was little else that he cared to do and time moved slowly for elves. Their pace of life was far more sedate, not like the mad rush of a human life. That rush also applied to him, as he had not inherited his mother's longevity. Though he might look like a young elf of a few hundred years, in reality he was a man of thirty years old and his features would keep aging in human terms. Try explaining that away.

'Speaking of which, we've been in here for a while. What say we get back out into the open and have a gallop? See how you do at that,' she said.

'I'll try not to disgrace you,' he replied.

She walked her horse towards him, stopping when they were shoulder to shoulder. Fillion half expected Amice to give her mount a nip.

'I've known these woods all my life but do you know your way out?' she asked with a gleam in her eye.

Of course he did, he was a captain of the Imperial Scouts. He didn't get lost.

'If I'm any judge,' he pointed a finger to his right, 'it's that way.'

Nadena raised a pencil thin eyebrow.

'Very good. But then I expect nothing less from a borderlands elf.'

'Masters of the forest, so we are,' he replied, grinning.

'Come on, then, let's stretch our legs a little and see where it takes us.'

'After you, my lady.'

'So gallant.' She laughed gaily and turned her horse. She tapped her feet into its flanks and it moved off at a steady trot, moving through the trees with confidence. He let her get a little way ahead then leaned forward in his saddle, bringing his mouth to Amice's ears.

'Listen to me, you little shit. You can forget all that elf training you've had. You work for me now. You follow orders, run when I say, stop when I say and kick any bastard who looks at me the wrong way. Do that and we'll get along fine. Piss me off and I'll break your legs. Understand?'

Amice's ears had pricked up and he snickered in response.

Fillion sat up and patted the horse's neck. 'Good lad. Consider yourself a member of the Imperial Scouts. Now, after them.'

He touched his heels lightly against Amice. The horse reacted instantly. Fillion held tight and let the horse run. He wanted to see how well this horse could move. It was quick, sure on its feet, and smart, anticipating well and maintaining its pace.

They burst out from the woods, just as Nadena emerged, with somewhat more control and grace. He heaved on Amice's reins, fighting against the stallion's instincts to run.

'You all right?' she called over.

'Yes,' Fillion said, a little breathlessly. He was still out of shape and his arse and thighs were aching. They were a little further south from where they had started. The road and gate were away to their right, a half-mile or so across a green, rolling pasture.

'Ready for something more exciting?'

'Ready when you are,' he replied.

'Good. See you back at the gates!' she shouted and kicked her mare into a gallop.

'Right, Amice, now you get your way. Heeyaw!'

He kicked hard and was jolted as Amice cut loose. He overtook the mare halfway back to the gates.

CHAPTER 15

Owen could appreciate that it was a gorgeous day, warm with a gentle wind and a sky covered in small, white fluffy clouds. Even so, you didn't go flying in the Highlands without proper clothing, something he ought to have remembered before getting on his bird without his headscarf. They were already several miles out and didn't have the time to turn back. They had a long way to go today and he wanted to make sure they had put some proper distance between them and home territory. Arno was having a good time, riding the thermals, whilst their new eagle companion, Ayolf, was working hard to carry his rider, young Jussi.

Hunched up, his body tensed, he was a good boy, doing as he was told, keeping Ayolf tight on his flank. Jussi was dressed in a thick cloak, high boots and at least three layers underneath. He had a mother to fuss over him, to make sure he was properly prepared, but who did Owen have? He was the chief now, the Head Man, and he had to think about everyone else's comfort first and his own last. At least he had Murtagh and Naimh to keep him honest. Murtagh had a look he'd give Owen whenever he started to voice a disagreeable notion. Owen had learned that the day-to-day stuff was best left to the big man and his sister. And it gave him more time to fly.

'*How is it going over there?*' he pulsed.

Jussi looked over. He wore a scarf around his lower face and his hood was up.

'*I'm okay.*'

'*Sure?*' The lad was barely ten and had had almost no time to develop his Gift before the Highlands were overrun. Owen felt a little guilty. From the time Saul had led his people in, he had just expected Jussi to

234

take on the mantle of a Rider. It would have been better if the lad had a choice but they wouldn't have that luxury for a long time to come.

'Yes, just … I'm holding on tight.'

Owen could see that. The boy was holding on damned tight and staring straight ahead. *He needs to relax, his bird needs to feel that.* They had been fortunate Jussi had already named the eagle and had spent a fair bit of time with him. With a bond already forged, Ayolf was happy to rejoin his friend even though he'd become used to fending for himself, finding and catching prey. It was another thing to not have to worry about, though it left Ayolf with an independent streak. The eagle hadn't been pleased when they'd tried to get a saddle on his back. A week's worth of effort and a lifetime of scars and scratches spread between Owen, Erskine and Jussi. No wonder the boy was stiff as a board.

'*That's fine. Ayolf is a good bird, he'll look after you. Just keep sending him your thoughts like we talked about. Lots of encouragement. Don't let him hear your fear. He is still young, it'll spook him.*'

'Yes, Owen. I will.'

'*Good lad. Keep it tight, stick with me.*'

Ranging a little ahead and high, Em and Taru soared along with powerful beats. Owen looked on with admiration at the way she had taken to the sky, with no doubts and no fear in her. She loved flying and she loved her bird. All summer they had been working together. She was becoming proficient in handling her eagle and Taru was growing stronger with each flight. They had the drills down and she handled her as well as Owen had when he had been at the same stage of training. *And all of this without the aid of the Gift.* She made up for that by spending every spare moment with Taru, mucking out her stall, bringing her food. She had even taken to sleeping with her in the roost. Murtagh hadn't been happy about that but Owen had talked him round with the help of Naimh. He'd explained it was no different when they were out in the field. The payoff was worth it and the two lasses had forged a strong bond. The only problem as far as Owen could see was that Em was still very young and headstrong. She had no sense of the dangers this world posed. Owen could talk until he was blue in the face but only experience could teach her that. There was another problem too: it was a bloody pain not being able to speak to her at any distance.

He put his fingers to his lips and blew a long, high note. Em turned her head and he raised his hand and beckoned her close. She waved. Taru's wings tilted and she drew back, gliding in close to his left side. Em had a big grin on her face. Damn but how could he blame her for that. It was the best feeling in the world.

'Em, you are getting too far ahead. Remember what we talked about. Someone needs to watch our rear,' he shouted.

'Sorry. It's not like there's anyone about.'

'That's not the point. Now get your arse back.'

'Yes, Owen.'

'And don't fall too far behind either. I can't help you if I can't see you.'

'Yes, Owen.'

She pulled lightly on the reins and they peeled off, dropping behind.

Owen shook his head. Em would, should, hang back, a little higher than them, flying in a wide circle. It was a standard drill. The best way to stop anything coming at them from their blindside. Each Rider would take a turn, dropping out of formation, scouting behind them then pushing their eagles to catch up with the rest, A few minutes later another Rider would pull out of formation and repeat the move, nice and slick. That was the theory anyway, but the practice of it with their fledgling group would take a little longer.

It was going to take a long while to put together a functioning squadron, but he had to start somewhere. This was Jussi's first long distance trip and his first night camping out. *If we don't count the months living in fear for his life.* Ayolf was big enough now to bear his smaller frame but it would be a test of his endurance. The other two birds from the 'Rest were growing fast but he still had no riders for them. No one else had come forward with a Gift. Perhaps some of the younger babes had it but they'd be no use for years. He needed somebody fast before the birds got too big and too wild. Whoever it was also needed an ounce of common sense, you needed that before you went anywhere near an eagle, friendly or not. He'd have to think about that.

He turned his head. Good. Em was completing a circle. She and Taru had put some distance between them even though they were flying at a sedate pace. He watched Taru's wings beat faster as she sped to catch up.

'No one but a flock of geese to the west,' she shouted back.

'Watch them. Crafty buggers,' he advised.

Em stuck her tongue out.

They landed a few hours before dusk. Owen had spotted a wide valley nestled between two peaks, running almost east to west. Perfect for catching the last of the sun's rays. He also caught sight of a stream, pouring down from the slopes, glistening in the fading light. As he led them down, it looked like a peaceful spot. A good place to live a life.

It turned out it had been. They glided over the burnt out remains of a small hamlet of no more than a dozen houses. He pinched his lips and snorted gently through his nose as they passed over them. You just couldn't escape it. Wherever you went, the war had left its mark. He took them further down the valley, landing them near to a small copse of trees, just yards away from the water. He settled Arno and went to supervise the youngsters. Em was fine, she was fussing over Taru, nattering away about how pretty the bird was. He would have had the crap ripped out of him for doing that if Bryce had been anywhere near. Young Jussi was having trouble with his saddle so Owen helped him undo the straps and lift it off.

'I don't think he likes wearing it,' said Jussi.

'It's just a little uncomfortable. He's had it on all day. Trust me, if he didn't want you to put it on him, he'd let you know.'

'He had a peck at my hand the other day.'

'Draw blood?'

'Yes, a little.'

'He's young, still trying to work out who's the boss. You'll be fine, just remember to tell him off next time he tries it.'

'Should I feed him?'

'Yes, I'd say he's earned it. Remember, we don't carry any bowls out here so just stand back and throw the food at him.'

Jussi nodded and went to his saddlebags and removed a sack. He stood in front of Ayolf, dug his hand into the sack and withdrew a hare, freshly killed and skinned. He held it by its hind legs and as it swung gently, Ayolf eyed it with interest.

'You get him to pluck it from the sky and I'll let you off watch tonight,' said Owen.

Jussi looked at him, doubt in his eyes.

'Really?'

'Really.'

Jussi screwed his mouth up in concentration.

'Ayolf! Here!'

He underarmed the hare, releasing the swing far too early. It landed a few feet short of Ayolf. The eagle looked at it for a few moments, cocked his head to one side and took a step forward. Head lowered, he started to peck and worry at the animal. Then his beak pierced the skin, and he started at it with gusto, tearing at the flesh and throwing back pieces of meat into his mouth.

The boy looked at Owen with disappointment, a red flush playing around his cheeks and neck.

Owen laughed and rustled his hair. 'Next time. Besides, there's nothing better than keeping watch in the middle of the night, with a fire to your back and your friends curled up beside you.'

'Yes, there is,' said Em walking up behind them. She was brandishing her crossbow.

'Ah. Fancy some practice, then?' he asked, having had every intention of making them do it anyway.

'I think you need some,' she replied.

Cheeky mare.

'Jussi. Go and fetch your bow.'

The boy raced off to dig out his crossbow. It was far too big for him and he did not have the strength to pull back the string yet. It was lucky enough that they had been able to find any bows at all amongst their hotchpotch armoury of weapons that folk had brought with them.

'What we going to shoot at, Owen?' asked Em.

'Let's set something up on that tree over there.' He pointed to a solitary pine a little way off, standing near to the stream. They couldn't afford to lose bolts, so better to find them in the grass than blundering around within a wood.

He went to retrieve his own bow from his saddle, grabbed a handful of bolts and followed Em. Jussi, clutching his oversize weapon tight to his chest, brought up the rear.

'I was thinking,' said Em.

Oh yes? Here we go …

'Why don't we set up some kind of moving target range. Something to practice on. Shooting at a tree isn't like shooting when you are moving.'

Quite the veteran. 'You're not wrong. It's nothing like it. It's about time you learnt.'

'I've been practicing anyway.'

'Really?'

'Yeah. I've been throwing rocks and stones at things as we fly past.'

Got to give her credit for trying at least. 'Any success?'

'Not really. By the time I let go we're usually past the target. I can't make Taru go any slower.'

'You don't want her to. You have to lead the target, work out where bolt and body will meet. Estimate your speed relative to theirs. It's not easy but you can get your eye in with practice.'

They stopped a little way from the tree and Em placed her bow down, put her foot in the small stirrup and hauled the string back.

'Ever hit anyone?' she asked.

Good question. Had he? Except for the wood elf, but that didn't count.

'I've fired a few bolts in action. It ain't easy.' *Nicely evaded.*

'And a spear?'

'Oh, I've broken a spear in battle.' He wasn't lying.

Em seemed satisfied. 'Shall I shoot first?'

'Go ahead.'

She raised the bow to her eyeline, sighted along its length, breathed deep and pulled the trigger. The bow twanged and the bolt gave a dull thud as it hit the tree a little left of centre.

She turned her head and smiled smugly.

'Hmm, not bad. At twenty paces you killed it dead,' Owen said, keeping his tone neutral.

Her eyes narrowed.

'Jussi. Your turn.'

Jussi stepped up and Em scowled at him. He brushed a lock of hair away from his face and raised the bow. He held his breath as he sighted, his face puffed out. He fired, the bolt going well wide. Owen watched it land thirty yards beyond the tree almost at the water's edge.

'See where it landed?'

'Yes,' said Jussi, pouting.

'Know what you did wrong?'

'I missed?'

'Don't get all sullen, Jussi.'

'Sorry.'

'You held your breath and you took far too long aiming. Your hand was shaking all over the place. Here, watch me.'

Owen pulled his own bow back, felt the string catch and placed a bolt into the groove.

'When you fire a crossbow, especially if you are moving, never take so long to fire it. The longer you leave it, chances are that you'll miss. Look at where you want to hit and bring your weapon up to meet your sight. Watch the target, not the bolt. If you want to and you have the time, take a breath. Relax, breathe out, then shoot. Chances are you won't even have time for that in a fight. Just think about where you want it to go. It sounds a little like Shaping, but it's not, it's instinct.'

He sounded like someone else. He remembered when the same advice had been given to him. He sounded like his father.

He fired. The bolt slammed into the wood three inches to the right of

Em's. He relaxed his shoulders. If he'd fluffed that he couldn't have borne the smirks. He had a command presence to maintain. *Thank you father. Your training worked. I can still beat children in a shooting contest. You'd be so proud.*

They carried on with practice for another hour, by which time the sun was truly low on the horizon and they risked not seeing where the bolts fell. Owen decided it was best to call a halt. Em had started to get a bit sloppy towards the end. She was tiring but blamed everything else for it; it was too dark, Jussi was putting her off, her bow wasn't working right. For his part, Jussi did improve a little; he started hitting the tree once he'd gotten the hang of the breathing. Owen was getting hungry and set to building a fire whilst Em collected more firewood and water and Jussi prepared the night's dinner. It was not long before they had a decent blaze going and a pot suspended above the flames.

'Nice work on this hare,' said Owen running his finger round the bowl and licking off the last of the stew.

Jussi shrugged. 'I learned how to do it last year.'

'Good skill to have.'

'Can we make him the squadron cook?' asked Em

'We could. I haven't seen you cook yet.'

'You don't want to.'

Owen smiled. He sat back against a tree, looking into the fire. A few yards away the flames gleamed off Arno's eyes, the bird watching him.

'You alright old friend? Happy times eh?'

Arno blinked.

Owen looked at the two youngsters. Em was in her element, happy and relaxed. Jussi was doing okay too. Between the pair of them they made one halfway decent rider. Or at least one as good as him.

'What do you think of your first night as a rider, Jussi?'

He scratched his head.

'I enjoyed it. I liked it when we just flew straight. I always feel a little sick whenever Ayolf starts weaving about, like he does around the 'Rest. The wind helps though. I like it on my face.'

'I used to get that too. The world falls out of your stomach when they take off. It helps if you look straight ahead, keep your eye on the horizon. I heard it said that it's a lot like sea sickness. Not that we have many boats around here.'

He wondered about his friends and how they were coping with life on the open seas. He hadn't thought about Cadarn or the others for a long time. He had even stopped picturing Jenna. For all he knew they might have struck land. They might even be dead. It didn't do to dwell on these things. Here and now was what mattered.

'You two both have your skills and I'm glad of it. But this is just your first taste of nights out. We need to train as a squadron. Learn to work together, anticipate moves, have each other's backs. That's only half of it though. You both had to live rough not so long ago but you also had help, folk who could do things. I'll expect you both to learn to be self-sufficient, learn how to survive in the wild, catch food, build fires, find shelter. When you are ready you will be flying patrols, watching our borders, looking for any signs of survivors or the enemy. There won't be enough of us to fly in pairs for a while, so you will have to rely on your own wits, judgement and most importantly, your birds. Look after them and they'll get you out of trouble.'

Both of them nodded, solemn expressions on their faces. Then Em grinned. 'When can I start my first patrol?'

Owen sighed. 'Not yet, you can't. You get that range built, get some shooting practice, get better. Then I need to teach you the basics of spear work.'

'I get to learn to fight?' Em rubbed her hands together. 'I'm already looking forward to it.'

'Can I learn too?' asked Jussi

'Yes, you too. But not yet. You and your bird need to grow a little first.' Jussi looked crestfallen.

'Tell you what, though. We made good time today, faster than I thought. We'll have some time in the morning. Why don't we try some shooting on the move? We've got a good strafing run along this valley and you can follow the line of the stream to the tree.'

'Now you're talking,' replied Em.

Owen stretched and stifled a yawn. A wave of tiredness washed over him and suddenly his eyes felt very heavy.

'Right. That's it. I'm done for the night. Jussi, you get the first watch.'

'Oh, yeah, right.'

'Next time, make sure your bird catches the food,' he suggested. Owen winked at Em and lay back on his saddle.

Owen opened his eyes and gazed into the night sky. He studied grey clouds that hung in the air, holding their station amidst the stars. One of the two moons glowed bright. It was Bendis, rather than Arma, because of the large black mark visible to the bottom left of its sphere. Highland legend said they were the homes of the Gods, two families that each held a moon and waged war against each other. But that never made sense to Owen because all the Gods were supposed to live on the sun and that's where the Emperor ascended to on his death. And to add to the confusion, he was sure the Celtebarians said the Gods lived on other worlds that could only be reached by sailing off the edge of our world. Well, whoever wanted to undertake that voyage was welcome to it. The world he knew was big and dangerous enough as it was. The thought struck him that maybe the fleet had done that very thing. That Cadarn, Bryce, Jenna and the others were looking down on him. Bryce was probably making a sarcastic comment about Owen's current state, and the bugger would likely be right.

He hadn't been woken up and Em was due to rouse him when it was time for his watch. A glance at the small shape swaddled in a blanket on the far side of the fire confirmed that Jussi had handed over to her. He looked for Em. She wasn't sitting next to the flames even though it was her job to keep the fire fed. It still crackled steadily and the wood looked like it had not been burning long. Perhaps she was behind the tree they had camped under or maybe she'd gone to relieve herself. That was probably it. He rolled his body over, his face catching the heat of the fire. He closed his eyes and listened to Jussi's heavy breathing which was punctuated by the occasional grunt or snuffle. At least he wasn't snoring.

He opened his eyes again. He couldn't relax. He wanted to check to see if Em had reappeared. She was light on her feet so it was simple enough to believe he hadn't heard her come back. There was still no sign of her. He pushed himself off the ground by his elbow to get a better look. He opened his eyes wide then squinted, directing his gaze towards the eagles. Em might well be visiting Taru and he could imagine them huddled together for warmth, but it was impossible to tell from where he was lying. *Right. Fine.* He was wide awake now so he pulled the blanket off him, wrangled his boots on to his swollen feet and stood up. Damn but it was chilly. He gathered up his spear and thought about taking his crossbow, but it seemed like overkill. The fact of the matter was, the fire would have already seen them dead if they were truly in danger.

He walked across to the eagles, and gently probed Arno's mind. He was at peace, the bird fast asleep, no doubt dreaming of high, soaring peaks and tasty rabbits. Taru and Ayolf were just the same. He circled round the trio but there was still no sign of her. *Where are you, Em?* He pulsed his questions around him, hoping he might catch her. He didn't want to start shouting out for no reason. There was no movement, nothing to suggest she'd heard him, but that might just mean she wasn't close enough.

They had the stream to one side and the valley ahead and behind them. The eastern edge of the valley was fifty yards to their right. He might as well start there. As he approached, he zigzagged, studying the ground, looking for signs of disturbance. Not far from the slope he found what he was looking for, grass had been bent and squashed into a footprint sized shape. Up ahead the ground started to rise gently, and was sparsely covered by trees, bushes and shrubs. He followed the direction of the footprint and headed up the slope. Here and there he saw evidence of Em's passing: scuffed soil, a broken flower stem. Yet still no sign of the girl. Halfway up the slope he came upon a rocky outcropping, little more than a thin ledge of soil and stone that jutted out from the slope. He climbed up on to it, using his spear as a support.

From the ledge Owen looked out across the valley. He could see the stream, a gently sparkling vein tracing its way from the valley head and disappearing westwards. The fire was a warm glow, constantly shifting in the shadows of the tree above it. The eagles were an indistinct but obvious shape. Anyone that flew above or passed over into the valley would spot the camp instantly. He shook his head. Maybe he had been too careless in his placement. They should have found something more sheltered from view.

'Nice isn't it?' came a quiet voice behind him. He turned quickly, his spear dropping into a guard position. Em was perched just above the ledge, kneeling against a boulder that looked like it might roll off at any second. Her crossbow was cradled in her arms.

'Em.' He shook his head, allowed his racing pulse to settle, the burst of cold dread to fade. 'You scared me.'

'Sorry.' Em jumped down on to the ledge, a few small pebbles and chunks of soil following in her wake.

'What are you doing up here?'

Em shrugged.

'I thought I saw something up here. Watching us.'

'And?'

'Nothing. I saw some animal tracks, probably a deer.'

'Lucky for us.' His shock was gone. It was replaced by anger.

Owen dropped his spear and stepped in close to Em, placing his hands on her shoulders, gripping them tight.

She made a pained face. 'Ow.'

'That was stupid, crazy and dangerous. If you thought you saw something, then you should have woken me.'

'But nothing happened.'

'That's not the point!' He dropped his hands and breathed deep.

'What if there had been something there? It didn't need to be an elf or a gnome. It might have been a wolf, even a bear. You think your bow would have stopped it?' He slowed his voice, trying to stay calm, thinking how Cadarn used to handle matters.

'If I had got a shot off … '

'Just one shot isn't going to bring down a bear and I would have been too far away to do any good. And I have to think of Jussi and the eagles. What should I do? Do I come save you and risk them instead?'

Em was quiet a moment. 'Sorry, I didn't think.'

Owen shook his head. 'You are too damned brave for your own good, Em. You need to think about the consequences. We have to look out for each other, watch each other's backs. I can't do that if I don't know where you are.'

'Yes, Owen.'

'Now, come here.' He held an arm out. He needed a hug, a chance to show her that he cared.

Em lowered the bow to her side and stepped in close, putting an arm around him and resting her head on his shoulder.

Owen smiled.

'Sorry, Owen,' she whispered. 'I don't want to let you down.'

'You didn't.'

He squeezed her a little tighter, and she squeezed back.

'You know, you sounded just like my father, then.'

That shocked him a little. *Me, a father?* Now that he thought about it, Em did feel like family to him now. There was an obligation, a desire to protect as well as nurture. *Is that good in a Squadron Leader, or a Head Man?* Carrying the burden, knowing that he would have to ask folks to put their lives at risk, brought home just what was expected of him now.

And how do I protect her when I let my fear get the better of me?

'So does that mean you are going to listen to me when I tell you to do something?' he asked.

'I'm not sure of that, Owen. I seldom listened to him.'

Owen laughed. 'There's a surprise.' He let her go and looked out across the valley. His eyes caught sight of a spider's web, revealed by moonlight, almost circular and strung between two unearthed roots. A few drops of moisture were held within the strands. He smiled again.

'Come on. Let's head back and you can get your head down.'

Em scratched her nose.

'You sure? I don't think it's time yet.'

'Trust me, I'm in no fit state to sleep. You scared me good.'

'Silent and stealthy killer, just like Taru, huh?'

'Something like that,' he replied. As they worked their way down the slope, he wondered what would happen to her when she was asked to make her first kill. A part of him hoped it wouldn't change her, wouldn't harden her, but war did that to everyone.

CHAPTER 16

Father Michael warmed himself by the fire even though it wasn't cold. The late summer days were being kind to them but Baron Ernst liked to maintain a fire throughout the year. To enjoy such comforts as a roaring fire, to be bathed in its heat and protection, was a feeling Father Michael had not enjoyed for a long time, nor had he been sure he would again. For too long his nights had been bitter, often wet and fearful, stuck in the bowels of a pitching, rolling ship. He stood and retrieved from his pocket a small object wrapped in cloth. He turned and looked at Baron Ernst. The Scotian sat on his chair, eyes wide, yet staring at nothing. Father Michael unwrapped the cloth, revealing a pebble-sized chunk of meat covered with gristle and fat. He gently laid the cloth on the chair's left armrest and knelt over Baron Ernst, studying his face. Father Michael knew of two death faces: the face of surprise and the face of calm that often descended on those with a chance to comprehend what was happening. Death had come as a surprise to the Baron.

Father Michael took hold of the Baron's chin in one hand, tilting the head back a little. With the other hand he forced the meat into the Baron's mouth, using his fingers to push it back, deep into the cavity, down into the neck. Once the chunk was lodged securely, he withdrew his hands, let go of the head and wiped his fingers on the cloth, throwing the material into the fire once done. He watched it catch and flare briefly before shrivelling and burning away to ashes.

He looked around the room. It was very well appointed for something so quickly constructed. A large bed sat in one corner next to the fire, a writing table and a bookcase in the opposite corner. Behind Father Michael a wardrobe was up against the wall beside the door. A small table beside the Baron's chair held two fine decanters and a carafe of ruby-coloured wine. There were two small crystal wine glasses, one of which was half-full of the red liquid. He had been poured a glass even though he had declined. A second was empty, the mark of greasy lips around its rim. Father Michael took his glass and carefully poured the wine back into the carafe. He then he returned the glass to the table. Father Michael took one more look around the room and nodded. Everything seemed in order, nothing out of place, no signs of a struggle. It was the best he could do, he was no assassin.

Father Michael raised his arms high, his sleeves dropping back, revealing a number of gouges, raw and wet upon his right arm. The Baron had struggled but Father Michael had gotten a good grip around his neck. The wounds stung a little, but he was easily able to ignore the pain. Years of conditioning had made him very good at that. A notion struck him. The Baron looked too peaceful. He returned to the body and picked up the Baron's hands. The nails were well kept but not short and they had served well enough to tear his own skin, a little of his blood and skin was packed under the nails. He dropped the left hand, and using the right alone, started picking out the fingers and digging them forcefully in the flesh around the Baron's neck, scratching and pawing against the skin. A little blood oozed from the vertical marks. He switched to the left hand and did the same to that side. Once done, he stepped back to survey his work. *Better.* That's how a dying man should look. Fighting for life.

Father Michael turned away and strode to the door, stepping out into the night. A short distance away, a guard stood by a small, desultory looking brazier. He looked around as Father Michael approached. He was a hard looking sort, displaying no deference or manners to a man of the faith.

'The Baron bids that he is not disturbed further this evening,' said Father Michael.

The guard nodded. Father Michael could feel the man's gaze upon his back as he walked away from the Baron's modest but solid cabin. It irked him a little. *Why do I feel so damned uncomfortable? What I did had to be done.* He had killed so many and the death of this man should have meant nothing to him. Perhaps his faith had altered his point of view. Maybe that's what happened to you when you found your God.

Around him the town was quiet. There were no lights but for the occasional fire in the distance. He could see one or two people out on errands. He strode along the muddy trail, keeping his head down, passing crude lean-tos, shelters and cabins. The past two months had been a flurry of activity as the survivors had disembarked and set about building a new home. The Emperor had named the place New Tissan. It was a name with a lot to live up to.

The Church had displayed great foresight during the evacuation. Tradesfolk and their families had been accommodated aboard the Imperial ships, and the lords had seen fit to do the same. A small force of carpenters had begun work on constructing dwellings. The makings of a town, not unlike the countless small communities that lay upon the old King's Highway, had appeared. There was a temple, a granary, stables, smithy and even a tavern, all set around a central square hub. Even with all this industry, things came together slowly. Most people still lived under canvas, placing their homes along routes heading east, west and south from the square. Some had even elected to stay aboard those ships that still floated. Of the fleet, only the Emperor's fighting boats and the sturdier merchantmen remained, numbering no more than a dozen. All the rest had been beached and stripped down for their timber, their sails and ropes being put to good use in the building effort.

Father Michael entered the square from the southern side and cut across, heading north. There were lights and voices coming from the tavern, off-duty sailors and soldiers for the most part. There was a bark of laughter as the tavern door opened, and a man in the livery of the Emperor's guard staggered out and around to the side of the building while undoing his britches. Father Michael had not realised just how much ale had been salvaged in the evacuation. He had mentioned this to the Admiral, who had laughed and clapped him on the back. 'You think the love of the Emperor will keep these men warm at night? You have to be pragmatic, Father.'

Opposite the inn, on the eastern side, was the temple. It looked little more than a long, low barn. Father Michael turned towards it and entered through the single door, into an interior lined with benches. At the far end was a crude altar and upon it was the sun symbol. Taken from the old chapel in the Imperial palace, it had survived the evacuation and had made it unscathed across the seas. Almost a foot in diameter, the sun was made of gold, its base silver. There was a time when he would have been more impressed by the sheer value of the thing rather than what it represented. The temple was dark and a little cold as he made his way along the central aisle. He navigated by the single candle upon the altar directly behind the sun that made the symbol look like it was glowing, its meaning and power emphasised. Behind the altar was another door. He knocked and waited. He heard footsteps on the other side and the door opened inwards, a little more light spilling into the temple. Arch Cardinal Vella stood in the threshold.

'Come in, Father.'

Father Michael bowed his head and stepped through into the Arch Cardinal's cell. Like the Emperor, he had chosen to live simply, the room containing a bed taken from *The Fist of Tissan,* a chair and table, and a chest containing his few belongings.

'Would you like some water, Father?' asked the Arch Cardinal.

'Yes, I would.'

Vella went to the table, where a clay jug and two cups rested. He filled one and handed it to Father Michael who drank deep.

The Arch Cardinal lowered himself into the chair and clasped his hands together, resting them on the surface. 'I am sorry I have nothing else to offer you, but at least water is one commodity we are not short of.'

'Thank you, it is all I need,' replied Father Michael.

There was a pause.

'Is it done?' the older man asked.

Father Michael nodded. 'Yes.'

'Are you well?'

'I … I feel uneasy about what I have done tonight.'

'Go on.'

'My Blessed Emperor is my salvation and his light fills me with joy and purpose. But to kill a man in such a manner, it feels … wrong. Before, my opponents have always faced me. This is work I feel ill-suited to.'

'I understand. However it is work that must be done and you are the one who has been chosen to do it. Were you seen?'

'Yes, there was a guard out front. I behaved as a visitor might and left calmly.'

'A shame but we always knew that may be the case. We could not risk bribery or persuasion. There must be no one else who knows or even guesses at the work we undertake. The Gifted will likely investigate this, and a servant can easily expose their knowledge, drawing unwanted attention.'

'Then will the Gifted not find the guilt in me?'

'You are a man with a lifetime of burdens. How can they tell the difference? You were sent to speak to Ernst by me. You will be the last man to see him alive but you are a man of the cloth and that will protect you. You are trusted and for those that look, the Baron will appear to have died of natural causes. That is what will be believed.'

Father Michael nodded.

'You are right, of course.'

'Only you and I will ever know about this. Fifty years from now, it will not matter. Hmmm?' The Arch Cardinal sighed. 'Perhaps it is over. Baron Ernst was always the chief agitator, the one who had the most influence. I believe, without his voice, the other lords will fade away.'

'Will they not still be on the council?' Father Michael asked.

'For now. But I am certain the Emperor will start to see things differently. We already have far more influence with the court than we have ever had before. We have Llews to thank for that. The Empress has become most reliant upon him.'

'That is good.' Father Michael was relieved that there was another, more intelligent mind who could help advise the Imperial family, someone clearly more suited to the role than he could ever hope to be.

'Indeed it is. I was fearful that we might become a people obsessed with vengeance and retribution. When the Emperor talked of returning home to Tissan, I thought we would have to undertake far more extreme action. Yet he has quieted, has he not?'

'The Emperor is certainly most interested in this new land. He wants us to go riding the day after tomorrow.'

Arch Cardinal smiled. 'How are your riding skills?'

'I have none. Perhaps I shall ride in the wagon.'

'Just as long as you stay close. I have listened to the reports brought back from the eagles. This land is benign. It resembles the Riverlands in so many ways. Yet we must stay alert. We do not know what creatures have thus far stayed hidden from us. Keep the Emperor safe. Keep his mind turned towards the possibilities this new land has to offer. Peace must prevail at any price.'

That price is high. The thought came unbidden and he had not expected to ever entertain it.

The Cardinal put his hand under Father Michael's chin. 'Go and get some rest. You have done good work this night.'

'I will.'

Father Michael stood to go.

'Oh, Father. I have one more thing for you.' Vella stood and went to his chest, rummaging inside it for a few moments. 'Here we are.'

He lowered the chest lid and turned towards Father Michael, holding a small book. He handed it over. It was covered in faded red leather. Gold stitching ran along the four borders.

'*The Journey of Simon of Stonebridge,*' said Vella. 'It seems appropriate that you read it now.'

'What is it about?' asked Michael. He opened the book, and found a folded folio, a map of the Empire. The script was small, the handwriting flowery and quite archaic.

'It is an account of one of the first true missionaries of the Church. Simon was a pious man who travelled across Tissan bringing the word of the Emperor's light. Indeed much of what was to become the Empire had yet to be conquered. Yet Simon was an eloquent and charismatic fellow. As we set out to tame this new land, you might draw inspiration from his words. His recounting of how he dealt with the savage tribes of the Plains is particularly interesting.'

'Thank you, Arch Cardinal' said Father Michael.

Vella waved him away. 'Enjoy it, and learn from it.'

Father Michael left the temple, heading north towards the Imperial quarter, as it was now known. It was set a little apart from the rest of the town, on a path leading towards the river. Ahead of him, ringed by torches, was the Imperial pavilion. No longer used as quarters, its role was to deal with the administration of the Empire, such as it was. Behind it were four structures, forming a crude parade square, with enough space for a large number of people to gather. The building at the northern end of the square was the Emperor's cabin, made from ship timbers with a shallow sloping roof, two windows and one door. It was raised a little above the ground and had a veranda on the front. The Emperor, in a show of modesty, had insisted his home not be too grand or overwrought. Once complete, it was no grander than the building the late Baron Ernst had lived in. The Emperor himself had dubbed it his 'lodge'. To the right of it was an almost identical cabin, although half again as large. This was for the Empress. It had, he was led to understand, three rooms rather than the two that the Emperor occupied. Running along the eastern side of the square was a barn that housed their small herd of horses.

To the left side was a far bigger building, a long, low construction with a flat roof. This was where the Gifted were quartered. They all lived in a communal space, bunks arrayed in a line. It was similar to how Father Michael used to live in the arena, the fighters of a specific stable would all be housed together. It was quite a strange sensation to have been given his own private space when he had joined the priesthood. Nothing more than a cell, with enough space for a bed and small wardrobe, at first it had felt more like a cage than a privilege. By the time the war had forced him on, he had rather begun to enjoy the solitude. Now he was fortunate to have a small tent to the rear of the Imperial buildings, one of a number arrayed along another track that led to the river. The tents housed the functionaries and remaining military personnel of the Imperial administration. That he had such a place was recognition for his role within the inner circle.

As he passed by the barracks block, the door opened and a short, hooded figure stepped out.

'Oh!' The figure jumped back. It had a young female voice.

'My apologies,' mumbled Father Michael. The figure raised a hand to its chest and laughed gently.

'No, Father. I am sorry too.' She pulled her hood back revealing a young woman, perhaps in her late teens, her dark brown hair cropped short into a bob around her ears. She bore the mark of a Speaker upon a delicate looking chin and her eyes, a startlingly deep green, regarded him with curiosity.

'I was just going for a walk. Sometimes my head hurts and I like the peace and quiet,' she said,

'I understand,' he said and continued on his way.

'You are the Prince ... um I mean the Emperor's priest, aren't you?' she called.

I'm tired. I want to sleep. He stopped. 'I have that honour, yes.'

'Ah, I thought you were.' She walked up to him, her head looking up at the night sky.

'I'm Ellen. I'm a Gifted,' she said, almost as an afterthought.

'I noticed,' he replied.

'Yes. You probably did!' she said with a laugh. It was a bright, happy sound, the like of which he had scarce heard since this journey had begun. It clashed harshly with his mood and the knowledge of the deed he had done this night. To take a life, even for the Emperor, should not be celebrated, or forgotten. He felt he had no right to hear such a sound.

'I am going back to my lodgings,' he said, hoping that would end the conversation.

'I'll walk with you.'

I am overjoyed.

He continued on his way, Ellen at his shoulder.

'Is it true what they say about you?' she asked.

'What is that?'

'You were an arena champion. You killed hundreds of men.'

And the occasional woman.

Father Michael shook his head. 'I was no champion. Just a killer.'

'But now you are a priest.'

'Yes. And the better for it.'

'I was just a girl until a year ago.'

You still are.

'Then the Cardinal found me and started my training.'

'Cardinal Vella?'

'No, Cardinal Yarn.'

'Have you ever been in service?' he asked, referring to the duties the Gifted undertook.

'No. I am still learning to control my Gift.'

The reached a row of tents. A gentle breeze blew across them, the fabric snapping and rustling.

'What about combat training? You will need that if you are to protect the Emperor,' he advised.

'I've learnt a little, but the Cardinal wanted me to focus on Speaking first. I've got a fair bit of catching up to do. She has been very good to us. All of us.'

They had reached his tent. He stopped and studied her.

'I am sure. There are so few of you left.'

'There are,' agreed Ellen. 'My brothers and sisters were all saved by the Cardinal when the Monastery fell. We owe her our lives.'

'We all owe the Blessed Emperor our lives,' he replied, sternly.

'Yes, of course,' she said with a smile.

He felt a little unnerved by that smile. 'Excuse me. I am up early tomorrow. The Emperor wishes to go hunting.'

'Sleep well, Father,' said Ellen, pulling her hood back over her head. She started walking away from the tents and out into the night. Father Michael watched her go and experienced a measure of concern.

'Hey,' he called after her. 'You should be careful and not stray far.'

She looked back, her face in shadows.

'It's fine, Father. If anything happens I'll shout. My brothers and sisters will hear me. I guarantee it.'

With that she disappeared into the night. He shook his head. She was an odd one, not like the other Gifted, and there was lightness to her humour. She reminded him a little of Cardinal Yarn.

Father Michael entered his tent and lowered himself on to his cot, reflecting on how truly odd the Gifted were. In his hand he still held the book. He had almost forgotten about it. He pushed his tent flap back in order to see better and opened the book again, selecting a page at random, scanning the words. The language was unusual, less formal than many of the texts he had learned to read with. His grasp of the written word had improved greatly and he understood many of the longer phrases and was able to appreciate tone and intent. He had even started to think differently, the new words helping to make sense of his thoughts. He decided he was looking forward to reading this tale. As long as he survived the investigation into Ernst's death and the horse ride the Emperor had planned.

CHAPTER 17

The flame coming from the small tallow candle was pitiful. It was smoky and smelly and gave about as much light as a star on a cloudy night. It flickered weakly in the small notch in the wall, just off to the side of the rock face where Hepton, his face a shadowed grimace, swung his pick.

Cade squatted and got two hands under the jagged, vaguely rectangular rock. She leaned back a little and pushed up with her legs, keeping her back straight. That was the way, always push with the legs never pull with the back. She'd learned that the hard way a long time ago. Having a strained back muscle was not fun. She'd been laid up for two weeks once and damned near starved to death in the process. There'd been no one to look after her and no one had cared. She was just another stray who was no use to anyone. Still it could've been worse. She made it through and knew better because of it.

Cade crab-walked away from the rock face back along the short side passage towards the main shaft. Theirs was a new tunnel, its height barely more than five feet. It was just as well she was so short. Her hair brushed the uneven ceiling above as she shuffled along in the near darkness. Behind, her fellow workers were not so lucky. Hepton was six foot if he was an inch and he had to work on his knees wielding his pick at odd angles, unable to get any real strength behind the swings. Rosta, the third member of the team, was shorter but clumsy. The daft bugger kept smacking his head against the ceiling and he had already bloodied himself twice. Though, to be fair, the passage was jagged and uneven and had been carved out by inexperienced human hands. It was, all things considered, a pretty shit job. But getting to the seam was all that mattered.

The main shaft was in a much better state. It had been hollowed out with far greater precision and, if not exactly smooth, it was well rounded. That was all dwarf work; they had pride in their business and they had an investment. Dwarves never used other dwarves as slaves, she knew that much. They treated their workers more like business partners. In that respect they were a damned sight better than any human merchant or businessman she had ever met. Not that those rules applied to the new workforce. Her dwarf masters didn't care about workmanship or their safety. Only results.

The main shaft was also well shored up by stout beams spaced out at regular intervals. It was not so with many of the human-made passages and the dwarves would hold back on making good until they were sure it was worth the effort. The tunnel she was in had yet to produce much of note, so no wood for them. At the end of the passage was a mine-cart. Emerich, a well-built farmer from the Celtebarian borders, stood behind it. She stopped by the cart and he moved around to help her lift it over the lip.

'Reckon that's enough,' he said.

'You want a hand?' she asked.

'Sure.'

Together they went to the rear of the cart and braced themselves against the weight. Emerich reached down to release the brake. Immediately Cade felt the weight pressing against her and she pushed back, locking her arms in place, her feet planted firmly on the ground.

'Alright?' asked Emerich.

'Yeah,' she grunted.

'Right and ... push.'

She leaned into the cart and took a step forward, her arms bending. She forced them forwards, feeling her chest tighten. The cart started to shift, slowly at first, then a little quicker as the momentum gathered. The slope of the main shaft was not too steep here and all they had to do was keep moving forward. Always keep going forward, that was the trick. There was another candle on the front of the cart, the light helping to guide their way. It flickered and flared as the cart wobbled and shook and its light played off the shaft's sides, the shadows weaving and shifting around them. Sometimes they passed the openings of further tunnels, either empty or worked out, just dark black holes that the light couldn't penetrate.

Occasionally they passed by another group within a side tunnel, their candlelight a flickering orb, their shapes flitting around it like moths. In other, deeper tunnels, there was just a faint glow and the sound of distant echoing voices and the clang of metal on rock. Sometimes there was no light at all and just the faintest rustle, like the scuff of a leather boot upon the floor. It was enough to make you believe in ghosts and the unquiet dead. Another light appeared ahead of them, nothing more than a pinprick, a point fixed in the dark. Yet as it drew nearer the light moved, swaying left and right with the rocking of the cart it was attached to. Within a few moments the lights met and merged, the other cart's crew thrown into shadowed relief.

'Afternoon,' called Issar. His face was a blotchy mess.

'Is it?' asked his companion, a sour faced woman called Miriam, who had long, lank grey hair, not that Cade could see it in this light.

'Yeah. Mid-afternoon I'd say,' replied Issar.

'How do you know that?' asked Cade as the carts continued past each other.

'Just got a good sense of time,' Issar called back. 'It's important to keep track. It lets me know when my next break is. Gives me something to look forward to.' His voice echoed back up the shaft towards them.

'Lets him know how much time he has for slacking,' muttered Emerich.

'I heard that!' Issar called back, his voice containing the faintest hint of wounded pride.

They continued on, the cart scratching and creaking as they went. The shaft started a gentle turn to the right and Cade felt the gradient increase and the pressure on her arms and legs starting to build.

'Last push,' growled Emerich. Together they increased their speed, gaining a little extra distance before the cart slowed on the ascent. Their breath was laboured. Cade felt a bead of sweat roll down her spine and into the crack of her arse. It wasn't a comfortable sensation. This part of the mineshaft was only a hundred yards long, but she felt every sodding yard of it. A glow emanated from the top where it opened out into the central chamber that all the shafts radiated from and where the carts were gathered.

With her thighs burning, they emerged into the chamber lit by several lanterns hanging off the walls. The difference they made was significant. Her eyes could make out every feature, every cart, every human going backwards and forwards from the shafts, every dwarf guard standing silent and grim. The floor here was roughly flat and level and Cade felt the relief in her legs as the strain disappeared.

'Thanks, Cade. I'll take it from here,' said Emerich quietly.

She nodded and released her grip, watching him push it onwards. Their Accounter, she had learned his name was Geir, was examining the contents of another cart and on seeing Emerich, beckoned to him. Emerich pushed it towards him and Cade walked along with him. Two guards stood a little ways behind Geir and one of them caught her eye. He scowled and made to take a step towards her. That was it, she had dawdled long enough, and they didn't like it when she dawdled.

'Yeah, yeah. I'm going.' She waved her hand in acknowledgment and made her way back down the shaft.

No guards were down there with them. There was nowhere to run or hide anyway. Geir would often come down to inspect progress, designate new digging points and examine likely veins. At first he had been rough on them if he felt they weren't working hard enough, the guards stepping forward to deliver an occasional beating. Nothing too extreme, just enough to cause a great deal of pain but not to stop someone from actually working. After all, that would be a waste and it was another example of their master's unusual approach to caring for his cattle. These days everyone had slipped into a happy routine, the beatings were less frequent and they were left to work and talk in relative peace.

The light from the chamber above guided her way back down to the curve in the tunnel. Once round that, she was in darkness once more but she knew her way well enough. She took her time, in no great hurry, taking measured steps and calculating her distances, she still had to locate her group and theirs was the fifth tunnel on the left. She passed the sounds of folk working, she couldn't see any candlelight but her hearing had become far more acute. She even picked out the deep tones of Devlin's voice, which meant she was passing the first tunnel.

She moved on once more and found her tunnel after a couple more minutes, a glow coming from the mouth. Cade's was the newest to be excavated. They were chasing a vein of silver, not much to be sure but the bosses were thorough in their pursuit of the stuff. The main shaft continued on, forging down and deeper into the mountain. She wondered where they were in relation to their stinking little city. She pictured in her mind the path of this shaft, thinking about where it started, where it wound down from the chamber and then past their tunnel. She thought they were somewhere under the great cavern, maybe two, three hundred yards down. Not that any of it mattered a fig but it gave her something to think about. You always had to know your bearings.

Further down, the main shaft was worked on by a crew of ten, as it had been since the day they had arrived. It was the one part of this mine that the dwarves had insisted on ensuring a better standard of workmanship. No doubt with an eye to the time they ran out of human workers and had to get their own hands dirty again. A few of the others had been shown how to construct the bracing. They spent a fair deal of their time transporting the beams down then shaping the wood before knocking them into place. Not a bad job. She'd missed out on that one.

Stopping at the entrance to her little world of pain she squatted down and peered in.

'Got anything?' she asked.

'There's another couple here,' replied Rosta.

'Right.' She stood up, placing her hand on the roof of the tunnel.

'Shit.' A small shower of chips and dust fell on her head. She shook them off and went inside. Rosta dropped a mid-sized rock at her feet; two more were already in front of her.

'Hepton's doing a great job here, one smack and these buggers just fall right out. '

'Hmm,' replied Cade. She really didn't care. She picked one up and made her way back to the tunnel mouth. She dumped her load just by the mouth, where it would stay until Emerich came back. She stretched, walked back inside and collected the next rock. Something was bothering her. *Wait a minute. Loose rocks …* She dropped her load and raised her arm and placed her hand on the tunnel roof. She felt the slightest vibration, a gentle movement against her skin. *Loose rocks …*

'Shit! Get out, get out of there!'

'What?' Hepton's voice came drifting back.

'Cade?' asked Rosta, his body blocking the light as he stood and turned to look at her. A loud crack rent the air followed by a deep rumbling sound. Then the tunnel roof collapsed. Cade threw herself out into the main shaft, everything turning black as a cloud of dust and debris engulfed her. She scrambled backward, smacking into the wall behind her. Cade's eyes were stinging and her mouth and nose were clogged up with crap. She coughed repeatedly, her throat dry and sore, her breath ragged.

Voices were coming from further down the shaft, more from above.

'Help me!' A faint, rasping cry came from the collapsed tunnel. She crawled forwards, scrambling over rocks and rubble, one hand held in front, feeling for the tunnel mouth. Her hand closed on the right hand edge and she pulled herself forward. The tunnel hadn't collapsed completely and she clambered a few more feet into the space, over rocks of all sizes, strewn across the floor. She was terribly aware of the pressure, the weight all around her. It was overwhelming and her senses were screaming at her to get out before she was buried alive. She stood up, desperate to rid herself of the sense of being confined. A hand grabbed her ankle. She gave a yelp and winced at the pain.

'Cade? That you? Help me, I'm stuck,' said Rosta.

She knelt down and prized the hand away from her.

'Rosta.'

The hand reached out again and touched her face. She jerked back a little, reached up and took it in hers.

'How far you in?' she asked.

'My legs,' he gasped. 'I can't feel them. There's weight on my back, a lot of it. You'll need to get it off of me.'

'Hold on.' She released his hand and probed her arms forward, striking a wall of rock. She felt for gaps or any kind of give, but the tunnel was full and packed in tight. Her arms dropped back down, tracing along the rock until she felt his shoulders. The rest of his body was covered. It would take a while to dig him out. It was also likely his body was too broken to be worth the effort.

'Cade. What is it? Can you get me out? Please?' he whispered.

She stood up. She felt another tremor. *Not good.* Behind her, the voices were getting louder. She knew how this might play out. Damn fools will try and rescue him and get more of them killed. *Fuck that.*

'Sorry, Rosta.' She stepped back.

'Cade? Cade? Where are you?' he croaked. His voice was pitiful.

There was no point in risking her life, not for this one. Still in darkness, she reached down and got her hands around a rock. It felt roughly the size of a melon. She stepped towards Rosta, listening to his breath, his scrabbling hands, and knelt.

'I'm here, Rosta.' She felt his hands against the sides of her legs, holding them as if he were trying to hug her.

'Thank you, thank you. I think I can move a little …'

Cade leaned forward, raised her hands high and brought them down towards the sound of his voice. The rock smashed into his skull, the impact jarring her arms. She felt bone give way and Rosta's hands spasming against her legs. Then they were still. She dropped the rock and scuttled back out towards the shaft. She could see the glow of lights converging from above and below.

'Hello? Who's that there?' someone shouted.

'Cade,' she called back.

A crowd gathered round her, faces blackened and sweat-streaked, emerging from the shadows, a dozen voices speaking at once.

A hand touched her shoulder.

'Cade?' It was Devlin. 'You alright?'

'Uh huh.'

'Anyone else make it?' he asked.

A candle was entering the tunnel mouth. Folks were looking in.

'Not sure. Don't think so,' she replied.

'Anyone in there?' someone called.

The candle went further in.

'It's Rosta,' replied the same voice. 'He's dead. Whole damn lot fell in on him.'

'What about Hepton?' asked Meghan from somewhere in the shadows.

'If he's behind that, he ain't living,' said Devlin.

'They're coming!' shouted someone to her left.

Cade turned her head, trying to look beyond the press of bodies. There was another light coming down the shaft.

'Looks like our masters have come to take a look,' said Devlin. 'Let's get you on your feet. Don't want to give them an excuse to beat you for not having the good sense to die with your mates.'

'Ah, careful, you bastard!' moaned Cade as Devlin reached his arms round and under her armpits, lifting her upright.

'When Geir asks, just say you were on your way back down the shaft. You weren't anywhere near the cave-in,' he advised in a quiet voice. The light was close and three dwarves were marching towards them, Geir at their head.

'Damn straight I will,' whispered Cade.

Everyone made room for the dwarves as they arrived. Geir hooked his fingers in his belt and scowled.

'Any alive?' he asked.

Cade raised her hand.

He grunted when his gaze met hers. 'Everyone get back to work. Now!'

They didn't need to be told twice. The crowd quickly and silently dispersed. Devlin squeezed her shoulder and moved off back up the shaft. Meghan stopped in front of Cade, her face a picture of concern. Their eyes met for a moment and Cade nodded. Hell, she was the one in trouble and there she was trying to make Meghan feel better.

Once the shaft was clear, the Accounter looked into the tunnel. He tapped the walls with a small metal rod and sniffed like a dog searching for food.

He said something in dwarvish then turned to look at her. 'Ceiling collapsed. No bracing.'

No shit.

He stepped away and inspected Cade. 'Where were you?'

'On my way back. Got caught in the dust and rock as it came out of the entrance.'

He grunted again, his chest expanding wide.

'Dig it out.'

'What?'

'Good silver in there. Dig it out.'

'The roof is unstable, what if it falls in?'

The dwarf reached out and slapped her across the face. Her head whipped around, spittle flying from her open mouth. She felt a surge of energy, a desire to strike back. *Steady Cade. Keep it civil.* She tasted blood. She worked her tongue over her lips and found a split. She lowered her head, keeping her gaze fixed on her feet.

'Dig it out.'

'Yes, boss,' she muttered.

Geir turned to go, two guards falling into step behind him. Coming down the shaft was a cart, pushed by Emerich, and as it drew near it stopped and was pushed to one side to allow the dwarves past. Geir halted and looked back for a moment.

'Help her,' Geir ordered, then he continued on his way.

Cade stood and watched as the light shrank, then disappeared from view around the bend above them, a faint glow in the darkness receding to nothing. The cart moved down towards her, the candle flame a tiny, insignificant defence against the black. Emerich pulled the brake and walked around to join her.

'Cave in?'

'Yeah.'

'Others not make it?'

'Nope.'

'Guess we start hauling.'

'Yeah.'

Cade was exhausted. Her arms were scratched, her knees were scuffed and her back was sore. All she could think about was whether the next chunk of rock she moved was going to bring the whole mountain down on their heads. And all the while she had to work with Rosta's bloodied corpse lying directly in front of her. Even with Emerich taking turns she couldn't avoid it or the stink, that rusty, metallic odour, a mixture of blood and brains. Nor could she avoid standing in it or getting it on her clothes. By the time they'd been called back up, they'd cleared away all the loose stuff around the floor and a lot of the rocks at the top of the pile, creating a void they could work their way down from. It would likely take them a couple of days to clear if it was just the two of them. And at least another day before they might be able to get Rosta out. *Wonderful. Oh and let's not forget Hedron.* They'd have to deal with his mangled mess no doubt.

Her group filed through the Downside Gate and back into the cavern. Folk started to split up as they made their way to whatever piece of ground they called home.

'You okay, Cade?' asked Meghan, touching her elbow lightly.

'Um? Yes. Fine,' she replied, not really believing it.

'Lucky escape today,' said Issar.

'Oh, I was born lucky,' she said, sarcastically. 'Whole life I've always landed on the sunny side.'

'Just sayin',' said Issar, defensively. 'Could've been you back there under those rocks.'

'Could be any of us,' said Meghan.

'It wasn't. Best we can hope for, day to day,' said Devlin, his expression grim.

A horn sounded.

'Grub's up,' said Issar, his mood considerably brightened.

'Great. The free-for-all,' muttered Meghan.

'Guess we should hurry along before it's all gone,' said Devlin. He looked at Cade. 'You want to wait here? We'll grab you a share.'

Cade gave it a moment's thought. 'Go on, then. I'm shattered.'

Devlin nodded and her three companions left her to it. She was in no mood to brave the food queues. Like Meghan had said, it was almost a damn free-for-all. Each branded group was allocated its own amount depending on their numbers. Like everything, the Assessors made sure it all added up. It all worked fine with her bunch after there'd been a few words, one or two cracked heads and then everyone agreed to play fair. It had taken a little longer with many of the other groups. Self-preservation had kicked in and folk had become little better than dogs fighting over scraps of meat. As she'd expected, food was becoming the currency of necessity, and some were starting to suffer because of it.

She fell on to her blanket and lay back, her hands behind her neck. She looked up towards the roof of the cavern. Most of it was too dark to make out, though she could see a little, ridges, folds and protuberances, stalactites and such.

Damn. I need to piss.

She rolled over on to her front, drew her legs in and pushed off with her hands, springing upright, her knees complaining, a sharp pain pulsing in her back.

'Shit.' That was dumb.

She made her way through the cavern following the wall around rather than going straight through the settlement. She looked up and spotted a pair of legs that were dangling from the tier above her. Boots, the treads almost worn away, kicked against the rock behind them. A few small stones detached and fell away. Cade dodged them and a vision of the cave in came to her mind. *I can't keep working down there. I don't want to die buried alive. No way I'm going out like that.*

To her right she heard a noise.

'Ahh ...'

A release of air. A sigh.

She stopped and chewed her lip. None of her damned business, folk were still folk. But she took a step towards a sheet draped over a wooden pole. Behind it there was whispering, urgent and fierce.

'We promised we'd protect you. Did that, didn't we? Now you owe us.'

She pulled back the sheet. Two figures lay on the ground.

One was a brown-skinned woman, likely an Erebeshi. Her face was a picture of fear. She was pinned by a far larger man whose nationality she couldn't guess. He looked at her with something like annoyance.

'Fuck off, bitch,' he spat through a gummy mouth missing most of its teeth. His hair was greasy and fell across his eyes in thick clumps.

'That's not a nice way to talk to a lady. Have I intruded on something?' she said brightly.

'Nuthin' for you to worry about. Not yet anyway. This lady agreed for us to look after her. Keep her safe. But she needs to pay.' He grinned.

'Food?'

'Or her cunny. I don't mind which but the boss would rather have the food. I might just take both.' His grin turned into a leer.

'Right then, I'll be off,' she said and turned to go.

The man looked away, Cade already forgotten. Perfect.

She took three paces forward and delivered a kick to the side of his temple.

'Opph!' He rolled off the woman, who promptly screamed.

'Shut up,' Cade ordered. She stepped over the panicking woman and stamped her heel down the man's exposed stomach. She felt it sink in a little way.

'Arrgh.'

He doubled up, mouth open wide, his stained and stinking gums on display. She leaned over him. 'I need a piss.'

She turned away and resumed her walk towards the Heights. That felt good. She'd needed to let off some steam.

Folk were starting to drift back from the food delivery, clutching small loaves of bread, vegetables, and what passed for meat around here. At least no one had thought to resort to cannibalism. Yet.

She turned on to the slope that was the start of the Heights and climbed the short distance to the stream tunnel. She stopped a woman carrying a small pot from entering.

'Need a moment, love.'

The woman halted with a petulant 'tut', her eyes rolling.

Cade ignored that and went inside. A candle was burning at the end and several more were left unlit beside it. Evidence that people could get along if they wanted to. She undid her belt, unlaced her britches and squatted over the water. She mused as she listened to the gentle tinkling sound. There was probably gonna be something made of what she'd just done. *Ah well.* She'd deal with it later.

Someone had left a small waterskin on the floor, just below the candle. She made her own 'tut' and shook her head. Didn't people know you couldn't trust anyone these days? She leaned over and yanked it towards her. She dropped it, splashed water over her arse cheeks then pulled up her britches. Then she took the skin, pulled the stop out and placed the opening upriver of her, letting it fill almost to the top. It would save one of her gang a trip later.

She returned to the tunnel exit and back on to the slope. The woman was still there and still scowling.

'All yours,' Cade said. Her attention was already fixed on the man waiting for her. She rolled her eyes. *What a bloody day.*

He was slender-looking, short, a streak o' nuthin. He had all his teeth though, and a slim moustache, which must've been the best he could manage. Everyone else was looking a lot hairier these days.

'Have you paid for that?' he asked. He had quite the accent, educated by the sounds of it.

'What?' she asked.

'That water. You need to pay.'

Cade just stared. He reddened but didn't back down.

She shook her head. 'Just fuck off. I'm not in the mood.'

She stalked past him and his stuttering protestations.

'You have to pay. That's the rules now.'

'Is it, indeed?' she muttered.

Civilisation was trying to assert itself, just like it always did. Shit on that. She was tired. And hungry. Her store of goodwill was used up for the night and woe betide anybody who even looked at her funny. She wandered back to her bed in a foul mood.

Part Five

AUTUMN

CHAPTER 18

Father Michael counted a dozen Gifted formed in a battle line, fully armoured, shields locked together, wearing sheathed swords and carrying short throwing spears. They were facing off against a line of narrow wooden posts driven into the ground about one hundred paces away. Standing ten paces behind the first line were another twelve Gifted, similarly armed. Father Michael took a moment to study the faces and the tattoos behind the helmets. The first line was made up entirely of Shapers. The second line was a mix of all four Schools. He stopped to watch.

At a shouted command the Shapers pulled back their spears and released. At that distance, with such small targets, their weapons should have been all but useless, but they were Gifted. As the spears left their hands, instead of describing a shallow arc in the air, these shafts stayed straight and true, hurtling towards the posts at a speed no normal man could have generated. Each and every one embedded itself into the wood. Another command and the Gifted turned around. The other twelve marched towards them, swords drawn. In the space between the two lines, the ground was littered with small chunks of wood. As the two lines closed, many of these chunks lifted into the air and flew forwards, bouncing off raised shields, knocking into helmets. One or two flew back the other way in response. Then the fighting proper began. The lines joined and started the dance of the melee.

Apart from that first order, both sides fought quietly, no one spoke, grunted or shouted. The strangest part was the absence of swearing, curses or insults. The only sound was the ring of sword against sword, the crunch of shield against shield. Weapons flashed out, first a stab, then a block. An overhand strike, deflected off a shield, followed by a counter thrust. Figures spun and twisted, cut, clubbed and sliced. Emperor they were quick! It was like watching a fight in a dream. This couldn't be real for he had never seen humans fight like this. No one fell, no one lay bleeding out, screaming for mercy. His eyes kept shifting, trying to keep track of each fight as one couple moved into his vision, then was swallowed back into the shifting skirmish. There, a death cut, a weapon sliding inches away from an exposed throat. The victim stepped back, sheathing their weapon, withdrawing from the fight. Finally another fell to the ground, their feet swept from them by a low kick, the victor already moving away, looking for another opponent. The fight continued, the numbers whittled down.

Father Michael felt a presence next to him. Admiral Lukas announced himself with a short whistle of appreciation.

'Father. Will you look at this bunch?'

I am, aren't I?

'A pretty dance they make,' he continued. 'Not like a real fight though.'

Admiral Lukas leaned close. Father Michael forced his shoulders back. His natural instinct was always to tense up if anyone ever got too near him.

'You want to know how I made it through The Sound when so many others didn't? How the bigger ships, with bigger weapons and larger complements were overrun and sank to the briny depths?' Father Michael could smell the Admiral's breath, a mix of cabbage and the foul tobacco that he was so fond of chewing. 'I made sure that my ship carried the biggest, baddest pack of marines that I could find, from the darkest, dirtiest decks of the navy. Streetfighters, brawlers and nutjobs. When the first elven ship tried to board us, they didn't know what hit 'em. Last thing they expected was to see a bunch of bilge rats leap on to *their* ship. Hah!' The Admiral clapped him on the back and he took a stumbling step forward. It took all of Father Michael's self control not to lay the man out. 'You know what I'm talking about, Father. You get through this life by being meaner than the next man. Still ...' He pulled at the hem of his Admiral's tunic. 'I never meant to survive long enough to get this job,' he said, his tone a little surprised, and almost apologetic.

'Good Morning, Father!' said Ellen as she walked past.

'Good morning,' he responded, whilst eyeing her attire. She was wearing a sword belt and a breastplate, her face flushed with recent exertions.

'They've finally said I can start my combat training,' she said proudly.

'That explains it then,' he said gruffly.

She beamed at him and continued on. The girl always went out of her way to greet him and bring him up to speed on her progress. He hadn't asked for the attention but got it anyway.

'Well, well, got yourself an admirer there, Father,' observed the Admiral.

Father Michael kept his gaze fixed on the conflict before him. This dance was almost done. As a cloud drifted across the afternoon sun, bathing the ground in shadow, three Shapers stood facing off against a single, female Speaker, her breastplate shaped with a little more give in the bust. The three Shapers moved away from each other, and the Speaker thrust her shield forward. Three wood chunks lifted from the ground and flew towards the Gifted. She ducked low, one piece passing overhead. She met the flight of another, batting it away with her shield. The third did for her, adjusting its flight, following her down and striking her on the side of the temple.

Beside him the Admiral grunted.

'Unfair. She never stood a chance.'

'No,' responded Father Michael. 'She didn't give herself one. Why wait? She should have charged the one on her right. Kept her shield up and got the bastard turned around.'

'Oh, bastard, is it?' said the Admiral.

Father Michael flashed a look at the Admiral. He was grinning. 'You can take the man out of the arena ...'

'I'm sorry. I forgot myself,' said Father Michael contritely.

'Don't punish yourself over it. You're right. They were over confident and didn't expect anything else from her. That's the trouble with them. Great fighters, great training, no instinct.'

The Speaker stood up and removed her helmet. The others were doing the same. Smiling faces appeared, flushed, sweating freely, energised by their exertions. The Speaker threw the helmet on the ground. It was Cardinal Yarn. She was smiling too, beaming even, her chest rising and falling with heavy breaths.

'I must say, I didn't expect that,' muttered the Admiral.

Her gaze turned towards the two men. Her broad smile changed, and she adopted the lop-sided, knowing regard she often wore. She nodded at the pair of them, stooped to gather her helmet and walked away, her fellow Gifted gathering around her, their course taking them towards the barracks.

'She was a warrior before she was a Cardinal,' said Father Michael, by way of explanation.

'What? No. I didn't mean that. It was their faces. Have you ever seen a Gifted look happy?' He paused. 'Ever fight a Gifted?' the Admiral asked.

'Once.'

'You win?'

'I'm still here.'

Father Michael pulled his hood over his head and went on his way. He heard the Admiral snort.

Father Michael did not share the Admiral's feelings. The Gifted were very good fighters. They coordinated well, and they knew how to use their talents. He was no general but he was sure if there had been but a thousand of the Shapers, let alone the battle-skills of all the other Gifted, then they could have decimated any army that tried to close with them. They could have turned the war. But there never had been a thousand Shapers, as Cardinal Yarn had once told him. There had never been more than two hundred serving outside the Monastery. Now there were no more than two dozen.

'Father!'

He turned to see the Emperor striding towards him, a large scroll tucked under his arm.

'Your Grace,' he said, bowing low.

'It's starting to get dark. I always think it's time to stop working when it gets dark. Some hope,' said the Emperor. He was wearing a red leather tunic, white cotton shirt and brown woollen britches, a sword strapped to his waist. 'Do you ever stop?' he asked.

'I am always in service,' replied Father Michael.

'Indeed. Just make sure you remember to sleep occasionally.'

The Emperor clapped him on the arm.

'Come along inside, I want to show you something.'

The Emperor led the way on to his veranda, passing a Watcher guard. Neither the guard nor the Emperor acknowledged each other's presence. Father Michael tried to get to the door to open it for his lord but was too slow, the Emperor getting to the handle first and ushering him in. Once the door was shut, the Emperor moved to his desk and placed the scroll upon it.

'Father, sort that fire out, would you?' he asked.

Father Michael bent down, found a metal poker and got to work shifting the small, smouldering pieces of wood around. He leant forwards and blew, conjuring a few licks of flame. There was some wood stacked to one side but he was loath to use it. Their supply was low.

'Don't worry about that, Father,' said the Emperor, helping himself to wine. 'We have a logging expedition out west. Mostly timber for building but they'll have firewood too. I intend to go and visit them tomorrow. We are getting serious about this now.' He drained his glass and gestured towards the scroll. 'Have a look.'

Father Michael picked up two logs and threw them on the fire. He then turned his attention to the table. The Emperor had rolled the scroll open and had placed weights on each corner. One of those weights was the wine bottle, another a small knife. Father Michael looked at the scroll and saw it was covered in curving lines and small annotations; a map.

'Here is our new Empire, Father,' said the Emperor, taking a gulp from his refilled glass. Father Michael raised an eyebrow and studied the map.

'This is the first to be produced. Our eagles have been conducting patrols of the area and we have collated everything into this. There we are,' he said stabbing a finger towards a point on the right hand side of the map. A circle had been drawn and letters scrawled in a flowery hand beneath it, spelling *New Tissan*. Two wide, curved lines ran just above that circle, and these lines widened out to form an open-mouthed triangle, the river and the estuary. On the far side of the river, arrows and sharp-sided marks indicated higher ground. Below and to the left of the river were large circles with tree symbols, and lines representing further tributaries and other curving markings resembling hills.

'We have been very fortunate, Father. Our little town is well situated. The ships have a good berthing here and the soil is fertile so we can begin planting seeds. We've already cut down all the available wood in the vicinity but further south and west are sizeable forests. There are even fruiting bushes and trees. Cadarn brought back apples. That means we can make cider.'

'The soldiers will be happy at least,' said Father Michael. He had given-up alcohol willingly, but there were times, certainly on their voyage, when he wished he hadn't.

'We'll need something to keep the citizens happy. The Gods of Old know we will soon be out of wine and I doubt there are any vineyards nearby.' The Emperor raised his glass in a toast and emptied it for a second time.

'Our food supplies are limited. We can survive off our stores for a few more months, supplemented by the fish stocks in the river. However, I want to get a sense of the game out there. There is no substitute for fresh meat. The carpenters have built a couple of wagons. We have a few draught horses and we'll use those to start a regular run to the forests. Admiral Lukas says that, barring the storm, we were heading in a due westerly direction since leaving Tissan. We have to assume that the winters here will be just as wild as back home.'

'We could sail south. The climate may be better for you,' said Father Michael.

The Emperor smiled.

'I never travelled to the south of the Empire. Erebesh always sounded like a grim place, far too hot. I was raised in the Riverlands. I am reminded of it here. I plan to send a flotilla south after the winter. Admiral Lukas was agreeable. His ships could do with some work anyway. I'll also be sending an expedition to the west, along the river, to see what the interior may be like.'

Father Michael nodded. He felt invigorated and excited by the Emperor's enthusiasm.

'What are those symbols, Your Grace?' he asked pointing at place in the bottom part of the map.

'Those are horses, Father. Our scouts spotted a herd. They got a little spooked when the eagle overflew them, but the rider swears they had four legs, a tail and pointed ears. Their colouring was different, a new breed or related species perhaps. Good news, nevertheless.'

That reminded Father Michael. 'This visit tomorrow. Are you still intending on riding, Your Grace?' he asked.

The Emperor nodded, picking up the wine bottle and pouring the remaining contents into his glass. The scroll edge curled over, obscuring the detail.

'I don't see why not. I had thought to go with the foresters, see the lie of the land a little. We have half a dozen palfreys that survived the journey. It's about time they stretched their legs a little. I forgot to ask. You can ride, can't you, Father?'

'I have little experience of horses. But I know one end from the other.'

The Emperor laughed. 'It's a start. We'll take it steady, we don't need to gallop there. We can enjoy the journey.'

'Your Grace. This trip, there is still so much we don't know about the land. I fear for your protection.' Father Michael had to say it, after all that was his task.

The Emperor's face clouded for a moment, his smile faltered.

'I understand your concern, Father. You are as bad as my mother. I will be taking two Gifted. You'll be there and I know you are no stranger when it comes to a fight. There will also be two Eagle Riders above our heads and Cardinal Yarn has already had a Watcher travel to our intended location. The Watcher will be keeping an eye on us from back here. They will know when we arrive and when we leave. I am confident that no harm will befall us.'

Father Michael conceded with a bow of his head. 'Then I have nothing more to worry about.'

'No, you don't! Now, I want to get at least a little sleep before tomorrow.'

'Of course. I will bid you an early good night, Your Grace.'

'Good night, Father,' replied the Emperor with a nod of his head.

Father Michael left the cabin with an image of the Emperor with his glass to his lips. As he stepped off the veranda, he saw the Empress pass by, heading towards her cabin. Father Llews was at her shoulder, speaking softly. He couldn't make out what he was saying, but the Empress was listening intently. Behind them followed two ladies-in-waiting.

Father Michael bowed and said loudly, 'Your Grace.'

Father Llews turned and looked at Father Michael, his face frowning. Recognition passed across his features and he waved. The Empress did not even bother to look. Father Michael watched the entourage enter the cabin. The two women were dismissed at the door as the Empress went inside. Father Llews followed her in.

Father Michael was a simple soul with limited experience of the world, but he felt it wrong for a man, even one of the Imperial faith, to be alone in the Emperor's mother's chambers. There were ... rules. He shook his head. *Don't be a fool, Michael. The world has changed.* It was his natural distrust that made him think that way. Father Llews was an ally and he could be trusted. Father Michael returned to his tent and while there was still a little daylight, he decided to try to read a little. He sat on his bed and removed his boots and socks. Gripping his toes, he wriggled them about then wrenched them down hard, hearing and feeling a satisfying click as he straightened the joints. He lifted the pillow and retrieved the book. He had nowhere else to hide it, yet another habit from long ago. He opened it to the first page and started to read. But soon his mind started to wander. He kept thinking about the Gifted and their training. He had done no serious physical activity since he took the cloth. Only his abstinence and years of training had kept him in reasonable condition. It was high time he started working his body again.

CHAPTER 19

Arno flared his wings and touched down lightly on the ledge in front of the roost. Owen climbed off and instead of using the reins touched Arno lightly on the beak. The eagle followed him into his stall and turned himself around, unbidden. Owen was glad finally to be home from the day's patrol. The morning air had been crisp, a real bite to it. Owen gave an involuntary shiver. He really ought to have dressed more warmly. He'd become too used to the summer days and the bright sunshine. It was funny how he had dismissed all recollection of the previous winter, the vicious cold that sucked the life out of you, the freezing nights where he fell asleep wondering whether he'd wake up again.

With the change in the seasons, he felt a sense of expectation. The last time he felt that, they had been winging towards Aberpool, screening the retreat of the last few units of the Imperial army. *My Gods. It was almost a year. How did it go so fast?* Though in truth, they had accomplished a few things, including the rebuild of Eagle's Rest. And they weren't just surviving anymore, they were now thriving, against all the odds.

'Good lad, Arno.' Owen reached for the doors, closing them tight. The evening was shaping up to be a chilly one and whilst he was sure Arno would be comfortable enough, he liked to keep him out of the elements as much as possible. Owen knew his bird had suffered enough on his behalf.

'How'd it go?' asked Erskine, walking into the stall.

'Not bad,' he replied. He pulled the bar down and gave the door a shake. Nice and tight. 'Em is getting to be quite the marksman.'

Erskine grunted. 'She should be. If she's not with her bird, she's with her bow. Here, I got some grub.' He lifted up a bucket. 'Arno, got you some nice blood and guts. Perfect for a growing eagle.'

284

Arno made a gentle squawking sound.

'You're welcome, big lad.' Erskine dumped the bucket in front of Arno.

'The others settling in?' asked Owen, as he started to unbuckle the saddle.

'Yes. No worries. They are good with their birds. Let me help you.'

'Thanks.'

Together they lifted the saddle off Arno and took it to the corner.

Owen stood and folded his arms. He had a notion.

'Erskine?'

'Hmm? Oh, I know that look. It means you're thinking.'

'Really, I have a look?'

'Yeah. We all know it. You make it at every town meeting.'

'Shit. I never knew.'

'It's all right. Murtagh says at least it means you are *actually* thinking before something comes out of your mouth.'

Good point.

'Out with it, Chief. What are you after?'

'How are the other birds?'

'Good. But they need riders. They are getting too big. Before long they'll be too old to train.'

'You are right,' said Owen. 'I was wondering about that. Maybe we could ask for volunteers. Get a couple of the youngsters to look after them. We need the eagles to stay friendly.'

'With each other as well, yes? I guess we need them to start breeding soon.'

'Right, but that's not what I was thinking about right now. Is your brother showing any interest in the birds?'

Erskine grunted and placed his hands on his hips.

'Ah. I get it. Answer is no.'

Owen folded his arms.

'You know those two better than anyone.'

'A bit big for them, aren't I?'

'Right now but they grow fast. Thing is, I don't have to spend the time teaching you half the stuff I need to teach Em and Jussi. You know how to look after yourself and take care of a bird.'

Erskine scratched his arm and hemmed.

'I've gotten used to working on the edge out there. I suppose the heights don't bother me. I'm still likely to shit myself.'

'No different to anyone else. 'Cept maybe Em. That girl knows no fear. I'd say you take the female. She'll grow stronger and will take your weight easier.'

'Right. Want me to ask about, see if anyone else is up for it?'

'Go ahead. I trust you to make a good choice.'

Erskine smiled mischievously. 'Oh, Murtagh wanted a word with you as well.'

'When doesn't he want a word with me?' smiled Owen.

Owen clapped Erskine on the back and left the stall. He walked the length of the rookery, looking in on each eagle in turn. Em and Jussi were both busy settling and feeding their birds and he let them get on with it. The other two eagles were also comfortable in their stalls, and he pulsed greetings to both. Each one recognised his voice and reacted with warmth. They needed names and fast. The closest thing they had to family was him and Erskine, but they had to have someone closer, someone to truly connect with. He wished he knew whether Taru and these two shared any parents. Ideally not, he needed the breeding pool to be as wide as possible. Arno would do well no doubt, perhaps with Taru, and next spring they should get a couple of pairings. There must be more eagles out there. They were likely to be wild, but if he could get hold of a few eggs, it would give them more than enough to build a self-supporting community of eagles. When the 'Rest got too full of people they could relocate folks with their own squadron. By the Emperor. Listen to him. They were still struggling to find enough people to fly the birds they had. Time was everyone wanted to be an Eagle Rider and you couldn't be that if you didn't have the Gift. His father had said that only one in a hundred folk had it. Not such a problem when you had a whole nation to pick from. They had one hundred and fifty waifs and strays, so they were lucky to have two. He emerged from the rookery into the cooling evening air. He walked up to the gate and greeted the woman, Rencha, on guard.

'All well?'

The squat, compact woman leaned on her spear.

'Aye.'

'Everyone in for the night?'

'Aye.'

He nodded, opened his mouth, and cut it off when he realised he had nothing else to say. He smiled encouragingly.

'Right. Have a good evening.'

He turned and headed for the hall, feeling his face burn. He had it in his head that being the leader meant having the right words to say to everyone. He was buggered if that was the case.

He saw smoke rising from the central hole in the roof. He had been worried about using the hall fire pit. That line of smoke was a beacon for anyone looking. In the old days they'd navigate between settlements using those beacons. Murtagh had been belligerent, protesting that they were in the middle of the bloody Highlands and there was not a soul left to see it. Against such unyielding good sense, Owen had relented. He recalled he'd been hungry at the time and the thought of missing out on that stag roasting over the firepit had pushed him over the edge.

Crossing over the square he heard hammering coming from the smithy. The door was open and he peered inside. The coals within the brazier were glowing red. A shadow was cast against the far wall, defining an arm raised then brought down, the ringing sound of metal on metal following after. Next to the smithy was the newly erected cattle shed. It held no cattle, but did have several pigs. The Gods knew how they had chivvied them up the slope. He didn't need to know. A young girl was hauling a bucket of feed towards the entrance and he hurried over to her.

'Here, let me help.'

The girl looked up, her face turning panicky when she recognised him.

'It's okay,' he assured her. He knew she was one of Saul's bunch but couldn't remember her name, something else he had to work on.

'I can do it, my lord,' she stuttered.

Owen raised an eyebrow. 'Less of the lord, young lady. The name's Owen.'

He took the bucket from her and she hurried to the shed door and opened it. An earthy stench hit his nostrils, swiftly followed by a chorus of grunts and snorting.

'I'll take it, my lord,' she said. Was that a curtsey?

He handed the bucket back over. He wasn't sure who felt more embarrassed.

'Look, if you want, call me Chief. I'm no lord. Alright?'

The girl swallowed.

'Yes, Lord, umm … Chief.'

Owen ruffled her hair and headed back to the hall. As he climbed the stairs a figure moved up to his side.

'So it's Chief, now, is it?' Naimh asked.

He shot her a look. She was smirking.

'Oh Gods, don't you start as well.'

'Me?' She placed a hand to her heart. 'I'm just a simple woman of the Highlands. What do I know about rule?'

'Between you and your brother, you got this place working better than I ever saw it before.'

She nodded, her mouth a tight line. 'I'm as surprised as you. I think everyone is so desperate to make it work. It is a chance none of us thought we'd have again.'

'We have to make it count, don't we?'

'We do. Tell that to my war-mongering brother,' she said, pointing her chin towards the top of the steps.

Murtagh was watching them, arms folded. 'What's she saying about me?' he asked, his voice gruff.

'I'm saying you are a bloody war-monger.' Say one thing for Naimh, she was not shy in coming forward.

'Chance would be a fine thing,' Murtagh grumped. 'Our Chief here has me run ragged. I never get time to think about war. Too busy worrying about organising everything whilst he gets to gallivant around on his bloody bird.'

Owen reached the top step and stood in front of him. He grinned.

'My loyal steward and seneschal. What would I do without you?' He meant it. Owen placed all of his trust in the older man. If the day came that Murtagh wasn't being a moody, grumpy sod, then the world would come to ruin.

Murtagh punched Owen in the arm. Hard.

'Ow!'

'Just reminding you what it's like to be human and not the bloody Emperor.'

'Okay. I'm reminded.'

Murtagh smiled back and placed a fatherly hand on his shoulder, guiding him inside, Naimh following on behind. Owen glanced over at her and she rolled her eyes.

'How was your trip?' Murtagh asked casually. Not a hint of concern over Em. Owen knew better. Murtagh took his role of surrogate parent seriously.

'It was good. Em makes it all look easy and Jussi is shaping up well. He's still young but he'll grow into it. I just asked Erskine if he wants to become a rider.'

They entered the hall, where the atmosphere was smoky, hot and busy. People bustled about preparing the evening meal. A large cauldron sat over the firepit, something bubbling away within it. Tables were arranged in a horseshoe around the pit on the far side of the hall. Three kids ran up the stairs from below the hall, tearing past Owen and the others, hooting and screaming into the night.

Murtagh grunted his approval. 'About time you asked him. That lad has been after a go for months now. What with all the time and effort he has put into that roost.'

I hadn't noticed. So damned wrapped up in my own cares I hadn't stopped to think. Stupid.

'We need one more rider, for the male eagle. I asked Erskine to think about it.'

'We could ask for volunteers?' said Naimh.

'Just don't make it one of the adults. We need them to work for a livin',' said Murtagh. He took them round to the centre table and seated himself. There were jugs and mugs already laid out. He reached for the mugs, setting one out for each of them. Owen sat next to Murtagh and Naimh next to him. Murtagh grabbed a jug and sniffed it, his face turning sour.

'Water.' He reached for another. 'Ah.'

He poured, and ale came out. Once he'd filled his, he also did Owen's. Owen took his mug and had a long drink. It was cool and hoppy.

'Erskine said you wanted to see me,' said Owen.

Murtagh drained his mug and went to refill it.

'Nothing you don't know about already. Nights are starting to draw in now. Just wanted us to think about the winter and how we get through it.'

'Can't be harder than the last one,' said Naimh.

'True. But with the last one we only had a few mouths to fill. This time we got a whole village of hungry souls.'

Owen reflected on this. After the arrival of Saul and his people, there had been a constant trickle of survivors. Larsen and the hunting parties had ranged out a long way, finding small groups of Highlanders holed up in cave systems and deep within the darker woods and isolated valleys. There was still more ground to cover, though anyone else left out there would struggle to last another Highland winter without proper food and shelter.

'Do we have enough stores laid in?' Owen asked.

'We've got a fair supply. Vegetables, some fruits. Meat shouldn't be a problem. We've got those pigs, a score of goats. Plenty of water.'

'Tell you what we don't have,' said Jenni as she passed by carrying several loaves, 'is grain. We won't have any bread this winter, not if we want to keep some seeds and such for planting next season.' She stopped and placed a loaf on to a wooden chopping board on the table in front of Owen.

'It's worse than that, love. We don't grow any hops. We won't have any beer,' said Murtagh solemnly.

'The Emperor save us from that disaster!' said Jenni, smiling at Owen before she moved on.

Owen reached out and tore an end off the bread. 'I was thinking about that,' he said. 'We used to grow oatmeal down below the 'Rest, on the ground out to the west.'

'I know. We didn't do a very good job of harvesting it this year,' said Naimh. 'We concentrated on the vegetables instead.'

'We'll have to change that next year,' said Murtagh. 'We've got some scythes and we have the granary patched up.'

'More work for willing volunteers,' said Owen. He picked at the bread, tearing off a chunk and compressing it into a ball between his fingers. He popped it into his mouth and pressed down. It was thick and a little chewy and had small gritty pieces it in. He reached out and collected his mug, washing down the bread with a healthy glug. 'Is Larsen heading out again before the winter hits?'

Murtagh grunted, his own mug to his lips. 'He's thinking of leaving tomorrow. Hang on.' Murtagh turned in his seat. 'Hey, Larsen? You here? Anybody know where he is?' Murtagh gazed about and a few folk shake their heads. The door to the hall opened and Larsen strolled in followed by Saul, Ernan close on his heels.

'Great Gods, Murtagh. I swear I can hear you halfway to the bloody Riverlands,' said Larsen.

Murtagh grinned.

Larsen and the others took seats at the table.

'Murtagh tells me you are heading off tomorrow,' said Owen.

Larsen scratched at an angry looking red welt on his check. 'Weather's drawing in. Time we got some fresh pelts. Lot of people need to keep warm.'

'Good idea. Where you heading?'

'We've been spending a lot of time nearby, just a couple of days away. We thought we'd strike out east,' said Saul.

That surprised Owen. They normally never went that way. East was heading in the wrong direction if you didn't want to meet the enemy. It didn't matter that there was nigh on a thousand miles between them and the borders of the other races, it made him feel uneasy, and he wasn't the only one who felt it.

'You sure you want to head that way?' he asked.

Larsen and Saul shared a look. Owen felt foolish for even asking.

'I guess we've all been avoiding it,' said Larsen after a short pause, making Owen feel a little better. 'There is a lot of land that way we haven't seen. There should be plenty of game and maybe some folk holed up.'

'Larsen was saying he didn't want to hunt locally anymore. We don't want to thin the beasts too much,' added Ernan. He was becoming a fair hunter and idolised Larsen. He'd also lightened up a little as far as Owen's role was concerned, as long as Owen didn't tell the hunters their business. That suited him just fine.

'We can't stick to one place. It's not long since the bastards rolled over this way. They needed meat as much as we did and there were a damn sight more of them than there was of us,' explained Larsen.

'Do we have anyone who knows the territory out that way?' asked Naimh. Owen didn't think anyone did.

'No, there's no one from the east of the Highlands here. You'd know it better than anyone like as not, Owen. This is your land,' said Saul.

Owen nodded. Saul was right. He'd flown these peaks for years. It was just that he'd never walked them. Things looked a little different from a mile up.

He smiled at them all. 'Sorry. I have a different perspective on what's out that way. It's been a while but you should head north east, following the old trail, and get yourselves over the next range, the one with the three peaks close together. We used to call them the Three Chiefs. Then you'll hit a valley heading almost directly east. It will take you a couple of days, maybe three, to get there, but there's good game from what I recall. Nobody lived out that way, so there's a fair chance it was left untouched.'

'Good enough,' nodded Larsen. 'We've been getting our kit sorted. Five of us and three mules heading out tomorrow at first light. The plan is to stay out a few weeks, maybe a month, catch as much as we can before it gets too cold. We've got a bunch of game traps set up in the valleys north and west. Owen, make sure someone checks 'em daily. Your eagles get through hares faster'n we can catch 'em half the time.'

'I know,' said Owen. 'I appreciate the work you do for that. It's the younger ones I need to domesticate a bit first, get 'em used to thinking of us as family. Then we can start letting them look for their own supper. Arno's better. He can catch his own meals most of the time and I know he'll always come home.'

Larsen sat back.

'Anyway's just get someone who knows what they are doing.'

'I will. In fact, I'll get my Riders to do it. They need to learn about hunting and trapping. I'll show them myself.'

'Fair enough,' said Larsen. 'Right.' He pushed himself up. 'Things to do.'

'Good luck and stay careful,' Owen said to the three of them.

Saul and Ernan stood and followed him. They headed for the stairs leading down into the caves. Larsen was probably going to sharpen his knives, Saul to see the young woman whom he'd taken a shine to and Ernan to sleep. It was his second favourite thing after hunting.

'Owen!'

Erskine came bustling into the Hall, Anneli hot on his heels.

'I've just been speaking to Anneli.'

Owen looked at Anneli, red-faced and bright eyed, standing right by him.

'I gathered.'

'She'd like to learn to ride.'

'Is that so?'

Anneli nodded, 'Can I? I don't mind taking my turn on the wall and doing chores but …' She shrugged. 'And I've been learning with my spear.'

'Have you ever shot an arrow?'

'Er … no.'

'Ever ridden an eagle?'

'Um … no.'

'Sounds like you are as qualified as Erskine then,' said Owen.

'Hey!' protested Erskine.

Owen laughed and raised a hand.

'Sorry.'

'True though,' said Murtagh trying to work a finger under one of his torcs.

'Hey!' spluttered Erskine.

'Anneli,' said Owen, speaking over Erskine before he got too riled. 'I know you've been trying hard and want to help. Looking after an eagle is a big responsibility. They become part of your family, closer even. You start as their parent then they become like a brother or sister to you. Do you understand?'

'Yes.'

'Good. Then tell you what. Tomorrow come over to the roost and I'll introduce you to a fine young lad. He's a good bird but will need a firm hand. Then I'll take you for a ride on Arno, see how you like heights. After that, we'll see.'

Anneli smiled. 'Thank you, Chief. I won't let you down.'

'Sure you won't. Speaking of which, you are still holding your spear. Does that mean there is no one on watch?'

Anneli's face flushed a brighter shade of red. 'Oh. Yes. I'd better get back.'

'Off you go, then,' said Murtagh. 'If I hear there's an army of dwarves marching up the hill, you'll be in trouble, young lady.'

Anneli sprinted out of the hall.

'Cruel bugger,' said Owen.

Murtagh smiled an evil smile and took another drink.

'Thanks, Owen. I think she'll do a great job,' said Erskine with a big grin. He followed Anneli out at a more sedate pace.

'Do I see another love match?' muttered Murtagh.

Love. I wonder what that is? Owen pictured Jenna. It seemed like a boyish infatuation to him now.

Owen looked at Naimh and Murtagh. 'I feel exhausted. I've only been away a night and suddenly everything is happening at once.'

'You're the Chief. Comes with the territory,' said Murtagh.

'I guess.' Owen shook his head. 'This morning I had two youngsters learning to fly and now I've got a squadron to look after.'

'And a fearsome bunch they are,' said Murtagh. 'We'll strike fear into the hearts of any shitting elf looking for trouble.'

'I doubt they'll ever be that. I just want them to be good Riders, learn to take care of their eagles. That way we can pass on what we know to the next generation.'

'Just don't forget to teach 'em how to fight.'

'Trust me, Murtagh, I'm on it.'

Sometimes Owen felt he was the only one who was looking beyond the next battle.

CHAPTER 20

Fillion hurried along the street and leapt over a puddle of water. The heavy red cloak he wore restricted his legs a little and he didn't quite make the distance, causing a splash as his heel landed heavily.

Shit.

It mattered little, as his boots of supple leather were protection enough, but it did reflect on his fitness. He was growing soft. He had gotten far too used to the good living, and the fair weather. A wind blew into his face, pushing back the hood. He felt a few splats of moisture against his skin. Reaching up he tugged the hood into place, keeping his hand on it. The skies were leaden grey, the clouds thick and in places, almost black. It had been raining for nearly two days and it was as miserable a day as he could remember since his arrival in the city. The concourse he was on was almost empty of life. A single wagon rolled over the cobbles, its driver hunched forward, obscured by a heavy woollen cloak, covered with beads of water. Spray flew from the wheels, some of it reaching the pavement, as Fillion strode by going the other way.

The weather had robbed the houses of what little life and light they may have had and Fillion felt his own spirits dampen down. Today was supposed to be a good day, another step forward. But the depressing, soulless world he inhabited had robbed him of any optimism. He found himself thinking about Patiir's house and a hot, steaming bath. The Emperor knew how good that would feel right now. He'd happily hide himself away until the sun came out again. *On, Sabin, on. I do not have the luxury of turning my back. Not today.* At the very least he could content himself with a small measure of comfort when he arrived at his destination. Once there he could have a goblet or two of wine, though it was weak, watered down and lacking flavour. These city elves didn't know how to drink properly and certainly didn't approve of the good stuff during the working day. Still, any port in a storm would do.

The sign he was looking for appeared on the other side of the street. A silver chalice against a field of green. Stepping off the pavement, he made sure to avoid the stream of water heading towards the drain. The cobbles were slick yet hard against the soles of his feet. On the other side, he took another exaggerated step, back on to the pavement and through the door under the sign. A gentle murmur greeted him as he entered the spacious room within. The Silver Chalice was a tavern, though of a type he had never experienced before. It had the atmosphere of a sitting room rather than a drinking house. It was far too brightly lit, far too fresh smelling and far too clean. He took his time to get his surroundings. Several round tables filled the centre, each of them with four chairs. At the back was a long counter, behind that another counter where a large number of bottles were racked. To the right was a line of three alcoves, each with a table and rounded benches covered in leather. To the left was a large fireplace, unlit, and flanking it on either side were more alcoves. Two high-backed leather bound chairs sat in front of the fire. He counted potential threats. There was one elf behind the bar and seven other patrons, six of which were paired up. One pair at the counter, one in the centre and one in an alcove on the right hand side. The seventh, solitary elf, stood up from the one of the chairs and beckoned Fillion over.

'Simeon,' said Fillion with a smile.

The elf smiled back. 'Sabin. Come join me. It's good to see you.' The young elf extended his hand. Fillion took it and shook it firmly.

'My apologies, I may be a little moist.'

Simeon waved his hands dismissively. 'Don't worry about it.' He looked Fillion up and down. 'So you have your new robes of office.'

'What? Oh, yes.' Fillion looked down at the red sash tied around his waist. Along with his cloak, it marked him out as a Servant, a functionary of the Parliament. He had noticed that all but Simeon and the bartender wore the same.

'Honestly, I haven't left the city yet and you have already usurped my position!' Simeon said with a laugh. 'Come, sit. I was lucky, I got the best seats in the house. This place won't fill up for another hour or two yet.'

Fillion removed his cloak and looked around for somewhere to hang it.

'I'll take that, sir,' said the bartender. He hadn't seen him come up.

'Ah, thank you.' He handed him the cloak.

'Markos, this is Sabin. He is taking over from me,' said Simeon, by way of introduction.

'Very pleased to meet you, Sabin. Your master is one of our finest politicians.'

Master, is it? He's not my fucking master, you creeping piece of shit.

'And I am pleased to meet you. Patiir has been a gracious host to me and I hope to serve him well.'

'Markos, could we have some wine? Something a little stronger. I no longer have to worry about drinking whilst working and Sabin here could probably do with it on his first day.'

Markos inclined his head. 'Of course.' He retreated to the bar, hanging up Fillion's cloak on one of several numbered pegs.

Simeon settled back into his chair and Fillion followed suit. The chair was comfortable and he sank into its embrace.

'Thank you for suggesting we meet before you left. Any guidance you can give I would appreciate most strongly. I value your experience,' Fillion said.

'It is a pleasure. And welcome to the Silver Chalice. We like to think of it as our place of refuge and second office,' replied Simeon.

Fillion raised an eyebrow.

'This is where you'll find most of us go after we have finished for the day. All the Servants that is. And as you can see, some of us come here earlier than that. If you want a bit of privacy or somewhere to let off steam, this is the place.'

'I'd have thought even here you'd have to watch your tongue.'

Simeon shrugged. 'True enough. Each of us has a loyalty to those we serve. Sometimes it is better that we deal with things more informally than for the Members and Ministers to have to thrash it out in the Chamber. We can talk more freely here, gauge the mood. Then we pass it back to our Members. You'd be surprised how much business gets done here.'

'You sound proud of it.'

Simeon smiled. He oozed smugness. 'I have played a part.'

'Then I admit to being surprised that you would wish to leave,'

'It is not entirely of my doing. I have to go home, my parents want me back. Perhaps in the future I'll return. Life at the centre of Elven politics is far more interesting than managing the estates of my father. Ah, thank you, Markos.'

The bartender had returned with a tray bearing two fine crystal goblets and a carafe. He set it down on a small table next to Simeon's chair and poured out pitifully small measures. With a nod he retreated and Simeon passed one glass over to Fillion and took one for himself. He swirled it around and took a sip.

'Ah.'

Fillion didn't bother with the preamble. He took a gulp and washed it round his mouth before swallowing. It was rich, fruity and with a bit of bite. Better than the swill he was expecting.

Simeon sported a raised eyebrow and a wry smile. 'I knew you'd be needing something stronger.'

'Always.'

Simeon tilted his head. 'That must be the soldier in you. It might serve you well with some of the Members. Take Randyl Thrawn, he was a general for many years. He's getting on a bit now but likes nothing better than to bend a Servant's ear over a glass or two. More importantly, he was the King's sword tutor. Patiir has a soft spot for the old elf, and even lets him indulge in a bit of royal ear-bending on occasion. And you might like to meet Member Dalas. She is an important wine trader, owning many vineyards. You are drinking some of her stuff now. You know the merchant class is looked down on, so she'd be most pleased if you were to voice an appreciation of her wine. No doubt she would see you as her means to Patiir. No bad thing to have her as a friend.'

'It sounds to me as if this patronage goes beyond the masters we serve.'

Simeon took another sip of wine and gazed thoughtfully at the glaze, rolling the stem through his hands.

'It's true. I won't deny it. All of us follow two paths. The first path is one of service to our King and to our people. The other path is of service to ourselves. Being a Servant can give an elf power and prospects. Some Members gain their place because the King has commanded it. Others have earned it through acts of great renown or, like the merchants, through their money. Most Members are in Parliament because they always have been, their places determined by a hereditary line of succession. And a Member can serve for hundreds of years. Patiir himself has been a Member for at least nine hundred summers. When a Member makes the decision to stand down, they choose their own replacement.' Simeon placed the glass down on the table and crossed one leg over the other. 'I won't lie to you. I had hoped that Patiir would ask to keep me on. But it was not to be, and no point in dwelling on it. I'm not the first Servant he's had, not by a long margin. And the old elf has never once looked like giving it all up. He is a determined and devoted Member. So I'm leaving the lists and passing the torch to you.'

'I doubt I can do better than you, or any Servants that have gone before.'

'Oh, I think you may.'

'Why would you say that?' asked Fillion, making sure his face had the proper frown.

'You happen to be very close to his daughter. He's not blind to that, yet he asks you to take over from me as a Servant. Do you know how many elves would've wanted that position? Would have happily entertained the notion of killing someone for it?'

'I'm just a simple soldier,' protested Fillion.

'And a likely future son-in-law. Patiir offered you the role because he wants you around. Because Nadena wants you around. Well done, Sabin. You are either an incredible actor or the most genuine and un-effacing elf I have ever met. In which case, thank all the Gods that Patiir is your patron. The Parliament is no place for the faint-hearted.'

Fillion shifted in his chair and tried to show enough grace to be embarrassed. It was hard. He felt a rush of excitement, a surge of energy. He had nobody to share his plans with but hearing this from someone close to the heart of matters was a vindication of his efforts. He had wheedled his way into the house of one of the most powerful families in the city. He was one step nearer to his goal. He could scarce believe it himself.

Fillion entered the Temple. It was the first time he had visited it, or at least, the first time he had gone inside. He had never been a religious man, he got that from his father. Celtebaria was awash with Gods of all kinds and creeds, and the other nations of Tissan had been little better. His father had said it didn't matter which God you prayed to, none of the bastards listened. He had become worse after his wife had left, his bitterness turning him into a sour old man.

Fillion's mother on the other hand, had always maintained her link with her Gods. He'd learned about them, had come to understand they were all linked to one greater power; that they were just facets, manifestations of some greater life force. He didn't pretend to understand it. He certainly didn't try to accept it. The Emperor himself was the one true God and no others need be worshipped. As religions went, it was a different kind of faith to what had come before. Only the Ogres had a single God, and theirs wasn't a particularly pleasant one.

One true God, the Emperor, yet the Imperial religion taught that his power was derived from the Heavens, given to him from all the other Gods to be their instrument on earth. If you looked at it, it was a clever piece of work, taking all those old Gods and saying they were letting the Emperor run things. Of course, he could never have said that out loud, even amongst his own men. They'd as like to burn him as a heretic. No, his devotion to the Emperor was far more pragmatic. The elves hated the Emperor and Fillion hated the elves. It was a perfect match.

The Temple was rectangular on the outside, in contrast to the Parliament and the King's palace. As he stepped under the wide lintel, he was met by the warm glow of flaming torches, placed at regular intervals along a broad corridor running the length of the building. He was within a reception hall, the only place where daylight filtered in from small windows set high in the front façade. To his left was a stone statue of a noble-looking female elf, three times his height and twice as broad. She was dressed in a simple shift that covered one of her breasts, the other conspicuously bare. Vines had been carved around her arms and legs, leaves sprouting off to either side. Her similarly bare feet rested upon a carpet of stone flowers. She was looking down at Fillion, her face set in a maternal, caring frame, a gentle smile, her eyes half closed. Both her hands were open as if she wished to gather up a child in her arms. She was the Mother. To the right was her counterpart, the Father. A male elf, dressed in the same white shift, his countenance stern, gazing down upon him with fierce judgement. He carried a bow in one hand, a spear in the other. One sandaled foot was resting upon the body of a deer. Together they were the highest lords of the elven pantheon.

A black-robed priest stood to one side of the Father. He was watching Fillion, a knowing smile playing on his face.

'This is your first time,' the priest said.

Three elves walked past Fillion, bowed to the priest, who nodded his head in return, and proceeded along the corridor.

'Yes. How could you tell?' asked Fillion.

The priest took two steps towards him. His hands clasped together, resting easily just below his belt.

'You have the look,' said the priest. 'Your mouth is open and you are staring at the Mother and Father with a look of wonder.' The priest laughed gently. He looked well into his middle age, his features still firm and unblemished, though his hair was starting to grey about the temples.

'I am sorry, I do not mean to mock you, but I don't often see such a face from those who come to worship here regularly. It is quite refreshing.'

'You have the right of it. This is my first time,' said Fillion, feigning a smile.

'You are from the borders, yes?'

'Yes. Is it obvious?'

'Your accent is a strange one, it is rather coarse.'

'I am sorry if it offends you,' said Fillion. *Cheeky fucker.*

The priest raised his hands. 'No, no. It does not offend me in the slightest. It pleases me to hear it. I lost my accent a long, long time ago.'

'You are from the borders too?' asked Fillion.

'Yes. Though I come from the east, whilst I would presume you have come from the west?'

'You are right.'

'Hmm. Quite so. The eastern elves have an accent that is far more … musical in its cadence. Strangely, it has a strong similarity to the speech of the wood elves.' The priest sighed. 'Sadly, I have acquired the more formal rhythms of the central Heartlands, the tones of the royal court and the inflections of the citizens of the capital.'

'You do sound a little regretful.'

'Yes, a little.' The priest smiled and placed an arm gently on his shoulder. 'But I could not ignore my calling. And what a reward I have gained, to be accorded a place in the Temple of the Gods, at the heart of elven power.'

He patted Fillion's shoulder.

'Now, forgive me. We have not been introduced. I am Penitent Welland, and you are?'

'Sabin.'

'I am truly pleased to meet you, Sabin. And what brings you to the capital?'

Fillion shrugged. 'I was wounded in the war, I made friends with my carers and decided to travel with them.'

Welland nodded, his face intent, holding on to Sabin's words as if they carried great importance. 'The war. Yes. I had hoped to travel with our armies but my duties here prevented me. I am glad you have recovered.'

'As am I.'

The priest stepped back. 'Do you know which God you wish to pray to?'

Fillion had no idea. He thought a moment, trying to recall what he knew of the elven Gods. 'Yes. Mardock.'

The priest raised an eyebrow. 'The God of Justice is visited by many petitioners, but I am surprised you would choose him. What has been done to wrong you?' Welland stopped, shook his head. 'I am sorry, I am far too inquisitive. You do not come here to answer to me. You come here to answer to your God.'

'There is nothing to apologise for. I am coming to give thanks.'

'Ah, then, your prayers have been answered.' Welland nodded. 'That is good to hear. Let me show you the way. Look down the corridor, you will find his chapel on your left side, almost two thirds of the way to the end. He is between Hera and Centa. As I said, he does receive visitors but usually first thing in the morning or later in the evening. This afternoon, it is quiet. Please.'

The Penitent lowered his head and stepped to one side.

'Thank you, Penitent, it has been good to speak to you.'

'For me as well. If I am not here on your return, I hope our paths meet again.'

'As do I.' Fillion nodded to the priest and moved past him and into the corridor.

His steps echoed along the flagstone floor, worn smooth and scrubbed to a shine. The corridor must have been a hundred yards long, and spaced evenly on either side were archways. He glanced left and saw a chamber, dimly lit by candles that were clustered at the feet of another statue. It was a male God. He had no idea who it was. An elf was kneeling before him. Fillion moved on.

As he continued, he looked left and right into the chapels, many empty, some holding one or two elves. Some Gods had a number of candles placed at their feet, the wax having melted and spread over their plinths. He smiled at a young, female elf, dressed in black priests' robes as she passed him by. She smiled in return. He stopped to allow an old elf, using a walking stick, to shuffle by. The elf mumbled his thanks. He looked into another chapel. It held an image of the goddess Hera. He knew she was related to rivers, streams, lakes and such. What gave it away was her fishing net, carried over her shoulder.

The next cell was indeed Mardock's and he stepped inside. The chamber was empty and quite dark. That was a relief; he was tired of being respectful. As he approached the plinth he counted four candles upon it, all but one already burned out. The last one was down to an inch or so, its flame flickering and weak. Fillion, his vision accustomed to the shadowed gloom, inspected Mardock. A well-defined male elf, he wore a breastplate and greaves, though his head was bare. Grim-faced and of middle age, he carried a sword in his right hand and a purse in the other. So that was what justice meant to the elves. You either got it at the end of a blade or you got it through coin. *Fair enough.* Punishment and enrichment, and as he had no desire for payment, the blade would do just fine. *Do you listen to human prayers, I wonder? If so, hear mine. I plan to take justice for what your people did to mine. Do you believe in justice for all? Not that it matters if you don't.*

Fillion stood there for some time. He watched the candle burn down to the barest stub. He looked around and saw a small alcove set back in the wall behind him, next to the archway. He went to it. Inside were a few candles, next to them a bowl. Inside the bowl were four small coins. He reached out and took a candle. Should he pay? Did they count the coins and the candles? He wasn't going to bloody pay for one if they would never know anyway. He took the candle back to the statue and used the last of the dying flame to light the wick. He let it catch and burn for some moments then tilted it, letting wax drip on to the plinth. As it pooled and started to cool, he placed his candle on top. *There you are. Have a candle on me. You can't say I didn't ask nicely, you bastard.*

He exited the chapel and looking left, saw the corridor ended at a stout, iron-banded door. There was nothing else of interest, so he made his way back to the entrance. As he passed through the hall of the Mother and Father, he noted that Penitent Welland had gone and was replaced by the female priest he had greeted earlier.

'Did your God answer you?' she asked politely.

'I am sure he will,' he replied, not smiling.

Fillion went out into the fading light. Across the plaza, torches that flanked the entrances to the Parliament were being lit. On his left, further down the parade, the palace was blazing from a dozen different points.

He crossed the parade, heading for the Parliament. The rain had slackened somewhat and he pulled down his hood. He stood there, just looking. *What am I now? A Servant to the Parliament of the Elven Court. Not bad going for a scout captain. Father. If you could see me now, what would you say? Probably accuse me of being a traitorous son of a whore. Well, in a way I am. I just hope you know whose side I'm really on.*

'Sabin?'

An elderly elf walked slowly towards him. He wore a red cloak like Fillion, his arms folded within the sleeves, the folds wrapped tightly about him.

'Lenard?' asked Fillion. He had been told to meet this elf here and was glad he had not had to wait

'That is my name, yes,' said the elf, with a warm smile. He withdrew a hand and held it out. It was wrinkled and gnarled. Liver spots decorated the skin. Fillion took it and Lenard then placed his other hand over his.

'Well met, Sabin.'

Lenard was the oldest elf he had ever seen. Older than Patiir, and that bastard was old. Sabin studied Lenard's face. His hair had greyed to white yet was still worn long. There were wrinkles around rheumy blue eyes and veins stood on out on his forehead amidst skin that was stretched taught. His cheeks looked hollow, the flesh caving in a little when he spoke.

'You look a little surprised,' said Lenard. 'Have you never seen an old elf before?'

Sabin the elf would have. Fillion the Imperial Scout had never seen one in his life before. It was said that there was no such thing as an ugly elf but he was reassessing the truth of that statement.

'Forgive me,' he said with a slight bow, collecting himself. 'It's just I had not thought to see someone of your age here. This place seems so full of …'

'Youth?' said Lenard, the smile unwavering.

'Yes. I thought politics required energy and vigour. From all I've seen it is quite exhausting.'

Lenard released his hold on Fillion and placed his hands back into his sleeves.

'Trust me, you have no idea. But power brings its own vitality. Once you have experienced its caress, it is hard to give it up. It sustains you, as much as it feeds off you.'

'Sounds wonderful,' said Fillion.

Lenard chuckled. 'I'm sorry, I have been around orators for far too long. Their words and mannerisms have rubbed off on me a little, I think.' He looked around the steps and up at the sky. 'Shall we go inside?'

'Yes, of course.'

Fillion followed Lenard into the Parliament. Inside was quieter than usual, as if the weather's gloom had robbed this place of its urgency and life. Servants and functionaries hurried past but with none of the usual chatter or sense of purpose.

'As to your initial question, you are quite right,' said Lenard.

Fillion didn't recall asking one.

'There are not many elves of my age working in the capital. In fact, I am quite sure I am the only one. I had thought that perhaps you might have heard of me? I am something of a minor legend in these parts.'

'We don't have much to do with the King's business out on the borders, I'm afraid.'

'Ah, that explains it. I am, I confess, a glutton for punishment. I have been here longer than any elf now serving, if you can imagine that.'

By the look of you, yes.

'Most elves would have returned to the loving warmth of their families by now, ready to embrace their passing. Honestly, I'd find that dull. And I can't imagine what my family would say. They wouldn't know what to do with me.'

Fillion half listened, bored, and half looked at where they were going. Lenard had taken them a short way around the circle concourse and was now leading him down a set of unfamiliar stairs. What was unusual was the absence of any other floors or exits off them. They just led straight down. Fillion's interest picked up.

'I've been here so long I've served under two kings! Our current lord and his father before him, almost his entire reign at that,' said Lenard.

Good Emperor Above. How old was *this coot?*

They arrived at a set of double doors set in an archway of marble, with delicate scrollwork carved into both the pillared sides and the curving lintel. The doors bore similar work, sets of intertwining leaves and branches, green and brown against a sky blue background.

Lenard stopped.

'It is no surprise that I am the most suited to fulfil my current duties.' He paused and a thin, white eyebrow rose. At the same time his eyes squinted suspiciously. 'Did Patiir tell you what I do?'

Fillion shook his head.

'He told me I would meet an elf called Lenard and that there was no one better suited, no finer elf in fact, more respected and revered, to guide me in learning my duties.' That was a slight embellishment. There'd been no mention of respect and reverence but this old bugger appeared to like getting his ego flattered. Fillion could see it worked as Lenard had grown a little in stature, his chest puffing out. 'Unfortunately,' he continued. 'He had not mentioned anything about what your business was.'

'No matter, no matter,' said the elf waving his hands. 'Perhaps it makes this sight all the more impressive.' He placed a hand on each door and pushed. They swung forward easily and Fillion felt a slight rush of air. Beyond the doors, a large, cavernous room opened up before him. Rows of shelves and bookcases spread out and away from the doors in orderly lines towards the far wall. That he could see it at all was thanks to the beams of weak, grey light, slanting down from openings evenly spaced around the edges of the ceiling, another set of ingenious passages that funnelled and reflected the daylight into the recesses of the building.

'This is the Great Library,' announced Lenard. 'The repository of all the history of the elven race since we first began to record and remember such things.' He walked through the archway and beckoned to Fillion. 'It's a shame the weather is not better. I do love the sunlight streaming in. I imagine you never thought you'd ever get to see this. Not many elves outside of the capital do.'

No, I never thought I'd see this. Probably because I never knew it existed.

'This place is marvellous,' he said, and meant it.

Lenard nodded. 'Is it not?' he pointed to a table set off to the right. Fillion noticed as they moved towards it that the circular walls were covered with bookcases, while the nearest sets of shelves held scrolls placed on racks, one to a slot, much like bottles in a wine cellar.

'You are the librarian?' said Fillion.

'I am. Astute fellow, I can see why Patiir wants you.'

Lenard settled down into a simple chair of carved wood. A large white cushion rested on the seat. Fillion took a similar chair on the opposite side but this one had no cushion. The table was empty except for a quill, ink and several flat pieces of parchment. All very orderly.

'I've served as the Librarian for most of my life. First as an apprentice then, much later, I was given responsibility for all of it.'

'And you look after this place by yourself?'

'I do. I suppose I ought to get round to training someone else, but I rather think everyone believes I will live forever. I certainly do, all appearances to the contrary.'

'And this library has all of our histories?'

'Yes. It charts the reigns of all our Kings and Queens and provides narratives for all of the events that have shaped our peoples. The King has his own library. Full of learning and science, awash with texts of magic and myth. This place,' he said, tapping the table, 'is the heart of who we are. It is priceless. A jewel!'

Fillion gazed about him. He pictured the place going up in flames. It would be easy to do it. Something to think about.

'You might have already worked it out, but the Parliament sits above us. I believe it is important the Members understand they are supported by the histories of all who have gone before them. It makes them think about the responsibility and the duty they bear to the generations of elves who have assisted in building our society.'

Build a big bonfire. Make the whole thing burn. Let the Members roast.

'I can understand why Patiir wanted me to come to you. The politics of today are informed by the politics of the past. I can learn about how the Parliament works by understanding our history, how the Members form the decisions they have made,' said Fillion.

Lenard clapped his hands. 'You have it!'

He pushed himself back up and walked around to stand by Fillion. He placed a withered hand on his shoulder.

'From what Patiir tells me, you have little experience in politics or governance. This puts you at a disadvantage. Many Servants have been prepared for their roles before taking their posts. They understand the issues and have been tutored in the histories, albeit abridged versions. You will have to do this at some speed if you are to be of value and serve your Member effectively. Up, up!' He squeezed Fillion's shoulder.

Fillion stood and allowed himself to be guided along an aisle.

'I can help you along the way by furnishing you with the most appropriate knowledge. The most timely and efficacious examples of historical precedence. I can show you decisions and directions that were undertaken a thousand years ago and why they have resonance today. In short I can ensure you are the most well-versed and effective Servant this Parliament has seen in centuries.'

Fillion had stopped listening to the old codger. He looked along the aisle. He'd better not be expected to read all of this shit.

'Where do I start, Master Lenard?'

'Ah, a good question. Perhaps you need to start with something relatively recent?'

He wandered down the aisle, crossed a junction and proceeded onwards to the far side. He stopped and withdrew a scroll from its place on a rack. He handed it over.

'This is the history of King Anai, father to King Lujan. It is the first scroll of his ascendancy to the throne. Hence it is as you see it.' He pointed behind Fillion. 'We did not start binding books until the five hundredth year of his reign. As you know King Lujan has sat on the throne for three hundred summers. I don't deny, books and folios are far better records to use but ...' He shrugged. 'We work with what we have. That scroll will start you off then all these others ...' He ran his hands over the rack. 'They will take you the rest of the way.'

Fillion couldn't help make a face. 'This might take some time.'

'Oh we have all the time we might ever need. You are, however, right in your obvious concern. Patiir needs his Servant now. So each morning you will attend him and run his errands until midday. Then you will come here and read.'

'And how long do you think it will take me before I'm done?'

'That's up to you. I can see this taking many, many months before I'd be satisfied to tell your Member that you are ready. You are young and eager. All Servants are when they start. Do not concern yourself with speed. Concern yourself with becoming the best Servant you can be.'

Young and eager? I'm older than you know and getting older by the minute, I'll likely be dead before I'm done here.

Lenard clapped his hands a second time. 'Time to start, I think. I'll leave you to it. There are reading tables arranged along the sides. Please find yourself one. I have lanterns for when it grows dark.'

'Thank you, Master Lenard,' said Fillion, bowing his head.

'Don't thank me, Sabin. We are all Servants here. Doing what we can. Oh, be careful with that scroll, it's delicate.'

Time passed slowly. The reign of King Anai was boring. There was no war, no natural disasters, outbreaks or intrigue. He decided that if this was to be his fate, he wouldn't even die of old age. He'd top himself first. The only thing he had found of any note was the occasional mentions of relations with the humans. The Tissan Empire had not been established yet and instead the elves had made contact with many of the Plainsfolk, Erebeshi tribes and Highland peoples. They had trading missions in many of the cities of the Riverlands, dealing with local lords, petty kings and merchant princes. The information recorded was little more than a list of goods bartered and bought. Every now and then there would be a reference to local disputes and skirmishes but only in how they had affected commercial activities.

There was no talk of alliances or interventions with the humans. The elves seemed content to live and let live. If only they had continued that course. Their dealings with the other races were a little more detailed. Diplomatic relations with the dwarves and ogres were well established and the comings and goings of gnomes, wood elves and others were mentioned. Nothing juicy though, nothing that was useful to him. Fillion looked up at the windows. It was pitch black out there. He hadn't eaten since his meeting with Simeon and his hunger for justice wouldn't fill his belly, but some wine from Patiir's cellar wouldn't hurt. He'd had enough religion and history and other shit for one day. He stood and stretched, his muscles complaining. He rubbed his eyes, which felt sore and strained. Lenard was still at his desk. He looked the type to be wholly devoted to his work. Perhaps he lived here? He returned the scroll he'd been reading, the fifteenth of the day, and headed over to the old elf.

'Master Lenard.'

The elf looked up, smiling. 'Master Sabin. I had almost forgotten you were here.'

'I have to concentrate when I'm reading,' he said. His aching head proof of that.

Lenard smiled. 'Good, good. Did you enjoy it?'

'Very much so. I have made some inroads into King Anai's reign.'

'Instructive?'

'Indeed.'

'King Anai was fortunate to rule during a time of growth and political stability. There was even some talk of attempting another embassy with the Hebbarite nation far to the east. An exciting prospect! But I don't want to spoil it for you.'

No please don't. Who the hell were the Hebbarites anyway?

'I look forward to it.'

'I'm sure. Now, off with you and I'll see you tomorrow afternoon,' said Lenard, with a wave of his hand.

'Good night,' replied Fillion.

He made his way back up the stairs and along the empty concourse to the exit. Two guards were stationed next to a brazier just inside the middle entrance. They looked him over with polite indifference. He nodded to them both and hurried down the steps. That was new. They had guards stationed here at night. Perhaps that meant there were less of them inside than in the daytime. It made a kind of sense, as there would be few if any Members working late and doors would be locked. He would have to check that, it might prove useful to know in the future.

The walk home was brisk, the night colder and more unpleasant than the day. The only positive was that he couldn't see the oppressive architecture surrounding him, or the grey clouds of daytime that put him in such a funk.

'Are you well, Master Sabin? A good first day?' asked Rabi, standing at the entrance to the house as Fillion hurried into the courtyard.

My head fucking hurts.

'I am well, though tired. My eyes are fit to burst.'

Rabi laughed as he helped Fillion off with his cloak. 'I heard that might be the case. Master Patiir warned me you might need a pick-me-up. The bath water is hot. Mistress Nadena suggested you head straight there.'

Did she?

'Then I'll take her advice.'

Rabi handed over his cloak and Fillion bid him good evening. He climbed the stairs and went straight to his room. Entering the hall and climbing the stairs, the house seemed empty. It was certainly very quiet.

He imagined Patiir was still up the hill. There ought to be some life, Hedra and Alica were usually chattering about something, somewhere in the house.

He undressed, placing the cloak on a hook, unwinding the sash and draping it over the cloak. He shed his shirt, britches and boots, then his undergarments. He sat on the bed, leant back and threw his arms out.

'Ahh.'

For a moment he allowed himself to drift off. *Wait. Bath.* Reluctantly he rolled over and pushed himself off. From the wardrobe he took a white robe, put it on and headed out of his room, padding barefoot to the bath wing. The building still felt eerily quiet. As he'd been told, on entering the bathing rooms, he found them warm and hazy with steam. He made a beeline for the hot pool. Undoing the robe he threw it into a corner and stepped into the water.

'Ahh.'

It was hot. It lapped over his chest. *Oh that's good.* He settled into it, dropping his body so only his head was dry.

'That is not very respectful.'

'What is?' he asked, turning to watch Nadena emerge from the far side of the room.

'Throwing your robe in the corner like that. Anyone would think you grew up with humans.'

'Oh.' *Guess what.*

'Yes. Oh.'

'Sorry. I forgot myself. It was a long day.'

'I'm sure it was.' She stepped around the bath, undoing her own robe. She slipped it off and made a point of laying it on the nearby bench.

Fillion studied the outline of her body. He did that a lot of late.

'I'm starting to treat this like my own home.'

'You are.'

Nadena slipped into the water. 'Turn around.'

'Huh?'

'Don't argue. Turn around.' He watched her settle on the ledge that sat midway under the water level then shifted his position. He felt hands on his shoulders, a gentle pull. He shuffled back a little.

'Better.'

Her hands got to work. Kneading the muscles, applying pressure on his knots, rubbing his skin with soft, delicate strokes.

'Oh. Ah.'

'That working?'

'Ah.'

'I'll take that as a yes.'

Fuck yes.

'I didn't think reading could be so tiring,' he murmured.

'Don't take offence but it's not something you've had to do much of before, I imagine.'

'True. I'm more the practical sort.'

Careful. He had almost said man. It was an expression that had no place in elven society. Even after all these months he still had to watch himself. *Get too relaxed and see what your big mouth will drop you into.*

'That you are. A reason my father likes you. He thinks your … rough and ready nature, will be a breath of fresh air. You don't come to the role with any ambitions.'

'You make me feel so special.'

She laughed and squeezed.

'Ow.'

'Hush. You know what I mean. Father likes you because you are honest and you have no agenda.'

'Not true. I have ambitions.'

'Me too.'

Her hands pushed and pulled him around so that he was facing her once more, her face a little higher than his. She looked down at him with a strange half-smile. She placed a finger on his cheekbone, ran it down to his chin and when it reached the bottom, applied pressure, forcing his head up. She leaned in and kissed him. She pulled back, her head tilted to one side.

'Is it me or has your face grown red. There is definitely more colour in your cheeks.'

'Must be the heat,' Fillion replied, certainly feeling something.

'Hmmm.' She leaned forward once more. She kissed him again. This time she lingered. Her mouth parted a little, her tongue pressing forwards, pushing lips apart. He opened his mouth wider, letting her in. Putting his arms around her waist, pulling her off the ledge. She pressed against him, her small breasts crushing against his chest, her arms wrapping about his neck, her kissing becoming more insistent.

Fillion felt himself respond, felt his cock grow and press against her belly. He hadn't been sure, when the moment came, whether it was going to work. Whether he could do it. Problem solved. She shifted in his arms, pulled away.

'Get up.'

She pulled him on to the bath ledge. Straddling him. Guiding him inside.

'Oh, oh,' she whispered. The water barely moved as she rode him.

Fillion held on to her tightly, face buried between her breasts. If he kept his eyes closed, he could block out what he was fucking.

Patiir was sitting by the fire as Fillion entered the study. After the bath he'd dressed in loose fitting green cotton trousers and an oversized eggshell-coloured tunic. His hair hung limply across his shoulders, still damp from his earlier activities.

'Sabin. Are you well?' Patiir indicated he should join him.

'Yes, thank you.' Fillion said, seating himself opposite. He was still flushed from his bathroom exertions and the heat from the fire made him a little uncomfortable.

'How was your first day with Lenard?'

'It was … interesting.'

Patiir laughed. 'A fine answer. Already you are talking like a politician.

My apologies for not explaining his role to you in any great depth but I thought it would make for a more interesting experience for you.'

'Indeed. I do understand his value. I can learn much from him and his books.'

'That is good to hear. I have absolute confidence in your ability to be a good Servant in the practical sense, but perhaps you are learning that there are more subtle demands expected of you.'

'That much is evident.'

'Good. I don't expect you to have to do my job for me, but I need you to be aware that nothing is ever as it seems.'

'I believe you. Yet I always thought the King through Parliament governed our people. That there was never any discord.'

'But the King has the last say on all things,' said Fillion. His mother had never taken the time to explain elven politics to him. So he tried to relate it to how the Empire was run. From what he was hearing, there was little difference.

'If His Grace wishes a path taken, then we set the course which provides the least disruption. He has his advisors and ministers who will assist him in his decision-making. Sometimes he pushes, sometimes we pull. It all works but like any construction it must be constantly attended to. Checked for flaws, cracks and wear. And, if I may mix my metaphors a little, it is also like an animal. You have to understand its moods, what it needs and when. Feed it when hungry, starve it to keep it in line.' Patiir stopped and smiled ruefully.

'Sabin, my apologies. I am lecturing you on politics. We are at home and at leisure. We all need time to rest our minds.'

'My mind truly needs rest. I have been working through the histories of King Anai.'

'Lenard has taken pity on you, then. He would have been just as likely to have started you ten thousand years ago, rather than more recent history. You have many elves still around who can remember well Anai's rule. If you have any questions, I will be happy to answer them for you.'

'Thank you, Patiir.'

Voices echoed down the chamber.

Patiir looked around. 'Ah, I hear the young ones returning. That is our cue to attend dinner.' He stood and Fillion followed suit.

'They went out riding today, down to the river, I believe. They'll no doubt have worked up quite an appetite,' Patiir continued, leading the way out into the hall. 'It was curious, though, I could have sworn that I saw Nadena's horse already stabled when I returned.'

Fillion was glad he was in the rear as his face had started to flush again.

'Ah, good evening, everyone,' said Patiir, as he entered the dinner room. A long table ran away to either side of them, covered with glowing candles and autumn flowers. On the far side, several sets of thin double-doors opened out on to the courtyard. On warmer and lighter nights they would be thrown open so the family and guests could enjoy the evening. Tonight, thankfully, they were shut. Two identical fireplaces sat within the walls at each end of the room. Neither was lit even though it was a miserable night, but it was not cold. Hanging along the length of the inside wall were a number of portraits; Fillion had already learned they were members of the family. Some of the pictures were thousands of years old, the oils used were faded with age. In the Empire, such a portrait would have been worth a fortune. Over the left-hand fireplace sat a small silver frame holding an image of Patiir's wife. She stood in front of a large tree, the branches, thick with leaves, spanned out to either side. She was dressed in a simple, unassuming white robe, her left shoulder bare. She held a child in the crook of one arm and looked out of the picture towards whoever might be watching her. The similarity with Nadena was obvious. They shared the same, almost coy, smile. The same one that her daughter wore now. She sat to the right of the portrait and she was watching him.

'Father!' cried Alica, getting up from her chair and flinging her arms around Patiir.

'Have a care,' he laughed, gently pushing her away. 'You almost crushed the life out of me. Honestly, it's as if I'd been away for a hundred years. Go on, sit down.'

'Sorry, Father,' she said. The look on her face said otherwise.

Patiir took his place at the head of the table. As the guest, Fillion sat next to him on his right side, Nadena was on his left. Their eyes met briefly.

'Nadena, good to see you.'

'And you, Sabin. How was your first day?'

'Most productive. I met with Simeon, he bids you all farewell, and then I spent the afternoon in the library.'

'Oh, I love that place,' said Hedra. 'There are some incredible books in there.'

'You've read most of them, haven't you?' asked Nadena.

Hedra shrugged. 'Most.'

Fillion figured that Hedra must have spent most of his childhood in there to do that. At least twenty years of it.

'And what of your day?' asked Patiir.

'It was good. Apart from the weather,' said Alica.

'Yes, we decided to go along the river then stopped off at that farm where they make cider,' said Hedra.

'Nadena! You weren't encouraging your brother and sister to drink during the day, were you?' asked Patiir, with genuine concern.

'Of course not. I just let them try a little with lunch.'

'Hmm. I don't approve.'

'Yes, Father.'

Fillion watched the exchange closely. Nadena had looked shocked by Hedra's remarks but had quickly disguised it. For his part, Hedra looked directly at Fillion and winked. Of course, they had to know. In fact, come to think of it, everyone at this table knew. And nobody was going to say it. Yet.

CHAPTER 21

The queue for food was an orderly affair. If this had been left to them to organise, Cade had no doubt that there would have been chaos, fights, deaths and a lot of hungry people. Say this for the dwarves, they kept things neat. Each group was lined up, as per the Accounting, and called forward by their owner's mark. That group would step forward and walk down the line receiving their food allowance, dropped into whatever cup, plate or bowl the human happened to be carrying. Once each group was done, the next would be called forward. All this was carried out under the ever-present grim-faced gazes of the guards. They watched each human carefully, as if they might try and steal more than their share. Cade would have liked to try but she hadn't seen a way to do it yet. The process was too simple and they were too exposed.

She stood behind Issar as her group was summoned. The Erebeshi shifted nervously, like he was feeling guilty about something. Cade had learned that when he wasn't jittery there was something up. She shuffled past a guard. She kept her head low, flicked a gaze in his direction, too quick for him to notice. She saw his hand resting on the pommel of his sword and that his hand moved a little, poised to whip that sword out and take her head off. She knew this one, he was not one of her boss's. She'd taken to learning about the guards, who they belonged too, who the sadists and bastards were. There were a lot of those.

Up ahead there was a shout, a scream. A figure fell to the ground, a plate clattering on the floor. Who was that? Ah, Friede, probably looked at the cook the wrong way. She couldn't help it, her face looked like a slapped arse at the best of times. Friede picked herself up, gathered the plate and what was left of her food, and hurried away from the table. Cade's turned arrived and she stepped forward. A large, dirty looking

320

dwarf wearing a brown leather jerkin over mail was doling out today's meagre offering. She got a chunk of flesh, an onion and a hunk of bread. A veritable feast! She took her bowl, walked away from the table and studied her meal. The meat was of unknown origin, cut off from who knows what. She couldn't recognise the meat but it didn't look like any reproductive organ, so that was a happy outcome. She could swear she'd had a bollock of some kind a week or two ago. That was the exciting thing about their mealtimes, every day brought a different adventure in food.

The dwarves had served them hot food on the long trek here. A thin gruel, but it was hot. Since arriving, that had all changed. The underground stream meant they didn't have to worry about providing water and the dwarves now expected the humans to cook for themselves. No great drama for Cade as she and the others could combine their stuff and produce a passable stew. It still tasted like shit, but it stayed down and filled a hole.

She took a bite of the bread, tearing a piece off with some effort. It was hard and gritty and chewing it was slow going but at least it wasn't mouldy. Issar was waiting for her at the edge of the open area by the gate. Others were walking by, heading back to their little camps. A new group was being called forward.

'Going to fetch some water,' he said, holding up a small pot. 'Want to come along?'

'No.'

'Oh.' His face was a picture, he looked like he was about to cry. Dammit, was she a bloody nursemaid now?

'Oh, for crying out loud. That is a face only a mother could love. Okay, I'll come with you.'

Issar smiled happily as Cade joined him. They fell in behind some others making the short journey to the Heights.

'Nice little routine this,' she muttered.

'It is. You get to know people, listen in on the gossip.'

'Gossip?'

'You'd be surprised. I get a lot of my information on these water runs.'

Cade shrugged. She supposed it wasn't so different from the rookery. Her information of choice was gleaned from a dozen dirty-faced snitches who lived on or under the streets. She really hadn't gone up in the world at all.

'What's this?' asked Issar, stopping in his tracks.

A large crowd had gathered at the start of the slope. There was an argument going on, voices raised in anger. Interesting.

'Let's listen in,' she said. The crowd was split into two distinct groups. The first were the Heights dwellers, she recognised them all. They formed a loose line and looked like they weren't intending to move. The other, larger group was gathered at the foot of the slope. Cade noted that behind the Heights dwellers, a few large boulders had been put across the path, not much of an obstacle to be sure, but it was a start. She was sure it would get bigger given time.

'Just let us pass,' shouted someone they couldn't see.

'We will. You just need to give us payment,' said someone from the Heights just as loudly. A big man and the largest in their group.

'Why should we?' called another voice.

'Because we have the water. Which we are willing to share with you. But we need to protect it, keep it clean in there, make sure we don't over overuse it.' That was another voice from the back of the Heights crew.

'Overuse it? What in hells do you mean?'

'It's simple.'

A figure stepped out from the crowd on the slope and hopped up on to one of the boulders.

'Our water comes from one little stream, flowing from who knows what to who knows where. We have been using it to drink from, toilet in and wash our clothes. But how many of us are there? What if it stops, or slows down. How do we control its use? How do we ration it?'

'Quite the smart bastard, isn't he?' said Issar.

'Oh yes, he's smart,' Cade replied. She knew him too, his name was Arren and he had shoulder length hair, a long straight nose and thin arms. His voice was loud and forceful, projecting out across the crowd.

Cade noticed he kept tilting and turning his head, so his people could hear what he was saying. He was an agitator, a rabble-rouser. Cade knew his sort, he would play on people's fears, talk them into frenzy. *Wouldn't get his hands dirty though, oh no. He's just saying what everyone is thinking. He doesn't want trouble he just wants justice.*

'Ration it? Who's rationing it?' asked one of the women in the crowd below.

'We are,' said the first Heights dweller. 'We make sure everyone gets a fair share, so we control access to the water, make sure people who want to shit don't go in at the same time as people who want to collect.'

'We can do that ourselves,' she responded. A chorus of agreement bubbled up.

Arren raised his hands. 'And you're doing a terrible job. Why, just yesterday, I found a turd sitting in the middle of the stream. It hadn't swept away and the culprit never bothered to clean up after themselves. We know how quickly a pox can spread. If I hadn't done something, why, who knows how many of you would have drunk tainted water.'

'You need us to keep the stream clean and protected,' said the big Heights dweller.

'And what do you expect for this service?' Cade called out.

Arren looked at her and smiled, lowering his arms but keeping his hands spread out, palms facing the crowd.

'If we are going to protect the water so that all of us can thrive, then we will need some … exchange. I suggest that whoever wants water, gives us some food. Not too much. Half an onion, a piece of meat, nothing that you would miss day to day.'

'Shit on you!' shouted someone from the crowd. 'We ain't paying!'

'No, let us through, damn it!'

'Come on, they can't stop us all.'

The Heights dwellers stepped back a pace. Cade could see doubt setting in. They started looking at each other, looking for direction.

'Please, it doesn't have to be this way, we only want to do what's right!' shouted Arren.

The crowd moved closer.

'Wait. I'll do it!' shouted a female from the crowd.

That stopped everyone in their tracks.

The woman stepped forward. 'I'll pay. I want my water clean, I don't want to die. Here,' she stepped up and handed over a piece of bread to Arren. He smiled warmly, bowing to the lady as he took the food.

'See? Take her bowl, ensure it is full to the brim,' ordered Arren.

A Heights dweller took her bowl, walked around the barricade and up into the water tunnel.

'This is a bloody stupid idea,' whispered Issar.

The problem was there were fewer folk wanting to do something about it now.

'Maybe this is for the best,' said someone else. And with that Cade knew their moment was lost.

'Everyone, trust me, this is for the best. All our lives will be better for this. Now, form a line and we will get all of you the water you deserve,' said Arren.

The crowd had quieted, was starting to follow Arren's direction. Smart.

Issar leaned in close. 'I know that woman. I saw Arren talking to her a couple of days ago. They looked pretty tight.'

Bet they were.

'Proves Arren's been planning this,' she said.

'And he got all his people on to the Heights, been doing it over the last few weeks,' said Issar. 'That big bastard and his mates threw out the last couple who weren't part of his work gang just the other day. Wasn't anyone able to stop them.'

'Arren had to make sure he had some muscle first. If he'd left it as a mixed crew of branded, then they could have been picked off during the shifts by the rest of us. He'd not have the strength to hold on to the Heights.'

'What are we gonna do about it?' asked Issar. Cade studied the look of expectation on his face, like he was waiting for orders.

'Nothing yet. We start trading food for water, just like everyone else.'

'Doesn't sound right,' said Issar frowning.

'It ain't. Fact is, we can't start a fight, too many of them, not enough of us. You know I said this would happen. Food and water are the currency now.'

'Shouldn't be,' Issar grumbled as he went to join the rest of the crowd, now quietly queuing for water.

Cade shook her head. Issar ought to know better. There's always the smart ones, the clever sons of bitches who get to the top. Happens everywhere. And they leech off the rest. *We're just going back to what we've always done. We'll keep doing it until it's too late to change.*

When they got back to their little slice of home, Devlin already had the fire going and was slicing up an onion with a relatively thin sliver of rock.

'Getting quite handy with that,' she said.

'A knife would be better,' he responded with a raised eyebrow.

'If only.' She passed over her offerings and Issar carefully threaded their pot on to a length of metal. It was held over the fire by two sticks that threatened to snap under the weight at any moment.

Meghan appeared and sat down next to Cade. She pulled her knees up to her chest and wrapped her arms about her knees. Cade noted she was quiet, just sat there, looking into the fire. Usually she had something to say.

'What's up with you?'

'I don't know whether to feel happy or sad.'

'The latter is more likely,' said Issar.

'Yes.' Meghan looked up and smiled weakly. 'I was up by the stream. Went with Jessene. We got talking. She's pregnant.'

'Oh,' said Issar.

'Shit,' said Devlin.

'Well, that was bloody stupid,' said Cade.

'I know. I asked her what she planned to do.'

'How far along is she?' asked Devlin.

'Long enough. She's starting to show.'

'She's married, ain't she?' said Cade.

'Yes.'

'So, if she's showing, sounds to me like it happened on the road here.'

'Reckon so,' agreed Devlin. He shook his head. 'Bloody stupid.'

'She's been wearing a larger shirt, been hiding it for as long as she can. Jessene says maybe she can hide it 'til the birth. Maybe the dwarves won't care.'

'They will,' said Cade.

'This will end badly,' said Devlin. He leaned back, pushed his legs forward whilst rotating his feet. 'You can't hide a baby in here. And think about it. Think who they spared. No children. No old folk.'

Issar placed a hand on Meghan's knee. He smiled awkwardly.

'Sorry, Meghan, we aren't sharing in the joy very much, we're just trying to be realistic.'

Meghan nodded. 'Like I said, I don't know whether to be happy or sad. I wouldn't wish this life on anyone.'

'Could be for them,' said Cade. 'When the dwarfs find out, they'll be pissed.'

'Can you not speak to our boss? Maybe we can talk him into something?' pleaded Meghan.

She's joking, right?

'Come on, think about it, "Hey, boss man, fancy having a baby on the payroll?" Meghan, that is a stupid, stupid idea. Don't think for one minute about ever asking a question like that. He'd give you such a slap you'd still be spinnin' a week from now.'

'She's right, Meghan,' said Devlin. 'The only reason we aren't beaten daily is because this dwarf of ours has a different way of looking at his business.'

Meghan sat back, her face contrite.

'I know. I hoped.'

'Don't,' said Cade. 'Don't ever do that.'

She poked at the fire with her boot. Things could be worse. She could be the one who was pregnant.

CHAPTER 22

The day was bright, if a little chill. A flock of birds passed overhead in a crude 'V' formation. They were heading south – winter was coming. Father Michael stretched his shoulders, stamped his feet a little. Around him, their small party gathered. The Emperor was in very good spirits. He was decked like a huntsman. He wore thigh-high leather boots, a rich brown in colour, supple and comfortable. He had matching gloves of the same leather, thick brown woollen trousers and a green tunic, open at the neck. He clearly wasn't feeling the cold, or at least wasn't showing it. He was already mounted on a chestnut horse. Father Michael knew little about the different breeds.

'Father! Good morning to you. Here is yours,' he said pointing at a dun-coloured beast. He tilted his head to check. It was a male and ungelded.

The Emperor followed his gaze and laughed.

'Someone had the foresight to think that we may need to breed these.'

'You said this horse was a palfrey? What does that mean?'

'It means that you are fortunate to be riding one. They are trained to walk at a comfortable pace and do not jar or jolt as others might. The ride is smoother. These horses are most favourable for an enjoyable day out. Not so good in a charge, though.'

'I should hope we aren't planning on doing any charging.'

'I doubt there is much call for it,' replied the Emperor. 'Here, young Uther will help you up.'

The Emperor's gangly servant beckoned Father Michael over with a knowing smile. It was almost a grin. Since the Emperor had awakened the lad had grown in arrogance.

'Don't be afear'd, Father. This one is broken in nicely.'

'Right.'

'You might want to adjust your robe a little. You don't want it getting caught up. Good. Just place your foot in the stirrup. That's right. Hand on the Pommel. Yes. Now, just haul yourself up and swing your leg over. One smooth movement. I've got the reins and I'll catch you if it goes wrong.'

He was already self-conscious enough. He didn't need this snot of a lad to rescue him. He pulled himself up hard with his arms, pushed down forcefully with his leg. He was still strong and supple and he accomplished the movement with ease. His leg clearing the horse's back with room to spare. He landed on the saddle hard. The horse shied away, snickering.

'Whoah!' cried Uther, the reins slipping from his hands.

For a moment the horse continued its sideways movement. Father Michael clung on for dear life.

'Gotcha,' said Uther, collecting the reins and slowing the horse down to a standstill. 'There you go. There you go.' He ran his hands along the horse's neck, whispering in its ear. 'Don't worry about the Father. He is a holy man. You'll need to do the thinking for him.' Uther was grinning now. 'Father, here you are.' He handed over the reins. 'This one will be fine now. Just go gently when you climb aboard. He can carry your weight but you don't need to throw it around so much.'

'Thank you,' Father Michael replied stiffly. 'I will try to remember that.'

'Well done, Father. Your first lesson,' said the Emperor. 'Ah, here is our escort.'

Two Gifted rode around the corner of the cabin. Helmeted and armoured, their sheathed longswords tied lengthways on their saddles, shields strapped to their backs. They still had the shortswords on either hip. Very impressive but it must be uncomfortable.

'That's an appraising look, Father. Do they look effective enough?'

'They look fine, Your Grace. They look quite intimidating.'

The Emperor rode his horse past him, leaning in close.

'But you don't,' he said with a smile. He leaned back in the saddle and announced loudly. 'All here? Now, let's be off!' He turned his mount and took them along the westward street leading out of the settlement. Father Michael pulled at the reins, and kicked at the horse's flanks. It refused to move. Damned beast. The Two Gifted rode by. They did not acknowledge him or the difficulty he was having.

'Father?'

'Hmm?'

'You need to be gentler.' It was Uther, leaning in close and resting his hand on the pommel. 'This horse knows how to ride and take commands. You just have to give the right ones. Keep your feet against his flanks, if you want him to move, just squeeze. You want him to turn, you squeeze with the left or right foot.'

'Right,' he was half listening. The others were getting too far ahead.

'And if you want to stop, just lean back and pull just a little on the reins.'

'Right. Squeeze his flanks.' Father Michael, squeezed. The horse started and jerked into a gentle gallop.

'Don't squeeze that hard!' called Uther.

Father Michael pulled back on the reins. The horse whinnied and came to a stop, its head swinging violently, pulling against his grip.

'Don't pull so hard!' Uther called.

Father Michael felt a surge of anger. He didn't do delicate. He swore, if those he'd fought in the arena could only see him now. *Right. Gently.* He pressed with his heels. The horse started to walk. He squeezed harder and it picked up its pace. Easy.

'Father!' he looked around. Uther was jogging along behind.

'One more thing. This horse is trained but even the best of them can be a bit wilful. It'll want to fight you. Just be firm.'

Father raised his hand in farewell.

'Ah, he wants to fight me?' he muttered. Good. He knew about fighting.

The sun was well past its zenith when one of the Gifted dropped back to join Father Michael who, despite his best efforts, was constantly in the rear. The damned creature never wanted to keep pace with the others and he was applying 'gentle pressure' every two minutes. The thing would speed up then slip back into its ambling pace. Father Michael could walk faster without it.

The Gifted walked his horse slowly, allowed Father Michael's to draw level and then urged his to maintain the same middling speed.

Father Michael scratched his chin and glanced over. The Gifted stared straight ahead. He fancied he was the same one that had stood guard outside the Emperor's cabin more often than not. He hadn't noticed it before but half the man's left ear was missing.

'I saw you fight in the arena. A few years back,' said the Gifted.

Father Michael didn't have an answer. Lots of folk had seen him.

From the corner of his eye he saw the Gifted look over.

'I was still young. I hadn't been found. Still free from the Schools. I watched you, wanted to be you. You were magnificent. A magnificent animal.'

Father Michael turned and saw the Gifted was smiling. There was a time he would have smacked the man down for that. If it had been the arena, he would have killed him. But then, he killed everyone in the arena.

'When I was found, and I learned to use my Gift, I realised there can be beauty in combat. It is a dance, a melding of mind and body, forms, shapes and symbols woven in the air at speeds most men cannot fathom.' A pause. He looked away, like there was something more interesting to watch. 'You never danced. You never had that grace. You just killed.'

Did this idiot have a point he wanted to make?

The Gifted deigned to meet his gaze. 'Look at you now,' he said. 'A man of faith. Just like me. What turned you?'

'I had a second chance. The Emperor saved me.'

The Gifted's mouth sloped downwards. 'Did he? Then you are truly blessed.'

'Yes.'

'And you ride with the Emperor.'

'There is need of me.'

The Gifted smiled again, amusement sparkling in his eyes. 'Do you advise him spiritually? Or are you simply a notary?'

He had no clue what a notary was but doubted it applied to him.

'I serve my Emperor with the skills I have.'

'Cardinal Yarn told me as much. I don't think you are the type to deliver sermons. She told me you are a protector, and I had to accord you respect as a Father of the Church.'

Accord me whatever you want. I don't care for it. The man smiled.

'My name is Eidion. I was a Scotian.'

I was a bastard.

'In my old tongue the name means "anvil". The Church councils us not to have pride, but I am proud of that name. Michael isn't your real name, is it?'

'No.'

They ambled in silence for a moment.

'I am devoted to His Grace. I will kill anything and anyone who would dare threaten his life. I am a Shaper, a warrior born. I regret that I did not fight for the old Emperor. My training and duties kept me away.'

Good for you.

'They say battle is not something you can truly train for. Not until you have been in one can you understand. At least that is what I hear the soldiers talk about around their camp fires as they share a cup. They sound defeated.' He hissed scornfully. 'They should be more thankful.'

'There have been hard times. They have a right to let off some steam.' Father Michael wondered why he was defending these men. *Probably because I understand what it's like to feel there is nothing left to you. When the world has sucked you dry and there is no purpose to life.* 'We all have our own ways of dealing with our burdens. Allow them theirs.'

Eidion bowed his head. 'As you say, Father. I was coming to a question, actually. We train for battle, have learned our dance, but you can never learn too much. Perhaps you would be willing to face me. I would value the opportunity to try my sword against yours. You have no problems facing a Shaper, do you?'

Father Michael closed his eyes. *So you are taunting me. You want to test yourself. I am not sorry to disappoint you.*

'I do not fight others for sport. I gave that up when I took my vows.'

Eidion frowned. 'Oh. That is a pity. I must have been mistaken. I had thought otherwise.' Eidion made a clicking noise. His horse responded and moved ahead.

'Do not fear, Father. We Gifted have been the Emperor's protectors for a hundred years. We will not fail him,' Eidion called back. The Emperor and the other Gifted were far ahead now. They were unlikely to have heard the exchange.

Father Michael watched the back of Eidion as he rode on.

What had that been all about? Some kind of cockfight? He resolved to speak to the Arch Cardinal about this. There should be no room for this kind of behaviour in the Church. Especially not now, not when there should be unity.

The day was late when they finally made it to the logging camp. The sun was low in the horizon. Father Michael reflected on the fact that he must be getting old. There was a time when he could survive on only a few hours rest a night. A mixture of early mornings and long days did not agree with him anymore. His thighs were sore, chafed even. Earlier that day during a rest stop the Emperor had echoed his squire's words, patiently telling him that the horse he rode was not bred for war and had been much favoured by the women of the court for their gentle demeanour and ease of travel. If that were so then he had a new-found respect for the Emperor's cavalry. They must be men of iron.

The Emperor was already off his horse and leading it towards the small encampment that had been constructed at the edge of the forest. Father Michael slid off the saddle and followed, inspecting the camp, such as it was. Two wagons, both empty, their horses grazing placidly nearby, were parked next to a faint trail. A pile of tree trunks, stripped of their branches, rested next to them. There were four tents set up in a circle facing a central fire pit. One tent was larger than the others, as tall as the height of one man, with plenty of room inside.

Two eagles were settled on the ground. He'd spied one in the air earlier on their journey to the forest. Their Riders were walking towards the Emperor. He did not see anyone else about, though he could hear voices coming from the forest.

'Leader Cadarn, Rider Bryce.'

Both men dipped their heads.

'Emperor. The skies are clear and there is not a soul to be seen,' said Cadarn.

'I did not doubt it for a moment,' replied the Emperor. 'I wondered where you two were. Hadn't seen you in the skies for an hour or so.'

'We were nearby,' said Cadarn.

'My thanks for providing the accommodation.'

Cadarn nodded. 'One of us will maintain a constant vigil. If we spot anything, I'll ensure the message is passed back to you. The Watcher back home should also be maintaining their sight on this location.'

'Thank you, Leader Cadarn.'

Cadarn bowed again and turned to Bryce.

'You can take the first turn. I want to make sure everything is settled here.'

'Alright. Just don't forget I haven't had supper yet,' said Bryce.

'I'll save you some.'

'You better. You know how grumpy I get.'

'I know how more grumpy you get, if that's what you mean,' said Cadarn.

'Pah.' Bryce waved his hand dismissively and stalked over to his bird.

Father Michael watched the man mount his eagle and launch into the skies. He was slightly in awe. He wondered whether he could do such a thing. Then he remembered his thighs. How much worse would it be up there? He scratched at the cloth bandage he had wrapped around his forearm. He'd cleaned and dressed the wounds and he was confident there was no infection, but they were a little itchy. An itch was good, it meant the skin was healing. He doubted the Baron had ever gotten his hands dirty enough to carry infection.

The Gifted dismounted and led their horses towards a rope that had been suspended between two younger trees. They tied the horses off and took post to either side of the larger tent. It was then that he noticed the Speaker mark beneath the faceplate of the second Gifted. It was not like him to miss a detail like that.

'Father?' called the Emperor. 'Can I interest you in some ale to line the stomach before supper?'

The Emperor was kneeling by the firepit, filling a mug from a clay jug.

'No, Your Grace. Just promise me, no more riding.'

'Huh, that I can do!'

'Speaking of which, what is for supper?' Father Michael found he had a mighty hunger now he was off that beast of his.

'I suspect it might be that,' the Emperor indicated with the jug.

Behind Father Michael, two hunters emerged from the trees. Both were men well into their later years, hard and grizzled. They had long leather bags on their backs, probably their longbows. One was also carrying a brown sack over one shoulder. They dropped to one knee on reaching the Emperor.

'Your Grace,' they both intoned, heads down which muffled their voices a little.

'Stand up, please. We are a long way from home.'

The huntsmen stood. One crossed his arms. He had a squint in his right eye, a patchy brown beard and looked like he never smiled. Father Michael was led to understand both men were long-time servants to the Imperial family, helping to manage their old estates and forests. He wondered what they made of this new world.

'Did you find anything promising, Reese?'

'Plenty of game trails, my lord. We were just out setting some lures,' said Reese.

'Excellent. It's a pity we didn't get here a little earlier. We might've caught something for supper. I don't relish another night of fish and hard bread.'

The huntsman unfolded his arms. 'No fear o'that. We already caught you some birds. Found 'em lurking just inside the trees. Easy.' He pointed to his companion who produced two large fowl from his sack. They looked a little like chickens but were twice the size. 'And there's this.' They both retreated into the nearest tent. He heard some heavy rustling and then a breath being blowed out.

They emerged with a prize.

The two huntsmen had a crudely cut branch resting on their shoulders. Suspended from it was a deer carcass, its fore and hind legs bound together by leather straps, its head hanging low, not far from the ground. Its neck had been cut.

'Thought we'd keep it in there. Just in case.'

'See that, Father? We will be feasting tonight,' smiled the Emperor.

'If it please you. We'll be getting on with it,' said Reese.

'Oh, it pleases me.'

The huntsman bowed his head to the Emperor and flicked a glance Father Michael's way. It wasn't suspicion, just mild curiosity. The Arch Cardinal had told him just to accept the looks. A man of faith wasn't supposed to be such a large a brute like he was. Unless he was one of the Gifted.

'Father?'

'Yes, Emperor?'

'Have you seen where they put the wineskins?'

'I'm not sure. Perhaps one of the tents?'

'Hmm. They aren't going to do much good in there, are they?'

The Emperor stood up.

'Your Grace, I'll get them.'

The Emperor threw his hands up. 'Father, I am entirely capable of getting my own drink. If they're lucky I might get some for these lads as well,' he said loudly, indicating several of the woodsmen who were emerging from the forest. His comments drew smiles.

'It's thirsty work, Your Grace. You pour it. We'll drink it!' one of them shouted back with a grin on his face.

The Emperor waved them off and continued to the tents.

Father Michael was impressed by the easy manner in which the Emperor endeared himself to his people. It was an expression of his godly powers. Proof that the Emperor truly was divine. He felt a sensation of warmth well up from his stomach. Looking up at the sky, at the darkening blue, at the stars already visible scattered widely across the firmaments, he smiled.

'You've got us dinner, then?' said another one of the woodsmen, his axe in one arm, a log balanced on his shoulder.

'I'll trade you some for wood for the fire,' the Emperor called back, emerging from a tent, a wineskin in hand.

The huntsmen lowered the carcass next to the fire. The Emperor stood and supervised as they took out small skinning knives and got to work preparing the animal for cooking.

The evening was far more pleasant than the day. Father Michael sat a little to one side of the fire, away from everyone else, and watched them all. The company of the woodsmen and hunters was easy, they laughed and joked and accepted the Emperor as one of their own. For his part he drank, and laughed and joked right back. Behind him, one of the Gifted stood guard, hidden within the shadows of the largest tent. At least his presence was not overly intrusive. Later, once the sky had lost its colour, he watched Bryce's eagle come in. The night was still bright and the stars shone amidst a waxing moon. Ten minutes later Cadarn's took off.

Bryce took a seat next to him. He carried a bowl of steaming stew in one hand and a piece of the deer in the other. He nodded at Father Michael and got to work. They sat in companionable silence.

'You had any?' said Bryce

'What?'

'Any of this?' Bryce waved the deer meat at him.

'Oh. No. Just the stew.'

'Good choice. This is bloody tough, I almost lost a tooth just now.'

'Uh huh.'

'Always look after your teeth,' continued Bryce, ignoring his own advice and taking another nibble. 'You only get one set.'

'True.'

'Heard you were a fighter. Arena man.'

Father Michael paused. Even now, even a thousand miles and another life away, he couldn't escape. 'Yes.'

'Huh,' said Bryce, nodding his head as he sucked a finger. 'Never went to the arena. Grew up in the Highlands. You get tough by living, no time to go watching a show. Reckon you got tough by living too.' He threw the last bit of meat back towards the fire.

'Time for a nap. Good talking to you, Father.'

'Yes. Good night.'

'Reckon not. I'm up again in four hours. But that's life.' Bryce disappeared into the night, heading towards his eagle.

Had he just been given a compliment? Had they even talked properly? Still, it had been a far warmer encounter than with Eidion. Bryce's idea of sleep had taken root. There was a tent he could use, but he was happy enough to sleep by the fire. He spread out the blanket he had retrieved from his saddle. Lying back he turned away from the chatter. He could feel the heat against his neck and head. It felt good.

Father Michael felt his heart pounding, his breath ragged. He was not sure how far he'd run but the sun had been little more than a distant glow in the horizon. He'd had to take care, unsure of his footing. That was no bad thing as he'd been labouring as it was. Too out of shape, too long forgetting what he was and where he came from. The camp was before him, the pickets watching his approach. He raised a hand, saw one raised in return then he dropped the hand to his waist belt. His fingers wrapped around the pommel of the blade held close to his side. He pulled, hearing a gentle scraping sound as it slid out of the scabbard. He leapt high in the air, tucking his feet under him, then, as he landed, he let his legs collapse and he dropped low. The tips of his fingers brushed the ground as he pushed forward into a roll. As he came out of it, he thrust forwards and upwards with his blade. He pulled his arm back, rising and twisting, cutting the air behind him with a backhand slash. Upright once more, he advanced against an unseen enemy. Cutting, stabbing, feinting, swerving, swaying, always changing his approaches, never using the same attack twice.

Move right when they expect you to move left, slice left when they expect right. Don't become predictable. Let them tire as you remain strong. Then step close and finish them quick.

It was a mantra he had repeated most of his adult life, though it had been some time since he'd last used it. He finished his routine and stood in the chill early morning light, sucking in air. As he blew it out, his breath misted and steam rose from his bare chest. He knew it was cold, but he barely felt it thanks to his exertions. That would change soon enough when his body cooled. He was tired, more so then he should be. There was a time he would barely break a sweat with a routine like that. Age and his new life had done that to him.

He gathered his undershirt, placed it over his head and then reached for the sword's scabbard, replacing the blade. He would return it to Bryce along with his thanks. Finally he collected his robes and tucked them under his free arm. He needed to piss before he put them on. He walked towards the trees and ducked round the nearest, hiding himself from the camp. He released his fly and watched the clear stream splash against the bark.

'Morning, Father.'

'Oh, good morning, Your Grace.' He felt embarrassment wash over him. He'd thought his place in the trees would have been more than adequate.

The Emperor stood beside him and fiddled with his trousers.

'Ahh.'

Another stream of steaming urine fountained on to the same tree Father Michael had used. He stepped back, allowing the Emperor some privacy as he tucked himself back in.

'You went to bed early,' he said over his shoulder. The piss continued.

'Um. Yes. Tired. And my thighs are still aching.'

'Ah, well. We all had to start somewhere.'

He hitched up his britches, turned and clapped Father Michael on the back.

'Though I have to say, my head is a mess. Those lads can drink. Heading back?'

Father Michael felt the Emperor's eyes on him as he steered them back towards the camp.

'Quite a combat routine you have worked out there. I couldn't tell what you were going to do next.'

'That's the idea, Your Grace. Even I don't know.'

'And if you don't know, how is your enemy supposed to.'

'Yes.' Father Michael was impressed.

As they drew near, one of the Gifted moved close and bowed. It was Eidion.

'Your Grace. Leader Cadarn asks if you might speak with him in private.'

'In private, you say?' replied the Emperor. He looked at Father Michael, an eyebrow raised.

'Very well. Far be it from me to ignore such a summons. Father? Please attend me.'

Together they walked the short distance to where the Eagle Riders billeted. The Gifted hung back, taking his station near the Emperor's tent. Father Michael noticed how both of the creatures were on the ground; settled, resting easily, heads jerking and shifting as they watched their approach.

Leader Cadarn stood in quiet conversation with Bryce. He turned. His face was grave. 'Your Grace.'

'Leader. What is amiss? I understood that a constant vigil was to be maintained,' said the Emperor.

'I felt, given the circumstances, it was better to report to you.'

'Circumstances?'

Captain Cadarn nodded. 'It was Bryce who found it. Best he tell you.'

'Go on,' commanded the Emperor.

Bryce scratched his head.

'I was out this morning. I thought I'd do a circuit of the forest. We kept low. Figured Odolf would like some breakfast.'

'Who?'

'My eagle.'

'Ah.'

'Anyways. This forest ain't that big, least not as the eagle flies. I reached the far side of it after an hour. Realised I needed to piss, begging your pardon, Your Grace. So I landed and wandered over to the nearest tree. And then I saw it.'

'Saw what?'

'A lean-to.'

'A lean-to?'

'Yeah. You know. Not a cabin, just a shelter really. A bunch of thicker branches tied together, held up on a slant by a crude frame.'

'I understand what you mean,' said the Emperor a little testily. 'But are you sure? Could it not have been just a jumble of old trees, perhaps blown down from a storm?'

'I checked. It was old, covered with moss. Easy to miss. But unless squirrels have learned to make rope and tie knots, it was built by somebody.'

Father Michael smiled in spite himself. He liked Bryce, even if his comments were bordering on disrespectful.

The Emperor looked at Leader Cadarn. 'Really?'

The Eagle Rider nodded.

'I don't doubt the honesty of my Riders, but in this case, I thought I'd better check. He's right, Your Grace. It was there.'

'Damn.' He shook his head.

'We have only just returned,' continued Cadarn. 'I wanted to do a little more scouting around, see if we could find anything else.'

'And?'

'Nothing. No trace of life or further habitation. No firepits, no tools left behind.'

The Emperor tapped his lip with his index finger. 'Father? Your thoughts?'

Father Michael pondered the implications as quickly as he could.

'Someone else got here before us?'

The Emperor nodded. 'And?'

'Perhaps they were the survivors of a shipwreck. There have been attempts to cross the seas before.'

'There have,' the Emperor confirmed.

'Maybe someone already lived here?' said Cadarn.

'Maybe they still do,' added Bryce. He leaned over and spat. His eagle followed the jet of phlegm and eyed it.

'How long to ride around?' asked the Emperor.

'Half a day or so,' said Cadarn.

'I would like to see this for myself. How could I miss it? We can start out this morning and be back before dusk.'

'Of course. Perhaps you'd rather fly? I could take you up myself. We'd be there and back before midday,' said Cadarn.

'Fly?' The Emperor shook his head. 'I never even considered it. Yes, why not?' He beamed at them all and clapped his hands. 'This is a most diverting mystery! And I feel my mouth could do with a wash out. Leader Cadarn, Flier Bryce, join me for ale?'

The two riders exchanged a look and Bryce shrugged. Father Michael suspected they might be Speaking. Leader Cadarn turned to the Emperor and bowed his head. 'I will join you for a drink Your Grace, just the one however. I will need a clear head to fly.'

'Alcohol messes up our thoughts and gets the eagles all confused,' added Bryce.

'Very good. Let's see what's for breakfast. Oh. One more thing. Let's not share this with the rest of the men. Not until we know for certain what it is we are dealing with. Our people do not need to fear any more bogeymen. They have had enough of that back home.'

'As you wish,' said Cadarn.

'Aye, damn right,' said Bryce.

Father Michael just nodded.

'Good.' The Emperor turned and headed back towards the fire pit. Father Michael stayed. He couldn't say why, but he needed a little space. Time to think.

'I could do with a bloody ale,' said Bryce. 'I bloody found the thing and instead I have to get back to sentry duty. No justice in the world eh, Father?'

'Was there ever?' He couldn't remember. He didn't know what it looked like.

Bryce gave a grunt. He turned about and started to adjust the saddle on his eagle.

'Good point you make, Father.' He hauled himself up. His eagle, Odolf was it? stood up and stretched out its wings. 'Let me know if you spot any, I'd love to know what it looks like before I die.'

Father Michael watched as the eagle took to the skies, the downwash of the wings blowing a little dirt into his eyes. He shielded his face, watching as the bird and rider grew smaller, curving left and passing in front of the sun rising in the east. A lean-to. Life. Something none of them had been expecting. What would this mean for them all? It all made sense, this trip out to the forest. The Emperor was truly leading them to a new future.

CHAPTER 23

'Sabin?'

Fillion turned to watch Ezra jog along the corridor towards him.

'Morning, Ezra. You feeling all right?' he asked. The Servant looked a little out of breath. He smiled and put a hand up.

'Sorry, just give me a moment.' The black haired elf was almost as old as Patiir, although seemed to carry it with a greater burden. His shoulders were permanently sloped and his eyebrows had gone grey. No doubt working for Member Tekla would do that to a man. She had a fierce mind. Ezra inhaled deeply and blew out. Fillion smelled garlic.

'Better?' he asked.

'Yes. Thank you. Here you are.' Ezra handed over a leather bound sheaf of documents.

'And these might be?' said Fillion.

'Oh. I thought you knew. It doesn't matter. Member Patiir requested some reports of taxation levels for the last fifty years. Member Tekla has approved their release. So here they are.'

'Right.' Fillion found himself a little annoyed. He had expected to be made aware of all Patiir's business and requirements but found he was always one step behind.

'Did you speak to Marmus?' asked Ezra.

'What about?' *Something else he hadn't been told about?*

'Oh, nothing much, I'm sure. He was asking for a meeting with Member Patiir.'

'Then why didn't he come to me?'

Ezra put his hands up.

'Oh, I'm sure he will. I heard it in passing. Ambassador Marmus was in Member Wheyburn's office. I was just walking by.'

'Right.' He had yet to personally meet Marmus, the dwarf ambassador, but had already developed a healthy dislike. He spent most of his time wondering around the Parliament pontificating to anyone who would listen. Fillion supposed that when you are that short you have to make a bigger noise.

'I'll wait for him to make a formal request then.'

He nodded at Ezra and continued on his way.

'Mind if I walk along with you?' asked Ezra.

Piss off. 'Not at all.'

He slowed his pace a little and Ezra drew up alongside him.

'How are your studies proceeding?' asked Ezra.

'They go well. Although I find my time for reading is becoming less and less. Patiir has me running messages for most of the day.'

'Such is the life of a Servant,' Ezra responded with a wry smile.

'I suppose,' said Fillion.

'I have heard it said the King is soon to be leaving for his winter residence.'

'Uh huh.'

'So I imagine there'll be a gathering of Parliament.'

'Isn't there always?'

'Ah, another new event for you. The King always attends a special session before he departs. It is quite the affair. Things get very exciting.'

'Do they?'

'Oh yes. It's his chance to tell Parliament what he expects of them over the cold months.'

'I thought we recessed during winter?'

Ezra bobbed his head. 'We do. The Members all return to their estates, manor houses or city residences. But government continues. It depends on what is required but a few ministers and Members will be going nowhere. That's the excitement. Finding out who that will be.'

'Sound exciting. Surely the likes of Chancellor Nazar and Member Tekla are required to stay?'

'No, not often. Taxes are never collected this time of year. At least, none are delivered to the Treasury. The merchant lanes are mostly closed. So Member Tekla likes to return home. She has much to organise and inspect. Very much like Member Patiir.'

'I suppose so.' Did that mean they were leaving the capital this winter?

'I imagine Patiir will want to discuss matters pertaining to war reparations?' asked Ezra, gazing at a window.

'I'm sure he will.' It had gone very quiet over that matter. Even Patiir had not mentioned it since Fillion's first visit to the Parliament.

'Ah. I think our paths diverge here,' announced the elf.

'Yes.' They were on the steps leading down to the lower levels.

'Well. It was good to see you.'

'And you, Ezra. No doubt I'll see you later.'

'No doubt.' Ezra bowed low and bustled off.

'You look like you've just had a fight with an angry bear,' said a cheerful voice.

Fillion looked down and smiled. Coming up the stairs was another elf wearing a red sash over a worn, sleeveless leather jerkin. He had short blond hair, left to grow thick and spikey. Braids were woven into those clumps and tassels hung from them. His ears were prominent, each one pierced many times with metal and bone and even a small bell, so he jingled a little as he moved. His arms were covered in bands, bracelets and bits of material. To cap it all, most of his skin was covered in tattoos. A mass of curving twisting lines, eldritch symbols and abstract pictures of wild creatures. Fillion had learned not to focus on them too much as the mess of shapes hurt his eyes. The elf's name was Kanyay, and he was a wood elf.

'I'm not sure Ezra could do angry if he tried. It would exhaust him too much,' replied Fillion.

'True enough,' said Kanyay with a thoughtful look. 'Maybe a lazy bear then.'

'I was thinking more a sloth.'

Kanyay grinned. His teeth were bright white and sharp, the ivory tapering down into wicked incisors. Fillion had always thought they filed them down on purpose, but Kanyay had told him it was all natural, they were born that way. It did not make him feel any more assured. Wood elves were prone to eat their enemies.

'Are you going to the Chalice later?' asked Kanyay.

'I might go after the library today. I am almost halfway through the histories now.'

Kanyay frowned.

'They work you too hard. Besides, who cares about what happened a thousand years ago? Why would I want to fill my mind up with such nonsense.'

Fillion agreed wholeheartedly.

'It is a burden I must bear to serve my people.'

Kanyay sighed dramatically and slapped him on the arm.

'I know, my friend. I feel it too. And you have the added burden of having me as a bosom companion.'

Fillion was surprised as anyone that he had formed an alliance with this wild creature from the west. He expected it was because Kanyay was an outsider like him. At least Kanyay could admit to it, and do so at every opportunity. He was so unexpected in this place and so utterly welcome. Finally Fillion had someone he didn't have to maintain an air of formality with, like he did with the others. The wood elf was accorded the rank of a Servant; in reality he was the closest thing the wood elves had to an ambassador. He acted as the messenger and mouthpiece for his tribes and sent news from the more cultured nation of the Heartlands. They clearly had a problem raising a wood elf to Member status and Kanyay did not want to be considered an ambassador. He said it sounded far too pompous. Instead he wore the sash, and only then because he liked the colour.

'It is a burden I can live with.' Fillion smiled back.

'Just don't spend all evening amidst the dust,' said Kanyay, his face a frown.

'I can't imagine I'll do too much. It's been a long day already.'

This time Kanyay clapped him on the shoulder.

'Good. I hate to drink alone.'

Fillion knew he'd happily do it anyway.

Fillion staggered home well past midnight. He was sure it wasn't the wine, though he and Kanyay had gotten through enough of it. He was just tired. When he got to the archway, he took a moment to straighten himself up. He untied his sash from where it had slipped down over his arse and retied it back around his waist. He yanked at his tunic, trying to straighten out the folds and creases. He could do little about his wine-tinged breath.

Walking into the house proper he saw a light coming from the drawing room. He shut the door and made for the stairs.

'Sabin.'

Shit. Patiir. Doesn't that bastard ever sleep?

He turned around and prepared himself for a browbeating. Patiir was in his usual place at the fire, which was burning merrily, a pile of logs stacked neatly beside the hearth. A small table held a carafe of red. In his hand Patiir cupped a glass, a third full of the stuff.

'Sir,' said Fillion.

'Sit down.'

Fillion took the seat opposite. He realised he was still wearing his cloak. Patiir raised an eyebrow.

'I'd offer you one of these,' he said raising his glass. 'But something tells me that you have had quite enough already.'

Fillion knew better than to respond to that, even in his muddled state.

'I imagine you have been consorting with the wood elf again?'

'Yes.'

Patiir shook his head. 'I ought to be annoyed at that, but having him close does have its uses, I suppose. Just watch yourself with him. He might be the most civilised member of his race I know, but he still has the potential to cause havoc and mayhem given half the chance.'

One of the reasons I like him. It was a shame he was an elf.

'I understand.'

Patiir looked into his glass.

'Tekla asked when I would be scheduling my request to speak before the King and Parliament.' He left the comment hanging. Fillion had to think. Patiir wanted a response ... Oh.

'Ezra.'

'Yes. You spoke to him earlier today no doubt.'

'I did.'

'I have not told you about any plans to talk to the King. So I can only assume you suggested the idea yourself?'

'Umm. Not exactly. Ezra did the suggesting for me.'

'I'm sure he did.' Patiir sighed. 'The fact is that I *am* planning on speaking before the Parliament. I had not publicly pursued the issue since my initial proposal. It is a common practice of mine to wait, to go patiently whilst I built a body of support. These things take time and persistence.'

'Patiir, I am sorry, I did not realise.'

'No, you did not.' Patiir's voice was stern, the admonishment clear. He took a sip of wine, his face softening. 'No harm done. Ezra was fishing. It's what he does. Tekla is, for the most part, an ally. It doesn't matter overmuch that she knows my plan. She would have expected nothing less of me.' He placed his glass on the table, folded his hands under his chin and leaned forwarded a little. 'Sabin. You play the part of the bluff borderlands soldier well, but you must learn to be more guarded, more circumspect. You cannot take anyone at their face value. Except perhaps Kanyay. He is as transparent as they come. Politics is a game. I have played it all my life. I am good at it, but I must know that you will not become a weak link.'

Fillion nodded. It felt strange to be chided in this way. This man was a sworn enemy, not a senior officer, not his Emperor.

'I know it cannot last as an excuse, my being new to all of this. I was tired and distracted. It won't happen again. I promise to be more guarded in my dealings. This place is more complicated that I gave it credit for,' he said, with as much humility as he could muster.

Patiir smiled. 'That it is. And I do want you to do well. I need to be able to trust you with my plans and intentions more openly. I need someone to work with. You are family after all. Almost.'

'Sir?' Something was coming.

'It's about time that you and my daughter stopped the pretence. I would have you marry her. And quickly. Your courtship has been fast but it is publically acceptable, considering the circumstances of your meeting.'

'Courtship?'

'Honestly, Sabin, don't looked so shocked. Everyone in the city is like to know of it. I would have you marry Nadena in the Spring.'

'Patiir, I don't know what to say.'

'You have nothing to say to me. You have something to say to my daughter.'

'Yes. Yes, of course.'

Patiir collected his glass and took another sip of wine. 'Now off to bed with you. Another long day tomorrow no doubt.'

Fillion took his leave and walked slowly and deliberately upstairs. That was it then. Everything had come together. There was nothing more he could do. He had the access to the inner circle of the Parliament and the ear and potential trust of one of the most powerful elves in the realm. All that mattered now was what he was going to do with all of that.

He entered his bedroom. It was dark. He shrugged off his cloak, undid his sash and threw off his boots. He felt his way over to the bed and crawled on top of it.

'You are late,' murmured Nadena.

He hadn't noticed her. He reached out with his hands, tracing the shape of her body under the blankets.

'Yes, I'm here,' she said lightly.

'You know your father is still awake don't you?' She was taking a risk coming to his bed like this, even now. It wasn't done.

'I know.'

He felt her shift position. When she spoke again her face was not far from his. 'You talked to him?'

'Yes.'

'You know that I love you?'

'Yes.'

'We are to be married.'

'I thought I had to ask you first.'

'Like you have a choice, Sabin.'

'Still, there is a form to these things.'

'Sabin. We must marry soon.'

'The Spring. It seems a little …'

'Sabin. I'm pregnant.'

'Uh … Um … Oh.'

'You are so eloquent.'

That explained the need for haste then.

'I … I don't know what to say.'

'You start by saying how happy you are.'

'Ah. Right. Yes. Yes, I am happy. I'm happy. I'm …'

'Speechless?'

'That too.'

She laughed softly. 'It's okay. Just sleep. I'll be here. We can talk in the morning.'

'Yes, um. Good.'

She kissed him lightly on the check.

Fillion couldn't move. He just lay there, gazing up into nothing. Speechless didn't cover the half of it. Oh sweet Emperor. What had he done?

Part Six

ANOTHER YEAR
OF LIVING

CHAPTER 24

The two guards moved down the line, Geir at their head. He paused at each person, looked at his or her face, then made a mark in his ledger and moved on. He arrived at Jessene, looked her up and down and made a mark. He turned to one of the guards and spoke a few indistinct words. The guard drew his sword and stepped up to Jessene. He pulled her tunic up, exposing her rounded belly. She tried to take a pace back.

'No!' she blurted out, part sob, part scream.

Gwillem was two spaces to her right and leapt forward.

'Wait, stop!' He reached for Jessene but the second guard moved into his way and slammed a fist into his side. Gwillem doubled up.

The first rammed his blade into Jessene's belly. She let out a soft grunt that trailed to a gasp. The dwarf pulled his blade out, blood streaming from the wound. Jessene's legs gave way. She fell on to her knees, her hands trying to block the flow of blood. Gwillem crawled forward, trying to reach for her.

'Jessene!'

The second dwarf pulled out a knife and smashed the hilt into the back of Gwillem's head, knocking him cold.

Blood was pouring through Jessene's fingers, pooling around her knees. Her mouth was open, a strange mewling sound coming from it. The first guard stood beside her and rubbed the flat of his sword across the top of her shoulder, one side, then the other, removing the blood from the blade.

Geir was already continuing his work, moving along the line. There had been not a murmur, not a ripple of movement from anyone within the group. Only the eyes had shifted, glimpsing the action from the edges of their vision. No one dared to turn their heads. Everyone knew what happened if you did. It was simple survival. As he passed by Cade, he looked up at her, his dark eyes moving swiftly across her face, looking for Emperor knew what. He turned to his ledger and made a mark.

'Collect Gwillem when we have finished, get him up. He has work to do,' he said, his voice a quiet yet authoritative growl. *Great.* With that he moved on as the two guards caught up with him and fell into step, looking for all the world like nothing had happened. Once they had moved beyond her, she flicked her eyes back to Jessene. She was still on her knees, her top half had folded forward, her head resting upon her chest. Cade knew that position. She was already dead and gone. Damn it all, why did that bastard dwarf have to stop and speak to her? It was one thing to try and butter up the boss, but now Geir had made her look like she was a toady, that she was their bitch, someone to clean up their work. Folk would pick up on that, some would start whispering, start spreading the word she wasn't to be trusted. This kind of thing was liable to get her dead.

Once the Accounting was complete, the parade broke up and started to make its way to the Downside Gate. Cade made her way across to Gwillem. He was sprawled on the ground, his arms flung wide. She hunkered down and checked him over. There was a dark moist patch under his hair, gently glistening in the firelight. Maybe his skull was cracked? It was always hard to tell with a head wound. She placed a hand on his neck, felt a pulse. Damn, she'd hoped he'd be dead. Another problem.

'He okay?' asked Devlin. He was standing by the woman, his feet just outside the pool of blood.

'Yeah.'

'Jessene's dead, or she will be soon. You can't lose that much blood and live.'

'No.'

'Want a hand with him?'

'Yeah.'

Devlin took up position on the other side of Gwillem and placed a hand on his shoulder.

'Gwillem. Hey.' He shook him gently. 'Gwillem. You need to get up.' Gwillem moaned in response.

They needed to move faster. Most of the group were already through the gate and the dwarves weren't likely to be patient.

'We need to get him up, carry him if we have to,' she said.

'Alright.' Devlin, picked up Gwillem's right arm, draped it round his shoulder and reached his arm round the unconscious man's back. With a grunt he pulled Gwillem up into a sitting position. He looked at Cade.

'A little help?'

Cade repeated the motion on her side. Together they hauled and got Gwillem draped between them, hanging limply. They started to drag him towards the gate, his legs scuffing uselessly along the ground behind them, head lolling from one side to the other, still groaning, spit drooling from his mouth.

'Damn, he's bloody heavy,' said Cade. 'I thought we were all supposed to have lost weight.'

'You've just gotten weaker, is all,' said Devlin. 'Gwillem. Wake the fuck up and start using your legs. We ain't carrying you all day.'

Guards looked on with disinterest as they pulled him through the gate and into the passage leading to the mines, the slope helping to take some of the pressure off her aching back. Midway down the lad had recovered enough that his legs were moving, albeit unsteadily.

'Jessene,' he whispered. 'Jessene. Where is she?'

'She's gone,' said Cade.

'No, no, she's not.'

'She's dead, Gwillem,' said Devlin gently.

'Bastards. Bastards. Fucking bastards. I'll kill them. I'll kill them,' growled Gwillem.

'Good luck with that,' muttered Cade.

Gwillem started to sob. 'I'll fucking tear their hearts out.'

'Nothing you can do,' Devlin counselled, his voice calm. They were entering the chamber leading to the various mines. A lot of people were there, still gathering their tools for the day. 'Leastways not about that.

It's your choice. You can decide to live or you can take up one of those picks over there and take a swing at one of those guards.'

Cade watched Gwillem closely. Emotions were flickering across his face at speed. He was weighing his chances, deciding whether to live or die. His lips were pinched, his eyes narrowed. She felt his body tense next to hers. Then the moment passed. His tension faded. His body went limp once more. He let out a shuddering sigh.

'Good choice,' said Devlin. 'Stick with me today, when they come to check on the work, stay back, we'll cover for you.'

Gwillem nodded dumbly. Cade stood behind him as he was issued his pick, watched him stumble along behind Devlin as they entered the depths of their shaft and disappeared from view. She was glad of Devlin's help. She'd never have been able to handle Gwillem by herself. What a fucking way to start the day. It was a lesson they all needed to learn. No matter what concessions they gained, no matter if they got better treatment, they were still just tools. The dwarfs didn't want them to breed and weren't interested in creating fresh slave labour. When they were done being useful, they were done. The future truly was grim. The game now was seeing how long you could stay alive. It could be worse. She was good at that game.

Her day didn't improve when a younger woman with drab blonde hair and washed-out blue eyes grabbed her arm with both hands. She'd only just walked through the damned gate. A bit of peace and quiet would have been nice.

The woman looked frightened, her hands squeezed a little too tightly for her liking.

'What?'

'Someone wants a word.'

'Do they?'

'You've got to come.'

'Do I?'

'Yes.'

Clearly Cade's natural sarcasm was lost on this one. 'Alright.' She shooed the woman forward.

Cade followed her into the heart of the chamber. It was a maze, a labyrinth of thin wooden walls, dusty, dirt-stained sheets and shit-strewn pathways. It also stank more than she was used to. The air couldn't get inside here so easily, so the stench couldn't get out. As the woman led them into the winding mess, Cade made sure to keep her bearings. It wasn't hard. If you looked up you could see the Heights, get a sense of where the Gates were in relation. Not that she'd be able to find a straight route out of here.

The woman stopped outside a crudely built hovel. It had the look of having been there for a while, a dwarf-made one. It had three walls and a sheet doubling up as a curtain.

'In there,' said the woman. She was already backing up. Honestly, what was she afraid of? They were all dead already.

Cade nodded and pulled the sheet back.

'Knock, knock.' She looked inside. It was gloomy, but then so was everywhere. A figure detached itself from the darkened rear of the structure.

'You Cade?' said a low, deep voice.

'Depends.'

'Yeah, you're her.'

The figure got close, a face appearing. Features became clearer, a stern visage, big bushy eyebrows that met in the middle, eyes a little too close together. *Anzo?*

'I'm Herrick.'

Not Anzo.

'Herrick. Not heard of you.'

'No? Good. I like it that way.'

'What do you want, then?'

Herrick paused, pushing his lips and mouth out. It made him look petulant. He stepped around Cade and she got a whiff of stale sweat. It was powerful. It had to be to have any effect in this place. Herrick twitched the side of the sheet, popped his head out, and looked left and right. He withdrew, letting the sheet fall back into place and returned his gaze to Cade.

'You attacked one of my people.'

'One of your people?'

'Don't play smart. I know it was you.'

It was funny, she didn't know him, and she thought she'd worked out who was who. *Getting sloppy.*

'You stopped him doing his job. That's annoying. It makes me look bad.'

'Sorry to hear that. What's it to me?'

A hand shot out, closing around her throat. It was big, the fingers thick and she felt her herself being raised off the ground. Her heels lost contact with the floor, her straining toes barely touching it. She gripped the hand with hers, trying to pry it loose. Emperor he was strong! She could barely breathe. She felt the constriction, the pressure. She wanted to choke, to gag. All that came out was a gurgle.

He leaned in and whispered in her ear. 'You want to think very carefully about what you say next.'

He let up, releasing his fingers and pulling his arm away.

Cade dropped down. She staggered back, breathing deep, trying to get air back into her lungs. This met the overwhelming desire to cough, and for a few moments she was fighting for air again. Herrick waited for her to gather herself. Cade stood up straighter and wiped spit off her chin. 'Alright. Let me put it another way. What do you want me to do?'

'I want you to work for me.'

'Huh?'

'I know you got a way about you. I've been watching you. I like how you handled yourself with my man. I want you enforcing for me.'

With a grip like that, he could do that by himself.

'Just me?' she asked.

'Got a few people signed up. You already met one. I need more. There's others who want a slice of the pie.'

Yep, she could guess who.

'You not thinking of throwing your lot in with them?'

Herrick made that pouty face again. 'Why would I do that? I want it all for myself.'

Cade nodded. 'Thing is …' She started to cough, rubbing her throat again.

'Yes?'

'Thing is, I'm already spoken for,' she croaked.

Herrick closed in again. His eyes were so close together that Cade was having trouble focussing on them.

'Anzo. He's already got me on board.'

'What?' Herrick growled. Cade could feel violence ooze from him.

'Anzo. He already got to me. Said I had to work for him. Said he ain't looking to share. Said he is gonna kill anyone who tries.'

'That so?'

'Yeah. Look, Herrick. I like livin' and I know you can squash me like a bug. But Anzo's got a big crew now. I don't reckon anyone can stand up to him.'

Herrick had pulled back. He was frowning.

'I need to think about this.'

Cade took a deep breath. As she did so Herrick leapt forward and grabbed her shoulders. His breath stank worse than his odour, and spittle covered her face as he spoke.

'Don't try and do anything fucking smart. Keep your mouth shut. Get out.'

Cade didn't need to be told twice. She backed up, felt the sheet behind her, and kept pushing. The material passed over her head and she spun around, moving fast to put distance between her and Herrick. A man and a woman were standing on the path ahead of her. They didn't look friendly.

'Evening,' she said, lacking her usual charm and cheer.

They didn't get any friendlier. She pushed past them and jogged on, trying to recall the route out. *Nice work, Cade. Now you've done it.* She wasn't sure why she had, maybe she'd just been pissed with Herrick, but she'd seen an opportunity to stir things up. If she'd played it right, she might just have started a war.

CHAPTER 25

Owen climbed down the ladder into the storeroom in the roost. He found Murtagh and Larsen waiting for him. They looked grim-faced and their bodies oozed tension. Larsen must have returned from hunting sometime during the morning. He did a quick calculation, trying to remember when they had left. They'd been gone for some time.

'What is it?' he asked, looking from one man to the other.

Murtagh pointed at his companion, 'Larsen needs to talk to you. We needed somewhere private. That's the problem with this place now. Too many folk around.'

Owen laid his gloves on a shelf and shrugged off his jacket.

'Go on.'

'Larsen, you tell it,' said Murtagh.

The wiry old hunter folded his arms.

'We were out east. A long way out, took the way you said. The weather wasn't as harsh as I expected it to be, some early snow but nothing too heavy, so me and Ernan thought we'd push on a bit, see what we could find. Saul and the others were happy hanging back, using the grounds you'd pointed out to us. We found a couple of villages, some farmsteads. All deserted. Nothing new. Thought we'd check out the peaks nearby. Look for any signs.'

'You find some?'

'Aye, we found some.' He picked at a tooth, flicked something away. 'We started looking for caves. Always the likely place to find people. First major one we found, there were carcasses. Fresh kills. They hadn't been mauled, so we figured there might be someone still alive. We carried on, hit upon some fresh trails, no attempt at hiding. They led us to a camp, almost on the borders of the Highlands.'

Owen guessed the rest.

'Not human, were they?'

Larsen shook his head and spat on the ground.

'Gnomes.'

'Fucking little brown-skinned shits,' added Murtagh.

'What were they doing?' said Owen.

'Looked like a small hunting party. Not unlike ours. We watched 'em for a while. They looked settled.'

'Do you think they were fixing on staying long?'

Larsen shrugged.

'Couldn't say for sure, but I reckon they'd been there a while. Winter is here and they aren't clearing off.'

'They are hill dwellers, so they like the territory. But they've always stayed away before because we laid claim to the Highlands. Might be they are fixing on moving in, staying on the borders and in the valleys,' said Murtagh.

'If so, that's a problem. They do that, they could just as well decide to just take the whole Highlands all for themselves,' said Larsen.

'Maybe,' said Owen. He had hoped this wouldn't happen. The gnomes lived a way east. They'd come along with the dwarves during the war, but had no reason to stay. They didn't mine, didn't manufacture the way the dwarves did. 'Even if they stay on our borders, they will still send in hunters, just like the ones you found. '

'We could stay away from that area, keep hunting to the west,' suggested Larsen.

'I'm not giving up the Highlands again,' growled Murtagh.

Owen was waiting for Murtagh to suggest an attack. The thing was, he didn't have an argument that could sway him. If the gnomes were planning to settle in the Highlands then there would come up a day when their paths would cross. And the gnomes wouldn't want to play nice.

'We can't give up the Highlands, there's nowhere else for us to go,' he said. 'This is our home.'

'Hah!' Murtagh slapped a hand against a shelf.

'Larsen, you wanted to tell me first. Does that mean the rest of the hunting party knows?' asked Owen.

'Yeah, they all know. Me and Ernan got ahead of them. They're still humping our furs back, should be here before nightfall.'

'Murtagh, I want to take a look first,' said Owen.

Murtagh scowled. 'What's to look at? We know where they are.'

'I want to see for myself what their plans are. Gauge their strength. We might get lucky and they head home for the winter.'

'I doubt that.'

'Maybe, but it's what I'm going to do. I'll head out with Em and maybe take Jussi too.'

Murtagh shifted uncomfortably. He was worried for the young ones.

'We'll just take a look. No heroics. If Larsen is right, then we'll come back and talk about a plan of action.'

'Seems like a lot of talking,' Murtagh grumped.

'Better than dying, Murtagh,' said Owen. 'Speaking of which, what do you think we should do? Our people need to know what Larsen and the others found.'

'They'll know soon enough when the rest of the boys get back.'

Owen had considered asking them to stay silent, wait for him to get back. But that wouldn't work. It also wasn't fair.

'Then when they do, we'll call a town meeting. We'll let everyone know what's happened and what I intend to do. '

'Some folk are liable to get a little skittish,' said Murtagh.

'We been skittish for a long time,' said Larsen. 'We all shouldn't need to worry about everyone getting fearful. They want to run, fine.'

'Let's hope nobody does. Murtagh, you spread the word. Larsen, you and me need to spend a little time working out just where you found them. If we get it right, I can get us there and back in a day.'

'Right.'

'First up, I need to let my Riders know. They'll be having an early start tomorrow.'

'What happens when we find them, Owen?' asked Em.

'You know what happens. We stay and watch them for a while. See what they are up to.'

'Then what?'

'Em, we talked about this at the meeting last night,' sighed Owen. 'We don't need to do anything else right now. We have time.'

'But what if Murtagh is right and they invade and start taking over the Highlands?' Owen looked over at Jussi. The boy was watching the exchange with his mouth open, his eyes betraying his fear.

Bloody Murtagh! He hadn't quite said that but he'd implied it plenty. His talk had given everyone the notion that this was the start of something bigger. A remorseless push into the Highlands to wipe the last traces of humanity from the peaks. He had lost the people of Eagle's Rest when Murtagh had started speaking. He'd heard the voices of those in the hall: they were fearful, angry, eager to do something. His words of caution were drowned out, as were those who might have agreed with him, all lost in the hubbub. Thank the Emperor for Naimh, she'd stood up and explained to everyone a little more about what they faced. She had spoken of how the Gnomes were tribal, that they had no kings, no leadership. They had joined the war against humans because every other race had. Owen had seized on that, said they could stop this incursion and not worry about reprisals. They do it right and word would never get back to the dwarves or the elves. Gnomes were superstitious creatures and they could play on that. At least Murtagh had supported his recce. It gave him some room to manoeuvre, try to regroup, and form a plan before he had to face everyone again.

Owen took a drink from his waterskin. The liquid was icy cold.

'Em, they won't invade the Highlands. We'll see to that. Trust me. Now, are you going to finish that cheese or do I give it to your eagle?'

'They don't like cheese,' said Em.

364

'I do,' said Jussi. 'I'll take yours if you don't want it.'

'Fine. I'm not hungry anyway,' said Em, tossing him the half-gnawed chunk.

Jussi snatched it from the air and bit into it. Owen had wondered whether it was a good idea to bring the lad, but this was valuable experience. They could only pretend for so long. He wanted them both to feel a little fear. They had to learn it wasn't a game.

'Let's go.' He stood and walked to Arno. Within a minute they had lifted off from the small cleared hilltop rising from the valley where he'd sent Larsen and Saul. He turned them northeast, the Three Chiefs just behind his left shoulder. The sky was grey, but it was dry and the clouds were high up and moving slowly. They had been lucky with the weather so far, but it couldn't last. In eighteen years he had never known a winter that had not turned the Highlands white. They left the valley and flew through a range of high hills, climbing up into peaks and across meadows. They stayed low to the ground for much of this journey. It was still their land and it was safe enough to do so, but an hour later he took them up. They were in the area where the gnomes had been ranging. He didn't want them spotted as Eagle Riders. Take them higher and they could be mistaken for their wild cousins.

Jussi, peel off and head south. Stay as far from us as you can. Fly random, put some turns and circles in, okay?'

'Yes, Owen.'

Jussi waved and pulled away. Ayolf was turning into a powerful and magnificent looking bird. Arno was still the best of course. He turned and beckoned Em closer. Taru beat her wings and brought her level.

'Em, you head north of me, follow my line of travel, keep me in sight but stay as far away as you feel comfortable. If you spot anything, head my way. We'll go and look together.'

Em nodded and pulled at her reins.

Owen watched her go then adjusted his own course, turning Arno on to an easterly direction. They were not far from the border, where the high country became hills, which in turn became rolling pasture. He had not been here for a long time. He felt a strangely unfamiliar sense of caution. Almost like he was flying over enemy territory. That was foolish, he'd never really been over enemy territory. Yet he *had* felt this caution before, over Aberpool, in the blasted heaths and mountains of the north. Those weren't his lands, these were, and for the last few months he had felt content and safe. *Now for the second time we are under threat and if we make a false step, if I make a false step, nowhere will feel safe again.*

Arno flew across a saddle between two low mountains. If he had the right one, Larsen had spoken of this landmark. As expected, the land opened up before him, dropping away into a range of hills. They were thickly forested, marked with steep rocky gullies, where numerous streambeds had cut into their sides.

Arno was scanning the ground keenly for signs of life, preferably life he could eat. His bird didn't differentiate between the races, not at this distance, but he could recognise civilisation.

'Owen!'

He looked to his right. Jussi was winging towards him.

'Jussi, what you got?'

'I saw smoke, in the trees!'

'Alright, let's take it slow.' Owen wanted to keep Jussi's excitement contained. *'That was good work. I'll take a look, but you stay here. I'll send Em your way.'*

'Yes, Owen.'

Owen swung around, heading north. There was a speck in the distance. He could hardly see it himself, but Arno confirmed it. Trust Em to push it so far.

As they drew nearer, Em spotted them.

'Keep heading that way,' shouted Owen, as she sped past.

Arno turned sharply and brought them next to Em and Taru.

'We found them. I'm going to go in closer. Head south and west, you'll see Jussi. I want the pair of you to circle and wait for me to come back.'

'We'll come and get you if you get into trouble,' she called.

'I feel safer already!' he said with a smile.

They flew on for another half mile. Ahead of them a lazy trail of grey/white smoke rose from the forest.

'That's it. Stay here you two,' he shouted.

He pushed on towards the smoke. He kept Arno high on his first pass, wanting to be as inconspicuous as possible. There was a clearing from where the smoke issued. It was large, likely widened by its occupants. He relied on Arno's vision to give him more. He saw a number of structures, at least a half dozen. He thought he spotted movement, but they were too high to see who it might be.

'*Come on Arno, let's chance our luck a little.*' They spiralled down, slow and easy. Owen wished it had been a clearer day, as they could have used the sun on their backs to keep them hidden. He lay low on the saddle, his head almost resting on Arno's neck. The clearing grew larger and widened out before him. Touching Arno's mind, he saw three huts, made of crudely cut wood, roofed with interwoven branches. In the centre of the clearing was a pit, the smoke rising from the fire within it. Arno could already feel the thermals rising to meet him. He used them to slow their descent. They now saw several tents, circular and high-sided, their frames meeting at a central point. They were scattered around the edges of the clearing, a little way from the forest. He saw movement by the fire and by the buildings.

Owen pulsed Arno to head west, he'd seen enough as he cared to, from the air at least. They flew for a minute, losing sight of the clearing as they went over a hill thick with spruce and birch. He could see Taru and Ayolf in the distance, circling each other, looking to the unsuspecting eye like two normal eagles searching for prey. Owen wanted to land. Larsen had been right and he had no reason to doubt that they were indeed gnomes down there. But he needed to be sure. He needed to see for himself that this wasn't just a precursor to a larger force. If it wasn't then they had a chance to survive this. *Where to land?* A little way on the far side of the hill the ground started to rise climbing in a steady but irregular pace towards the first peaks to the west. He spotted another clearing, not too far from the back of the hill, only a hundred yards away. He turned Arno around for a better look. The clearing was almost circular, sloping upwards west to east, covered with low-growing bushes and weeds. It had all the signs of being man-made. The growth told him it was at least a year old. He pulsed Arno to land, and the eagle put down easily. Owen climbed off and withdrew his crossbow and spear. On the clearing floor, he found a number of tree stumps, small mushrooms and mosses sprouting and growing over them. Whether it was a human or something else that had cleared this place, he'd never know. He waited a moment, listening for sounds of movement, trying to sense any danger. He looked at Arno. The eagle was calm, watchful but not tense. That was good enough for him.

'Jussi? Jussi, can you hear me?'

Nothing.

'Jussi, I might be able to reach you, so listen to me. I'm going in on foot. Keep your station. If I need help, I'll holler. You can come a little closer if you stay directly west of the smoke. Just make sure you keep enough distance so they can't make you out.' He reach out and clapped his hand on Arno's neck. *'And you, Arno. Stay here.'*

Arno cocked his head and looked away.

Owen started out of the clearing, walking down the slope until it met the hill, then he started to climb. He used the spear as a crutch, to keep his balance as he negotiated the incline. He kept his crossbow in his other hand, which made the endeavour more cumbersome than he would have liked it to be. Once at the top he walked around the crest, trying to find a good place from which to view the settlement. The trees were thick and mostly pine. Their thin branches spread out low and wove into each other. It was hard, annoying work to have to push through them. *Damn, looks like I might just have to climb one of them.* That would be no fun. He thought a moment. *No, bugger that. I'll just have to get closer.* He found a small game path, little more than a faint winding line of bare earth, running down from the top of the hill. He forced through some branches.

'Gah!' A branch swiped him in the face and he threw his arm out in a useless warding gesture. He kept his eyes squeezed shut, waiting for the sting to pass. He opened one eye, stretched the muscles of his face, and then opened the other. The branch was still in front of him. He dropped low, placed his weapons on the ground, then reached up and snapped the offending limb. It hung limply, still connected by a piece of bark. He crouched back down, gathered his spear and bow and started forward once again, turning sideways to force his way out. On this side of the slope the trees were more spaced out, birch and ash dominating. His arms were getting tired, the muscles starting to complain. He hadn't thought this through, had too much to carry. He stopped and looked for a good spot to leave his spear, something obvious. There wasn't much, but there was a small indentation on the ground not far away, like a groove in the soil. Next to it was a fallen branch, quite thick, with small branches, still covered with growth. That would have to do. He placed his spear under the branch, and covered it with some loose leaves and dirt that were sodden with recent snowmelt. He stepped back, satisfied with his work.

He cradled his bow. He wasn't going to bury that anywhere; they had been through too much together. He took a moment to regain his bearings. The smoke was covered from view, the branches blocking out the sky, so he had to make a guess. Straight down was a good start. He pushed on. Ahead of him the ground sloped steeply down. As he reached the edge, he caught a scent. It reminded him of burnt wood and something else. Meat, acrid, like when it gets charred through too much cooking. If he could smell that, then he was close. As he started to negotiate this new slope, where it dropped away steeply, he caught a glimpse of open ground through the trees. He dropped to one knee, reaching out take hold of the thin trunk of a younger ash, craning his head left and right. He could make out one of the tall tent-like structures. Long and thin pine trunks had been cut down and tied together into a frame that met at the top and fanned out at the bottom, making a solid base. Around that frame a number of animal hides had been stitched together and wound around the wood to create a waterproof skin.

He needed to see more. Staying low and leaning his body towards the slope he scrambled further around, so that the tent moved to his left and he could get a better look within the clearing.

He could see it now. A cleared channel between the trees afforded him a view of almost the entire camp. He could see figures. There were two standing by the fire, their backs to him. Another emerged from one of the structures not far from his position. It shouted something, its voice high, almost shrill, and Owen had no idea what it was saying. The structure itself was crude, a simple log cabin with a low ceiling, too small for a human to stand in. He wondered what was in them. It would be good to know and he was also feeling a little exposed. If he could see them, then they, if they happened to look his way, could probably see him. He worked his way along a little more so that the back of the cabin was now facing him. He crept forward, holding his crossbow tight to his side. He stepped lightly, scanning the ground for twigs that might snap, and watching ahead for anyone coming his way.

He made it to the wall of the cabin without incident and crouched down. He realised he'd been holding his breath and he let it out slowly. He could hear his heart thumping in his ears. For the first time he realised what he was doing.

Alone. In daylight. Sneaking into a camp full of how many gnomes? Each one of which would take great delight in skinning me alive. Nice move, oh mighty warleader, the Imperial Scouts would be proud of me.

He leaned against the wall, and studied how the logs were stacked one on another, tied together with thin straps of hemp. The logs had not been shaped or finished particularly well, with plenty of gaps left between them. He placed an eye close to one of those gaps, peering into darkness. At first he couldn't see anything. He kept shifting his vision, left and right, trying to make out shapes. The cabin was quiet at least. There was no sound from within. He could still hear talking from the centre of the clearing. Just as long as those voices stayed where they were.

It took several more frustrating moments before his vision adjusted enough for him to start to make sense of what he was looking at. Inside he could see things hanging, each one a different shape, rounded and rectangular. Small patches of light from the many holes in the walls played against their surfaces. Skins, had to be, left to dry and cure.

He sat back and though about that. Definitely a hunting party, forging new ground now that they had nobody to compete with. He crawled to the wall's edge and peered round. The three gnomes were still talking, gesticulating at the fire, making hooting noises, punctuated by screeching, growls and purrs. Was that truly a language? He watched them as they talked.

They were short, shorter than dwarves, who at least could stand to the shoulders of a teenage boy. Gnomes were no taller than his waist. At a distance they could be mistaken for children. Get close enough and you could see they were anything but, with ugly, pug faces, wide snouts and beady eyes. They reminded him a little of a bat, though their pointed ears sat in the same place as his own. They were dressed in the same furs, leathers and weaves that his people might wear. They might seem brutish, but they were still intelligent creatures.

The two by the fire didn't appear armed, though there was a long knife on the belt of a third one, who had just emerged from this very cabin. As he watched, that third gnome raised a hand, lifted his head to the air and started sniffing. The two watched him then started to speak, more softly than before. He growled a reply. The bodies had stiffened, their stance grown more alert. They all started to look around them. Owen ducked his head back as one turned his way. *Enough was enough.* He ran back up the slope, keeping the cabin between him and their line of sight. They must've caught wind of him.

He got to the top of the steep incline, breathing heavily. Where was his damn spear? He'd have to angle back, try to find the place.

He jogged on, breathing hard. He heard something. Was it a voice? One of them? He couldn't be sure. It might just as well have been a damned warthog. He paused, gaze trying to locate anything out of the ordinary.

Owen felt himself becoming disorientated, his breathing fast and uneven. Nothing seemed familiar, he had no idea which way to go. He shook his head. He had to get a grip of himself. *Stop it. You know which way is up, which is down. Bugger the spear. Just move!*

He started off once more. Heading up the slope, angling to the right, hoping to cross the path of the animal run, or at the very least get to the hill.

Thank the Gods! There it was, rising ahead of him.

He set to it, scrambling up the slope, his free hand grabbing hold of rocks and roots, his crossbow waving in the air. He felt exposed again, just like he had in Scotia against those wood elves. He reached the top, spied where he had exited, the branch still dangling. He crouched low and pushed inside the tangle, keeping his head down, the branches shifting and rustling with his passage. It sounded like he was making a right racket. That wouldn't do, he was going to give himself away.

He stopped and took a deep breath. Leader Cadarn had once told him that a Rider was his own worst enemy. You dwell too much on what might be happening, you start to fret that something is coming in on your blind side, making it impossible to think straight. Owen had been drowning in a rising tide of panic. It might have given his legs some speed, but for a few moments he'd lost all reason.

That's going to get you killed easier than anything the enemy might be fixing to do.

He needed to get a handle on what was happening. Owen got down on the ground and crawled to the edge of the pines, looking down the slope. He exhaled. There was no pursuit. The trees swayed a little as a breeze played over their taller branches. A bird swung low and landed on the branch of a birch. *Stupid idiot, Owen.* It seemed like he'd got his britches soiled for nothing. *That'd be a fine way for you to go.*

'Jussi, I'm on my way back. I'll be with you in five.'

Owen backed up, pushing the branches away and got free of the tangle of pines. He turned and walked into a gnome.

'Huh?'

'Ahg?'

Owen stumbled back a little. He looked at the creature, aware that his mouth was hanging open. The gnome stared back, its eyes wide, the black pupils so expanded, only the barest hint of white orb showing. It was carrying a small spear wrapped in the same leather strapping he'd seen on the cabin. A bow rested on its shoulder.

Owen moved first. He fired his crossbow.

'Urk!' The creature fell backwards, the bolt slamming into its neck. The spear flew up into the air. He pushed past the gnome as it writhed on the floor. He heard a shrill cry behind him and the sound of something pushing through the trees. Another spear clattered past, smacking into a tree. He increased his speed. His weapon was useless and he wished he still had his spear. He careened down the slope, taking long strides, caring little for his balance. Slipping and sliding, he bounced off another tree, moving his head just as an arrow embedded itself in the wood. More shouts. Where had they come from? Certainly not the camp. They must have found his trail or heard his crashing through the trees. He reached the bottom of the hill and picked up speed. At least he could outrun them, as long as they didn't shoot him first.

'Jussi, stay back. They are after me. Don't come any closer.'

Owen charged through the forest. It was only a hundred yards, but he had to duck and weave all the way, the trees slowing him down. There must be at least two more after him. He could see the clearing ahead. Another arrow brushed his arm.

'Shit!' He didn't mean to shout but he couldn't help it. Just speaking meant he was still alive.

He reached out a warning to Arno. The eagle already knew. It had smelt them out.

'Watch for them Arno, I'm coming.'

A vision entered his mind. Arno had seen something. A gnome waiting for him in the bushes. 'Get him!' he shrieked.

Arno moved quickly, smashing into the forest's edge. The trees were too tightly packed for him to get in very far but it did the trick.

The gnome darted from its hiding place, a bow in its hands. Owen changed his direction, running straight for it and swinging his own bow in an overhead arc. It struck the gnome in the face, the head whipping round in a spray of blood. It was red, and a small part of Owen was surprised at that. He wasn't sure why. The gnome collapsed to its knees. Owen kicked out, connecting with the jaw. There was a crack and the gnome fell on to its side, its head at a strange angle. He heard a hoot and then a growl. Owen turned. Another gnome rushed at him, a wicked dagger in its hands. Owen held his crossbow out as a shield. The gnome ducked low and slashed at his leg.

'Arg!' Owen felt a sharp burning pain just below his right knee. He lost his balance and fell back on to the ground with a thump, the breath knocked out of him.

The gnome leapt forward, the blade coming down towards his face. He put up his hands, stopping the knife an inch away from his eye. For a few moments they wrestled, then the gnome swung a fist at him.

'Oof!' He felt the impact, once, twice.

His vision was a mess. Owen rolled over, pulling the gnome with him. He kept his grip on the gnome's knife hand. The creature, now beneath him, was snarling and spitting, its face a twisted ugly mass of hate. His legs and free arm worked frantically to pummel Owen, to kick him off.

Owen lifted the hand holding the knife and slammed it down hard. The hand spasmed, the knife falling away. He clasped his hands together and swung them into the side of the gnome's head, then he switched, lifting them straight up and down.

He landed a blow on to the nose and felt it collapse under him. He lifted his arms again, slammed down harder. Blood splattered. He did it a third time, the blow landing lower, smashing into its teeth.

The gnome looked dazed, its face a mess.

Owen leaned forward, gathered up the knife. He jammed it into the gnome's neck, meeting resistance, he pulled it out, a gush of blood followed, and he drove it home a second time. Blood frothed from the gnome's mouth. A hiss issued from the gaping maw. Owen looked behind him. There were more small shapes running through the trees. He pushed himself off the body, leaving the knife where it was. He reached out, grabbed his crossbow and staggered out into the clearing.

Arno, wings spread, stood high on his feet. He screeched when he saw Owen, who hobbled towards him, his leg screaming. Something entered his right eye, blinding him. He wiped it away. Blood.

'Settle down, Arno, I need to get on you.'

Arno's discomfort was palpable; he was fighting his every instinct to flee. He was vulnerable on the ground.

'It's alright, lad. Just let me climb up.' He pulsed soothing emotions, desperate to disguise his own panic. Arno lowered himself down and Owen limped around to his left side, reached up and pushed his bow into a saddlebag. He placed his left leg into the stirrup and swung his right leg over.

'Ahhh!' A wave of pain, sharp and vicious. His leg felt so heavy. More blood was pouring into his eye.

'Go, Arno. Go!' He shook his head. Stars were flashing before his eyes. Underneath him the eagle bucked, Owen swayed, and realised his right leg was dangling free. He vision cleared a little. Arno was climbing, gaining a little extra height with each beat. Three gnomes emerged from the treeline. They had bows and they were aiming right at him. A flash of colour passed by, a blur of wings and feathers and outstretched talons, heading right for them. Who was that? He lost sight of it as Arno gained height, turning away rapidly.

'Shit!' he forced his right foot into the stirrup, his leg sending another stab of pain through him. Owen shifted in his seat and tried to look back. The blood was in both his eyes now. He saw motion, frantic and impossible to make sense of. *Damn this blood.* He wrapped his hand tight around the reins, grabbed hold of the pommel and used his free hand to wipe the blood away but his sight was still blurred. He blinked, but his world was shrinking. Everything was going black. He felt exhausted, it hit him like a wave. Pitching forwards he felt his head hit the pommel. He was so tired. He just needed a moment.

'Owen? Owen? Can you hear me?'

A voice inside his head. It was young, panicked. He thought he recognised it. Then it all went dark.

CHAPTER 26

'I forbid it! You cannot go.'

There was a collective intake of breath. The mother of the Emperor she might be, but no one would dare question him so publicly. It was unheard of and was, as far as Father Michael could see, the sort of thing that could rapidly lead to one's death.

'Mother, I do not believe that you or anyone else is in a position to forbid me anything. That is what being a Living God means, does it not?'

Emperor Tigh smiled and sat back. He appeared amused rather than outraged. A few members of the council chuckled.

The Empress, red-faced and agitated, stood up.

'You are also my son and the last member of an illustrious line. You cannot risk your life. Who would take over after you? There are no heirs, no children.'

'At least none that we know of,' whispered Admiral Lukas under his breath. Father Michael cricked his neck and steadfastly refused to acknowledge that comment from the old seadog. They stood next to each other in the shadows of the Emperor's cabin. It barely had enough room to accommodate the circular table that had been taken apart, brought from the ship and reassembled here. The Emperor's throne, was at its head and every other spare inch was filled with chairs and each chair held a member of the Council.

Apart from the old chamberlain, Aban, the balance had shifted. Most of those around the table were members of the Church, like Father Rossart, who'd been raised up by the Arch Cardinal to become the Master of Supply. That meant little to Father Michael, but he knew that the man looked after the food and told folk what to do with it. Other servants of the Empire, such as the Admiral and Leader Cadarn, had also been invited in at the Emperor's request. Father Michael had approved, even if the Arch Cardinal had not. They needed men of more practical minds for a discussion such as this.

'I understand the implications, mother, but your judgement is clouded on this issue.'

'You expect me to feel otherwise?'

'I expect your blessing. Now, sit down. Please.'

Father Michael suspected he wasn't the only one feeling uncomfortable for having to witness this dispute. It wasn't right to see anyone question the Emperor so publically, even if it was his mother. She had given up any say when he had ascended the throne.

Father Llews took the Empress's hand and pulled her back into her chair, his smile broad, knowing, strangely at ease.

Cardinal Yarn coughed politely.

'Your Grace. You called this council to discuss a proposal, one I must confess that I myself feel a little uncomfortable about. Surely you must understand if some of us have … reservations?'

'I understand that some of you are still a little raw from our voyage and the last few, frantic days of the old Empire,' replied the Emperor.

Arch Cardinal Vella leaned back, his lips pressed tight. 'We are still recovering, Your Grace, that is fair to say. The people are just starting to rebuild, to get their lives back. They need time to heal, to grow strong again. This will take many years. They need you here to give them guidance, for you to lend them your strength, for you to give them hope.'

The Emperor slammed his fist on to the table. Some of the Council jumped in their seats.

'Exactly! Hope! That is what I plan to give them. What better way to fire their imaginations? A grand expedition to learn more of this new world. To bring them back tales of wonder, stories of adventure, strange new food, animals even.'

'But you wish to seek out the makers of that shelter. That is the truth is it not? To find what intelligent life might be out there?' asked Cardinal Yarn.

The Emperor pulled his fist back.

'That is true, I will concede that. We found evidence of life, of civilisation. We should strive to learn more. Perhaps there are fellow humans out there. Perhaps a new nation, descended from early explorers like us. It would be like the first days of the Empire, when my forefathers sought to unite all the peoples of humanity.'

'That was a bloody cause,' said Cardinal Lucien.

'And a long one,' added Aban.

'But no less just!' cried Father Llews, finally rising from his beatific trance.

The Emperor pointed a finger at Father Llews.

'At last, someone who agrees with me.'

'Your Grace,' said Arch Cardinal Vella, rising from his chair. 'We are here to advise you. Our agreement is moot. Your decision is and always will be final. All I can do is counsel caution. We do not know what is out there. Perhaps it is best it stays that way. If we disturb the hornets' nest, there will be little we can do to stop it. We are so few now.'

'And how long do you expect to be gone for?' asked the Empress. She looked no calmer, but her voice had lost its hysterical edge.

'Leader Cadarn? How far have you flown westwards?' asked the Emperor, ignoring her question. 'How far before we hit virgin territory?'

Cadarn stepped forward from the shadows, light from the window throwing his face into drab relief.

'Not much further than that forest, Your Grace. It sat on the edge of our ranging. We can go further if you wish. My Riders are used to living off the land. We could bring you the information you need.'

'There, my lord. Perhaps that is your answer?' said Cardinal Lucien.

'No, no, no,' replied the Emperor. He was looking at Leader Cadarn with irritation. Clearly it was not the answer he had wanted from the Rider. 'The eagles can cover ground but they cannot hold it, cannot examine it the way a man on foot can. There must be an expedition.'

'Then let the Riders and others go in your stead,' pleaded the Arch Cardinal.

'If I may?' Father Llews stood up. He was smiling again, but this time he appeared focused, his manner and bearing exuding confidence. *By the Emperor, this man's mood was more changeable than the weather.*

The Arch Cardinal sat down, yielding to Llews. 'My friends. There is much wisdom in what you say. Your concern for the Emperor is most admirable. Yet you miss the very point of this endeavour. Our people follow because they believe. They believe in the sanctity of the Emperor, in the preaching and teaching we administer to them every day. We talk of his Godhood, of the inviolate line of his forefathers. Their God's-given right to rule. Because they achieved *miracles*. Our Emperor has brought us to these shores, has saved humanity. But what stories do we tell the children of our children? That the Empire was destroyed, that we pathetic few were allowed to survive? Or do we tell them the stories of how the Emperor himself dragged humanity back from the brink. That by his example, his courage, his bravery, his vision, he saved us all. He would not sit idly by as his people scratched a life from this new soil. He marched into the west, to discover, to subjugate, to claim all the land for the New Tissan Empire. These,' he thrust a finger into the air, 'these are the stories we must tell our grandchildren. Not myths, not legends, but the truth. That is how our new Empire will grow. By the example set by the best of us. Our Emperor.' He finished and looked into each face. His eyes moved to Father Michael's, they were shining.

The room was quiet for a moment.

'Thank you, Father,' said the Emperor. Even he looked a little taken aback. Father Llews nodded graciously and settled into his seat. His wistful smile had returned, his eyes gazing into empty space. Father Michael swore that only the Emperor could know what that man was looking at.

The Emperor leaned forward in his throne. 'Now. Are there any other objections?'

'Your Grace, how many Riders will you take with you?' asked Arch Cardinal Vella.

'We'll need to set up way stations. Use my Gifted to act as a link back to the city,' added Cardinal Yarn.

'Provisions, Your Grace. We must plan for proper provisions, and what of horses, pack animals?' asked the Chamberlain.

'I can assist with providing those,' said Father Rossart.

And like that the decision had been made. Father Llews had spoken passionately, had delivered his absolute support to the endeavour and that was all the Emperor had needed. They were all falling over themselves to get behind this ... expedition? He didn't understand it himself. Hadn't they just done that on a fleet of ships across a thousand miles of ocean? Wasn't that enough?

'Looks like I'll be staying out of this one,' said the Admiral quietly in his ear. 'Though I imagine you'll be going along. Lucky you.'

Of course I will be. How could I not?

'Father? A word.'

Father Michael, hands deep inside his sleeves, bowed his head. 'Arch Cardinal.'

The old man bowed back, placed an arm around his shoulders and led him away from the hubbub outside the Emperor's cabin. Father Michael was thankful for it. Well-wishers, Council members and common folk alike surrounded the Emperor. Word had spread fast and he had not seen such a level of enthusiasm since the crowds in the arena. At least no one was baying for blood. Tomorrow they were leaving, an expedition heading into the winter winds to find evidence of life. A worthy and noble cause. But first he had to endure a night of noise and shouting and drinking. Was there ever a greater way to test his faith? They walked quietly for a few moments, heading along the main street, such as it was. Many of the common folk watched them, though none came close enough to listen.

'You are ready?'

'Yes, Arch Cardinal.'

'Feeling buoyant and confident?'

'Yes.'

'Sure that this is the right thing to do?'

That threw him. 'It is the only thing to do. The Blessed Emperor has commanded it.'

'Yes. Indeed he has. I fear for him.'

'Why?'

'He puts himself in harm's way when he has no need to.'

'He has me. He has the Gifted.'

'Yes. He has the Gifted. He has you.'

They walked on in silence. Cardinal Vella turned his head towards Father Michael.

'There are those who think this trip is folly. That now is not the time. It is … dangerous for him to be away.'

'I will protect him.'

'Yes, you will. But it is here that I fear for his rule.'

'I don't–'

'Understand? It is a simple matter. You and I have struggled for the cause of peace. To put aside all thoughts of vengeance and retribution. There are those who do not agree. Those within our Church who harbour thoughts at odds to ours. I thought I had done sufficient to remove them. I was wrong.'

'Who? I can deal with them.'

The Arch Cardinal shook his head.

'It is too late for that. You are going on a long journey. You have no time.'

'Then what must I do?'

'Protect the Emperor. Against anything and everyone.' The Arch Cardinal stopped and looked down at his feet. They had moved beyond the outskirts of the town and now stood on bare grass, sodden from the cold rain moving in from the north.

'Gah. Why he does not wait until the spring I do not know. The impetuousness of youth, even in a God.' He placed both of his hands on Father Michael's shoulders.

'Life is not as simple as we'd like it to be, Michael. When people get together, start to live with one another, you will find their behaviour changes. The worst kinds of human emotions rise up. Jealousy, anger, greed. We are all imperfect. That is why we need something to look up to. A perfect role model. That is our Emperor.'

'Praise him,' said Father Michael.

'Yes.' He removed his hands. 'I will await your return. I can but hope that your endeavour meets with disappointing results. '

Father Michael smiled and nodded although he was utterly confused. The Arch Cardinal was far too clever not to notice it. He laughed.

'Let us head back. I confess to being a little famished.'

They walked back in companionable silence, bearing left at the barracks block and making their way around to its rear.

The Arch Cardinal clapped his hands. 'Ah, here we are. And here comes the Emperor.'

A feast was laid out. Half a dozen tables, fashioned from lengths of freshly cut timber, were set out in a horseshoe. Upon them were set haunches of venison, still dripping with fat, bottles of wine, jugs of ale, fruit and some of the vegetables that, through trial and error, they had found to be edible.

A large crowd had gathered, though no one had started on the food. This was probably because just behind the tables, arrayed in two lines, were the Gifted. Father Michael did a quick headcount and decided it looked like all of them, they were armoured though their heads were bare. Father Michael spied Ellen in the back rank. She looked odd in her armour, and he thought it didn't sit well on her. Then there was the expression on her face. While the rest of her kind stood stock still with hardly any emotion, she wore a wide smile, like she was enjoying the spectacle. Her joy gave him a pleasant warmth inside and, strangely, he felt sadness too. It would be a shame when she assumed her duties fully. Her dedication to the Emperor would become everything. There would be no love or laughter in her future. Just devotion. Then again, perhaps it was just him and his own choices that made his life the way it was. He had never been one for levity. The Church did not prohibit laughter and clearly made allowances for those with certain types of humour. *Speaking of which …*

Cardinal Yarn stepped forward to greet them.

'Good evening to you both. What do you think of our leaving present for His Grace?'

'You did this?' asked the Arch Cardinal.

Cardinal Yarn shrugged. Her lips stretched into her usual sly smile.

'My School did most of the work, I just provided the direction.'

'Cardinal, what's this?' said the Emperor. He was astride his horse. Father Michael could have sworn he had been on foot just a moment before. 'I wondered where you had disappeared to. I was concerned you would miss this feast. Now I know why.'

'Yes, Father Michael, I can see your face. Someone suggested he should ride. It looks more … impressive does it not?' whispered the Arch Chancellor.

'Quite so, Your Grace,' said Cardinal Yarn. 'I thought I'd come ahead, and prepare this welcome for you. I regret I cannot promise this every night.'

'Hah, nor would I expect it. I thank you all the same.' The Emperor dismounted. 'Uther?' The servant jogged over. 'Here. Make sure he's taken care of. He has a long way to ride tomorrow. Don't worry. I'm sure there will be food enough left for you.'

'Sire.' Uther gathered the reins and led the stallion away.

'This is quite a send-off.' The Emperor commented as he surveyed the scene. 'Is it me or are there a lot of Gifted here?'

Cardinal Yarn nodded.

'They are arrayed for your inspection. They are all anxious to join you on your quest.'

'All of them?'

'All.'

The Emperor looked a little anxious. Doubtful even. 'Is that wise?'

Cardinal Yarn spread her arms wide. 'We are the Emperor's servants and protectors. Where else would we be?'

Father Michael had to agree. She had the right of it. It was their role and responsibility as much as it was his.

'Even so, I am concerned. When we discussed the size of the expedition I had of course expected some Gifted to come along.' He shook his head. 'But the settlement, the people, need protecting.'

Cardinal Yarn lowered her arms and clasped her hands

'And it is. You have your loyal soldiers, and I have Watchers. They can see if anything is amiss.'

'I understand that, Cardinal. But it does no good watching from afar and being able to do nothing about it.'

The Cardinal smiled easily, though Father Michael didn't see anything close to it in her eyes.

'Of course. My apologies, Your Grace.'

'Accepted. I appreciate your sense of duty to me, but that must extend to my mother and the rest of the people of Tissan. They need your School as much as I. The Gifted can be of best service to me by serving everyone.'

'Yes, Your Grace.'

'Good,' he reached out a hand and patted her shoulder. Father Michael swore she looked a little taken aback by the gesture. 'That said, you can send six Gifted along with the rest of my party. That will prove more than sufficient for the task at hand. And I have Father Michael, my ever-present shadow.' The Emperor turned to look at him, a strange cast to his face.

'Yes, ever-present,' said the Cardinal giving Michael a hard look.

The Emperor nodded to them both and took his leave.

Cardinal Yarn turned towards Arch Cardinal Vella.

'Please excuse me. I must go and select those who will best serve the Emperor.'

Was that annoyance in her voice? He had never thought Cardinal Yarn could ever suffer from such emotion. She was always in control.

Father Michael watched her walk away and shared a look with his mentor. Vella smiled thinly.

'Pride, Father. Did I not say? Pride.'

Father Michael felt well rested and ready. He had not expected it after the feast had been such a busy, raucous affair. He'd felt totally out of place, but then he always did. Fortunately, as darkness fell early, he could stand back in the shadows whilst the Emperor enjoyed himself. *The Emperor's ever present shadow.* Once he stood centre stage where everyone could see, see what he was and what he did. For a short time, he was the most important thing in their lives, as long as he killed someone. Did he miss it? Yes, in a way he did. It was *his* burden of pride.

He emerged from his tent into a dark, gloomy morning. At least it wasn't cold. He carried nothing with him, just the clothes on his back. There were a few people around, quiet figures creeping through the damp air. The barracks block was also empty of life. Likely the Gifted were all up and about. He was proved right as he walked into the square. Just like the night before, the Gifted were lined up as if awaiting inspection. This time they stood to one side of the Emperor's cabin. There was another, smaller group of eight Gifted gathered opposite them. He recognised Eilion standing slightly ahead of the others in that smaller group. So he was their leader. That was unfortunate. Father Michael knew he would have to bear that particular burden as well. Eilion gave him the slightest of nods. As acknowledgements went, he'd had friendlier.

He decided to take a path past that group of Gifted, flicking glances at each one, never staying long, moving his gaze this way and that. He knew that to others who did not know him well enough, he looked like he was unfocussed, nervous even. The truth was he was assessing those he passed, what weapons they carried, where the hidden ones may be, any scars, old injuries, likely places of weakness, points to target. Which side did they favour? How did they carry themselves? What thoughts were going through their minds? Confidence? Arrogance? Fear? Each one could be used against them. It was a tried and tested method of appraising his opponents. Old habits died hard and this one was something he needed to keep alive.

As he continued his inspection he didn't spot much that he hadn't seen already. All that was closed to him was the extent of each individual's Gift. Until they used it he had to rely on what he had already seen. And the best fighters always kept something back for when their lives truly depended on it.

The square was busier than the feast the previous night. The expedition group was gathering. Voices spoke softly, things jingled, jangled and clunked. Horses snickered and swished their tails. The Emperor had yet to emerge from his cabin and awaiting his presence stood most of the Council. He spied Cardinal Yarn at the end of the line, standing a little apart from the others.

Father Michael stepped towards her and bowed.

She inclined her head in return.

'Father. I imagine you never expected to be going on such adventures.'

'I hardly dreamt it possible.'

'Why, is that sarcasm? Are you developing a sense of humour?'

'I think it might be too late for that.'

Her mouth quirked.

'Perhaps.'

'Cardinal. I looked over the Gifted you assigned to the Emperor.'

She raised a delicate eyebrow.

'Yes?'

'Six Shapers, a Reader and a Watcher.'

'Just so.'

'No Speaker.'

'Yes. Ah. Now I see it … continue,' she said raising a hand in offering.

'We have two eagles. Both can speak to each other but what if neither is on the ground?'

'Yes! Father, you make quite the tactician. It was an oversight on my part, I must confess. There are so few Speakers that I did not consider sending any with you. I shall rectify this immediately.'

Father Michael nodded. He was satisfied and had nothing else to say. He'd decided to let slide that there were two Gifted more than had been asked for. He moved to step away but her hand grabbed his arm.

'Father. Can I ask you a question?'

Why does everyone want to speak to me today? I wasn't even this popular in the arena.

'Cardinal?'

'Father, why don't you join me? You can help in my selection.'

'As you wish.'

She kept her hand on his arm as they walked towards the lines of Gifted. He looked over at her. She wore a contented smile, as if nothing was amiss.

'Cardinal. Why the secrecy?'

Cardinal Yarn let go of his arm and tucked her thumbs into the belt of her robes. Her manner reminded him of a soldier.

'I wanted to ask your opinion on something. Well, someone, actually.'

'My opinions do not tend to be thought of that highly,' said Father Michael. He suspected that he wasn't going to like the question.

'Even so, you are one of the few I can ask. What is your … view, of Father Llews?'

Ah. 'He is a most dedicated servant of the Emperor.'

She nodded. 'He is.'

'And he has provided the Empress with much spiritual guidance and support.'

'He has.'

And?

'And he is an ardent enthusiast for the rebirth of the Empire. A worthy cause.'

'Yes, yes.' There was a flash of irritation in her eyes. It passed quickly. He hadn't thought of it before, but her dark eyes, the way they slanted, made her look like a cat. Cats were cunning. 'I see that I will have to be less circumspect and more to the point with you, Father. I will be blunt.'

'I am a blunt man.'

'Indeed you are.' She stepped close, just a few inches away from his face. It made him feel uncomfortable, unsteady. There was only one reason anyone ever got this close to him and it usually ended up bloody. 'Father Llews is a most fervent, fanatical member of the Church. But I do worry. He has gained a great deal of influence. You saw it yourself at the last Council meeting. Did you see him with the Empress? The way he touched her? I fear that he has a hold over her that goes beyond … just the mind.' She leaned in closer, almost whispering in his ear. 'He speaks to her of the injustice of the war, how humanity was punished for being idle. That the Emperor must be aggressive in his pursuit of vengeance.'

Father Michael could sympathise with some of her concerns but Llews? He was hardly a force to be reckoned with. He wasn't even a true member of the Council.

'Cardinal, he is but one man. The Arch Cardinal leads the Council now. He does not believe in that path.'

Cardinal Yarn drew back and sighed. 'The Arch Cardinal is a good man. No less fervent. No less fanatical in what he will see done to keep the peace.' She looked at him hard. *She knows. Has she had someone read my thoughts?*

'Cardinal, you speak of treasonous things. How can you be so sure of Father Llews's intentions? Why don't you use a Reader?'

She shook her head. 'It is a bitter irony, but it is useless. His mind is closed to us.'

Closed? 'I thought that was impossible,' said Father Michael.

'It is another Gift. There are those few who we cannot Read. They have a wall around them. It is a useful ability if someone wanted to keep secrets from us. I have known a few merchants hire such people as their staff to manage their accounts, to keep certain dealings protected.'

Another Gift? Why had he not heard of it? 'But there are none within the Schools,' he said.

'No. It is a Gift which we have never thought to utilise. We do not want secrets within the Church nor the Council.'

'Can you not use a Watcher?'

'Father! You forget. The Imperial family is sacrosanct. Now *you* speak of treason. We cannot dare think of Watching them, or using a Reader.'

Father Michael was at loss. 'What is to be done, then?'

'We cannot touch him. The Empress would be outraged. The Arch Cardinal would, I think, have already spoken to you of this?'

Yes. She knew he had.

'This expedition does have one redeeming value. It puts distance between His Grace and the good Father. Whilst he whispers words of war to his mother, her influence cannot reach her son's ears. I hope your trip is a failure, Father. But perhaps it will take some of the fire out of the Emperor's belly. Now is the time for wise heads, patience and forbearance. The Arch Cardinal and I are in agreement on this. We need a ruler who knows that our survival as a species must come before all other considerations. If we cannot have such a ruler, then we must make another.'

Father Michael drew himself away. He was shocked. She *was* talking treason, against the Living God. 'What are you saying?'

She placed her hands out, palms spread, in a calming gesture. 'Peace, Father.'

'Don't act so outraged, Father Michael. You have done terrible things. Things you did willingly in the name of the Emperor. You are not the only one who is prepared to do what is necessary to keep us all alive.'

He shook his head. 'Get out of my mind,' he hissed.

'Gladly.' Cardinal Yarn smiled sadly and reached out a hand and touched him lightly on the arm. He shook her off.

'I ask but one thing of you. If the moment comes, sometimes the best course of action is to do nothing.'

She withdrew her hand, folded her arms and pressed her lips together. 'On second thoughts, Father, I think I shall pick the Speaker myself.'

She turned away without ceremony, ending the conversation.

Father Michael had always thought there was more to her, yet he had always believed the Church was in concord, a strong bastion, serving the Emperor's will. Was Father Llews the enemy now? If that were the case, then who was he to trust?

An hour later the expedition departed. They were sent off to much cheering and good wishes from the assembled citizens of New Tissan. Yet again, Father Michael was minded of the crowds that used to greet his arrival. Their wishes had not been so well meaning.

Hundreds had gathered to either side of the short, muddied stretch of a street that led out to the west. Lines of soldiers and guard lined the route keeping them at bay. The expedition was small, only twenty souls. It looked a lot like the party who had returned ten days earlier. Besides himself and the Emperor was Reese the hunter, eight Gifted, two of the woodsmen they'd encountered at the logging camp now acting as drivers, and the Emperor's squire, Uther. The Eagle Riders, Leader Cadarn and Bryce, were already in the air. Finally, four marines had trooped up just before they had set off. They had marched in a loose square, adorned in worn but serviceable leather armour, swords buckled at their sides and carrying crossbows on their backs. They were a surprising last minute addition, as Father Michael knew the Admiral was usually quite protective of the duties of his men. Father Michael couldn't recall them being volunteered during the planning.

Then there were the animals: there was the Emperor's horse, a spare mount, two wagons pulled by bigger draft horses carrying the supplies, with drivers and spaces for two others. Everyone else was on foot, except the two Eagle Riders of course, as they couldn't spare the horses for such a potentially long and arduous trip. It bothered him little as it was better to be foot-sore than arse-sore. He'd picked that up from Bryce.

One last member had joined the party just as the Emperor was making his final goodbyes, the young Speaker, Ellen. She looked a little breathless, as she handed up a small sack to one of the wagons. She nodded quickly to Father Michael and fell in with the other Gifted. An interesting choice by the Cardinal. Perhaps she wanted the girl to be toughened up a little. Either way, Father Michael was heartened to see her join them, he had grown … well, fond of her, he enjoyed her good humour and her company, felt protective of the secret they shared. It was another emotion he was unused to.

The Emperor kissed his mother, waved at the crowds and rode to the head of the short column. He was dressed in his hunting garb, unassuming, except for his blue cloak edged with a brocade of gold.

He raised his hand and shouted, 'Forward, for Tissan!'

And off they went, the cheering reaching new heights of noise. The two eagles patrolled the skies, screeching as they did so, going in a wide curve in the air then swooping down on a low-level pass over the crowds.

'Stop showing off, you bastards!' shouted someone. Father Michael looked for who had spoken. Ah, young Harwen. He was laughing and gesticulating to an older woman who was shaking her head. That was Jenna and she looked exasperated. In which case, he could allow them their crudeness in front of the Emperor. They were Riders after all.

As grand spectacles went, he had seen better, done better in the arena. Though as they walked slowly out of New Tissan and followed the rutted path heading westwards, he reflected on what Father Llews had said about the stories that would be told. Fifty years from now, when most who then lived would be too young to remember it, they would say the Emperor led a hundred men. A hundred years from now it would be five hundred, and he wore a silver crown and armour of gold. And in three hundred years he would have conquered the entire continent and slaughtered thousands. That's how it went. He'd heard similar stories about himself floating around the arena. That he killed over a hundred men – it was no more than eighty – that after the fights he feasted on their flesh, growing stronger with each heart he ate (he didn't, he got older and slower). Perhaps it didn't matter that the truth was less than the legend. Stories mattered, people liked to believe in stories. Otherwise why spend so much time telling them to each other?

He walked behind the last wagon, amidst the marines and Reese. He listened idly to their chatter, one of them was whistling. Most of the Gifted walked behind the Emperor, their spears barely moving as they marched, shields held tight to their bodies. Their swords were sheathed, oiled and sharpened, ready for war and battle. Two more Gifted walked behind, a little way back from everyone else. Watching their rear. They weren't talking.

The whistling had stopped. He felt a tap on his shoulder. One of the marines. He had a patch over his left eye, a long drooping black moustache and a shaved head. His skin was dark and leathery, a rough looking sort. He leaned in close.

'Corporal Fenner. The Admiral sends his regards.' His one good eye winked. 'Any trouble, you just holler.' The corporal eased away and carried on like nothing had happened. His lips pursed together and he started to whistle once more.

CHAPTER 27

Fillion yawned.

'You'll catch a fly,' observed Lenard.

'I would like to see one try and make it into here.' He had seen not one insect, flying or walking, since he started coming to the library. The place was truly lifeless.

Lenard chuckled. 'The Gods forbid that I would be so derelict in my duty.'

'The Gods could not do a better job at keeping this place so tidy,' said Fillion. The elf was so fastidious he must have some magic about him. 'You sure you're not a sorcerer?'

'Humph. I should be so lucky. I have no talent in that direction.'

Fillion stood from his desk and returned a scroll to the rack. That was all the history of King Merene's life, done and dusted. It had been dull, instructive to a very small point, but still dull. There was one more section of parchments that he had not opened. King Merene had died in the last scroll, so what were these? He pulled out the first.

'Lenard, what's this one? You didn't put them out of order, did you?'

'Insolent elf! Of course not. This is the history of the Cleansing.'

'Cleansing?'

'Honestly, Sabin, I do despair of your ignorance. Though I suppose the event is seldom discussed these days. Many Members have moved on since then.'

'I was never very good at listening.'

'As you often say.' Lenard Walked towards him and took the scroll. 'The Cleansing. It was an event of such importance it was given its own place in the histories. It was the source of much loss and grief for so many elves. Why would we wish to dredge up memories of such an event? It took us so long to recover. Who'd have thought we would need to do the same so quickly?'

So quickly? Was this Cleansing another conflict? Fillion wondered if perhaps it had been a civil war, the name suggested as such. He realised Lenard was still gabbling on.

'I suppose that someone will write the account of the war with the humans. Remember the histories of our land are often recorded many years after the events they recount. Sometimes a decision is made to tell those histories in a certain manner. The issues around the Cleansing were removed from the general histories so they could be addressed separately.' Fillion had to supress a frown. How can you give an accurate account if you keep chopping and changing the story? 'I am sure once our present King passes, a chronicler will undertake the recounting. Sadly it will not be I who stores it as part of King Lujan's life.'

With a loud sigh, he handed back the scroll and walked away. Fillion went to the rack, collected the other scrolls and took them to the table. For the first time he felt genuinely interested. He unfurled a scroll and laid it out before him. The familiar flowery script of the King's historian looking no different from every other scroll he had seen before. He began to read:

'This is the true account of the noble undertaking that became known as the Cleansing. In the three hundred and fifteenth year of the reign of King Merene it was decided that action must be taken against the Nidhal. It had been fifty years since the ambassadors of the Heartlands first encountered them as the Nidhal spread east, a race of green-skinned creatures that walked on two legs but had the manner of beasts about them. At first they had lived in peace with the elves, even though they were given to much barbarity and savageness. A land dispute between the wood elves and a nearby tribe of Nidhal, led to bloodshed. Whilst many believed this was an inevitable outcome considering the nature of both peoples, it was said that simple mediation could quickly address this issue. A second party argued most vociferously that this was the precursor to far greater excesses

that had the potential to spill over into the Heartlands. After much debate, this second party, led by the insightful and impassioned oration of Patiir of Fairfields, gained the ear of the King.'

Patiir. Yet again Fillion was amazed by the longevity of the elves. Patiir had been a Member for longer than the Empire had existed. What had the bastard been up to all those years ago? More importantly, who the hell were the Nidhal? Fillion continued to read. The account suggested this race shared a smiliar heritage to humans, presumably with origins in the west, but whereas humans had had a chance to evolve and develop civilisations, the Nidhal did not advance a culture more sophisticated than the Plainsfolk. Further descriptions emphasised their animal features: muscular limbs, broad snouts, large mouths and a gutteral style of speech.

Time passed, he had no idea how long. He looked up from the parchment. He had to place his hands flat on the tabletop. It was the only way to stop them shaking. He breathed deep. His eyes were aching from the strain of reading. He hadn't taken a candle and the library was already a gloomy place, and the days were short. Yet it seemed darker somehow. He felt the walls closing in on him. He could sense the weight of the ceiling, carrying the Parliament above. There was a pounding pressure on his skull. He clutched his head. His breathing quickened. Standing, he started to walk to the door. His pace increased, his strides lengthening. It wasn't quick enough. Fillion was running as he passed Lenard.

'Sabin? Sabin, are you …?' His voice was lost. The pounding was too great. Sabin took the steps three at a time. Up and up, his legs burning. He reached the top and turned left. His lungs were screaming, there were beads of sweat on his forehead. There were others watching him. The Parliament was still busy at this time of day. He passed them, their heads turning, watching him, their faces frowning and concerned. He had to slow down, he was drawing too much attention. *Dammit. Slow down, you fool.*

He forced himself into a brisk walk, arms swinging. *There*. He came to the exit, then on to the steps, moving away from the centre, away from everyone, into the shadows. He kept walking to the edge of the steps, looking over into the ground below. He hunkered down, wanting to be sick, but it wouldn't come. Fillion raised his head and forced air into his lungs, taking three deep breaths. In through the mouth. *Hold it.* Out through the nose. He felt his heart starting to slow. He forced himself up and looked around. The steps were almost empty and the promenade was quiet. He saw no one taking an interest. That was something at least. A bead of sweat rolled down his neck. 'I need to get fitter,' he said softly, wiping it away. He felt a gust of wind. It was cold against his skin even though he was warm from his exertions. *Oh.* No cloak, he'd left it in his office. He had to go back inside anyway. He could hardly run. Where would he go?

Making his way back to Patiir's offices, he had time to gather his thoughts, but they were jumbled, racing. What he had just read was shocking. It was almost unbelievable. *Almost.*

He reached the outer office. The door to Patiir's was shut but that meant nothing. He knocked lightly on the door and there was no response. *Fine.* He took his place at his own desk. There were some leather wallets, documents delivered in his absence. He pulled them over, undid the tie on the first wallet and slipped out the contents. He looked at the lines of script. Something about a delegation and another Member requesting a meeting. He tried to focus. After a minute he realised he was just staring at it. He heard footsteps and voices, and he looked up, holding the paper in front of him, trying to look busy. Two purple-sashed elves walked by deep in conversation. A Servant followed behind them, looked Fillion's way, and nodded. Fillion nodded back feeling strangely relieved. Patiir walked through the entrance. Fillion jumped.

'Sabin? Not at the Library?' Patiir stopped, concern on his face. 'You have gone white as a sheet.'

'Oh. I have not been feeling well. I couldn't concentrate so I came back, thought I'd try and do some work.'

'I doubt that's possible. If you can't concentrate on reading, you can't work.' He continued past Fillion, opening the door to his office. 'Perhaps you should go home?'

'I will.' Fillion stood went to the threshold of Patiir's office. 'Patiir?'

'Yes?'

'I was reading about the Cleansing.'

The briefest pause. 'What about it?' said Patiir as he continued into his office. Fillion could see something in his manner had changed. There was a stiffness to his walk.

'I never really knew much about it,' he said.

Patiir sat at his desk, took up a quill and started writing.

'I suppose not. Before your time. Even elves do not live forever.'

'I saw your name. You were involved.'

Patiir placed his quill on to his desk. He aligned it with the left side of the sheet he was writing on then he pushed the sheet away. He did the same with the quill. Slow and exact. He sat back and steepled his fingers.

'Yes, I was. And you have questions.'

'The war against the humans. It was my first. I had not thought …'

'That there was another?'

'It was a terrible thing.'

'I agree. It was terrible. But it was no war. A war implies two sides fighting for gain. One side wants one thing and the other doesn't want to give it to them. Once the war is done one side gets what it wants and the other agrees to it. We have fought wars before, against ourselves, against the wood elves, and others.' He sighed. 'We did not fight a war against the humans. It was an extermination. No negotiation, no agreements, no peace. You know that, Sabin. Every elf who marched into the Tissan Empire understood why we had to. Sabin. Sit down. You look like you might fall over.'

'I prefer to stand.'

'Sit.'

Fillion chewed his lip and took the chair facing Patiir. Truth be told his legs were feeling weak.

'Sabin, you are surprised that you were not made aware of my involvement. Perhaps you think I might have told you?'

'Yes. I suppose. You must have known I would find out.'

'I expected you to. By reading our histories, you can at least place it into perspective. I know the war damaged you, Sabin. I can see it in your eyes. You have a sadness and a rage. Perhaps you think you hide it. But it is part of you now. That is why, to a point, I agreed to let you stay with us. Why I wanted you to become my Servant.'

Fillion felt some of that rage flare. 'Pity?'

Patiir shook his head. 'Responsibility. I know my role in this. I hoped to provide for you a measure of peace and … healing. Nadena loves you and so my responsibility to you is now greater, for you are my son.'

You are not my father, you son of a bitch. Your kind killed my father. He fought a ferocious urge to leap across the desk and throttle the elven shit. *Steady, Sabin, don't lose it.*

'I don't know what to say.'

'What is there to say? I bear responsibility for much of what we did. I was the one who argued that we must do something. When the dwarves came to us and spoke of what the humans had done, I knew then that after almost a thousand years, I was compelled to speak to the King and Parliament. The humans were a pestilence, a blight. Under a veneer of civilisation, they were greedy and ambitious. They had expanded to fill every space, be it the tallest peak or the driest desert. They were even starting to conquer the seas. Their ships were the finest ever designed, robust and able to sail away far from shore. And their Gifted? What if they continued to evolve and grow in power? Perhaps one day they could challenge our sorcery, and rid us of our greatest weapon. It was only a matter of time before their arrogance persuaded them that the other nations of this world might be too weak to stop them. They were wrong. We united all the races against them. We fought for our very survival. The temples spoke of it as a holy crusade.' Patiir's smile was wry. 'I'm a politician and do not subscribe to that sort of rhetoric. There was nothing holy about what we did. It was entirely pragmatic. Entirely essential. Entirely the right thing to do. This world and its cultures are many and varied but each must be protected, allowed to thrive and survive. There is a balance that must be maintained. But there is price to be paid.'

'We have paid this price before.'

Patiir nodded. 'The Cleansing. Those elves who remember it do not wish to speak of it. We are a good people, Sabin. But sometimes the greater good may seem as the greatest evil. Depending on your perspective. I go to sleep every night remembering my part in the Cleansing and the destruction of the Tissan Empire.'

'Who were they? This race we fought in the Cleansing?'

'The Nidhal. Theirs was a culture far removed from the Tissan way. At least with the humans we could understand their politicking, their agendas. For their part, the Nidhal had their own twisted sense of integrity and honour. They were *uncompromising*. That was their problem. They lived for war and conquest. They did not understand that conquest is never an end unto itself. They would have burned the world and not realised how pointless their own existence had been.'

'So we destroyed them too?'

'We drove them from all the lands west of the Heartlands. Pushed them to the edge of the sea. All traces of them were erased. Their villages burned, their markers brought down. It was not difficult, they made little that was permanent or made to endure. When the humans rose, they would not have known they walked on soil that had once been ruled by the Nidhal. But were they destroyed? I doubt that. I am sure that some of them escaped. The Nidhal knew how to sail. They had magic, of sorts. Perhaps somewhere in the world they found a new place to call home.

'I am not a monster, Sabin, though I might understand how those who do not have to make these decisions would think me as such. We know a fleet of humans escaped. The last of their kind. Perhaps there are still some left out in the wild places of the old Tissan Empire. We could have pursued them, made sure of our work. But in the end, perhaps mercy got the better of me. I persuaded the King and the other races to recall their armies. We had bled enough, our work was done. The dwarves were satisfied, the others had enjoyed the chase, and taken what booty they wished. For the elves, it was never about gain. If any humans do still live, I wish them luck. If the species survives, it will take them another thousand years to recover. It will take us just as long. I hope the humans will take a different path if they do survive as a species.'

Patiir sat back, placed his hands on the rests of his chair. His face set hard, his eyes like flint. 'And in a thousand years, if necessary, we'll do what we have to again, if any human or whoever comes next, decides to tilt the balance in their favour.'

Fillion sat quietly. He didn't trust himself to do anything else. *You bastard. You bastard. I want to rip your throat out. I want to burn your cities to the ground. I want you to know what it feels like. I want to shove your greater good up your fucking arse and I want to see every single one of you die in screaming pain.*

'Sabin?'

'What? Oh. I am sorry, Patiir. I never realised.'

Patiir stood, walked around his desk and placed a hand on Fillion's shoulder. The flint had gone and was replaced by a familiar warmth.

'It is easy for us to let our shame and anger burn us to a crisp, to devour us from the inside out. Every day I look at my daughters, at both of my sons, Hedra and you. And I remember why I do what I do. So that they may never have to fear. It keeps me sane. Go home now, Sabin. You are a good elf and I know that you will find a way to come to terms with all of this. My daughter needs you.'

Fillion stood and allowed Patiir to guide him out the office.

'I'll see you later tonight,' he said.

Fillion was aware he was walking but he had no sense of his direction. He felt numb, like he was in a dream, the avenues, the Temple of the Gods, the houses, the streets, they all flowed by, glimpsed from the corner of his eye. His thoughts were a surging mix of questions, suppositions and confusion.

They did this before. How did we not know? We had an embassy for years and nobody ever cared to mention this to us? Do the other races have knowledge of it? They must do. The dwarves. He said the dwarves had come to them. What had happened for them to want to go to war. What did we do?

There had always been peace between the Empire and the other races. He had often talked with his men about what had sparked the war. Even his commanders had not been able to tell him. There had been speculation, but in the end it hadn't mattered. There had been no offers of negotiation and every delegation had been slaughtered out of hand. *They had done this before.* The elves had wiped out a race because they were afraid of what could have happened. *We weren't savages. We were not that different to the elves.* Maybe that was why. Maybe Patiir was just waiting for an excuse. A reason to convince the King and all the rest of them that extinction was the best policy. And all the elves, they just forgot about it, they hid it away in their long memories. They make a few bloody scrolls to record the death of an entire species. That's all it was worth. Some rolled-up pieces of dusty parchment hidden amidst thousands, in an ancient library that only the curious might find or care to read. A small note in the glorious history of the elves, who had walked this world for the Emperor knew how long. *They had done this before.* Maybe Patiir was not the first. Maybe others like him had argued the same course. *They worshipped a multitude of Gods and yet behaved like Gods themselves. What gave them the right?*

He stopped. He was under the archway that led to the house. There were lights on. He waked across the yard, opened the door and went inside. He heard voices and movement. He ignored them. He couldn't play act. Instead he took the stairs, walked the corridor and entered his room. It was empty but the bed had been made. He sat on it and looked blankly at the wall. He shrugged off his cloak, undid the sash tie around his waist and unwound it. There was a bowl of water on top of a small table, a mirror hanging above it. He stood up, went to the bowl and splashed water on his face. He looked in the mirror, studying the face. Water ran down his forehead, over his nose, dripped back into the bowl with a gentle plop. He looked at his features, the smooth skin, the ears and how they rose to a point. He felt trapped within his own body, a human cursed to walk the world as a grotesque. How had his men ever trusted him?

Is that why you left, mother? Did you leave because you knew what would happen to us? Was the guilt so great? Or perhaps you decided it had all been a mistake. Were you ashamed? Was there regret in having me? Did you look on my face and see a human underneath this elf skin?

A voice shouted down the corridor. 'Sabin? Was that you? Dinner is almost ready.'

He looked at the door. Reached out his hand, it was shaking. He closed his eyes, took a breath, grasped the handle, opened the door and stepped out.

Nadena stood near the stairs, her arms folded. She was trying to look stern but her face was a picture of happiness. 'Father should be home soon. You hungry?'

'Uh huh.'

He joined her. She slipped an arm through his and they took the stairs together. She was talking, Fillion could hear her, but the words made no sense. She squeezed his arm.

'Sabin. Are you all right? You look miles away.'

'What? Oh. Nothing.' *Come on, focus.* 'It has been a long day. I was reading in the library.' He had to ask. 'I found the history of the Cleansing.'

'Oh,' Nadena's face fell. 'A sad time.' *She knew.*

'It was shocking.'

'I know. My father told me about it. What choice did we have?'

Indeed. What choice? 'It threw me some. Awakened memories that I had started to forget.'

Nadena leaned in and kissed him. 'They will pass. It's done now.'

'Yes.'

They entered the dining room. Hedra and Alica were already there.

'Evening, you two,' the lad said, with a sparkle in his eye.

Sabin nodded to them both. He took his seat and Nadena sat next to him, her leg touching his beneath the table. Fillion filled his glass with wine and played at happy families.

Patiir entered the room ten minutes later.

'My apologies everyone. I was detained.'

'Father, you apologise every time. We *expect* you to be late,' said Alica.

'Just so,' laughed Patiir.

He took his place at the head of the table. He reached out and took the jug of wine.

'Sabin, you want some more?'

Fillion met his eye. 'Yes, please. I'm starting to relax now.'

Patiir narrowed his eyes for a moment. Fillion felt the judgement, the weighing. Patiir smiled and refilled Fillion's glass.

'Good. I know some days can be stressful. You'll get used to it.'

'He better,' said Nadena, nudging him in the ribs.

'Already she bullies me,' sighed Fillion.

'He learns, he learns!' laughed Hedra.

Fillion sipped his wine. *I learn all right, Patiir. You did this before. You are a monster. And I'll see you pay.*

After two hours of interminable good humour and inane banter Fillion was able to excuse himself to take in some night air before retiring. He was exhausted. This evening had been as great a test of his patience and deceit as any he had faced since he had started his self-imposed mission.

He needed time to take stock, to review his plans and decide what to do. But his mind was clouded, his thoughts drawn away from the tactical necessities to how incredibly complicated and problematic his personal situation had become. He had created a life with Nadena, and she would give birth to a half human/half elf child. The irony was not lost on Fillion; he had become his father. The most impossible, unlikely thing had come to pass. And what did that mean for him? The child meant nothing, it was a thing, a notion. When it was born it would be raised as an elf, as the enemy – and its coming was a potential threat that could reveal his true identity, his true nature. What if its human heritage was obvious when it was born? What if the child possessed no sharp ears, had human eyes, human hands? All eyes would turn to him, mages would be called to ascertain his heritage.

He would be arrested and detained at best, sentenced to death at worst. His plan would be in ruins. And with that thought, he focussed on what he must do. There were two options. He could remove the threat altogether: look for a way to kill the child in the womb, a poison perhaps, or he could just kill Nadena, take her riding, break her neck and blame it on a fall from a frightened horse. He shook his head. No, either one posed too many risks, would draw too much attention, too many potential questions. He had enough to deal with maintaining his persona as it was. He sighed, there was one other option. A pregnancy for an elf was similar to a human's, perhaps an elf would give birth a month or so earlier. That gave him seven months at best, seven months to see things done. After that, and the child was born and he was indeed a human child, then it would be over. So he had no choice, he had to accelerate his plans, he had to find a way to make the edifice of elven culture come crashing down.

Seven months.

For an elf, that was a blink of an eye. For him, it would be a relentless dash where one single, reckless mistake could see the end of it. He had thought he would have years to put everything into place, time to make sure everything was perfect.

Fillion swallowed and tried to steal himself for the road ahead. Seven months. Shit.

CHAPTER 28

'Owen?'

'Uurgh.'

'He's getting better then.'

'Not helping, brother.'

'Owen? Can you speak?'

Owen felt a cold pressure on his forehead. Moisture ran down his temples. At the point of pressure, he felt a stinging sensation too. He frowned, feeling a tightness, something pulling. It hurt.

'Ow.'

'He's awake.'

'Thank you, Murtagh.'

Owen opened an eye. It was gloomy. There was something. Somebody leaning over him. 'Naimh?'

'Yes, Owen.'

'I'm back?' his voice rasped. His throat was dry. He swallowed. That hurt too.

'Yes.'

He opened his other eye. The gloom resolved itself into the familiar shapes and proportions of his room within the bowels of the 'Rest.

'I'm on my bed.'

'His wits aren't back then,' said Murtagh. He leaned in close, his head next to his sister's as she bent over to apply another wet cloth to his head. 'You are one lucky son of a bitch.'

He couldn't argue with that. 'Gnomes. A hunting party, like Larsen said. I let them get the jump on me. Had to fight my way out,' he croaked.

'We know,' said Naimh.

'Took a few cuts, I think.'

'You could say that. You got a nasty one on your forehead. Your face was covered in blood when we got to you,' said Naimh, gently touching his cheek. 'We stitched it up. You'll have a scar.' She frowned. 'Your leg was a problem, though.'

Now that he was prompted to think about it, he could feel his leg wasn't right. There was a lot of pressure around his calf.

'That gnome sliced you open. Your muscle was spilling out. It was a mess,' said Murtagh. 'Don't know how you didn't bleed to death.'

Owen felt cold. *I haven't lost it?* He tried to move his head to get a better look but a blanket covered his leg. All he got was another pain in his head. He pulled himself upwards and felt a sharp, deep, tearing sensation.

'Arrgh.'

'Steady now, it's still there,' she said, pushing him back with a firm hand.

'Ah,' said Owen.

'We did what we could, cleaned the wound, cut away some of the flesh. Packed it and stitched it. It's been a few days, no rot has set in, and you had no fever, so you should make it.'

Days? 'Great,' muttered Owen.

Murtagh shook his head. 'It ain't gonna look the same and I doubt it'll ever be as strong.'

'I guess I got off lucky. Think I killed two of them.'

'Good for you,' said Murtagh with approval.

Owen tried to remember, there was a gap in his memory.

'How did I get here?'

'There's a question. I'll fetch Jussi. He can tell you how,' said Murtagh, his voice unusually gruff. He pulled away and left the room.

Owen was puzzled. 'I can't recall the flight back. I must have passed out.'

'You did, lucky for you that you were strapped in first. When Arno landed, your hand was wrapped around the reins, your legs were in the stirrups and your body had slumped right over your eagle's neck. Arno was exhausted but he must have flown straight and level all the way home. That bird loves you,' said Naimh.

'I love that bugger too,' Owen smiled.

'Owen.' Murtagh had returned, trailing behind was Jussi.

'Hey, lad,' said Owen. He was pleased to see him. 'Don't hang back there.'

'Go on,' said Murtagh, pushing him forward. Jussi stumbled as he came to the foot of the bed. He looked down at his feet, his face white, fists clenching.

'Jussi,' said Owen, still rasping. It didn't sound like his own voice. The boy looked up sharply, his eyes wide.

'Jussi, it's okay. Just tell me what happened.'

Jussi swallowed. 'We were both hanging back like you said. Then I heard you. It was real faint but I knew you were in trouble. I told Em. She didn't wait, turned Taru and went straight for you. I was following a little behind. I was shouting at her but I don't think she heard me. Next thing I saw, she was diving. Taru tucked in his wings and fell from the sky. It was so fast. You were airborne when they smashed into the clearing. I couldn't see what happened. So I flew towards you. I tried to pulse you, but you didn't reply. So I got closer, saw you weren't moving. I was scared, I panicked a little. I reached out to Arno, asked him to fly straight, not to wobble. I tried to send an image of you to him so he would understand.'

'I think it worked,' said Owen.

Jussi smiled thinly.

Owen frowned. Something was very wrong. Then it became terribly clear. 'Jussi. What about Em and Taru?'

Jussi was starting to well up. Owen frowned again, ignoring the pain it caused. He didn't want to hear what the lad had to say, as if by not knowing he could ignore the truth, ignore the coldness inside of him, the weakness he felt in his limbs.

'I looked back. I tried calling to Taru. The eagle lifted off from the clearing. It was a little way back. It wouldn't come near me. I guessed Em wanted to watch our backs. So I flew ahead. Pulsed to Arno and Taru to follow me and Ayolf. I kept going, didn't stop, not 'til we got home. I landed and got Arno to follow me in. Taru kept hanging back. I couldn't work it out. I pulsed and shouted his name. Erskine finally got them to come in when he started waving a dead hare backwards and forwards. But …'

'Jussi. Em wasn't with Taru was she?' said Owen quietly.

Jussi shook his head and the tears started flowing.

'No. I didn't think. I should have gone back.'

'You did the right thing, you saved Owen, brought all the eagles home,' said Naimh, putting her arm around the boy. He *was* just a boy, Owen could see that. Owen had still felt like a boy too, even when he had fought over Aberpool, even as the Head Man of Eagle's Rest. He didn't feel that way any longer. Em had been his responsibility and he had failed her. Brave Em, braver than he had ever been. She and countless others had died because he and his fellow Riders couldn't protect them. The hollow feeling in his stomach, the dread that smothered his thoughts, was gone. It was replaced by something harder, something icy. It was anger and rage and determination. If he had ever thought himself a coward before, that person, that part of him was gone. It was as dead as Em. *Time to grow up. Time to stop thinking they could all hide and let the world go about its business.*

'Murtagh, Naimh, she was your family. I let you down.'

Murtagh's face was hard, unreadable. Naimh's eye burned with fire, yet she reached out and touched his cheek.

'It wasn't your fault. We've had time to grieve, to say goodbye. She was happy, doing what she always wanted to do. She made us proud.'

Murtagh's mouth twitched. That man might have said goodbye but he wasn't going to forget his niece. He had promised to look after her as had Owen, and he wasn't going to forget, or forgive either.

'Murtagh. You got some folk ready to head out?'

Murtagh nodded. 'Aye, got a dozen lads, all used to ranging or fighting. We're already packed and set.'

'Good. Take Erskine and Anneli too. They need to learn how to take care of themselves.'

'Right … what about you?'

'I'm not going anywhere. Jussi can fly point for you.'

'Right.' Murtagh shared a look with Naimh, turned to go.

'Murtagh.'

He stopped and looked back.

'Kill them all. Burn their tents and cabins. Take everything you can find.'

Murtagh nodded. His smile was grim. 'Aye, Chief.'

Owen sat back and closed his eyes. *I'll make them pay. For Em. For everyone.*

He felt a hand touch his shoulder. Naimh had remained behind.

'Are you okay, really?' she asked. The fires had gone, but a warmth remained. 'I just ask because … your face. I've seen that face before. Anger, rage, despair. I've seen it in Murtagh and too many others. It'll kill you if you let it.'

Owen shook his head.

'I'm not going to let it kill me. I'm going to use it, Naimh. I thought we could rebuild, that I could bring back the home that I grew up in, that Eagle's Rest could be the haven of our future.'

'It still can be,' urged Naimh. 'We take our vengeance and they'll learn to leave us alone.'

'Yes. It can be,' agreed Owen, 'but not that way.' He turned to face her.

'Eagle's Rest will become the hope for all of what's left of our kind. We can't keep our heads in the clouds. We can kill all of those gnomes but more will come, eventually. And the elves and the dwarves and all the rest of them will try and finish us off. But we'll be ready. I found other survivors before, hard folk who know what it takes. Fighters. We find them and we organise. Let the enemy think they have won. And we'll make them believe it. We keep our heads down for another year, maybe two, and we prepare.'

'And then?' whispered Naimh.

Owen smiled and gripped her shoulder.

'We finish what they started. We take the war to them.'

CHAPTER 29

'What did you see today?' asked Reese.

'Snow,' replied Bryce.

Father Michael shivered a little and pulled his fur cloak around him. Everyone was similarly clad, it was too cold not to. The furs might have come on but they still didn't shed any armour.

'I saw a lot of that too,' said Reese.

'Anyone see anything other than snow?' asked Wendell, one of the marines.

'I saw my eagle do an almighty shit. Right into that.' Bryce pointed at the small round pot suspended over the fire they were all sitting around.

'Then tonight we'll feast like kings!' announced Bron, the driver and cook. 'I knew there was something special about tonight's stew.'

Bryce sniffed. 'Real shit can't be any worse than what you make for us most nights.'

'Speaking of which, what is the Emperor having tonight?' said Beautiful, another one of the marines, and their only female. She wasn't that beautiful. Father Michael thought her quite plain. If she didn't have shoulder length hair, he might have mistaken her for a man in certain lights.

'Bagged him a bird,' said Reese, picking at his teeth with a splinter of wood.

'What'd you get us?' she persisted.

'You get yesterday's bird. And extra birdshit.'

'I forget how lucky I am,' she muttered.

Father Michael gazed at the fire and smiled. He found he enjoyed the nights best of all. He could sit quietly and listen to this lot bitch and moan and swear all night. He'd found it didn't bother him like it ought to have.

'Hey, Father? What you smiling at? Looking forward to supper that much?' asked Wendell.

Father Michael rocked back and placed his hands on his knees.

'Just giving thanks for the Emperor's bounty and the fact that Bryce is a bloody liar.'

'See Bryce? You got caught out by the Father,' said Corporal Fenner, coming in from the dark.

'So what if I did? It'll still taste like shite,' grumped Bryce.

Corporal Fenner brushed some snow from his boots. 'I had a captain like you, Bryce. Moody son of a bitch. Remember him, Beautiful?'

'Yep. If I recall he was a little uptight.'

'That he was.'

'Used to give us a hard time alright. Nothing was ever good enough for him,' added Wendell, his face held up to the sky.

'And if I remember he was the one who left the door to his cabin open,' said Beautiful wistfully.

'Gave him the night of his life, didn't you?' said Corporal Fenner.

'That I did,' she said, still wistful.

'Never gave us any trouble after that,' said Wendell.

'So you want me to fuck Bryce, Corporal?' asked Beautiful. Her face was screwed up, contemplating the possibility.

'You bloody won't!' shouted Bryce.

'Wait 'til we go to sleep, Beautiful. I'm knackered out and your hollerin' will likely keep me up,' ordered Corporal Fenner.

'Right you are,' said Beautiful. She smiled sweetly at Bryce. One of her front teeth was missing.

'You have to get past my bird first!' said Bryce, standing up and kicking snow over Bron and the fire.

'Watch it!'

'Looks like you'll have to get in line, Beautiful. Bryce's bird has first dibs,' advised Corporal Fenner.

Bryce stalked over to his eagle, waving a fist in the air.

'Sorry about the talk, Father,' said Reese.

Father Michael shook his head and pushed himself up. 'Doesn't bother me. Just keep the noise down and don't upset the bird.' He turned to walk to the tent, set a little way apart from their fire.

'Hah!' said Corporal Fenner. 'Tantamount to permission that is.'

'Thank you for the blessing, Father!' shouted Beautiful.

Father Michael felt the snow crunch under his feet. He enjoyed the sound and the sensation. Struggling through it hour after hour was another matter. It was also playing havoc with his boots when it melted. The soft leather was getting badly stained and he feared for the stitching. At least he had worked out to stay in the ruts made by the wagons. Their weight packed the snow and made it easier to walk on. He made his way across the small hollow they'd discovered, nestled between three small rises a little way off to the south of their route. It gave them some cover from the wind and the snow flurries. Another small fire was built before the tent. Uther was fussing over it, and the bird spitted above. The Emperor stepped out from the tent holding a goblet in his gloved hand. He was wearing his blue cloak rather than the finely cut furs.

'They aren't teasing Bryce again?' he asked.

'Yes. It is their favourite game.'

The Emperor smiled. 'Anything to pass the time.'

'The nights are long.'

'They are,' he agreed. He hunkered down in front of the fire. 'Leader Cadarn should be back soon. Will you join us for supper?'

'Is there enough?' Father Michael didn't have the courage to say he'd had his eye on the stew. Dry meat was fine but if there was a choice …

'Of course. Young Uther here was saying he rather fancied the stew.'

'Then I shall be glad to join you.'

At first the Emperor had spent most evenings around the main fire, but had lately taken to keeping to his own tent, occasionally inviting Cadarn and Father Michael to join him. Neither he nor the Leader were adept at long conversations, but it seemed to suit his young lord. He remained in good spirits, certainly when amongst the men, yet there were times Father Michael had seen him brooding into his goblet.

'Can I tempt you, Father?' said the Emperor, raising his drink.

'No, thank you.'

'Of course. Uther, you can leave that and go and have something to eat.'

Uther looked up from the spit. 'Thank you, my lord.'

'The Gifted don't drink. Did you know that?' the Emperor asked, waving his goblet at a third fire, which made the point of the camp's triangle. Dark figures were gathered around it but occasionally the flame was reflected off bare metal, a gleam in the night.

He did know it. 'Do they never take off their armour?' asked Father Michael.

'Maybe they do but probably only to clean it. This weather plays havoc with our kit.'

'At least it isn't raining.'

'True. Wait until this lot turns to mud, then things will get interesting.'

'The wagons?'

'Yes.'

Father Michael didn't want to think about it. They were finding the going harder, the land less open, the paths more treacherous. Snow drifts threatened to engulf and trap their wagons. It was down to Reese and the flyers to pick the best routes. They were still heading west, after a fashion, but their path was no longer straight. The lands were also climbing, the slopes getting steeper, with more hills to navigate. It didn't help that they were looking for evidence of life, which was likely buried under a foot of snow. No one had said anything in front of him yet, but he knew what they were all thinking. *What did they hope to achieve?* His practical side recognised the futility of the search, but this was a test of faith. He understood that.

'I remember the rains at the end of the first year,' said Leader Cadarn, walking into the small circle of light.

'Leader, I didn't hear you land,' said the Emperor.

'Hilja is a quiet bird, we glided in,' he replied. 'The snow hides sound well.' He stood before the fire, his hands behind his back, waiting to be invited.

'Oh, please, relax. Join us,' said the Emperor.

'Thank you.' Leader Cadarn removed his gloves, hunkered down and placed his hands near the flames.

'You mentioned the war?' prompted the Emperor.

'The mud, Your Grace. I was attached to a division of your infantry, trying to get to the front.'

'Was there a front? I recall we never stayed in one place for very long,' said the Emperor gruffly.

'In that weather, we never made it anyway,' Cadarn continued on. 'The mud sticks to everything, gets everywhere. You get a train of wagons going over the same spot, which makes it worse, churns it up, makes it softer and deeper. Next thing you know wheels are axle-deep and stuck fast. Everything stops. You spend an hour trying to shift it. You get anyone standing by to lend a hand and they get muddied too. Then another wagon gets stuck and more people are called to help. Tempers are frayed, morale is dented. Before you know it, you've lost a day. In return you get tired horses and tired men covered head to toe in muck. When you stop for the night, the whole division is strung out over five miles.'

He withdrew a thin knife and looked at the Emperor, who nodded his assent. Cadarn leaned towards the fire, started stabbing the bird. Hot juices oozed out from the white and brown flesh. It dripped on to the fire, sizzling as it struck the wood, turning the glowing red to black.

'Wood elves hit us later that evening. They travel light and they don't care about mud. Savages but smart ones, they kept pricking us. Rushing in fast, overwhelming isolated groups and pulling back before anyone could react.'

'What happened?' asked Father Michael. He was intrigued and appalled in equal measure.

'We Eagle Riders did what we could to drive them off, but there were not enough of us. The decision was made to pull back and consolidate. By the time the division regrouped on higher ground it was three days later and we'd lost a third of our strength.'

'How many?' Father Michael had no idea about military organisation.
'I'd say about three thousand.'

'Sweet Emperor,' said Father Michael. He immediately felt foolish saying it. The Blessed Emperor was right next to him. He looked over at the Emperor and found his lord was quiet, thoughtful.

'The bird's almost ready,' said Cadarn.

'What's the ground like?' asked the Emperor.

'It's going to get harder now. Colder too, climbing all the way to the mountains. There is a river up ahead moving parallel to our line of travel. I'd say two days as the wagon rolls from here. Maybe it's spilling out from the ranges ahead of us, but could be it's coming from the mountains to the far north.'

'We can't we go round it?' the Emperor asked.

'We can try north but like I said, I couldn't say when we'd hit the curve. I didn't see one.'

The Emperor took a swallow of whatever he was drinking and placed the goblet on to the ground. Father Michael saw that it was empty and tried to smell what might have been in it, but all he got was wood smoke and meat.

'I'm hungry. Cut me a piece off,' the Emperor ordered.

Cadarn got to work, sawing a sliver of meat off the side, he didn't go too deep, keeping to the cooked sections of flesh.

'We could head south,' said Cadarn. 'The weather might let up a bit.' He held out the meat.

'Hmm.' The Emperor reached out, took it and bit away half. 'Oh. Hot.' His mouth was open, blowing air out, then closing, chewing fast, and finishing with a quick swallow. 'Damn.' He fished for his goblet and realised it was empty.

'Here.' Cadarn passed over a water bottle.

The Emperor took a swig, handed it back

'I see what you are saying. But I want to push on to those mountains. At least we should get to the foot of them. If we don't find anything then we go south.'

Father Michael nodded. If that was the Emperor's decision, then he would follow.

'Bryce and I will go up tomorrow, find a likely crossing point,' said Cadarn.

'Good.' The Emperor drew his cloak about him. 'It's cold tonight.'

'You should try up there, my lord,' said Cadarn, using his knife on the bird once more. 'It's bloody freezing.'

'Sweet fuckin' Emperor, I can't feel my fingers!' Wendell raised his hands and looked at them as if they were someone else's.

'Then don't wave them about you, bloody idiot. Stick 'em back in your pants,' shouted Corporal Fenner.

'Won't find nothing to warm him in there,' said Beautiful.

'You're not wrong,' muttered Wendell, pushing his hands deep into his pockets.

Father Michael didn't like to admit it, but he'd lost any sensation in his hands ages ago. He kept flexing them, wriggling the fingers, trying to keep the blood flowing. Standing out in this wind was sucking his energy away. It was painful.

'Can we move, already?' said Coyle, a heavyset marine who never stopped moving, even when he wasn't freezing cold. Right now he was jumping up and down on the spot.

'Reese is coming back,' said Father Michael. He watched as the hunter worked his way up the slope from the river's edge. He always planted his spear ahead of him, testing the ground before pulling himself up. It was a slow process, but a sensible one. They waited for him on a long rise overlooking the river that snaked its way along out of the white haze of the north before heading into the white haze of the south. Right now that river was frozen solid.

The Emperor nudged his horse forward to the top of the slope. Steam emerged from its nostrils and it didn't look happy, none of the animals did. At least the two draft horses had their exertions to keep them warm. Neither of their two drivers had that. Bron was hunched over his bench, lost in a mound of furs, his face hidden. The two eagles were both on the ground, their Riders talking quietly.

'Do you think they get cold too?' a muffled voice sounded from his left.

'Huh?' The hood on his fur coat was pulled so far forward he had no idea who had just spoken. He turned around to see the top of the speaker's hood barely met his shoulder. It was clearly Ellen, though they hadn't spoken much since they'd left.

'The eagles. Do you think they get cold?'

Father Michael shrugged. 'They live in the mountains. I imagine it must be cold there all the time.'

'Hmm.'

'You are a Speaker. Can't you ask it?'

'I could but I'd understand nothing. Flyers have a bond with their birds. They learn to communicate over years spent together, sharing feelings and emotions.'

'Oh.'

There was a short pause.

'Sorry I haven't had much time to talk to you,' she said.

'I wasn't expecting you to,' he replied.

'Still. It's rude. Eilion doesn't like us to … mingle.'

Arrogance. The Gifted was stood near the Emperor, his back to them. Reese had arrived and was in conversation with the pair.

'I understand,' he said. 'But it is good of you to say hello. There aren't many of us out here.'

They stood in silence for a moment longer, watching the discussion.

The Emperor turned around and beckoned everyone closer.

'Reese has scouted the river and been across to the other side. He believes the ice is thick enough for us to cross, though caution is advised. We'll drive the wagons down to the edge, offload them at the bank, then we'll drive them across and carry the cargo after. Eilion will supervise the work.'

Negotiating the slope was hard enough. The wagons threatened to slide through the snow, taking their horses with them. The drivers directed their horses to go zigzag down the incline and had men lean on the inward side. It worked well enough, but took them a good thirty minutes and some liberal cursing to make it down what was a run of no more than fifty yards. Uther had lost his footing at one point and rolled most of the way to the bottom. Luckily, he'd hurt nothing but his pride. Father Michael found it hard enough keeping his balance within his robes and was convinced he would join the young squire at any moment.

Eventually the expedition gained the bank, or where they thought it might be. It was hard to say where it ended and the river started. A few bushes and trees created a vague line of demarcation. He also saw the footsteps and rounded holes where Reese had ventured out. At first they were random, then started to follow a pattern, like the imprint of a paw. Two footsteps and three circles in front of them, like a great cat had stalked across the water.

There was little talk as everyone got to unloading their stores. The Gifted took the lead wagon, everyone else the second, and Father Michael helped with that one. Once their stores, weapons and food had been stacked, everyone gathered to watch the passage.

Eilion stood at the edge and waved the first wagon forward.

'Yentle, you can go first.'

Reese moved up to the wagon and looked at the driver. 'I'll lead you, just follow my footsteps.'

'Right. Gee up, you nag, let's get it over with,' said Yentle, a lithe and swarthy man from southern Scotia. He clicked his tongue and shook the reins.

The horse responded slowly and stepped out on to the river proper. Reese moved around it and took up position a few paces ahead. He walked on, placing his feet and spear in the marks he'd already created. The wagon rolled on behind him. Father Michael listened to the familiar and soothing crunch of snow compacting under the hooves and wheels.

The Emperor went to stand on the edge of the bank, perhaps a little way on to the river itself, his arms folded.

'This is slow going,' observed Corporal Fenner.

'We could make a fire? Make some tea?' said Coyle.

'No. By the time it's ready we'll be humping stuff across,' replied the corporal.

'That'll warm you up,' said Beautiful.

'Shame. I would've liked something hot,' said Bryce, coming to stand by Father Michael and the marines. 'Oh …'

'I can help you with that,' said Beautiful.

'Forget I said it,' said Bryce, his head in his hands.

Cadarn placed an arm around his shoulders in a show of support. It was an unusual display of familiarity from the usually serious Leader.

'Corporal, try to keep your people in line. My Riders are emotional people.'

Corporal Fenner grinned.

Father Michael turned his attention back to the crossing. They were over halfway along and moving steadily. Eilion walked back up the slope, signalling to Bron.

'Bring your wagon down. I'll walk you across when they are done.'

Bron sat up a little, his hands appearing from within the folds of fur. He jerked the reins and his horse pulled the wagon forward, the wood creaking in response.

A loud cracking noise made Bron shoot up from his bench.

'Shit!' he shouted.

'Oh fuck,' muttered Coyle

Father Michael was fast enough to see the first wagon disappear through the ice. One moment they were there, the next, the whole thing fell straight through, the horse dragged into the hole with it with barely enough time to scream.

Eilion ran on to the ice.

'Useff, Lendll, with me!'

Two of the Gifted split off from the others and charged after him.

'Where's Reese?' asked Wendell

'Can't see 'im,' said Beautiful.

'Bron. Can you see Reese?' asked Cadarn

'No.' The driver had a hand cupped over his eyes, straining forward atop his wagon. 'Can't see him. He must've gone in. The hole is pretty big.'

Cadarn ran over to the wagon, started to climb up. 'What about Yentle? Can you see either of them in the water?'

'No. Nothing.'

Eilion and the others were at the midway point. Father Michael could see no sign of Bron or Yentle. They had no idea how deep the river was, how strong the current under the ice.

The Emperor had not moved. Had said nothing. He just stood there, watching it unfold.

Uther, his face pale, joined Father Michael.

'What should we do?'

He had no idea.

'We wait here. See what the Gifted find,' he offered.

'Should we get a rope?' asked Uther.

'Too late for that,' said Bryce.

Eilion and the others were at the hole. They had spread out. Smart. Not a good idea to stick together what with all their armour on. It was a brave thing just to have gone out there, Father Michael had to concede. He'd never seen a Gifted lack for courage. The middle figure, he guessed Eilion, turned and waved back, shouting.

'Nothing!'

Cadarn jumped off the wagon, crunched his way down to stand by the Emperor.

'You Grace? What should we do?'

The Emperor was quiet, Cadarn even quieter when he leaned in closer. Father Michael had to strain to hear.

'Your Grace?'

'Get them back.'

'Yes, Your Grace.'

Cadarn moved away from the Emperor and whistled, raising his arms, signalling for the Gifted to return.

'Think we might have time for that fire now,' said Corporal Fenner softly.

Leader Cadarn was in conversation with Eilion when Father Michael found them standing just outside the camp's perimeter. They were still on the riverbank, having not moved, even though they'd had several hours of daylight left. No one had the enthusiasm to do much of anything after the accident.

'Father,' said Eilion. He had none of the usual mocking tone about him. He was sombre, serious. It made a change.

'How is the Emperor?' asked Cadarn.

'I have only spoken to Uther. The lad says he is brooding. And drinking,' replied Father Michael.

'I doubt we have much left for that,' said Cadarn.

'He's on the last of the wine now,' said Eilion.

'One less thing for us to worry about,' said Cadarn. He pulled at his earlobe. 'We need to get a decision from him. Do we push south, head back or try again.'

Eilion placed his hands on the pommel of his longsword.

'The Emperor will not want to head back. We have found nothing.'

Cadarn did not respond. He looked pensive. Father Michael wondered why. Surely the Leader was not suggesting they head back?

Eilion sighed. 'Father. The answer to the question your face is asking me is this. If we head back now, after suffering a minor reversal and having nothing even to show for it, what do you think people will say?'

Father Michael was struggling. He felt like a traitor for thinking it and was even more afraid to say it.

'The people will lose heart and they will lose faith.'

Eilion nodded. 'Yes, Father.'

Father Michael pinched the bridge of his nose. Surely the Emperor would not turn back. *No. He will not. He will lead us to a new future and we must follow, we must be worthy of him.* He looked hard at both of them.

'This is a test of our faith. This journey was never going to be easy. If we must sacrifice our lives to ensure we are successful, then that is what we will do.'

Cadarn and Eilion shared a glance. Cadarn wrapped his arms around his body and puffed out his cheeks. 'I've never once turned my back on my duty, Father. But I would like to know in which direction that duty is taking me.'

'Father, talk to the Emperor and find out what his orders are. It will help us with the men,' said Eilion.

'Very well.'

Father Michael took his leave and went directly to the Emperor's tent. There was a fire going, though this night there was nothing cooking over it. Reese's loss would be keenly felt. At first he did not see the Emperor, then as he drew closer he saw a boot sticking out of the tent.

'Your Grace?'

The Emperor's head emerged from the shadows.

'Father.'

'May I join you?'

'I can hardly stop you,' said the Emperor with a hard smile. 'Well, I could.'

Father Michael stood by the fire, looking into the tent. The Emperor was sitting on the ground, his back resting against his horse's saddle.

'Sit down, Father. Honestly, we are in the middle of nowhere. I don't mind and there is no one here to judge you.'

I can judge myself. He sat himself on the ground, on a patch of snow that had yet to melt in the heat.

The Emperor stared at the fire. 'A sad day, Father.'

'Yes.'

'It makes things difficult. Having lost a wagon.'

Father Michael decided it was important to sound positive. 'There is space on the second one and we still have all the stores.'

The Emperor sighed.

'True. We can pack them all on to the wagon, though the going will be slower.' The Emperor reached into the shadows, retrieved his goblet, and tipped it to his mouth. He upended it with a sour look and threw it to the ground.

'I am hungry. We caught nothing today or yesterday. Nothing fresh to eat.'

'Reese was a good hunter,' said Father Michael.

'That he was.'

The Emperor pushed himself up and stepped out of the tent. He reached down and retrieved a stick, snapping it in two against his raised knee. He threw both pieces into the fire. 'But so am I. Tomorrow, Father, we shall head south. I won't risk any more lives trying to cross that river. But first thing, you and I are going to catch us some meat.'

'Me? But I have never done such a thing in my life,' said Father Michael, feeling slightly put upon.

'Then it's time you learned. There's a stretch of woods just north of here that looks like we might find something. If you want to be my shadow, which you insist on being, then you can learn to be useful to this expedition. Now you can go and tell Cadarn and Eilion to stop fretting and spread the word to the men. I'm sure they will all be relieved.'

'Of course, Your Grace.'

Father Michael was a little relieved himself.

Father Michael sat by the small fire he had built for himself and used a nearby stick to prod some life back into it. The camp had long passed into slumber, bar him and the sentry, and Father Michael couldn't sleep, whether in spite, or because, of the day's activities, it didn't matter. It had been a hard day, the first true setback for the expedition. He was mulling over what might have happened if the Emperor had not been so positive in his decision. He was sure the point was moot, yet he also realised that worshipping a Living God could not blind a man to the harsh realities of life, especially when men such as Cadarn and Eilion questioned matters.

'Father?'

He looked up at Ellen, her face hidden within the shadows of her hood.

'Can I join you?' she asked?

Why not? He found himself looking forward to company. 'Please,' he replied.

She pulled her hood back and settled down next to him, arranging her robes over her crossed legs. They sat in silence for a minute before Father Michael decided he should say something.

'Are you having trouble sleeping again?'

Ellen nodded. 'I have nightmares sometimes. And no matter what I do, I can never make them go away.'

Father Michael believed he understood what was going on. She was wrestling with the demons of her past.

'You were you at the Monastery when it fell?'

Ellen nodded, her face troubled. 'I was there. It was terrifying. The flames were everywhere and there was screaming and fighting. I was still in my dormitory, with a few others and we didn't know what to do. An ogre found us. I saw a friend picked up and her arms torn from the sockets. I thought it was the end of us. Then the Cardinal appeared right behind the creature and drove a spear through it. You should have seen her face. She was drenched in blood, and she looked as frightening as the ogre she'd just slain. She got us out and led us through the fire and into the night.' Ellen shuddered. 'I still dream about it. Seeing the bodies, what the ogres had done.'

Father Michael reached out his hand, but stopped it for a moment, unsure about what he should do next. He wanted to offer comfort but he didn't think a pat on the shoulder would achieve much, and he was a long way from hugging anyone. He withdrew his hand and went back to stoking the fire.

'I have to live with my memories too,' he said. 'I almost allowed them to destroy me.'

'But they didn't.'

'No. I was saved by the Emperor.' Father Michael was going to say more about his redemption, but realised that there was something better to say, something just as honest.

'I wanted to forget who I was. I wanted to be a better man, different, new. But you can't pretend that the past didn't happen, or deny that what happened then shaped the person you are now. That will always be there. But you can decide to accept it and not fight it. Life is too short.'

He felt her hand touch his arm. It was a light pressure, barely registered, but it felt like a surge of energy had coursed through his body.

'Father. Can I tell you a secret?'

Father Michael nodded.

'I grew up on a trading cog, my parents owned it. I never spent much time on land, we were always at sea, going from port to port. And that suited my mum and dad. You see they weren't decent Emperor-fearing folks. They didn't hold with the Church, they were Celtebarians and still clung on to the old ways. I grew up thinking the same thing. They also knew I was a Gifted and they didn't want the Schools getting their hands on me. But then they got the flux, and I lost them. And their ship, which was mine by right, was taken by people who I thought I could trust. I found myself with no place to go. So what was I to do? I went to the Schools and found Cardinal Yarn. She took me in. So you and I, we aren't so different?'

Father Michael cocked his head and gazed into the fire. Perhaps not. She was right, they shared a similar path.

Ellen paused a moment and Father Michael could feel her eye upon him.

'I told the Schools I was a Speaker and I proved it to them, and

Cardinal Yarn said that even though I should have been too old to join, she wanted me to become one of them. She said she understood what I had been through. It was such a wonderful feeling, knowing I wasn't on my own anymore. But I do feel a little guilty. I still don't really believe in the Emperor or the Church. And I know that is bad of me, but I am my parents' daughter. We never needed either to get along.'

Father Michael shifted uncomfortably. What was he to do with this knowledge? Should he condemn her? How could he? She was not the first to have uttered such shocking words, even her own Cardinal spoke of matters that were treasonous. The fact was he didn't want to have to do anything. He didn't want to have to report her to anyone. He had his place and his role, and he had not been asked to root out those who disbelieved, only those that threatened.

'Ellen, are you loyal to the Emperor? Do you serve him gladly?' he asked.

Ellen bobbed her head.

'Oh yes. I told you, the School is my family now, though many of them are far too serious for their own good. Just because I don't believe in all that religious stuff, I am still loyal. I like being a Gifted and I owe the Cardinal. I don't want to let her down.'

Father Michael closed his eyes. Good. That was what he needed to hear.

'Ellen. I will keep your secret. But take a care never to say such things aloud and keep your thoughts guarded.'

'I will, Father. I knew you'd understand.'

She reached out and squeezed his arm. It was a pleasant sensation.

CHAPTER 30

Cade wiped her brow with both hands, forcing them through her long tangled hair. They came away wet. She felt patches of moisture under her arms and lower back as well. It all should have frozen in place but the work kept her body temperature up.

'Water?' asked Anyon, proffering a skin.

She took it with the slightest nod of her head. Opening her mouth, she tilted her head back and let the water fall into her mouth. It was cold and reminded her that she'd better not stop for too long. She let the water splash and fall from her lips, running freely down her chin. She handed it back to Anyon, stretched, and took a moment to look around. Everyone was hard at work, sitting or hunched over larger piles of rock, chipping away the waste to get to the ore within. There was little talk but here and there, someone asking for help or sharing a drink. There was a time, not so long ago, when water was rationed. Given only at specific times and watched over by guards. This was one of a number of minor concessions won from the boss. She felt pleased with herself. They also got to work out in the daylight for two days out of every three. All of them felt healthier for it, you could even say happier, but that was probably stretching matters. At the very least her group was suffering less for their troubles. They hadn't lost anyone in three weeks, even if it was bloody freezing out here. Leaden grey skies and the snow on the ground told them they must be in the thick of winter. They still took their beatings, but even the guards did it half-heartedly, like they were going through the motions.

Their boss was a smart one all right. He'd considered her comments about working the rocks and had taken the next step. He had offered the services of his humans to his partners in the mine and now they prepared everyone's stone for shipment. Just their group, mind, no one else was getting a look-in on this job. It had brought them all tighter together. People had started to watch each other's backs a little more, which was no bad thing. But resentment was building in the cavern and some folk didn't like the treatment her bunch was getting. They were still being brutalised, and they wanted to take that out on someone. It only needed a ringleader to get them started. She knew a couple at least who would happily fill that role.

The boss walked into view, looking the same as he always did. Hands on his belt, a permanent frown on his face. Cade knew he was capable of smiling he just didn't like to show it. He was heading towards her so Cade put on her game face.

'Afternoon, boss, good day, isn't it?' she asked.

He stopped and raised an eyebrow.

'Is it? It would be a better day if you stopped jawing and got on with some work,' he replied.

'I will do, boss, but I wanted a word with you.'

'So I understand. Geir said as much,' he replied.

'I was doing some thinking and I have a suggestion for you, boss.'

'Oh really? You are wasted here. Go on then. Dazzle me with your acumen,' he said, the edges of his eyes crinkled, showing some amusement.

'I was thinking about what we are doing here. You got it sewn up. Almost.'

The dwarf raised an eyebrow. 'Almost?'

'You know I mentioned to you about the smelting? I've found at least half a dozen folk who know how to do it.'

The dwarf grunted. 'And I assume that you might be one of them?'

Cade shrugged. 'I know a little. Just thinking, we could save you even more money if we did all the work for you.'

'And what would you want from me? A few less beatings? Your own cave to sleep in?'

'I wouldn't complain if you had a mind to set that up. Truth is, I want to survive. I daresay I'm speaking for everyone here.' She looked at Anyon, who was chipping away at a rock not five yards distant. The dwarf followed her gaze, as Anyon's eyes flicked up fearfully to hers then across to the boss, before returning to his work. The dwarf was silent for a while, watching her, calculating.

'These smelters. They aren't all mine, are they?'

'No, boss, Sorry. ' She'd had Issar check around the cavern. He hadn't got round to everyone yet but out of the five who claimed knowledge, only two really knew how to do it. Considering the pool to choose from, it was a blessing they'd found any at all.

'That's a problem, then,' said the dwarf with an air of finality.

'You could always buy them?' she suggested.

'I might. My business partners are getting a little antsy. They think I'm trying to take over the whole operation.'

'Good idea, boss,' said Cade.

'Is it?' he asked harshly.

Cade figured it was time to get back to work. She hunkered down and started to attack a rock with her hammer and chisel. The dwarf didn't move away.

'What's your name?'

She stopped and looked up. 'Cade.'

'Mine's Vidar.' He leaned forward and held her eyes with his. They were dark and dangerous. 'It was you who spoke to Geir. About the pregnant woman. You don't seem to care very much what happens to your own kind.' He said it softly, as aware of the other humans as she was.

Cade looked away and smashed the hammer down hard. A chunk of rock detached itself and dropped at her feet. 'I care about what happens to me,' she said.

'Watch yourself, Cade. You're too clever by half.'

Vidar turned and stalked off, his short, strong legs thrusting out and thumping down with each step. She watched him go, another successful negotiation completed. *Yeah, I'm clever. Thing is, am I clever enough?*

Her throat had gone dry again. There was a water butt just inside the cavern and she wasn't of a mind to wait for the usual water round, so instead she'd get it from there. No one was likely to question her as they still had people shifting stuff in and out of the lower levels. The butt sat in a nook just off the passage, the rounded wooden planks cold and slimy to the touch. The butt was filled by the steady drip of water falling down from the ceiling above. Cade peered up, watched another drop fall from the shadows and into the butt with a loud 'plink'. A second or two later, another drop, another 'plink'. She couldn't see where the water came from, likely the barest crack in the ceiling, maybe a stalactite or some such like they had in the main cavern.

She cupped her hands and leaned into the butt, scooping out some water. She bent towards it as the liquid escaped from her fingers, drinking it down quickly. A part of her did wonder if anything was living at the bottom of the butt, but they'd been drinking from this thing for long enough that any flux would have taken hold. Another 'plink'. She scooped up more water and splashed it over her face, rubbing the back of her neck. 'Plink'. She looked up, waited for the next drop. 'Plink'. She tried to gauge its location. 'Plink'. Another orb flew down, hitting the surface, its ripples joining the fading vibrations of the last impact. Plink.

A hand reached out of the shadows and touched her. She jumped back, looking to take a swing at however it was.

'Cade.'

It was Gwillem. He stepped out into the dim light coming from the tunnel exit. He looked terrible. His skin was a pasty colour and there was a sheen of sweat on his forehead. She hadn't spoken to him much since Jessene's death, she hadn't really wanted to. It wasn't her style to be the broad shoulder, leave that to Meghan.

'Gwillem. Gods Below, I almost dropped you.'

'Why do you do it?'

'What?'

'Speak to them, get friendly with them?'

Oh. 'You mean our hosts?' Cade had half expected this to happen.

'Those fucking bastards want us all dead. Don't think they'll treat you any different when the time comes. You're just an animal to them.' His features twisted, turned ugly. He spat.

'Maybe so, but there's a difference between living like a pig or living like a horse.'

'Others might think you are doing them a favour, Cade, but you're not. We'll all die down here. Least you can die with some dignity.'

'That's kind of my point.'

Gwillem shook his head. He reached out with both his arms and gripped her shoulders. Cade tensed, ready to fight or run. Whatever worked best.

'No. You don't get it.' There was a fevered gleam to his eyes. 'There's no reasoning with them. They are monsters. You can't be their friend. You need to stay human. That's the dignity I'm talking about. Remember which side you're on. When they finally slit your throat and let you bleed like the pig you are, at least you can say to yourself you never submitted, you never let them use you like a fucking whore.' He squeezed, the pressure painful. He pushed hard but didn't let go, and Cade rocked back a little. He released his hold, his arms dropping uselessly to his sides. He tilted his head and raised an eyebrow.

'Do you get it now? You can't have it both ways, Cade. It's wrong and one day you'll learn that.'

He smiled, but there was no warmth in his eyes. He turned his back and retreated into the shadows. She listened to him move away and chewed the inside of her cheek.

She debated whether to finish it now. Just pull out her knife and stab him in the back. He had decided to blame her for his troubles. It was always easier to blame someone else. Always easier to avoid the responsibility for your own actions. She was different, she never blamed anyone but herself, always would. This idiot killed his wife the minute he stuck his cock into her. Sad fact was, even though everyone knew what would happen, it wouldn't stop some idiots doing it. She was surprised that it hadn't started so much yet, but it would. And it'll be the single girls, the women who couldn't look after themselves, who couldn't fight back, who didn't have protection. She'd lived that life for a time. It'll be the desperate men at first, the ones who try and justify their actions, then it'll be Anzo and his thugs and they wouldn't care. But after a while they'll work it out. Learn to do it when a woman bleeds. Then they'll have a nice little whorehouse operation going on.

Gods she was good at this. *Makes you think, why am I not running the show?* It was a good question. She'd speak to Meghan, get her to spread the word about the bleeding time, might save a few lives. Not that she'd get any thanks. All she got was people like Gwillem. His guilt was eating away at him and eventually he'd do something stupid. Hopefully it would be alone and surrounded by dwarves. That way it would save her the trouble.

As the sun went down and the canyon fell into darkness, the humans finished loading the wagon train and were marched back down into the mountain. Once they were through the Downside Gate, Devlin joined her.

'You busy sucking up to the boss again?'

'Didn't you hear us? First name terms now.'

'Hah, things are on the up then.' He leaned in close. 'I think they'll make a play tonight. I just heard there was a ruckus. A few lives lost.'

'Who won?'

'Anzo and his crew.'

Cade nodded. She'd told only her three companions about her meeting with Herrick. Devlin hadn't been happy. He'd predicted there would be a reckoning. Looks like he'd been right.

'I'll be ready. Who can we rely on?'

'Amongst our lot? You got me. Meghan will help, not sure how long she'd last though. Issar won't fight fair but he might fight dirty if he gets a chance. I reckon a few of the others will. Ralph, Jape, Miriam, she's a tough one. They all know it was you who's been playing that dwarf, they appreciate it,' he said.

'I'll help too,' said Anyon.

Cade glanced back at the lad. Anyon was likely to piss himself at any moment. Still. The thought was there.

Cade looked around. They were heading along a central alleyway with dwellings on either side. After six months of habitation, the place looked a lot like the worst kind of hovels in the rookery, but they had a permanency about them now. Folk had made an effort to stamp their mark a little. Not all the other groups were back yet but still a fair number of people were milling around. There was something about the atmosphere: a tension in the air, a sense of expectancy.

'Hey, anyone seen Evan?' she asked.

'Yeah, he's back here.'

'Send him up,' she said. Cade slowed her pace. Ahead the alleyway emptied into a junction of sorts.

Devlin looked at her. 'I was right,' he said.

'Looks like it,' she replied.

Evan pushed through the crowd behind them.

'Cade?'

'I want you to head back to our spot, but not this way. Cut around the perimeter, and find my sleeping space. Look at the bottom of the firepit, you'll find something wrapped up in there. Bring it to me. Fast.'

Evan bobbed his head and shot off.

The group reached the junction, little more than a wide space where four lanes met. The route to their area was to the right. They found it blocked with people. Cade pulled up as soon as she saw them, everyone else gathered behind her. A chorus of whispered conversations filled the air.

Standing in the middle of the lane was Anzo. Cade looked him up and down. My but he was a big man. He wore a sleeveless leather jerkin. His skin was grey and black from working down the mines all day. He stood with well-muscled arms folded, his legs in a wide stance. She noted the snake tattoos curling around his biceps and neck. A gang symbol, the Vipers, from Aberpool, a small-time bunch that specialised in intimidation and protection rackets. She didn't recognise him from the rookery, but that just meant how low down in the food chain he'd been.

He grinned at her. His face was a mess of scars, lumps and bumps. His front teeth were missing, the rest looked black and rotten. Where his blonde hair was tied tightly back against his head, Cade saw his ears were swollen and misshapen like cabbages. His eyes were blue and cold. He was flanked by two others, both clearly crooks. Issar had already told Cade all about them. The one on the left was a wiry looking bloke with tattoos of fish on the inside of his forearms. His name was Chad. The other, Mostyn, was a slightly smaller version of Anzo but with a full set of teeth. He was bare-chested, revealing a horizontal scar running across the length of his stomach. Behind them were several more men and women, including the man she'd given a kicking to. They all carried the knowing, self-satisfied smiles of folk who thought they were in charge. More importantly, they were all carrying weapons of one sort or another, a couple of crude clubs, and the rest rocks. The three at the front, Anzo and the other two, his most trusted henchmen, they were the dangerous ones. The rest were just hangers on. None of those three carried weapons. They didn't need to.

'Evening, miss,' said Anzo. 'Thought we'd have a conversation.'

Cade scratched her head. 'Really? What about?'

'Oh, I just noticed how you lot have been going up in the world. Must be nice to see the sunlight once in a while, eh?' he said, the grin never leaving his face.

'I've had worse. You're not doing too bad yourself. A Viper if I'm not mistaken. Your lot were never big on ambition. The world must really have gone to shit if you're the best the criminal underworld has to offer.'

Anzo's smile faded a little, his eyes flashed.

'That's the thing. There ain't much crime to be had down here. Not much to control. Except people and food and water. Me and the boys here,' he said throwing his hands wide, 'we are fixin' at making sure the right folk are looking after everyone's needs.'

'Good of you,' said Devlin.

'Ain't it? Thing is, folk are getting jealous of you and yours. That flesh mark on your arm is giving you privileges we'd all like to share in. And everyone says that it's Miss Silver Tongue here that gets things done.'

'I'm just good with people, I guess.'

'Hah, that you are. Some idiot called Herrick said the same thing. He made a try for me the other day. Didn't go so well for him, but he told me about you. He wasn't happy. I like that, clever of you. So here's the deal. It's about time you and your gang joined up with us,' he said nodding at Devlin and Meghan. Issar, Cade saw, was nowhere to be seen. 'Get yourselves on the right side, so to speak.'

'That's a fair offer,' said Cade. Damn but this fella talked a lot for walking muscle. She was disappointed, she'd hoped for something more from Herrick, but it looked like he'd been worse than shit in whittling down Anzo's numbers. Either way, his prattle was giving her the time she needed to think.

'Oh, it's not really an offer,' said Chad, his face one big ugly slash of a smile.

'No, it ain't even a request,' said Anzo. 'That ain't all of it, either. I want you to speak to your boss. Arrange things so that we all get a piece of the pie, so to speak.'

Cade made a clicking sound. 'Not sure I can do that. Not really my place,' she said.

Anzo stopped smiling. 'That ain't the answer I want to hear. I know you've been asking around, finding out about metal workers. You got a scam going. You make it mine or we are going to have a problem.'

Cade shrugged and took a moment to look around. The other two exits were now full of bystanders, watching with that familiar fascination and revulsion that people had when they knew they weren't the ones in the shit.

'It's no problem for me,' she said casually.

'Yes, it fucking is!' Anzo screamed. He stepped forward and pointed a thick, dirty finger at her. 'You don't piss me off, bitch. I'll break your legs then give you to the lads as our whore.'

Cade heard a commotion behind her, felt movement as somebody shouldered their way through the crowd. She put her arms behind her back. Something covered in cloth, something hard and sharp, was placed into her hand.

'Back off, Anzo, we don't want trouble,' warned Devlin.

The grin returned to Anzo's face. 'You already got that. Mostyn?'

Mostyn stepped forward and aimed a punch at Devlin's stomach. The older man stepped back. Cade was ready, this was the moment. Anzo and his bunch would try to drop someone quickly and savagely, and everyone else would quickly lose heart. The cloth wrapping fell away from her hands and she leapt right at Anzo. He registered a flash of shock and threw his arms up. That was fine by her. She slammed into him and punched with her right hand into his stomach. She heard a loud 'oof' from the thug, then his hands were around her neck and she was physically lifted off the ground. As the pressure started to build she caught a glimpse of Chad moving to take her in the side. He was carrying a small, jagged looking piece of rock, his own version of a knife. A blur appeared, intercepted him and he fell away. Anzo was shouting at her.

'Bitch, fucking bitch, what have you done?' Globs of spit covered her face. He started to shake her.

She raised her right hand, the knuckles white, the skinning knife clutched tightly within it, blood dripping from its edges. She rammed it hard into his neck, just to the side of his adam's apple. She pushed it deeper and started to saw. Anzo pulled his head away, blood pouring from the wound. He dropped her, and his hands went to his throat. She looked away to see what was happening to the rest. Chad was down, Meghan was wrestling with him. Anyon and a couple of the others were ahead, trading insults with the rest of Anzo's crew. Devlin had Mostyn in a headlock and was shouting for help.

Anzo, a look of shock and panic on his face, was still backing up, his mouth working silently. He collided with one of his women. Nobody had realised yet that he was bleeding out. Cade still had the knife and she went after him. He threw out an arm to block her. She knocked it aside and leapt up again, wrapping her legs around his waist, her left arm around his shoulders, locking herself in tight. He staggered back some more, his hands clutching at her face. She thrust the blade back into the neck wound and continued to cut, moving the blade backwards and forwards as quickly as she could. Bubbles of blood and red saliva coated his mouth. Anzo's legs gave way and he fell to his knees, his torso falling backwards. Cade clung on and kept sawing, she was almost all the way through the neck. She felt something heavy smash against her back, the momentum knocking her forward. A second blow did not come. The knife came free from the flesh. She worked her left arm free, then her legs and rolled away from Anzo. She crouched low, holding the knife ready. The fighting was almost done. People were screaming and pointing at Anzo. His blood was pooling on the floor around his body.

Chad was not moving. Meghan had rolled away. She was clutching her side, a red stain spreading over her shirt. Issar stood over Chad, clutching a rock. It was covered with what Cade guessed were bits of brain and bone. Devlin had been right. The Erebeshi was a dirty fighter. Devlin was on the floor, Mostyn still in a headlock, and the man was struggling hard. Miriam was beating the crap out of one of Anzo's women. Cade winced. She was still mobile and her fire was up, but there'd be bruising tomorrow, maybe a cracked rib or two. Anyon was tussling with another one of the thugs, but that one didn't seem to have many guts about him. She forced herself up and took a running kick at Mostyn's balls. She connected and the man screeched. His hands let go of Devlin's arms. The Riverlander, his nose bloody, looked at Cade, his eyes wide, his face flushed.

'Finish it,' he shouted.

Cade stepped forward and brought the knife down hard, driving it through Mostyn's eye. It went deep, his body arched and spasmed. Devlin released his grip, pushing Mostyn off. Cade offered a hand and pulled him up.

Breathlessly she shouted, 'Who else wants some?' Nobody did. The fight was already over. There were only three of Anzo's crew left standing and it looked like they hadn't even raised a finger to help. Anyon, Ralph and Jape were facing them down and young Evan was with them. Miriam gave her comatose opponent one more kick, then spat on her face.

'Drop your weapons,' ordered Devlin. He had quite a commanding voice when he wanted to. 'Nobody tries it again. Let the word get around. There will be no more gangs, no more killing, and no more fighting for scraps.'

Cade bent over and wiped her hands across the floor. It didn't help much, their blood was all over her. She tucked the knife into the waistband of her trousers.

'Anyone wants to argue, you all know where to find us,' she said to nobody in particular.

'No,' said Devin.

'Huh?' she looked up at him. His face had a determined look, forceful and assured.

'We can't let this happen again. I'm heading over to the Heights.'

Cade wiped a hand across her chin. 'You going all public spirited on me? You go ahead.'

'Fine. Anyon, Miriam. Everybody who wants to make things better, follow me. And pick up those clubs, we might need 'em.'

Cade waited for the crowd to pass her by. It was just her and three bodies. *Oh, not quite.* She saw Meghan, still on the ground, and Issar standing fussing over her.

'What's up with you?' she asked, as she went to join them.

'Got a bit of a scratch,' replied Meghan, her face white.

'Lemme see,' said Cade. She hunched down, ignoring the pain in her back. She pulled Meghan's hand away from the red patch and lifted her shirt up. There was a ragged looking wound on her right side not too far from the edge of her waist.

'Chad got you with his little sticker, did he?' she said, peering into the hole.

'Yes, ahhh ...' Meghan hissed as Cade probed with her finger.

'Doesn't look too bad. Don't think it hit anything. Your blood isn't dark, see?' she said holding up her hand.

'She did good taking him on like that,' said Issar.

Cade looked at him. 'You finished the job, I see.'

'Had to bash his brains out. It was him or Meghan,' he said, a guilty edge to his voice.

'You won't get any complaints from me,' said Meghan.

Cade looked into her face. Meghan smiled back. Cade had to admit that the woman had more guts than she'd credited her. She owed Meghan and she didn't like owing anyone, but it would have been her with six inches of rock in her belly if it hadn't been for Meghan, for all of them if she was honest. They came through it without losing anyone. Looks like she'd made the right choice sticking with her little gang. Cade reached out and brushed a lock of greasy hair away from Meghan's eyes.

'Let's get you on your feet. We need to clean that wound and cover it up, best place is where everyone else is headed, to the Heights.'

She got a hand around Meghan's shoulders and helped her up.

'Issar, reckon you could scare up some clean rags to bind this wound with?' Cade asked.

'I can do better than that. Got hold of a small piece of iron, just a splinter, it'll do for stitching,' he replied.

'Sounds great. See you back by our beds. Get the fire going, we'll do it there. Let's go.'

Meghan hissed as she took her first step.

'You okay?' Cade asked.

'Uh huh. Just keep me moving, if I sit down I don't think I can get up again.'

'Good thing you're a girl. No way I'd be hauling Devlin's ass.'

They hobbled along the lane towards the start of the Heights. The place was empty of life, dark, dirty and desolate.

'Emperor, but it smells in here,' said Meghan.

'You only just noticed?' said Cade. 'This place always stinks. Still too many people living in their own shit.'

'Why don't they use the stream like we do?' Meghan asked. All of their group went to the stream to void themselves rather than use the buckets.

'Because a lot of folk have given up. They'll drift on 'til they drop. That's why people like Anzo can step up. This lot of have no fight left. Our bunch are fine, life's got a little better for 'em.'

'We can change that now, right?' said Meghan.

Cade stopped and looked at the woman. 'Listen, Meghan, you backed me up, so I guess I owe you. But don't think we are on a mission here. I'm out to survive this, not be some bloody hero. We just killed three men. They were bastards and had it coming, but it won't go changing who we all are. This is the life, you either let it drown you or you ride the wave.'

Meghan looked taken aback, her eyes wide, though that might have been the after-effects of the fight. 'I … I guess you are right,' she replied.

Cade started them walking again.

'I remember when my home city fell, everyone was in a panic,' said Meghan. 'The garrison, all the fighting men, had marched out in the middle of the night. When word spread, the streets were full of people trying to get away. There was looting, fighting. Everyone was looking out for themselves. I saw an old couple, they lived in a house the next street down from me. He was a tailor. His wife, she fell and must have hurt her head because she didn't get up. Her husband was asking for help, pleading for somebody to lend a hand. I watched it all. I could have run back but I was too scared. I just ran on by, got out just in time. There was cavalry behind us, they were circling the city, trapping those inside. And there were others, in chariots, they rode people down in droves. The screaming was the worst. I never thought such a sound existed. I got into a wood, they couldn't follow us in there. They torched the city. You could see it burning from miles away. A day later I could still see smoke. Wait.' She stopped and bit her lip. Her face was pained.

Cade waited. She wasn't interested in Meghan's chatter but it was probably stopping her going into shock. She nodded to continue their journey. 'Then there was the march to Aberpool. I saw one man kill another for the half a loaf of bread he'd been holding. And you know what that man did? He took it to his family and shared it out between his wife and two young children. He didn't even have any for himself.'

'That's life,' said Cade. 'You do what you have to do.'

'Life is hard,' Meghan sighed.

'Only if you make it that way,' replied Cade.

After that they carried on in silence until they arrived at the back of a large crowd. Cade figured it was damn near everyone in the cavern. More were arriving back from their shift, blackened faces confused and questioning. Looking up she saw another bunch standing on the slope, near the stream tunnel. They were Aaren's lot. They were facing off against Devlin and his crew.

'Coming through!' shouted Cade, pushing and shoving her way into the mass of the crowd. It got harder the deeper they went as the bodies pressed against them.

'Ow, shit, that hurts,' muttered Meghan beside her.

'Come on, move your shitting arses!' said Cade, grabbing a shoulder and yanking a man out of the way.

'Hey!' he replied, his face angry.

'Don't even fuckin' think about it,' she growled at him.

His face changed and he stepped back.

'Hey, Emerich!' she shouted, spotting a familiar face. The man turned and waved at them. 'Help us out here, huh?'

He nodded, touched the arm of a woman, Friede she thought it was, and the pair of them helped to clear a path through. Finally they got to the front ranks of the crowd. Up ahead, on the start of the slope, Devlin and the others were gathered together. They had armed themselves as best they could with Anzo's meagre weapons. There was something like a heated debate going on.

'Here, Friede. Look after Meghan.'

The woman nodded and put an arm around Meghan.

Cade walked up the slope to get a better view. 'Aaren, you are not listening to me. You don't have to move, we're not saying that,' said

Devlin to the man standing at the front of the Heights Dwellers. She noticed his followers also carried some makeshift clubs and rocks. They clearly planned to defend their territory. Quite right too. She would.

'Not yet, you aren't. I know how this'll go. We put down our weapons and everything will be fine. Then one night, you'll move in, take us out one at a time. Am I right?' said Aaren. Behind him, his followers were nodding their heads.

'Yeah, we got lucky and now you want a slice of the high life!' shouted one.

'You stay down the in the shit,' screamed a woman. 'We're not moving.'

Cade shook her head. *Did that bitch realise what she'd done?* She'd pretty much signed her own death warrant. Next time she came down from the Heights, she'd get jumped on. Nobody could escape the Accounting and there was no way she could hide up in her cave.

'Listen to me, Aaren.' Devlin turned to look out over the throng. 'All of you, listen to me. You all know what went down. Three men are dead because they tried to take over, tried to make an example so the rest of you would get the message. It didn't work.'

'Because your gang was bigger!' shouted Aaren. 'That's what this is about. Don't think they'll treat you all any better. They all wear that same symbol. They think it makes them better than us. Well, we have our own symbol and we deserve just as much respect.' Aaren pointed out across the assembled mass. 'Why should they get all the best work, eh? Maybe if there weren't any of them, we might all get a look in.'

Damn, nice move, thought Cade. There were stirrings in the crowd behind her. A few muttered words, a nodded head.

'Why should we listen to you? You want it all to yourselves,' someone shouted from the crowd.

'If we go down this road, then we are just doing what the dwarves have already started,' said Devlin. 'We'll wipe each other out. We need to stay organised, work together, not fracture into gangs.'

'And who'll do the organising? You? Big words from the man with all those clubs,' said Aaren with a sneer.

Cade shook her head. *Screw this, I've heard enough.* She stepped forward and held her hands high.

'Aaren, you're right. Look at my hands. Covered in blood. We were afraid, we had to defend ourselves.'

'Cade,' said Devlin, his arm coming out to stop her. She pushed it away.

Aaren looked at her suspiciously, but he didn't back off as she approached. 'Doesn't give you the right to tell us what to do,' he said.

'I know. We just want to talk,' Cade said. She had stopped in front of him, no more than a yard away. She dropped her hands down slowly and placed them on her hips. 'All we want to know is whether you can promise us you won't try and hog the water. I really need to clean up.'

Aaren smiled and folded his arms. 'Is that it? What makes you think we want to keep it for ourselves? I want us all to share!' he shouted magnanimously.

Cade's hands moved swiftly. She pulled the knife from her waistband and took a step towards Aaren. His head was turning back as she thrust it deep into his belly. He doubled over, his hands falling on to her shoulders as she yanked the blade out, fighting against the suction of the wound, and stuck it in again, then once more.

'What?' asked Aaren, his face a mixture of pain and confusion.

Cade smiled sweetly.

'Thank you for sharing,' she whispered. She caught a whiff of something acrid and looked down. Piss was dripping on to the floor. Likely he'd soiled himself as well. Cade stepped back, letting him tumble on to his side. His body was shaking, his blood running away down the slope. She looked up at the other Heights dwellers. No one had moved, they all stood with open mouths, staring at her and at Aaren.

That's the way you do it. How Anzo had wanted to do it, but he wasn't quick enough. You have to be fast and I'm the fastest.

Devlin joined her. 'Cade?'

She looked at Devlin and at the last of humanity. 'Right then. Here's how it's going to go. There ain't no gangs. Anybody disagrees can have a conversation with me. Start sorting your shit out.'

Speaking of which, she had to get cleaned up. She walked past Devlin, giving him a hard stare. In return he just raised his eyebrows. The gathering remained silent as Cade took charge of Meghan and led her into the tunnel and the stream.

Behind her, Devlin started to speak. 'There will be no more fighting and no more division. Each branded group will pick a representative. We will form a council that will decide what's best for this place. For this community. We'll meet back here in three hours.'

'He's quite the politician, ain't he,' said Cade, as she struggled up the slope.

'Makes you wonder,' said Meghan.

They arrived at the stream. She lowered Meghan down against the wall. Cade wanted to sort herself out first. She removed her top, working her back muscles to stop them seizing up after that smack. She placed her shirt into the water, using her hands and friction to work out the blood. She turned her head and saw Meghan watching her.

'Anything to say?' Cade asked, expecting some kind of shocked outrage.

'I know. I get it. You did what you had to do. If you hadn't, things might have gotten ugly. I know what I did when I thought that guy was going to get you. I didn't hesitate. Because you matter,' said Meghan. Cade smiled. Not often she heard that. 'I just think that … we are all that's left now. And maybe Devlin's got it right. We should all matter. There is no one else left.'

'Maybe.' Cade continued rubbing. 'All I know is today was a good day. No one died. Except those that deserved to. Devlin can crack on with his council if he wants. Can't see it changing much day to day, but if it keeps things quiet.' She raised her tunic from the water and wrung it out.

'Come on, then. Get that off you.'

She bent down and helped Meghan struggle out of her top, then brought her closer to the water. She could see the wound. It wasn't pumping out much, and the blood was clotting nicely, but they still had to catch it quick.

'This might hurt some, but we have to clean this before we stitch it,' said Cade.

'Go on,' said Meghan.

Cade reached down, cupped some water in her hands and pressed it against the wound.

'Ah,' replied Meghan, scrunching her face. Cade repeated the action, this time running her hands gently over the edges of the cut. Meghan's skin was soft, her stomach a lot thinner than it should be.

'You are right. Today is a good day,' said Meghan. 'You helped make it one.'

Cade shook her head. 'I helped myself. But if it makes you feel better about life. There, that's done. Let's get you sewn up.'

She retrieved her sodden shirt, pulled it back on then helped Meghan with hers. Together they walked back up the tunnel and into the cavern. The path was empty of life, the boulders pushed to one side. Aaren's body was already gone. She paused. At this elevation she could see across the cavern, the far side indistinct in the gloom. Cade took a moment to review her situation. She'd got her crew shifts above ground, she had weapons, a reputation, and the ear of their enslaver. Thanks to some smart work, and a little luck, was there anyone else left to challenge them? After today, probably not, and that made her Queen of Tissan, didn't it? Things could've been worse, hells she might've even settled for that.

She raised her gaze to the rock, overarching them all, its great weight a constant, oppressive threat. A promise of a future she wanted no part of. Yeah, she could've settled for being the queen. But not at any price, not anymore. She was tired of always being a prisoner in life. From the rookery, to the sewers, to the gaol, to the slave columns, to the mines. She wanted more than that. She wanted the one thing that she'd never had. Freedom. She had a plan to get it. And she would let nothing and no one stand in her way.

CHAPTER 31

Father Michael arose shortly before dawn. The sky had clouded over in the night and the sun was hidden behind a blanket of dark grey, with the barest hint of a glow in the far eastern fringes of the horizon. He could swear it was the coldest morning since they had set out. He felt it in his bones and in his muscles and even for all of that, he felt lazy and tired. Activity would warm him up, yet it was a struggle to get his limbs moving and shrug off his blankets.

As they gathered for the hunt, the Emperor was irritable, and had forbidden the Gifted from accompanying him, when Eilion had appeared with two of his Shapers. They hadn't liked it, but they could hardly ignore the command. Yet somehow Father Michael had convinced him to take two of the marines. At least, he argued, they were handy with their crossbows. In reality he had no idea, but he hated the thought of just the two of them heading out into a dark forest where he'd be nothing short of useless.

He quickly discovered he'd been right. He had little aptitude for hunting. He did not understand how to look for signs or how to move through the undergrowth. As the two marines, Beautiful and Wendell, ranged ahead, he took to trailing the Emperor. They were following game trails though he could barely see beyond a yard or two, the undergrowth being particularly dense. At least in the snow following tracks was easy, and that should mean all they need do was follow these tracks to their makers. They would stop often, crouching low, listening to the gentle rustle of leaves and branches. A few times he heard the scratching of the Emperor-knew-what moving through the smaller shrubs, bushes and weeds to either side of them. Apart from that, it was eerily quiet. He had discovered that this was quite usual when the snows fell. It seemed to absorb sound and everything became hushed and silent. It put him on edge and, not for the first time, Father Michael felt a little out of his depth. But having spent most of his life within the confines of one fighting arena or another, it was hardly surprising.

During another halt, he waited with one knee on the ground. He could feel the cold of the earth seeping through his robe and britches. He was thankful for that second layer under his furs. A few of the other brethren wore naught but their modesty underneath their robes, yet he was used to wearing trousers. He had never fought naked, and if he was required to do the Emperor's work, then he needed to feel ready. Up ahead he saw the Emperor lift his hand, making fast motions that he didn't understand. He saw one marine, Wendell, he thought, move past his eye line, left to right. He had no idea where the other had gone. The Emperor turned around and motioned him forward. Father Michael hitched up his robe and crept forward as silently as possible, keeping low to the ground. The Emperor kept his gaze fixed ahead. He had clearly been born into this, had hunted from a young age and carried himself well and confidently. Cradled in his arms was a loaded crossbow. He pointed with one leather-gloved finger and opened his mouth just slightly, tilting his head towards Father Michael. He caught a whiff of alcohol.

'We got one. There is a stream not far from here. The others are going to circle round. Stay close.'

Father Michael nodded but the Emperor was already off, springing up from his crouch and making his way along the trail. He stood and followed in the Emperor's wake, hitching up his robes and experiencing the familiar emotion of embarrassment. They moved quickly along the trail for a few moments, and then veered off left. They slowed as they pushed into the undergrowth, Father Michael trying to copy the slow, deliberate steps of the Emperor. The damned crunching of the snow underfoot didn't help. He put every effort into taking care not to step on a stick or branch, not to place a foot too heavily or brush past a bush with any force. Barely perceptibly, he picked out a new sound. At first he thought it was the wind in the trees, but as they drew near he recognised it as flowing water. Odd, he would have thought it frozen, like the river. The Emperor crouched low once more, made for a large tree directly ahead, and placed his back against it. Father Michael scuttled up and dropped down. The Emperor tilted his head to his left and smiled. He mouthed 'stay here' and pointed at the ground. Father Michael was happy to oblige.

The Emperor went on to all fours and crawled around the side of the tree through a mass of foliage, his head low, arms and crossbow out in front. He went slowly, scarcely making a sound. Once his legs had disappeared, Father Michael moved up to the tree and pressed his back hard against it. He wondered what to do now. He could just sit it out, which was probably the best and least stressful course of action, yet he did want to see what was happening. He hadn't come all this way for nothing. He twisted round and placed a hand on the cool, rough bark. He leaned out and around, straining to get a look at what was beyond.

It had grown a little lighter, and instead of the swaying, looming darkness, the world now had a grey, misty quality to it. No colours, but more clarity. He squinted, closed his eyes tight, then opened them wide. On the far side of the tree the ground fell away slightly towards a stream, running right to left, gurgling across a bed of rocks and soil. It didn't look deep, barely a yard wide. There was steam rising from it. A hot spring? Part of him desperately hoped that it was.

A little way to the right the stream curved away. As he moved his vision along it, movement caught his eye. A head dipped down, small, with high, sharp ears. A deer, or what everyone had agreed was a close enough resemblance to the Tissan variety, drank from the water. It lapped for a few moments then its long neck came up, the head looking towards his direction. He held his breath. He knew he hadn't moved, but something must have startled it. Perhaps it was their smell? Were they downwind of the creature? Seconds passed and the deer went back to the water. He breathed through his nose, slowly. This must be their prey. He just had to wait a moment longer and it would be over. They could collect it and head back to camp.

More movement out of the corner of his eye. The deer looked up again, watching a new arrival emerge from the bushes, almost opposite Father Michael's position. It was another of the creatures but this one was bigger, almost twice the size. Two large antlers sprouted from its forehead, a little forward from its ears, each one almost two foot high, with smaller, sharp looking stubs sprouting from the main stems. It worked its way down to the water stepping slowly, steadily. It was clearly a male so the other deer, he supposed, was a female, and it was ignoring the male. It was a stroke of luck that they now had two targets to choose from.

He heard a rustle down to his right amidst the bushes. The male had frozen in place, legs quivering slightly, eyes intent upon the source of the sound. Then it bolted. A 'twang' rent the air.

'Bastard!' shouted the Emperor, rising from his hiding place. 'I got it. Come on!'

He burst out of the trees and was across the water in one bound before Father Michael had a chance to react. He stood and followed, wading through the bushes and down to the stream. He tried to leap it, but got caught up in his robe. A foot splashed into the water. He looked right and the female had gone. The far bank was slightly steeper and he half scrambled up the other side. A waving branch marking the passage of both man and beast. He passed it and ploughed on into a darker section of the forest. He carried straight on, dodging around trees and thick branches, skirting a deep depression where a tree had collapsed, tearing up the roots beneath it.

The Emperor was lost from sight and Father Michael stopped. He tried to listen for the sounds of the pursuit. Nothing. *Damn it all. Where were those marines?* A white world of tree limbs heavy with snow, loomed above him and all around. Despite the growing light he had no sense of his surroundings, what direction he was travelling in. It all looked the same.

Wait a minute. Think about it. Follow the bloody footsteps, you idiot!

He started forward, trying to concentrate, looking for any signs of passage.

There. A broken branch. Follow that. See? Footsteps. Run faster.

He upped his pace, sprinting along what might be nothing more than a gap between the trees rather than an animal run, following the disturbed snow, the crunching playing in time to his breathing.

What was that?

He knelt and put his finger across a snow-covered branch that had a dark patch smeared across it. He smelt his finger. Blood. He was on the right track, he just had to keep following. He carried on, his breath laboured. He hadn't had to work so hard in a long time. He ran for what seemed like an age, forcing his way bodily through the snow. He emerged from a thick stand of trees and stumbled on the edge of a gully, the slope falling away before his feet. He allowed himself to drop, letting his knees bend beneath him, controlling the impact of the descent. He pitched forwards and sideways, putting his arms out, feeling his hands scrape against stone. His momentum was slowed and he let his lower half roll past him to the bottom of the slope, the snow acting as brake and cushion. He pushed off and stumbled along the gully. There were more splatters of blood, an uneven trail of spots, littering the sides and floor, running alongside the boot marks. A large stone sat in the middle of the path, another black mark prominent. Father Michael stepped over it and continued on. Both sides of the gully were still too steep to climb out easily, and he could see no signs of any attempt to do so. The path ahead curved and he started forward.

'Uh. Uh.' Someone was making a strange, laboured noise. He left the curve and found himself emerging from the end of the gully. It opened out into a slightly cleared area, the snow deeper with no trees to impede it. Before him was a truly unsettling scene.

A cloaked figure knelt on the ground, arm raised high. In his hand he clutched a thin bladed dagger. He brought the arm down hard, driving the blade into something Father Michael couldn't quite make out. A soft thud was accompanied by another 'Uh.' The arm went up again.

Thud.

'Uh.'

Thud.

'Uh.'

Father Michael saw droplets of blood fly from the dagger.

'Your Grace?'

Thud.

'Uh.'

He took a step forward.

'Your Grace?'

The arm stopped midway down. The head turned slightly. Neither man spoke. The head turned away again. The body started to shudder.

'Cuh, cuh, cuh ...'

Father Michael came closer. He stood above the Emperor. The buck lay on the ground before him. It was butchered, its guts had been torn open and its innards stabbed and raked repeatedly. Steam rose from the carcass as it started to cool. There was blood everywhere, moist and glistening. The stench was pungent. It brought back memories of some of his fights in the arena. Brutal and merciless, where his anger and desperation had given him reason to tear his opponents apart. It was only in his later years that he became more clinical, more economical. Just kill them quickly, as painlessly as possible, then leave them be for the animals to do the ripping. At least they had honest cause and no reason for remorse.

He stepped to his right and hunkered down next to his lord. The Emperor's head was in shadow. The arm still half-raised.

'Your Grace, let me help you.' Father Michael reached out and placed his hands on the arm, exerting a little pressure, forcing it towards the ground. It was trembling. The dagger dropped into the leaves and soaking soil. The Emperor's face turned to him. Splatters of blood, pieces of the deer, covered the pale skin. Lines of moisture ran down from his eyes, mixing with the blood, washing it away to fall to the floor. He wore a look of anguish, his features screwed up, like a baby when it was hungry, eyes wide yet barely recognising what they saw. His mouth was open, a mewling sound creeping from the throat. Father Michael knew this reaction, had seen it and had felt it. These was not simple tears of sadness. This was deeper. This was from the soul.

'I can't ...' whispered the Emperor.

'What, my lord?' asked Father Michael. Though he was, in truth, loathe to hear it.

'I can't ...'

The Emperor leant forward and spewed vomit, covering the carcass in acrid smelling bile.

'Ah, cah, cah.' A line of drool fell slowly from his mouth, falling on to the guts of the deer. His eyes were shut, screwed tight, his brows furrowed.

Father Michael was at a loss. Perhaps he should offer words of comfort? How do you comfort a Living God? He couldn't even suggest prayer to the Emperor. You couldn't pray to yourself.

He reached for his waterskin instead, a small bladder tied to his belt underneath his robe. It proved the good sense of his wearing britches. He undid the cord, drew it from beneath his robe and pulled out the stopper, handing it across to the Emperor, waving it almost directly beneath his nose.

'Your Grace? Drink this.'

The Emperor took a few deep breaths and opened his eyes a touch. He took the bottle and sipped. He grimaced and spat the water out. Then took another swig. This time washing it around the inside of his mouth, and then he spat again.

'Water,' he mumbled. 'I'd forgotten what that tasted like.'

'You wanted something stronger?'

'Huh? Oh, aye.'

The Emperor wiped a hand over his face, an odd look forming on his features. He held the hand in front of him, studied it like it was not his own and sniffed it.

'Huh.'

He rubbed his hand on his cloak, brushing it once, twice, then repeatedly, Forcing the hand down and along with heavy, jerking movements. Then he stopped and looked up. Father Michael followed his gaze. There was nothing there but more trees, a few rays of light slanting down from the right, small particles illuminated, drifting through the beams like insects.

'I ran,' said the Emperor.

'My lord?'

'I ran. How do you think I made it through? At the battle. Where we drew up to halt their advance. To smash them or die trying. No one believed that. How could we lose? My father, the Emperor, led our armies himself. At least sixty Gifted rode with my father as his honour guard. And his sons were right there behind him. I'm sure a few had doubts. We'd already lost the Plains and Erebesh. The Highlands were under siege. But now the Emperor was here and it would all be as he willed it. Our army was huge, impressive. And everyone looked so very smart. Flags and pennants, burnished armour, sharpened steel. The Tissan Empire at its finest. Then the first of the detonations happened. Great balls of flame arcing through the sky, tearing holes in our front lines. Clouds of buzzers covered the skies, you could hear their droning noise above the shouts of our officers and the cries of the dying. Our eagles met them mid-way. It was as if the buzzers just swallowed them up. You couldn't see what was going on, except when yet another eagle came falling back to the earth. Still we stood and weathered the storm. Our artillery started shooting. Great trebuchets launching their stones with a thump, our longbows singing as they launched volley after volley.'

The Emperor's voice was dull, lifeless, as he droned on. 'And still they came towards us. Ranks of glittering spears, cavalry and chariots skirmishing along our flanks, their own archers more than a match for our bowmen, launching two arrows for every one of ours. Men fell all around us, like wheat cut by a scythe. Then we got word ogres were bearing down on our left flank. A terrible mass of big ugly brutes charging in with their clubs, chanting their battle hymns. I saw a rider pulled from his saddle as packs of gryphons ranged behind our front lines. And you know what my father did? He sounded the charge. An advance on all fronts. Cavalry and infantry. So that's what we did. Horns sounded, signal flags were waved and Gifted sent orders down the line. We all drew our swords and pulled down our visors and kicked our mounts into a trot. We pulled ahead of our infantry as they stepped smartly forward, spears, pikes and halberds levelled. I was quite caught up in it all. It was splendid and glorious. And as we urged our horses into a gallop I felt a strange joy overtake me. You must know what that's like?' The Emperor smiled and took another drink. 'I wasn't even worried when the rider next to me got an arrow in his eye. It was just his bad luck. Then I saw three men to my right disappear in a cloud of flame and dirt as a spell hit them. It threw my horse off its stride, made it rear up in panic. It took me some moments to get it back under control, to get it turned the right way. As I made to catch up with the charge I saw it spread out in front of me. The ground was littered with our men and horses. Great smoking craters had appeared in the earth, pieces of … pieces of our men lay scattered around the rims. Others had become pin cushions for arrows. Some still moved. A horse lay on its side, whickering. A man was crawling towards me, his hand held out, beseeching me for help. What was I supposed to do for him? I saw the line of our cavalry disappear in a haze of dust and dirt. Behind me the infantry were coming up. They looked solid, orderly. Then I heard the shouts. I saw the confusion. Massive holes had opened up in the ground behind them. Some appeared inside their ranks. And as men spilled down into these holes, dwarves spilled out. They started to carve the heart out of our regiments. We were outflanked, the enemy in our rear. We couldn't hold the line, because there was no longer a line to hold.'

Another drink. He drew a hand across his eyes, flicking away the last of the tears.

'I didn't even have to think. I turned my horse and made for a gap in the lines. There was so much chaos. Maybe no one even noticed me. I rode as hard as I could go. I think I had cleared the front lines because all I could hear was the pounding of the hooves. Then I saw a flash to one side of me and everything went black. When I came to I found myself on a litter, part of a column of soldiers moving west. So, Father. What do you think of your emperor now? A coward, a craven?'

'My lord … I …'

The Emperor raised a warning hand. 'Don't say anything. I know what I am. I should have done the decent thing and died alongside my father.'

'But you didn't,' said Father Michael. 'You have ensured the line is unbroken. We have hope. The Empire has hope.' He knew this to be true. He knew that for whatever reason, this was meant to be. The Emperor was the Empire. Without it they, he, were nothing.

'The Empire? Our little band of adventurers? It will be a long time before we have an empire again,' the Emperor said bitterly. It struck Father Michael how young he looked at that moment. A young man who bore the fate of humanity on his shoulders. Just hours ago he had been the picture of confidence, a leader. The mask had slipped a little.

'We called this place New Tissan. I never asked you, do you approve?'

'How could we call it anything else, Your Grace?'

'Certainly a bold statement of our ambitions.'

They both turned their heads to the sound of something crashing through the undergrowth. The two marines emerged, bows held low but ready.

'My lord?' said Beautiful. 'We waited to catch the beast. Then we heard the ruckus.'

The Emperor turned away, his face in shadow. Father Michael could understand his wish to hide.

'I rather fear that this particular kill is spoiled. A shame, it was a fine looking stag. Go ahead and see what else you can root out. We'll meet you back at the stream.'

Wordlessly the Emperor handed Father Michael his waterskin. Gathering up his dagger, he wiped the blade on his arm then sheathed it. He stood, a little unsteady on his feet. He made his way around to the left of the gully mouth, following a slope up to the top. Father Michael followed as he led them along the gully edge, retracing their steps. Once beyond it, Father Michael lost any sense of his location. He could not recall the route of his previous passage. In the dim light of morning, everything looked unfamiliar. The Emperor did not seem in any doubt. Soon they reached the water, almost at the same place they had left it. Father Michael stopped and watched as his Living God knelt, cupped his hands and gathered water into them. He splashed it on to his face. Once, twice, three times. Rubbing his hands vigorously over his neck, cheeks and nose. Then he studied those hands, picking bits of dry blood, skin and offal out of his fingernails. He was slow. Fastidious.

Father Michael had believed an Emperor was beyond such emotions as fear, doubt and guilt. Yet in a few brief minutes, that belief had been shattered. His Living God had revealed a truth that had eluded him since his rebirth. The Emperor was as human as he and possibly just as damaged. *Did that change anything? No. It didn't. It couldn't. It mustn't.*

Father Michael squeezed his eyes a little and felt his brow furrow from the thoughts running through his mind. *What did I see back there? It was a moment and then it was gone. All day he has been himself. Who am I to judge? I well remember how I was found. It was little different, I had lost control. Me! The finest warrior in the arena, reduced to a slobbering mess. Nothing has changed.* And yet it had.

'Father?'

'Huh?'

The Emperor had a calculating look about him. 'You do realise that if you breathe a word of this I will have you killed.' The Emperor's tone was calm, almost matter-of-fact.

Father Michael was a little taken aback. What would he say? Who would care to believe his word over his Emperor's?

'Your Grace. I am your guardian. It is not my place to question or judge.'

The Emperor did not respond. He got to his feet and brushed himself down. Loose pieces of leaf and twig falling away from his leather britches. It was a little lighter now. Father Michael could see dark patches in his lord's jerkin. It would take more than a quick brush to remove those marks, he knew.

The two marines hove into view, walking along the edge of the stream.

The Emperor stepped up and clapped him on the shoulder. A smile on his face, the mask back in place.

'Come along then, Father. We still have to find ourselves something to eat. I can't go back to camp without a trophy. Can you imagine the grief I'd get from everyone?'

'Lead on, my lord,' he replied.

'Find anything else?' the Emperor asked of the marines.

Beautiful nodded and pursed her lips. 'Something big came this way not long ago, hard to say what ... oh.'

She stopped. Her mouth was open, her face shocked.

'Shit.' Wendell backed up, raising his bow.

'What?' the Emperor turned and Father Michael followed. Was it a wolf, a bear?

'Oh,' said the Emperor.

Father Michael couldn't even get that out.

At the top of the small rise on the far side of the bank stood a figure. Father Michael wasn't sure, but it had to be one of their party, who else could it be? Breath misted as it spilled from within a wide, deeply recessed hood. He was big, whoever he was, even underneath all those furs he was swaddled in. Eilion? The figure raised his arms revealing wrists covered by studded leather bracers, and pulled back his hood. No. It wasn't Eilion.

It wasn't even human.

Father Michael gasped and took a step forward. The Emperor, not once looking back, raised a warning hand, stopping Michael's progress.

'Everyone stand still!' he hissed. Then he walked slowly forwards, keeping his arms held out wide, palms up, in a non-threatening posture.

The creature studied the Emperor closely. Father Michael could hear its heavy breathing, regular and even. He could see misting air rising from its wide, swine-like snout. It regarded the Emperor with eyes that were framed by wide cheekbones and an overlarge forehead. Its ears were studded with metal and fetishes and its head was bare of hair except for a long tightly tied top-knot that fell back down behind its neck. Father Michael only then realised its skin was green and dark like the shades of the forest they were in.

The Emperor and the creature regarded each other for a few more moments then the Emperor slowly lowered his right arm and placed his hand on the pommel of his sword. The creature watched with interest but did not appear alarmed. The Emperor took a tight grip and pulled his sword free. Father Michael tensed, seeing the marines shifting their stance, ready to intervene. The creature cocked its head, running its eyes along the blade as it flashed in a ray of light penetrating the canopy. The Emperor brought his blade into a vertical position before his face and bowed low. The creature let out a grunt, reached into the folds of its cloak and pulled out its own blade. A wicked, heavy piece of metal that reminded Father Michael of the wide-bladed scimitars of the Erebeshi, though this had a row of saw-teeth along the bottom half of its leading edge. It adopted a smiliar pose to the Emperor, bringing its own weapon into the vertical and dipping its head.

It was only then that the Emperor turned to look at him. He was grinning, his face flushed with triumph.

'Everyone, stand down,' he ordered and the marines, grudgingly lowered their weapons.

Father Michael struggled to make sense of what this meant – and then had a moment of blinding clarity. He had been in turmoil, his faith in question. And now this. His Living God, his Emperor, who he had doubted, had revealed his true purpose. It was not just to save the remnants of the Empire, it was not about leaving a legacy for humanity to survive thousands of miles away in isolation. This great adventure, this exploration, was the reason why the Emperor had not been allowed to die on the battlefield. He had been given a higher calling. Father Michael felt raised up in hope and joy, for the Emperor had survived to find this creature and its kind. They were to be allies. They were going home and the Tissan Empire would be reborn.

THE END

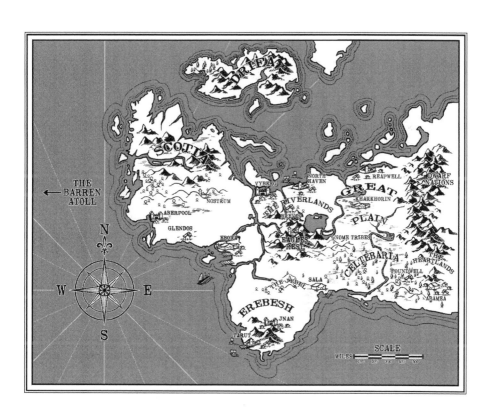

ABOUT THE AUTHOR

Alex Janaway is an ex-Regular Army officer having served in both the Royal Engineers and the Education and Training Services. He is now in the Army Reserve and is a lecturer at Cambridge Regional College. He has also written for computer games such as the BAFTA nominated *Merlin: the Game.*

Resistance – an excerpt from book two

Chapter One

Killen shifted uncomfortably. No matter where he lay his head he encountered bare, uneven rock or small stones. None of it was flat. He should have made more of an effort to clear the ground beneath him. He'd been living this life for long enough it should have been second nature, but some part of him must still be hoping it was all temporary. He sighed and rolled on to his side resting his head on his hands. In the shadowed gloom he watched the rise and fall of the camel's rib cage, expanding and contracting at a slow measured pace. At least someone was sleeping comfortably.

Its skin was mottled, the hair was thick and patchy, coarse to the touch. There were a few red patches where some insect had feasted upon its flesh. Perhaps it was one of those big ugly yellow spiders, aggressive, bitey and jumpy. He'd often fallen asleep wondering if he'd be feasted upon one night. The others had told him that they bit into the skin and laid their eggs in your flesh, and then they hatched and you got eaten inside out. What a way to go. He'd believed that for a good six months until eventually one of the native captains had grinned and slapped him on the back, assuring him they never used humans for hosts. Still, every night he made sure the edges of the blanket were weighted down, and that the blanket lay precisely over the back of his camel so there was no opening, the thick fabric stretched taut. Underneath it was a little cocoon of space; dark, cool and stinking of camel.

He hated his camel.

He hated it with a passion that defied logic. It was the embodiment of everything that was wrong with the world. Everything that had gone wrong for him. He should never have been here. He should have stayed in the capital. His banishment to the south was unwarranted. He remembered the summons, the colonel's smug look, his smart uniform, and his preening superiority.

'Here you are Major Roche. Your first independent command. The 3rd Erebeshi Scouts. Good luck to you. I'm sure your career will know no limits when your five years are done.'

Five years? Five Fucking years?

Killen had almost drawn his sword and run the man through, but he was not a fool. He should have known the good times would come to an end. It was cold comfort that this chain of events had kept him alive when everyone else was likely dead. Including that bastard colonel.

He'd never imagined in his worst nightmares he'd end up spending his nights in the desert. And he'd never thought it would get so cold during the winter months. That he could have stood baking in the sun one moment then shivering his ass off as soon as he stepped into shade. And the nights! They came in fast. Then it got really cold, a cold that could kill a man if he wasn't prepared. Such was the life in the Jebel, the high country of central Erebesh.

The camel made a whining, snorting noise. It was waking up. Its whole body shuddered, rose up slightly then settled back down.

He hated that camel.

It was lighter in his little hole now. The morning sun was making the edges glow. He knew he'd have to get up soon, even though he'd had no sleep. He was in charge. There was an image to maintain. Even though the whole bloody exercise was a waste of time.

He heard the scuff of boots; footsteps drawing near.

'Major?'

'Yes?'

'You are awake, Sir.'

'It would appear so.'

The blanket was ripped upwards, his small securing rocks flying all ways, many of them on to him.

Killen blinked at the burst of light. He was facing almost directly westwards, right towards the sun. A figure stepped into his vision. He recognised the outline as Hassan.

'Major. Come and look.'

'Yes. Right with you.'

Hassan smiled brightly, a look of excitement on his young features. He spun away, cloak billowing, his camel skin boots kicking up small dust clouds as he stalked off.

Killen pushed the collapsed blanket shelter away from him and stood up. His camel, its long neck turned to look at him, regarded him with disdain.

'I hate you,' he said forcefully.

The camel stared back, its jaws working. Killen suspected that the camel didn't care.

He stretched his arms and gazed around the camp. Everyone else was already up, packing away their blankets, taking a quick breakfast of dried meat or a sip of water. Killen worked his jaws and ran his tongue around his gums. They felt dry. He walked round to the saddlebags and pulled out a waterskin. He took a swig, sluicing the cool liquid around his mouth and spitting it on to the ground. The water was absorbed fast, leaving a dark patch. He ran over it with his foot, and when he lifted his foot the patch was gone. The desert had swallowed it, like it did with anything humanity tried to impose. There was no permanency to be had here, no stability, no growth. That was why the tribes moved on. It was impossible to stay in one place; the desert wouldn't let you.

He lifted the waterskin again and took several deep gulps. They had a good supply back in the caves. They'd been there longer than anywhere since they'd retreated into the high country. At first he had advocated strict rations, fearing that they would run out of water and food and be doomed to wander the wasteland until madness and death took them all. It was primal and instinctual. Yet the erebeshi were not bothered in the slightest. They had been born to this life and saw no future where they were not the princes of the desert. It was an alien culture but in the last year he had learned to trust their ways when it came to survival.

I may be a fool, but I thank the Emperor he granted me the wisdom to hide the worst of it.

When word had reached them that the last erebeshi city had fallen, that all pretence of imperial control had been lost, his command could have left him to fend for himself, they could have simply just slit his throat. And he wouldn't have blamed them.

'Major. Come along. You must see!' Hassan beckoned to him from the top of a small rise. Others were heading in that direction, a hubbub of excitement building. He quickened his pace, kicking up small puffs of red dust as he climbed the slope, part of a gaggle of scouts. He reached the top at the back of the group, who to a man were looking at the skies, hands raised to shield their eyes. He did the same, scanning the blue, and spied the smallest wisp of a cloud, high and far away to the east.

'What am I looking at?'

A few heads away Jehali, the native captain of the scouts, glanced at him and smiled.

'You are looking in the wrong place, Major. Up there.'

Jehali raised his hand and straightened his index finger.

Killen followed the line. He felt his eyes squint, his muscles pull his mouth into a frown.

'Do you see it, Major?' asked Hassan, his grinning teeth sharply highlighted against his dark skin.

Now that he had a name to give the dark shape in the sky, it made sense. The creature was little more than a dot, yet he could begin to make out a slight flaring to either side. No doubt wings.

'Yes. It's a bird. What of it? There are many predators out here.'

Jehali shook his head. 'Not like this.'

So this is what they were dragged out for, to look at a rare bird?

He sighed. 'Right. We've seen the bird. It's very nice. Let's go home.'

'No. Major Killen, you don't understand,' said Jehali. He turned to look at Killen with intense and intelligent eyes.

'That is not a bird. That's an eagle.'

Also by Alex Janaway

Redoubt
The Coming of Night
Tangier

Keep up to date with Alex's news on his website
www.alexjanaway.com

Printed in Great Britain
by Amazon

16248313R00269